THE WORLD
of
JENNIE G.

BOOKS BY ELISABETH OGILVIE

The World of Jennie G.
Jennie About to Be
The Road to Nowhere
The Silent Ones
The Devil in Tartan
A Dancer in Yellow
An Answer in the Tide
The Dreaming Swimmer
Where the Lost Aprils Are
Image of a Lover
Strawberries in the Sea
Weep and Know Why
A Theme for Reason
The Face of Innocence

Bellwood
Waters on a Starry Night
The Seasons Hereafter
There May Be Heaven
Call Home the Heart
The Witch Door
High Tide at Noon
Storm Tide
The Ebbing Tide
Rowan Head
My World Is an Island
The Dawning of the Day
No Evil Angel

BOOKS FOR YOUNG PEOPLE

The Pigeon Pair
Masquerade at Sea House
Ceiling of Amber
Turn Around Twice
Becky's Island
The Young Islanders

How Wide the Heart
Blueberry Summer
Whistle for a Wind
The Fabulous Year
Come Aboard and Bring Your Dory!

THE WORLD
of
JENNIE G.

Elisabeth Ogilvie

McGraw-Hill Book Company

New York   St. Louis   San Francisco
Toronto   Hamburg   Mexico

First McGraw-Hill Paperback edition, 1987.

1 2 3 4 5 6 7 8 9 FGRFGR 8 7

ISBN 0-07-047789-2

LIBRARY OF CONGRESS CATALOGING-IN-PUBLICATION DATA

Ogilvie, Elisabeth, 1917–
    The world of Jennie G.
    I. Title.
PS3529.G39W6   1986   813'.52   85-16629
ISBN 0-07-047789-2 (pbk)

Not in Utopia, subterranean fields,
Or some secreted island, Heaven knows where!
But in the very world, which is the world
Of all of us,—the place where, in the end
We find our happiness, or not at all!

William Wordsworth

THE WORLD
of
JENNIE G.

One

THE BRIG *Paul Revere* entered the St. David River on an incoming tide and a strong southwesterly breeze at a little past noon on a Sunday in late June 1809. Since yesterday at dawn the passengers had been seeing the coast of Maine, but that undulating heather-purple line was unimaginable as the eastern edge of an immense continent; reality was in the scatter of islands past which they had sailed on that long penultimate day. Some were no more than craggy islets where seabirds nested. Others showed log cabins and cleared fields, and children climbed on high rocks to wave at the *Paul Revere*. They had passed small fishing boats, in which the crews stood up and swung their caps over their heads and exchanged shouts with the brig's crew.

"Chet Mayfield, you have a son!" one man yelled between cupped hands, and aboard the *Paul Revere* a lanky young man with a big nose and hair like yellow straw blazed up in an incandescent grin, while he was slapped and pounded on the back. The nearest Highlanders, having some English now, shook his hand.

For the Highlanders these American fishermen were as exotic, if not as alarming, as the whales that had sometimes played about the vessel. A little more than a month ago they had sailed down Loch Linnhe with the bagpipes crying "We Shall Return No More," torn between grief and rage because they must go or be driven, trying to cling to the minister's affirmation that God had ordained this voyage.

"But how do we know that He is not ordaining the bottom of the sea for us all?" Alick murmured while the minister preached faith to his people. "The wee man is only trying to give himself courage. The great fear is at him, and he is trying to pray it away."

Alick knew all about fear. He had been living intimately with it for weeks. Sleeping with it. Waking to the ache of knowing it hadn't gone away. Jennie tucked her hand domestically into his elbow and gave him a pinch on the bicep.

"Don't be putting terror into their heads," she murmured.

"They have the terror already, if they are not daft entirely."

He was speaking for himself; he believed he had escaped the gallows for the privilege of drowning.

They'd made no stop at Oban or at Tobermory on Mull. All through the long summer evening, as the ship beat steadily to the southwest with a bone in her teeth and her American ensign snapping against the sky, the emigrants had watched Scotland disappear below the horizon, until the night filled in the place where their land had been.

If God seemed to be on the side of the landlords, He sometimes conferred blessings on exiles, as Mr. MacArthur promised; this time He was helped by a new and able vessel and an experienced captain who had been sailing the Atlantic ever since he was his father's cabin boy. Westward the *Paul Revere* flew like a gull, her new canvas swelled with fair winds. There was very little sickness. Jennie was astonished not to be seasick, even during the turbulent days when the captain ordered the passengers to stay below. Alick had had no appetite, and she suspected he was white around the mouth under his beard, but she laid that to fear and nerves.

One woman had a miscarriage on the voyage, and a boy just past sixteen went on deck during a time when everyone had been told to stay under cover, and he had been washed overboard with no one knowing just when it had happened. He left parents, younger siblings, and a fifteen-year-old virgin widow. Theirs had been one of the marriages arranged to conform with the General's edict about bachelors. The girl had wept herself sick for the playmate of her earliest memories.

In a few days each was left far behind, the missing boy and the little creature that had just begun to move in the womb. A healthy baby was born to another woman, and they all took heart from this omen. She was named Paulina Revere Mackenzie. "Because she is American, just," the mother said proudly in her new English.

Jennie taught English daily, from the first morning at sea. Mr.

MacArthur supplied paper and pencils from his trunk, and she compiled lists of the most useful English phrases to be learned. Alick was the interpreter between her and her pupils.

He didn't want to be, he preferred to be left to himself, but between Jennie and Mr. MacArthur he had little choice, and it took his mind off his certainty that they'd never reach America.

The children were quick learners; within a week they went back and forth between Gaelic and English with no difficulty, demanding new words as voraciously as infant birds demanding food. They were fearless and happy, except for the little widow. They would grow up as Americans, and they could hardly wait; all they knew of Scotland would come from their parents' memories.

Among the adults some learned as easily as the children did. Others, just as eager, had trouble but kept doggedly at it, practicing with each other or muttering phrases over and over to themselves. There were a few who wanted nothing to do with the language of the Sassenachs, as if to speak it would be to surrender the last particles of themselves, to have lost *everything*, not only their cottages and their valleys and their mountains forever. They were Highlanders, and they would speak as Highlanders wherever they went.

"I am a Highlander forever in my heart," Mr. MacArthur told them, "and I will always be remembering the old tongue, but I will be an American, too. And so will you be."

But that didn't move them. Even telling them that God demanded it of them couldn't fracture their granite opposition. They sat with the class but kept their mouths clamped shut and their eyes stonily distant. Alick tried to work alone with the men, in case Jennie, as a female and a Sassenach, put them off, but he got nowhere.

Some of them were quite young, whereas old Dougal MacKenzie, who had not a tooth left in his head, whose chin and bald crown were fringed in white, and who groaned and whispered lamentations to himself for an hour every morning until his rheumatism eased up, was as excited as the children.

"Good morning, sir!" he would call to the captain, lifting his bonnet. "It iss a ferry fine morning, iss it not?"

Captain Wells would respond with an austere nod. The first mate always smiled and agreed. For the most part the crew was good-natured, especially with the polite, soft-spoken children, and tolerant of the bagpipes, perhaps because Ruari Beag, the piper, was restricted to one hour in the morning and another in the late afternoon. He was composing a march to which the immigrants would disembark in America, and as it took form, it became more acceptable to the Americans as music. Sometimes he slid slyly into a jig, a reel, or a strathspey, which set the children dancing, and then there'd be some Yankee foot-tapping and appreciative grins.

Jennie and Alick, nominally part of the minister's flock, could not ignore the twice-daily devotions. Jennie learned to sing the Gaelic psalms, and if she gathered only a word here and there in the sermons and prayers, she could at least look attentive. Alick's expression was usually unreadable, and he wouldn't sing. He bore a grudge against the Landlord of the World, who bullied the weak in favor of His chosen ones. Jennie's theory of divine indifference was just as heretical, but she respected the others for their faith and the little minister for his passionate conviction. She didn't see her and Alick's lip service as hypocritical but as a necessary form of self-defense.

Ironically Alick's first real reading was the Bible. Elspeth Glenroy had insisted on their keeping her English Bible while she and Andrew retained their Gaelic one. "You *must* have a Bible. How can you be living without one?"

It had been given to her when she was twelve by the laird's wife on the estate where she had grown up. The elegant script ornamented the flyleaf: "To Elspeth MacKaye with kindest wishes from Emily, Lady Robertson. 'In all thy ways acknowledge Him, and he shall direct thy paths.' "

Jennie read that out to Alick in their box of a cabin. His response was a cynical sidewise glance.

"He is directing His own into some very strange paths. I am thinking of the Linnmore folk directed out to wander and starve and die."

Linnmore: the name that always crashed sickeningly into her midriff like a fist or a hurled boulder and with always the other name coming up behind it.

"Och, it's ill teaching a man to read from a book he is not believing!" she exclaimed in his own accent. "But there'll be grand stories of bloody battles in here, and sinfulness, and revenge, and you'll be meeting a most fearful Jehovah. You'll be believing in *Him.* God is not becoming the loving Father until the New Testament."

"Aye, when He betrays His son," he said. From a lifetime of listening to sermons and Scripture, until he'd finally refused to go to church, he was familiar with the substance, if not the printed word. But he was ready to learn to read well, not too proud to show his ignorance of long, hard words, and here was a book with weeks of reading in it. They worked steadily in the hours they could spend alone in their cabin. He would sound out a chapter to himself and then read it aloud to her for correction.

She had kept out some of the minister's paper for Alick's writing. With the dedication of a Michelangelo he copied the texts she chose for him. He was determined that he would set foot on America—if he survived—a literate man.

They also studied arithmetic. Mentally he was a swift calculator, but setting down problems and solving them on paper were new to him. He was fascinated with numbers and was soon working with large figures. Correcting his answers, Jennie never got the same result twice in succession, while he looked on, too polite to smile at her frustration.

"Arithmetic was never my strong point," she said once, hatefully flustered. "There must be a schoolmaster at Maddox who will tutor you and take you farther along than I ever could."

"You are taking me to America," he said. "How much farther could there be? Of course, we are not there yet," he added, being Alick.

She was on the deck very early one morning and saw a rampart of rock risen from the sea, burnished red-gold with the sunrise. It was like Venus rising from the foam, with gulls and terns flying about it instead of doves and cupids. Her first reaction was to rouse Alick out to see, but then she would lose this moment of particular glory.

"Davie's Rock," said Stephen Wells behind her. "It was St. David's Rock once."

She repeated it. "It sounds Welsh."

"Yes, and we'll be sailing up the St. David's tomorrow. Named by a Welshman, back a few hundred years."

"Did he name the town, too? Maddox?"

"You could say so, even if there wasn't any town then, just wilderness. He built a fort up the river, just below where the General's house is now, and called it after the place he hailed from in Wales, Portmadoc. I reckon 'Maddox' comes from that."

"What happened to him?" She kept her eyes on the rock, astern of them now but still glowing, wondering if the Welshman had seen the crag in such a light.

"He stayed for a year," the mate said. "Exploring up the river and trading with the Indians for furs. Then in one hard winter most of his crew were wiped out by scurvy because they wouldn't eat the way the Indians told them to. He and a handful survived by drinking this concoction of boiled white spruce bark, and they sailed home in the spring. He wrote it all up, but he never came back."

"It's strange that the name survives," said Jennie.

"It was recorded as Maddox on the maps that were made afterward, and when the later settlers came, nobody ever called it any different. When the town was incorporated about twenty-three years ago, there was a notion to pick a real Yankee name, but the General sent word from Saratoga that they ought to honor the choice of a brave man and leave well enough alone."

"The General sounds autocratic," said Jennie.

Wells smiled. "There were so many names put forth and everybody so violent for his own choice, they were carrying on their own war up here. The General put an end to the pulling and hauling—This has been an elegant changeover. So far." He knocked on wood. "It's his luck, the weather we've had, and she's a lucky ship, like everything the General owns or does. But your parson thinks it's all the doings of Providence. I don't have to know the lingo to guess what he'll be telling them today."

"Well, couldn't it be six of one and half dozen of the other?" Jennie asked.

"Now I never thought of that, ma'am." His grin made his long-jawed face boyish and filled his blue eyes with a mischievous light. He lifted his cap to her, and went aft to the helmsman.

Stephen Wells was her first American. He'd been the officer at the top of the ladder when she boarded the ship in Lock Linnhe, and they had become speaking acquaintances on the voyage because he handed on the captain's communications either to her or to Alick as the English speakers. Usually he managed to have a few moment's extra conversation with Jennie when she was the go-between.

The captain was his older brother. He kept a near-Olympian detachment and was respectfully referred to as the Old Man, even by crewmen with gray in their hair.

"Does your brother call you Mr. Wells on dry land, too?" Jennie asked once.

"You should hear what he calls me. And what I call *him*. No, you shouldn't. And what my father calls us both. 'Down east chowderhead' is the least of it. He doesn't want us to get too big for our breeches."

"Mr. Wells." His brother's barely raised voice. Stephen winked at her and smartly left. The summons had interrupted too many of their conversations to be always coincidental.

Davie's Rock was the beginning of those scraps of America scattered over a gentian blue sea. Passengers and crew prepared for tomorrow; not only would the brig be spotless, but so would the Highlanders. There was no need to stint on water now, and they had their Sabbath clothes in their chests; they were not paupers, even if the actual coinage among them was small. They had paid their passage, and they would not arrive looking like derelicts.

Hector MacKenzie, whose wife, Anna Kate, had suffered the miscarriage, clipped shaggy heads and trimmed well-established beards. The men who had grown beards on the voyage shaved them off, but Alick refused to. "Will you just be taking a look at Andrew Glenroy's razor?" he asked Jennie in exasperation.

"You could borrow one," she suggested. "Hector has given himself a beautiful shave."

His look put paid to that. Either men did not borrow razors, or women were not supposed to suggest it.

Most of the men and boys customarily wore the kilt; with fresh shirts, a change of hose, their hair cut, and their bonnets brushed, they looked amazingly well-dressed. The minister's black suit was old, but his linen had been bleached to a dazzling whiteness in Highland sunshine. Alick wore a pair of Andrew Glenroy's breeches, well belted in, a decent linen shirt, hose with feet in them. His boots and his bonnet were still whole.

The women's dresses were for the most part like the one Jennie had got from Kirsty, the wool and linen weave dyed in serviceable dark blue or brown, worn over a bright tartan or striped petticoat, and with the little plaid, the *guilechan*, fastened at the neck with the treasured brooch. Jennie had had to do without a brooch since the pin of hers had become a fishhook, but she knotted the *guilechan* as neatly as possible. Elspeth's second-best dress must have been made long before she became pregnant, and was only a bit large for Jennie. It was in better condition than Kirsty's dress and had been put away clean in the chest, like all the other Glenroy clothes and blankets. Some dry, fragrant leaves had been scattered among them.

She wore a mutch for the first time since she'd lost one running away from Jock. There were three left in the chest, as white as the minister's linen and the men's shirts. She'd gone bareheaded on the voyage, wearing the little plaid over her head for the daily service and letting it slide back for the rest of the time. No one ever criticized her to her face. She was forgiven such ways, along with being a Sassenach, because she was married to a Highlander and had given up palaces and dukes for him. So the young girls told her, and when she tried to dim the splendor of their fantasy, they thought she was being modest.

When they actually entered St. David River, a Sabbath service of worship and thanksgiving was held on the forward deck. After that there was nothing to do but wait while the brig raced toward home. Jennie and Alick stood apart from the rest, as they had stood when they left Fort William. Alick was as silent as before, and there was no way to guess his thoughts as he looked out on the sunlit banks, but Jennie brimmed with pagan rejoicing. "I did it, didn't I?" she said softly.

"You did indeed." He continued to watch the shore, but she felt that he was not seeing the land sliding by. Her euphoria collapsed like a hot-air balloon. It was not going to be right after all. It would be horribly wrong. But what choice had he?

"I have not the words to be thanking you properly," he said. "I have read thousands of words these weeks, but still, I have none to thank you as I should."

"Alick, we don't need words between us," she said. "Think what I owe *you*. We share too much that I will never want to forget, never in my life."

"Aye," he answered, "and too much that we will not be able to forget, though we would wish it."

For a shattering moment Nigel was there, and then everything went dark and silent, as if she'd been struck blind and deaf. Then gradually sounds came through to her, and her vision cleared. She blinked at an osprey riding the wind on motionless dark wings in blue space, above a sheltered cove glassy with hot noon.

"*Uisge-iolaire*," she whispered like an incantation. "*Water eagle*." She felt so sad, so tired; the weight of everything came on her so hard that the earlier instant of black silence seemed in comparison a refuge. What was Jennie Hawthorne doing *here*, so far from home and the people who loved her?

She'd have appreciated an arm to take or a hand to clasp. Alick was beside her but not with her, as if the final separation had already begun. The comradeship of the journey through the mountains, the shared suspense of departure, the hours of work in the cabin—all gone. Everything left behind, like the dead boy and the baby. Time rushed her on as the tide and the wind drove the ship.

But the ship was going home.

Then mentally she shook herself hard like a dog coming out of the water. She had done it; she had kept her promises; she should be proud. Here she was, about to step on American soil. Think of it! Jennie Hawthorne of Pippin Grange had crossed the Atlantic. And Ianthe considered herself cosmopolitan for merely traveling to Switzerland. *Just you wait till I'm back!* she threatened her sisters. *Will I have tales to tell!*

Hector MacKenzie came up to Alick's other side and spoke in Gaelic, pointing at a farm they were passing, and Alick answered. Hector, who had been always whistling and doing jig steps before they lost the baby, was smiling now. He hoped to be a farmer in America.

"Mistress Glenroy, will we be seeing Red Indians?" someone asked. It was Mairi, the fifteen-year-old widow.

"I hope so!" said Jennie. "What is America without Indians?"

"Oh, Mistress Glenroy, that is all Calum was talking about!" the girl wailed. "He was wanting to be a hunter and a trapper with the Red Indians!"

Jennie put her arm around the slender, bony shoulders while Mairi mopped her eyes with an edge of her *guilechan*. No one had been able to stop her weeping; it was as if she had come down with it as a chronic disease. The paradox was that during the hours when her mind was occupied with learning English, she never cried, and she was one of Jennie's best pupils. Her lower lip was raw from being bitten, and there were hollows under her high cheekbones. Soothingly Jennie put back the dark auburn hair from the girl's forehead. "Your hair is so lovely, so thick and long."

The sobs decreased as the child listened. "Was it a sickness you had," she murmured, looking at Jennie with drenched violet-blue eyes, "to be cutting off your hair like that?"

"Yes, love, it was a sickness." She sensed Alick's sudden move behind her, as if he'd heard. They had joked as he'd sawed off handfuls of hair with his dirk, and then she had never seen the hair again. Would it be woven into nests, she wondered, or be discovered in the depths of the cave by some traveler, to his eternal wonderment?

Two

THEY STOOD or sat quietly among their chests and baskets and bundles; most of the children were as subdued as their elders. For a little while the open ocean lay broad astern. Just inside the mouth of the river Jennie had seen a farmhouse cresting a green rise on the left, set snugly against a dark cloud of spruce forest with a view straight out to sea. Jennie saw it wistfully because she felt so tired, and the steep-roofed, gray, weathered house slumped so comfortably into its setting, like a hunk of granite that had been there since the world began. She thought achingly how deeply she could sleep under that roof. She'd hardly slept the night before, and now she had to endure the rest of a long, confusing day on an unknown planet, and she wished she knew where she was going to sleep tonight. As a high rocky point hid the house from her, she had an attack of homesickness for the cabin in which she'd slept for the past five weeks; if she could only sleep there tonight, she'd be able to face anything in the morning.

The ocean was gone now, but not the wind that filled the sails and whisked the water into whitecaps. Gulls still followed the brig on the chance that some orts would be thrown overboard by the cook, but the noon meal had been no more than what the Highlanders called a *strupak* and the Americans called a lick and a smell.

On either side of the broad blue tidal river there were open slopes with plowed fields and pasturage for healthy-looking cattle, a few horses, sometimes a small flock of sheep. The houses and outbuildings were log cabins or weatherboarded structures instead of stone and thatch. Almost every house had its orchard on the southwestern side and, where the

11

fields dropped to the shore, a little wharf with one or two small boats moored off it or pulled up on the shingle. There were belts of woodland between the cleared areas: spruces blued with distance and the bright green splashes of hardwoods. Oaks, birches, and maples were familiar, but it was the moutain ash which made tense faces break into smiles. Here was the rowan tree in good supply and still in blossom, a lucky omen if there ever was one.

There was a little quiet weeping, but nothing like the sound of mourning. The older youngsters clustered together, taut with suspense, eating up everything with their eyes. Mairi was not weeping now; she was too busy keeping her little brothers in one place. Two-week-old Paulina Revere MacKenzie was a tartan bundle in her mother's arms. Chet Mayfield, coming forward on an errand, stopped and touched the small face delicately with a big finger.

"My, that's a pretty one! What say we make a match of it, ma'am? Your girl and my boy, 'bout eighteen years from now?"

The mother beamed at him, not sure what he'd said but knowing it was well meant. He went on, saying over his shoulder, "I'll hold ye to it now! Remember!"

Jennie sat on a Glenroy chest, a Highland wife from the white mutch tied demurely under her chin to the brogues. Alick stood beside her, his bonnet tipped over his eyes, his plaid over his shoulder, and the leather satchel lying against his hip. They looked like any emigrating Highland couple. How long before everyone, including their sponsor, the General, found out how shockingly *unlike* they were? *It will be the instant I can take ship for home,* Jennie thought. Meanwhile, there was the rest of this day to get through. If only she could imagine a bed somewhere that would be hers, the vision would guide her like the North Star through the chaos to come.

The river swirled around a long arm of rock and daisy-flecked turf thrust out from the right bank, and a low, bleak barracks of a building appeared beyond it.

"Smallpox hospital," a crewman said. "Don't get to use it much since the General made everybody get inoculated."

This made no sense to the Highlanders, who wanted to be assured that this unsightly structure wasn't the General's house. Questioning faces turned toward Jennie. She had been inoculated herself a few years ago, but right now she couldn't think how to explain; she felt that if she opened her mouth to say anything, she'd burst into tears.

"There she is!" the American sang out. "That's the General's place! Look yonder, across the Pool!"

The harbor opened before them. Except for the clear avenue of the channel leading to the wharves, it was a leafless thicket of masts of all heights sprouting from craft of all sizes, from small wherries to boxy, broad-beamed cargo vessels. The land rose from the cluttered waterfront toward the northern sky; the mansion stood as if on a stage, with a broad wharf at its feet and a curtain of green behind it. In the full resplendence of a midday sun the first dazzling impression was of the luminous whiteness of marble or alabaster. The American flag flew as high as the chimneys from a mast on the lawn, the red and white stripes streaming out in the wind.

The Highlanders were mute before the irrefutable evidence that one of theirs, born under a thatched roof in Strathbuie, had risen to this. Into their silence came the first long summoning note of the bagpipes, echoing from bank to bank like the preliminary warning of a call to battle. Ruari Beag began to play his new tune, "The Strathbuie MacKenzies Arrive in America."

It was said that the pipes could tear the heart out of you with a lament and put it back into you ten years younger with a march. The *Paul Revere* left Scotland to the one and came home to the other, and the passengers stepped smartly down the gangway onto America with the piper leading the way.

If any of the crowd on the wharf snickered at their first sight of kilted men and groaned or grimaced at the sound of the bagpipes, they'd have been careful not to let the General know. The red-blond man in a brown coat and fawn trousers who stood bareheaded and radiantly smiling at the foot of the gangplank could be no one else. He was leaning on a stick, and his free hand kept time with the pipes, except when he stopped to wipe his eyes and blow his nose. A lanky black-haired boy stood beside him, holding two little girls by the hands. They were jigging up and down to the music. The boy, also in a brown coat but wearing knee breeches, looked unhappy.

Jennie and Alick stayed back in a silent agreement to let the bona fide immigrants go first. She was reluctant to leave the ship, and she wondered if Alick felt the same, but their relationship had so subtly changed in the last few days that she was too shy to ask. He moved away from her now and stood alone, and the literal distance emphasized the figurative one. *But this is how it was supposed to be,* she reminded herself. *We're each on our own now.*

The music had stopped, and the diminutive piper stood at attention, grinning, with his pipes drooping under his arm. Mr. MacArthur began to introduce the Highlanders, and the General handed his stick to the boy so that he could embrace Dougal and the two other old men who had known his father. He had leisurely words with everyone, hard handshakes, and claps on the shoulder. He prevented the men from pulling off their bonnets and raised the women from their curtsies with a smiling reproof. "None of that here!" The resonant voice carried to the brig. "I'm one of you!"

He shook hands with the older boys and girls, repeating their names and vigorously welcoming them. With the young children he spoke more quietly, caressing their heads, tipping up shy chins with a forefinger. The two little girls in muslin frocks and the Highland children stared at each other with a wholehearted objectivity which is beyond rudeness.

The skinny black-haired boy was introduced again and again; each time he looked more bored and sulky than the last. The only son of a man who had come up from nothing was likely to be badly spoiled, and Jennie guessed that this was the case here.

While the General was exuding Highland hospitality at the gangplank, there was a parting of the spectators and a dark blue open barouche drawn by two grays drove briskly out onto the wharf. The driver, in plain clothing but not livery, stepped down and came around to the horses' heads. The passenger was a woman wearing a flame-colored shawl and a hat with matching plumes. She carried an ivory white parasol, and even from this distance she had an air of imperious languor.

"Ah, there's the lady herself," Stephen Wells said behind Jennie.

"Mrs. MacKenzie?"

"She'd liefer be called Madam. But nobody remembers it much." He nodded toward the withdrawn Alick with a friendly curiosity. "What's your man's trade?"

"He is good at a number of things. He will do what honest work comes to hand first, while he's—while we are settling."

"Well, there's plenty of work, either for the General or for a man on his own, if he takes to farming or fishing."

"Does all this shipping belong to the General?"

"No, ma'am. About two-thirds of these are independent carriers. They've brought loads of wood from down east for the lime kilns, and they'll be going out with the tide today. See, some of them are ready to cast off now."

"All on a Sabbath, too," she said lightly.

He smiled. "Well, seeing that this Sabbath was about to be shattered anyway by us, and keeping the Lord's Day isn't much to some folks, especially skippers of down-east wood boats, I guess the hard-shells will just have to put up with an extra large dose of sin today."

Alick came over to them. He gave the mate a preoccupied nod. "Jeannie, we will be going ashore now." There were only a few left to be greeted; two were the couple with the new baby.

"Paulina Revere MacKenzie!" the General boomed. "That's magnificent!" He took the tartan-wrapped baby in his arms and moderated his voice. "I must tell Mr. Revere. She deserves a silver porringer from him!" The little girls pulled eagerly at his arm, and he bent down so they could see the baby. "Ah, she's a bonny one," he said to the parents, handing her back.

"Welcome to America, Mr. and Mrs. Glenroy," Stephen Wells said.

"Thank you," Alick said, looking strained and grim. He crooked his arm, and she put her hand through it; at the first touch she thought he was trembling, then decided she was the one. But she wasn't sure; she knew only that leaving the *Paul Revere* was as sickeningly suspenseful as the boarding had been.

"Mistress Glenroy," the minister said.

The wharf seemed to be heaving gently but treacherously under her feet, and when the General took her hand, she felt as if his clasp was all that held her upright.

"So you are the lady who has been teaching English on the voyage." Freckles spattered his big nose and broad cheekbones, and his eyes, set in sun wrinkles, were a light greenish blue under the bristly red eyebrows. "I am delighted to meet you!"

"Thank you, sir," she said. "I am delighted to be here. But my husband and I both taught."

"Admirable, admirable!" He released her hand and held his out to Alick. The white seam of an old scar slanted down one cheek close to the corner of his mouth and across his chin, but it did not impair the charm of his smile. It embraced them both with the conviction that coming to America had been exactly the right thing to do. "Alick Glenroy," he said. *"Ciamar a tha sibh an diugh?"*

"Tha mi gu math, tapadh leibh," Alick answered, and the General looked naïvely pleased with himself.

"There, you understood me perfectly. I was a little shy of trying it on the rest. But it's a lovely language—lovely!" he said fervently. "You know what they say, Mrs. Glenroy, that it was the language spoken in the Garden of Eden, and when I hear it again after all these years, I believe it. Here, you must meet my son. My little girls have scampered off after that baby." He drew the boy to him by the arm. "This is Anthony MacKenzie. You'll call him Tony. We all do."

Tony, fidgeting in his father's affectionate but powerful grip as if he had hair down his neck, met Jennie's hand with a limp, reluctant one. She looked into the drooping dark eyes and said, "How do you do, Tony? I'm sure you're happy to see the end of the line."

His long, thin mouth quirked in a surprising grin, and his clasp tightened. "It's a pleasure to make your acquaintance, ma'am." He then moved on to Alick and called him *sir*; it was a new experience for Alick, but he reacted with dignified equanimity.

"Now we'll join the others." The General swept them on to where the rest were clustering about Mr. MacArthur, keeping a tight hold on the children and looking anxiously back at the brig, where their gear still waited. The spectators watched every move with unnerving curiosity, but they kept to a distance probably ordained by the General.

"There is something you must explain, Alick Glenroy," he said, limping rapidly along. "By the law of this country, you must all be registered. Mr. Albion Hardy, our deputy collector of customs, the young man who boarded the vessel before anyone was allowed ashore, will take the names in our new lime shed here. And while they are registering, their belongings will be unloaded. Everything will be quite safe; assure them of that."

Alick repeated the instructions and explanation in Gaelic, and the minister and his wife led the move toward the open doors of the shed.

Alick stood back, looking around for Jennie, but the General began talking to him again, and Tony said to Jennie, "You aren't one of *them*, are you?"

"I am married to one of *them*."

His sallow cheeks flushed. "I was not being impertinent. Just curious. He's a mighty somber one, isn't he? But from what my father says, they all have reason to be. Well, Mrs. Glenroy, no one will do that to them here!" A proud and jaunty young smile changed his narrow dark face. "This is America! Welcome to Maddox, Mrs. Glenroy."

"Thank you, Tony," she said, wondering if the sensation of the world's shifting under her feet was the result of five weeks at sea or the word *registration*. Now Alick was coming toward her, his eyes on hers, and the message was a desperate one. To pass for a married couple while they were escaping was one thing; to be officially recorded here with pen and ink sounded like forgery or worse, as if the instant the lie were written down, they were inviting an ambush.

"Well, I'd better snatch my young sisters out of everyone's way," Tony was saying. He gave them a little salute and was gone.

She put her hand on Alick's arm, murmuring for her own assurance as well as his, "Nothing can happen here. No one can know."

"And what is one more lie?" he asked harshly.

She hushed him with a finger to his lips, and his head jerked back as if she'd scalded him. Behind them the General was sending men aboard the brig, and the wharf planks reverberated under hooves and wheels as the wagons came on, passing the barouche. "Come along, we will be getting this finished," Alick said.

The big shed, still empty of lime casks, smelled of new wood. A table had been placed just inside the open double doors, where there was plenty of light, and Mr. Albion Hardy sat behind it with his pen hovering over an open ledger. He was a stocky, pink-cheeked young man with tightly curly fair hair and spectacles which kept sliding down on his snub nose. He was as brightly attentive as a large, amiable baby watching butterflies.

"How is that name spelled, sir?" he was asking one of the men. Mr. MacArthur could not assist in Englishing the Gaelic names, and Mr. Albion Hardy half rose from his empty keg to shake hands with Alick gratefully. He registered Mr. and Mrs. A. Glenroy first on the page.

Once the crime had been committed without anyone's knowing it was a crime, Alick relaxed perceptibly and accepted a seat on another keg beside Hardy.

Jennie thought she must get into the air and sit down somewhere before she fell down. She avoided eyes as she passed the line; she knew some of the women would have detained her. Once they were outside the General's comforting aura, their anxieties returned. They didn't like turning their backs on their possessions; they were as tired as she was. But not in the same way; they had nothing on their consciences. How could anyone endure a life of crime? Hers was exhausting her.

"Mistress Glenroy!" Mairi's whisper followed her. She shook her head slightly and went out into the fresh, sea-scented breeze. Ignoring the crowd of expectant watchers, she looked for a place where she could sit down.

"Please, ma'am," said an urgent young voice at her elbow. She looked down into earnestly rounded aquamarine eyes under delicate little red-gold eyebrows. She had the General's coloring, freckles on a nose she'd live to grow up to, and a miniature of his square, cleft chin. "My mama asks will you come to her, please?" She spun herself around; her long, straight hair flying out shimmered in Jennie's vision like a flame paled by sunlight. She ran off to some other children, perfectly confident that her mama's command would be obeyed.

Jennie breathed deeply and took a step. *Good.* The motion was subsiding. She imagined balancing Papa's *Complete Shakespeare* on her head, fixed her eyes on the white parasol, and walked forward.

Three

M RS. MACKENZIE lay back indolently under the parasol and watched Jennie approach. The scarlet plumes quivered in a puff of breeze; black curls tumbled artfully out from under the narrow straw brim. She had a wide, bold face with well-marked black eyebrows and a large mouth so precisely cut and shaped as to redeem it from ugliness. The diffused sunshine sifting through the white parasol fell on the flame-colored shawl and reflected upward a rubescent glow that flushed her cheeks and deepened the redness of her lips.

Jennie had a horrid suspicion that this handsome woman was a more intelligent, more self-confident Christabel, but whatever the General's wife was, it could be of no concern to her and Alick. She nodded pleasantly to the pudgy, grizzled man holding the horses' heads, and he touched his hatbrim and said, "Good day, missis."

"Good day," she answered. "And good day to *you*," she said to the nearest gray, running a knowledgeable hand along the horse's neck. The gesture softened the driver's flinty eye. She looked up at the woman in the chaise.

"You wished to speak to me, Mrs. MacKenzie?"

"Yes. English, are you not?" Her voice suited her, deep and lazily arrogant. "I am curious about you. You stood out for me at a distance, before you left the ship. And then I saw the way you walked, even with those extremely odd objects on your feet, and your manner with my husband. I know a lady when I see one."

"I am English," said Jennie composedly.

"Married to that man who translated for my husband?" When she turned her gaze in Alick's direction, the pose showed her aquiline nose and strong white throat. "There must be more in him than meets the eye. A younger son, perhaps, with no prospects?" She looked back at Jennie. "Or in trouble of some sort, in disgrace with his family?"

Jennie neither answered that nor looked away. Mrs. MacKenzie's large, full brown eyes unhurriedly examined every visible detail of her appearance, beginning at the cap and then returning to it.

"Ah, well," she said negligently. "Whatever the trouble was, it means nothing here. Is your short hair a new fashion?"

"It had to be cut," said Jennie.

"It must be very easy to care for. Mine is miserably heavy and seems to take hours to brush and dress. I suppose you have felt less conspicuous in those garments, but now you will have no need to masquerade. If you've brought nothing suitable, we have a pair of quite good dressmakers in town. They're not up to elegance, of course, but they'll do to tide you over."

The urge to ignite into strident laughter was as strong as nausea. Jennie said, "If you will excuse me, Mrs. MacKenzie, I must see about my chests."

"And I must speak with my husband. Will you tell him that, please?"

As the Highlanders left the lime shed, they hurried across the wharf to be sure all their belongings were safe. They met with tolerant grins and good-humored assurances from the men who had now begun loading the chests into the wagons, but they were apprehensive until Alick came out with the last couple to be registered and passed on new instructions from the General. At once apprehension changed to an almost jovial relief, and the baggage fairly flew aboard the wagons. Tony and some other boys showed off their strength and vigor, as loud as young cockerels before the girls. The General looked on with satisfaction. Jennie went to him and told him his wife wished to speak to him.

"This is a grand day for me, Mrs. Glenroy," he said happily, and limped off toward the chaise. She looked for a Glenroy chest and found one just as Alick and Hector came to pick it up.

"Where are we going?" she asked.

"Shelter has been arranged," Alick said. "And then at four o'clock we will be gathering at the General's house for a meal."

"Oh, bliss!" She sighed. If shelter was only a little room with two pallets in it, she'd be satisfied.

"A *Dia*, the great hunger that's at me," Hector said fervently.

The driver of the chaise came stumping toward them. "The General says you Glenroys ain't to load your cultch yet," he said woodenly. "He wants a word with ye first."

Hector put a mute question to Alick's drawn and suddenly sweating face. Alick shrugged and said something in Gaelic which satisfied Hector's curiosity, and he left them. Alick's and Jennie's hands came together, compass needle to magnet. His were as cold as hers. *They can't know*, her lips silently insisted. *It's not possible.* But he looked as if he were hearing the exciseman's ghost or caught in a dream of the gallows.

The General was leaning against the barouche, wiping his face with a large white handkerchief. "I haven't run about like this since my leg was crushed under my poor Joshua in the Carolina campaign. Well, now, you two! The fact is, my wife has taken a fancy to you, Mrs. Glenroy, and she would like to have you closer, and I would like to talk with you, Alick Glenroy, about Strathbuie. My Gaelic and *their* English are too scanty."

"I am not of Strathbuie," Alick said stiffly. "I took the place of my cousin, who was not able to sail."

Mrs. MacKenzie gave him an amused glance as if to say, *I can see through your disguise.*

"But the way they are learning English," Jennie said quickly, "it will not be long before you can talk freely with them. And perhaps the Gaelic will come back to you."

"Dear God, I hope not!" said his wife. "It's hard enough to keep those featherheads of ours speaking an English free of the dreadful local accent, without their father taking up this new craze. Already they're quite demented."

"It's the Gael in them," he said.

The featherheads in their pink and blue muslins had joined up with other children and were watching the Highlanders leave the wharf. "Play more!" they shouted at the piper, who was walking with his pipe drooping and silent under his arm.

"No, don't!" shrieked another chorus, hands over ears.

"Now, Alick Glenroy," the General said genially, "there is a furnished cottage you can be using until you know what you will be doing here. There are many possibilities, and I know you have come to America to be your own man, as my father did. But meanwhile, it would give

Mrs. MacKenzie much pleasure to talk with Mrs. Glenroy, and you will be helpful when I interview the men. Now I must speak again to the Wellses; they'll be wanting to go home to Sunday dinner with their parents."

"Have Tony show the Glenroys to the cottage," said his wife. "He might as well be useful. Harvard may civilize him, but I doubt it. And send the girls to me, Colin. They've run wild for long enough today. Screaming like hoydens! Your Highlanders have sent them mad."

"My Highlanders," said the General, "are the salt of the earth. We have a scattering of Scots here," he said to Alick and Jennie, "but they are Lowlanders. They regard me as the Ninth Wonder of the World: a Highland barbarian turned into the facsimile of a civilized man."

"A *gentleman*," said his wife, "who has risen above his origins."

"My dear, I have never yet regarded my origins as low, and I never shall. Here come the Dalrymples. Be gracious unto them for thy husband's sake." He bowed to an elderly pair approaching the barouche and walked Alick and Jennie away in another direction.

Tony ordered his cohorts to find a cart and bring the chests to the cottage; Jennie softened this with a smile and thanks. He led her and Alick off the wharf through the thinning knots of spectators, who were now having a social time of it. They crossed a dusty road and went up three granite steps set in a grassy bank and through a white gate onto the mansion grounds.

A black Newfoundland dog named Oliver, ecstatically hospitable, joined them inside the gate. He padded along beside them with his red tongue lolling out past white teeth; he kept rolling a shining dark eye up at Jennie as if to say, *Isn't this splendid?*

After five weeks at sea it was exquisite to walk under green leaves and breathe the scent of fresh-cut grass. They came out to the flagpole, and now she heard as well as saw the flag snapping in the wind, as high as the balustraded roof.

"Here it is," Tony said. "Strathbuie House. Mama wouldn't have anything French if she couldn't have Montpelier, and the Knoxes already had that."

Afterward, no matter what else the white house came to mean to Jennie, the name always evoked the moment when she first stood by the flagpole hearing the halyards slap against the mast, and gazing at rows of long windows, the wide steps leading up to the front door, and the carved wooden eagle in flight, painted and gilded, mounted above the fanlight. The veranda was open to the sky and encircled the house, built on posts wreathed with honeysuckle and morning glories. They walked under it along the western side of the house. The ground-floor windows and doors opened onto this shaded arcade with its brick pavement and garlanded columns, and there were seats against the house walls, from which one could look across lawn to an orchard.

The cottage was about ten minutes' walk through the trees northwest of the mansion, but between Tony's rapid chatter and Alick's taciturnity she felt as if they were on a treadmill set against a painted sylvan scene and would never be able to stop. She knew that the boy was self-conscious and that Alick was being Alick; she knew fatigue and reaction were influencing *her*. If only she could be alone to collect her soul. Now she knew what Papa had meant by that.

"Now!" Tony stepped aside. "Behold!"

It could have been conjured up out of nothing by the snap of his fingers. Its very red brick, slate-roofed, foursquare solidity enhanced the illusion. Tony had been nonchalant about the mansion, hurrying them away from it, but now he behaved like a triumphant sorcerer. He sprang onto the steps between two sets of windows, opened the front door, and swept off an invisible plumed hat with a bow so deep his forelock almost brushed the step. *"Entrez, Madame et Monsieur!"*

A delighted Oliver bounded across the threshold. Jennie followed him into the hall, but Alick remained on the path, his bonnet over his eyes; she felt that if she hadn't looked around, he wouldn't have come in but would have walked off somewhere by himself.

On the west side of the small hall the parlor was all sunlit echoing emptiness. It had thrush-egg blue walls and a bloom of dust on the dark blue floor. A fireplace with a white-painted mantel stood between the end windows.

"Fairly grim, isn't it?" said Tony. "They flitted with the furniture. We'll save the kitchen for the last because it's best."

He went up the straight, narrow staircase three steps at a time. The dog didn't trust the steep stairs and flopped at the foot, staring yearningly after Alick and Jennie.

There was one large room over the parlor, painted apple green. The uncurtained south and west windows corresponded to those downstairs, but there was no window in the north wall; a plain pine wardrobe stood against it. The room was furnished with a double four-poster bed without a tester, a washstand with a flowered basin and pitcher, and a pine chest of drawers, above which hung a little, simply framed mirror. There was a small fireplace over the larger one in the parlor.

Across the stairwell one door led into a small room on the northeast corner, and another into a respectably sized bedchamber with an eastern and southern outlook. It held a narrow bed, a chest of drawers but no mirror, and a plain pitcher and bowl on the washstand. It had no fireplace.

Both beds had bare pillows and feather mattresses, and the ticking looked strong and quite new. Jennie was proud of herself for noticing that. "It's all very nice," she said while Alick remained uncommunicative.

Tony said loudly, "And now for the kitchen!" It sounded like a threat. He ran down the stairs, shouting, "Speak, Oliver, speak!" Oliver obligingly spoke in a reverberating bass bark until Tony yelled, "Enough!"

The kitchen was distinguished by a well-blacked stove with six covers, fitted into the chimney instead of a fireplace.

"Not many of those around," Tony said with an attempt at his earlier gusto. "My father had all our stoves shipped from Philadelphia."

"It's very handsome," said Jennie. There was a long harvest table with straight chairs on either side, and two rocking chairs. A covered woodbox under one of the windows on either side of the chimney made another seat. Across the room from the stove there was an incongruously luxurious note against the whitewashed plaster wall, a carved and gilded banjo clock with a colorful sea scene under glass at its base. It had stopped at seventeen minutes past eight.

The pantry-buttery, at the northern end of the kitchen, seemed to have everything necessary for cooking and serving meals: a large teapot with a picture of George Washington on it, a shelf of Staffordshire creamware, an assortment of cooking pots, and a drawer full of Sheffield cutlery. Jennie, rocking on her feet again, gave up trying to make polite noises of appreciation. At the northeast corner a door opened into a combined entry and woodshed. Tony took them out through the back entrance and flicked his hand at a little brick building tucked away among some spruce trees.

"The Necessary. And out there"—another limp wave of his hand toward the west—"the well."

Alick spoke for the first time. "I'll just be having a look at that." He walked away from them, with Oliver sociably at heel. Tony and Jennie looked at each other. She felt as if she should apologize for something. His face was flushed, and if he'd been about ten his sulkiness would have foretold tears.

"There's one more thing!" he said wildly. He rushed back into the kitchen and scrabbled behind the candlesticks on the mantelshelf, hissing angrily to himself. He pulled a chair over to the inside wall, stood on it, and wound the clock, then set it by his watch. That took time because he had to strike it through to ten past three.

Jennie sat at the table and rested her head in her hands. She shut her eyes; that made her feel as if she were waltzing in circles, so she opened them again but laid her palms loosely over them and supported her gently throbbing forehead with her fingers.

Three struck, but after a short interval she realized Tony hadn't moved. She took away her hands and looked up at him.

He still stood on the chair, facing the clock, stiffly erect, his hands clenched at his sides. The back of his neck and his ears were scarlet. "It's a Simon Willard clock," he said in a stifled voice. "I don't know how they forgot it."

It was the sight of those desperate fists that jolted Jennie out of herself.

"It's a beautiful clock," she said. "It's a beautiful cottage. Please don't think we aren't appreciative. It's just that I was anticipating a log cabin with a dirt floor, but this is so unexpected I'm beyond words."

"I thought perhaps it wasn't good enough for you, that it was an insult."

"Oh, *Tony!*" She laughed. "We've come with absolutely nothing but what is on our backs and in our two chests. Believe me, we'd have been grateful for that log cabin, dirt floor and all!"

"What about *him?*" he said truculently.

"Imagine being driven away from the only home you've ever had, knowing you can never see it again. He's a sad man," she said in a low voice. "What he is thinking now must be very bitter to him." She felt traitorous for speaking like this behind Alick's back, but it worked. Tony was immediately sympathetic. He jumped down off the chair.

"I am truly sorry. I wouldn't want even to *try* to imagine it. But he'll feel better by and by. I hope so. It can't be very pleasant for you." He cleared his throat. "Well, I had better see where your chests are. Stir yourself, old Oliver." He poked the Newfoundland with his foot. "It's an eight-day clock. You should wind it next Sunday."

"I shall."

"You'll be coming to the feed, won't you? It will be what the novels call a sumptuous repast."

"I can hardly wait," said Jennie. "I'm simply starved." He gave her a blazing grin and hurled himself out the front door and sprinted off along the path. Oliver's departure was more conservative. Jennie leaned against the doorframe; the floor was moving under her feet as the wharf had done, and the idea of a bed upstairs was a mighty temptation. But she was also hungry.

She walked into midafternoon sunshine and around the southwest corner. Alick had crossed a little field and was sitting on the stone well curb. His folded arms rested on his knees; his bonnet, his plaid, and the satchel lay on the grass among daisies and buttercups. She sat down beside him.

"So many changes in one day," she said. "I can't seem to catch up with myself."

"Jeannie, what do they want of us?"

"All I am sure of is that I know where we will sleep tonight. I shan't think of tomorrow until it is here."

"But what are you making of those two?" he persisted.

"Well, I think the General would like you to explain things and be a go-between until the men have more English. But you needn't live here to do that. As for me, I am just a whim of Madam's, and when she discovers I can't tell her what they are wearing in London and what the Prince of Wales is up to, we shall be out of here very quickly." Her earlier vision of a small room with two pallets in it suffered by comparison with the cottage, and she sighed, then roused herself to a fair show of optimism.

"But tonight we will have a good rest here and a good meal beforehand."

"Go without me," he said. "I have been with too many people for too long. You can be giving some reason. Say that I am ailing."

"No, Alick, I will not," she said flatly. "I will lie about some things like the worst sinner this side of hell, but I refuse to say that you're ailing. Mocking is catching, I was always taught, and I believe it. Besides, the General would probably come with a doctor to see if you should be quarantined."

He almost smiled. "Och, it's the domineering woman you are."

She said coldly, "I am *not* speaking as a woman! Being a man or a woman has nothing to do with it. I thought that we were equal partners in this—this venture, and that I could give an opinion without being called a domineering woman!"

"You are right," he said mildly, "and I am apologizing."

"You're not just humoring me?"

"No, woman or man, it should be left out of this." He squinted up at the sun through the leaves. "We have no timepiece."

"Tony started the clock. I would say it's about fifteen minutes before four now." When she stood up, the day dimmed to twilight and the birdsong faded from hearing as the earth began to fall away from her.

Alick forced her back to the well curb, hissing, "Sit, sit!" His hand on the back of her head pushed it down to her knees.

"Enough, enough," she sputtered. "It's over now."

He released her, and she sat up gradually. Nothing happened. She stood up as if balancing a cup of tea on her head. The sensation was entirely gone. Alick watched her with an aggressive intensity, his hands poised to seize her.

"I am all right, Alick. I am not a swooner; you should know that by now. It's just from being so long aboard ship. My equilibrium is still upset, and I stood up too quickly. And I'm *hungry*."

Four

AT SUNDOWN Jennie was making the beds. She had lost count of all the trips up and down stairs before she reached this summit of accomplishment. She had groped around in the dim entry and found a broom with which to sweep up dead flies. She had searched through pantry drawers for something with which to dust the washbowls and pitchers, and then she had carried up the pitchers half full of rainwater. She had brought up sheets, blankets, and two towels from the chests, which the boys had left in the parlor. Her intense rummaging through the pantry hadn't turned up any soap; if the mysterious *They* could leave behind all this useful, if humdrum, equipment, why couldn't They have left some soap? "Selfish brutes," she muttered. She wondered crossly who and what They were.

Nancy's soap was now a transparent wafer. Aboard the ship she'd used it only on Sundays, when enough fresh water was allotted for more than face and hands. The rest of the time she'd made do with salt water and no soap. A good hard rub with a rough towel each time took away the salt. Today she had leaned lustfully over a hogshead full from a recent rain and dabbled her hands and bathed her face with the soft water. Tomorrow a bath! And somewhere there must be soap. She would need to wash clothes, too.

They had a few coins left, and the General said his storekeeper would change their money for them; he would also extend credit to anyone who needed it. She was sure neither she nor Alick wanted that, but they might be driven to it or else go on very short rations for a time.

By now she was ready to fall onto one bed or the other and sink into a stupor. She was yawning so hard that she could barely see. Alick had gone for a walk after they had come back from the General's house; but she would go exploring tomorrow, and the anticipation showered sparks through her fog.

She was pleasantly full of food. It had indeed been a sumptuous repast spread for them on trestle tables on the veranda, for which Mr. MacArthur had offered thanks and asked blessings at length. Most of the food was good, plain, hearty, and familiar fare, even if most of them had never had this variety and this amount all at once. The leftovers were later parceled out to be taken away as a start for the next day.

Mrs. MacKenzie had not appeared. The little girls were there, eating like hungry gypsies and watching everything. They were in the charge of a rawboned young woman with tight yellow curls bobbing before her ears and a daintily sprigged dress with short sleeves that showed her sharp elbows and thick wrists. She helped with the serving, and her manner, though abrupt, was pleasant, especially with the children.

The General sat in his chair, eating little but smiling much. Tony was everywhere, transformed from uncertain boy to the glorious young squire, dispenser of good things. He kept going back to the table where Mairi and two other girls were in charge of most of the children. These looked up at him with silent wonder as he poured milk into their mugs, and the girls hid their diffident smiles behind their hands as he clowned. Mairi was quiet, but she was not tearful. Oliver, the dog, wandered around like an amiable bear; no one was shy of him.

"The Laird of Strathbuie is owning two like him, just," said Hector. "They are better liked than himself is."

His pale blue-gray eyes glistened with an almost manic excitement. He couldn't take the time to speak in English; he kept apologizing to Jennie and then going off into Gaelic again, while Alick gravely nodded at intervals.

Jennie asked Anna Kate about their quarters.

"Come and see. I am not having the words yet to tell you. It is called the Ark. But *you?* Is it in this fine house you are staying?"

"No, no! Just a cottage. Near the stables," she added to make it even less important.

"They are saying it is because you are English and a lady."

"I don't know why it is," Jennie said, "and we may stay there only tonight."

She finished the bed in the southeast room. She had propped some windows open with the notched sticks she'd found on each sill, and she knelt by the east window and leaned far out to look for Alick. She saw the glimmer of his shirt in the dusk under a belt of trees; when he came into the open, she called, "What have you found?"

"The stables. Gates. A lane that goes one way to a road and another way to a stream. I saw mountains from the ship, but they are a long mile from here, I am thinking."

"Are you disappointed?"

"It was not to find mountains that I came to America," he said severely.

Two mosquitoes settled on her arm, and she slapped them dead. "Will you come up, please?" she asked, and shut the window.

Alick inspected each bedroom without comment.

"Which bed will you take?" she asked. "Choose quickly because I am going to fall onto the other one and not stir until morning."

They were in the hall, and he pointed at the smaller room.

"Are you positive you don't want the bigger bed?"

"Positive," he said.

"About the covers, Elspeth expected to be making up only one bed, but I have divided the blankets between us. I thought you could use the plaid, and I've Elspeth's big shawl."

"*Jeannie,*" he said, "stop talking and go to bed."

"Oh, fiddle! And I'd like to say worse!" She leaned wearily against the doorjamb. "I forgot to take my nightgown from the chest."

"I will bring it."

When he came back, she was sitting on her bed untying her brogues. The dying embers of the sunset filled the room with a ruby light. She said drowsily, "Red sky at night, sailors' delight."

"Good night, Jeannie," he said, and went downstairs again. Before the afterglow had completely gone, she was asleep.

She woke up in the dark thinking she was in her berth on the ship, just as she'd waked often on the ship thinking she was in one place or another where they'd slept on the way to Fort William. She felt around for the boundaries of her berth. Then she saw the small panes framing stars, and she knew where she was.

The house was so quiet that she imagined she could hear the gilded clock ticking. She sat up and listened for Alick's breathing from across the hall. They had been sleeping so close to each other for so long that not to hear it now put everything out of joint. Besides, she needed to go to the Necessary. There was a chamber pot in the lower part of the washstand, but she didn't fancy emptying anything but wash water in the morning.

The floor was cold; she groped for her brogues and tied them on her feet and took Elspeth's long shawl off the foot of the bed and held it around her with one hand, leaving the other free to feel her way. But with so much white paint in the house it was not completely dark. She knew when she went out into the hall that Alick wasn't in his room, and she experienced the instantaneous, and familiar, creation of an arctic waste in her stomach.

He had gone as soon as he knew she was asleep. He had slung his satchel over his shoulder and struck out alone. No discussions, no good-byes. He had gone into America.

She patted the surface of his bed; the plaid was gone, too. She sat on the edge and breathed deeply until her heartbeat settled. By then she could wait no longer to go to the Necessary, but after that she should be able to think clearly.

She went downstairs with exaggerated caution; it wouldn't do to fall headlong with nobody there to hear her dying words. The clock struck once, and she jumped. She couldn't tell if it was a half hour or one o'clock. She felt her way through the entry and fumbled for the back-door latch. When she opened the door, she took long gulps of fresh air; a summer night in New England smelled much the same as a summer night in old England. Fireflies flickered on and off against the dark. Indians, wolves, catamounts, and bears were unimaginable in this setting. But what about out on the roads, away from the towns? There must be stretches of deep forest left where wild things lived, and Alick would have many a *mile dorcha* to walk before he reached where he was going, if he knew what that place was.

While she was in the Necessary, something sniffed noisily along the bottom of the door, and she could hear the movement of a body brushing the door, a clawing or scratching at the crack. There was a beast out there, and somehow she was not surprised. It was all of a piece with the way her life went these days.

The earth closet had a spacious seat for two with room to spare at either end and between the two hinged lids. At one end there was a small window, high up, and shaded by spruce boughs. She squeezed herself into the angle of the corner opposite the window side, hugging her knees to her chest and listening to the intermittent panting and snuffling and occasional scratching. Presumably the creature would be gone at cockcrow. If she had to sit here until then, so be it. She was warm enough in the nightgown and wool shawl. *Some day,* she thought, *I will be telling my grandchildren that once I went to America and spent my first night there crouched in a privy, listening to a wild animal outside the door. They will certainly be surprised at what their dear little granny had been up to, once upon a time.*

This is a good time to think, she kept insisting to herself. *I am healthy and intelligent. I am not spoiled. There must be something I can do.* But she never got any farther; clarity and creativity of thought seemed to have departed. After a time she realized the beast must have also departed, unless it was cannily lying in wait.

She unfolded herself, stood up very slowly for fear of creaks, and felt for the flat button and turned it parallel with the edge of the door. Then she walked her fingers toward the latch so as not to hit against it. Holding her breath, she lifted it and opened the door a few inches, thanking him who had installed squeakless hinges.

Outside, it was so quiet that she heard the stamp of a horse's hoof in the stable; the wild animal was probably prowling around there. She ran for the house and fell headfirst over a large, resistant, and hairy object. Crying incoherently for help, she tried to crawl away from it. It began swabbing her face with an enthusiastic tongue and smelled strongly of dog. Someone pushed it away, took her under the shoulders, and pulled her up.

"Is that you, Alick?" She squirmed around in his arms and felt his face. "It could be anyone with a beard."

"But it is not," he answered.

"And that dog could be a wolf or a bear. Could have been."

"But he is not. What are you doing out here in the dark, Jeannie?"

"That should be obvious." She released herself and settled her shawl like a hen arranging ruffled feathers. "What are *you* doing? Not sleeping in your bed, I know that much."

"It was too soft," he said gruffly, "and the ceiling was coming down on me. So I came outside to sleep."

"Did you find a bed of bracken in your wanderings? Show me. I can't go back to sleep thinking of you lying on the ground."

"I have the plaid, and the ground is not so hard."

They were walking around to the west side of the house. Close to the foundation there was still warmth coming from the brick and stone. He had been lying there on the plaid below her windows.

"Alick, I thought you had gone, and I didn't blame you," she said.

"I hope you are not disappointed," he said. "The General and his wife would be taking tender care of the poor lady deserted by her husband on their first night in America, and after she had been paying his passage, too. The man is the devil's disciple surely. You would be sent home in comfort, with their blessings."

"I don't want their blessings or their charity," she said. "Whether you leave or not, I am *earning* my way home. There must be something I can do. I am tough and willing. And Alick, I will never, *ever* say who paid our passage. Under *any* circumstances."

With a luxurious groan the dog fell over onto the plaid at their feet. There was nothing to do but laugh, and it was a relief. "Now, you *amadan*," said Alick, trying to move the dog while Oliver lay on his back and paddled his paws in air. Alick finally got the plaid out from under him. "Och, this one is a fool but a loving one!" He folded it and laid it on the ground. "Sit quickly, before he does."

They sat with their backs against the warm stone and brick, and the dog lay with his chin on one of Alick's ankles. The fireflies twinkled over the grass and against the trees.

"I think the dog has adopted me," he said. "He was here when I came out."

"Alick, *if* you stay, what would you like best to do of all the things the General had you telling about?"

"One thing I would not like is going to sea. If I was not sure I was born to be drowned—if I am not hanged first—I was hearing enough on the voyage to frighten me off the water forever. Lime afire between here and Boston; hurricanes, pirates, and killing fevers in southern waters."

"Not the sea then. I think I knew that already. But would you be an independent farmer, like Hector?"

He wasn't so quick to answer that, and then he spoke as if he were thinking aloud. "I would like it fine to *build* ships. But I am over-old to begin as an apprentice."

"You must begin somewhere, and if there are places in the shipyard, you should take one. . . . That's not a domineering woman talking."

"No." He agreed. "But for a long time we are rushing forward. For weeks, for months. Life made decisions for me. Now we are at a stop, and I must be making my own decisions. But I am hazy in my wits tonight."

"So am I, but at least the earth has stopped heaving under me like the sea. Whatever your choice is, Alick, I am glad you are free to make it. I only wish—" She hadn't meant to go that far and rip the scabs off old sores.

"You are wishing what?" he said.

"That the others could come. I wish I knew if they were all right."

"It is better that you aren't knowing."

"But I can't ever forget them, Alick. I knew them for such a little while, and yet Morag's smile and her voice in the morning, and Aili bobbing up and down and blushing, they will always be with me, and Morag on that last day, all tears and soot and pain, the way we parted with that little stream between us—it was the world dividing us, and we didn't know it." Any more than Nigel knew how soon he would be dead. She turned her head away and wiped her eyes on the shawl. "It will be like remembering Tamsin," she said. "Except that I know where Tamsin is."

"Tamsin?"

She told him, weeping softly before she was finished.

The dog came anxiously to her while she cried into the shawl. When she had control again, she said thickly, "That wasn't just for Tamsin."

"I know. I would be weeping myself if it came easily to me, but I have left only graves behind me. You have your sisters. I will give you all my earnings to pay your passage back."

"No, you won't," she said. The dog put his face to hers, and she scratched his broad head. "I came to help, not to drive a willing horse to death. I am not your responsibility. You must be free to go or stay without considering me."

"*Must?*" The soft voice was amused.

"You are understanding me perfectly. *Chust,*" she added deliberately. "But for practical purposes I may as well keep house for us both under the same roof until I earn my fare or you strike out for the high road.

There is no need in causing a scandal until we both can walk away from it."

"Jeannie," he said, getting up, "I will be seeing you to the door now, and you are to go up to your bed and stay there." He put a hand under her elbow and lifted.

"Are you going to lie out here for the rest of the night?"

"We are equal partners, are you remembering? You are not my responsibility, and I am not yours." He walked her around to the front door and saw her into the hall. "Good night, Jeannie," he said, and shut the door on her.

Five

S HE SHOT UP from oblivion like a cork suddenly released from under water. The thin, clear antiphony of roosters calling the sun put her back in Pippin Grange for an instant; next, the dawn chorus in the trees was being sung outside the windows of Tigh nam Fuaran. *But where is the blackbird?* she drunkenly questioned, and then fell back into the dark.

When she woke the next time, the refined chime of the clock came faintly up the stairs like a bell ringing in the elfland of her childhood. Anticipation of adventure quickened her; whatever happened on her first day in America was bound to be an adventure of some sort, if only because it would happen three thousand miles from home.

The General had asked all the men to meet at the store and offices at six this morning. It was eight now, and Alick should have finished with his go-between duties and be at some sort of work. She couldn't possibly imagine him doing whatever it was because she could not picture a background for him. The first thing she would do, as soon as she'd eaten, was to strike out and see for herself what lay outside this sheltered enclave.

Shivering, she bathed with the soft water in the basin. It made such an abundant lather from Nancy's soap that she decided to wash her hair, even if that was the end of the soap. Somewhere she'd find more. She rubbed herself warm and dry, dressed, and carried the basin downstairs; she emptied it out of doors and put it on the bench under the parlor windows. She washed her hair out here in the sun, lavishly ladling water from the nearest hogshead without having to worry about splashing.

When her hair squeaked under her palms and tangled around her fingers, she blotted it to dampness with her towel and spread the towel on the grass to dry. The rainwater made her hair feel as fine and feathery as a child's. It curled silkily around the comb, and she remembered Alick's cutting her hair with the dirk and saying it curled around his hand like a live thing. "It is not wishing to die," he said.

She tucked it behind her ears and went in to get her breakfast. She filled a plate with bread and butter, a chicken leg, a slice of cheese, and a solid wedge of the one American sweet they'd had at the feast, Indian pudding. "Och, it's a cup of coffee I am famished for," she said aloud. A mug of well water would have to do.

She took her food out to the bench and enjoyed it. A large American robin hopped up the path toward her; goldfinches fearlessly fed off clocked dandelions. From beyond the eastern belt of trees children's voices whistled and cajoled; calling to horses, she guessed. Tony MacKenzie appeared on the path from the mansion, head up, elbows well in, knees pumping, forelock bouncing, face agonized with the effort to reach an imaginary tape.

When he saw Jennie, all the energy went like a snuffed candle. He stopped running and tucked his shirt into his breeches and pulled up his stockings, scowling ferociously. Then he came on, chin up and belligerent.

"I must have looked like a lunatic."

"You did not. I was admiring your speed and silently cheering."

"I don't really believe you, but you're very kind. I might as well tell you that half the town already considers me a lunatic or a budding one." He dropped his eyelids, screwed his mouth to one side, nodded his head slowly, and tapped his temple. "French blood, you know."

"As bad as *that*?" Jennie gasped, and they both laughed.

"I'm doing an errand," he said in much better spirits. "My mother would like you to come to her. But you are not obliged. It's not a royal command."

"I *am* obliged, if only for the night's sleep I had here." Besides, she was curious.

"I'll show you the garden route this time," Tony said. "It's shorter. Everyone who comes by the back way uses it. Mrs. Glenroy, what is the name of that tall girl?" It came out in a rush. "The one with chestnut hair? She was leading two little boys ashore by the hand yesterday and tending them at supper. They aren't *hers*, are they?" He sounded horrified.

"No, her little brothers. She's Mairi MacKenzie."

He let out a long breath. "I *thought* she was too young, but I am not a very good judge of things. Mairi MacKenzie," he repeated slowly, as if he didn't want to relinquish the taste of it. "She's a very shy girl, isn't she?"

"Yes, and a sad one. Her husband was lost at sea during the voyage."

"*Husband!*" He stopped in the path to stare at her. He went red and then alarmingly pale.

"He was only sixteen," Jennie said. "It was the General's wish that there should be no bachelors over sixteen, so some marriages were quickly arranged. The married girls were sitting with their husbands yesterday at supper."

His color was coming back, but he was still upset. "Married, at my age! And now she's a *widow!*"

"Mairi and Calum had played together all their lives," she said. "So she lost a dear friend, and she was inconsolable. Everyone grieved for Calum."

He was glumly thoughtful for some time. A wrought-iron gate let them into the oval garden; it was young, as Jennie knew gardens, but well laid out and thriving. A sundial stood in the center, and at secluded spots among the shrubbery around the wall marble basins supplied water for birds. A bowed old man, who looked as dark, seamy, and scarred as an ancient decaying tree trunk, was hoeing along the perennial border. His pipe resembled a bit of branch left on the trunk.

"What ho, Truelove!" Tony hailed him.

Watery eyes rolled around at them under the dirty hatbrim; he made a rheumy sound in his throat and didn't stop working.

"*Truelove?*" Jennie whispered when they'd walked some distance.

"Yes. Truelove Adams. Not of the Quincy Adamses." He grinned. "I forget, you don't know our American aristocracy yet. Truelove he was christened, and Truelove he has remained. Difficult to realize he was once a dear little baby 'trailing clouds of glory,' isn't it?"

"Do you know Mr. Wordsworth's poetry, Tony?"

"I know what Mr. O'Dowda made us memorize. I don't say I adore him, but the odd quote impresses erudite young ladies."

"It has just impressed me," she said, and immediately he tripped himself on his own shoelace, swore under his breath, and hurried her through the opposite gate.

"My father is expecting me at the store, not to be running errands for his wife."

"Then, by all means, go. Someone will direct me to your mother."

"I shall deliver you," he said with frigid dignity.

The back door opened into a passage with the kitchen on the right and a stone-floored laundry on the left, from which came the steamy scent of hot wash water, splashings and the sound of scrubbing, and some vivacious female conversation. Jennie had received much earthy education in the washhouse at home, and this didn't sound very different, except that the accent wasn't Northumbrian.

"Greetings, Rose of Sharon, me darlin'!" Tony sang out. There was a shriek of laughter.

Another voice called sharply, "Anthony MacKenzie, you jibe over onto another tack! This is no place for you."

"Don't I know it? I've been blushing ever since I came in the door! . . . Mrs. Frost," he said when they'd got by. "Bark's worse than her bite. Benoni Frost runs the stables."

They came out into the large central hall, flooded with light from the glass in the roof three stories above; it reflected up from the parquet like sunshine from dark water. A staircase with a white balustrade spiraled in two airy curves to the second-floor balcony. She felt an immediate shock of pleasure; Papa would have loved this, she thought.

Across the hall a girl in a print gown and a starched apron was arranging white peonies in a sapphire blue vase. She watched Jennie and Tony in the oval mirror over the console table. She had a round, pinkly blooming face, with a little retroussé nose and a dimpled chin, and curly hair the color of bracken in winter frothed around her cap. Jennie remembered her from yesterday; she'd been serving, and not happy about it.

"Well, Hannah, m'dear," the boy said. "And what have you been doing that you shouldn't? Or to put it another way, what would you like to do but you dassn't?"

"None of your sauce, young feller, me lad," she said robustly. "And none of your hints and whispers. I'm not a cradle robber."

"Like the boy in the song, Hannah, love, I'm young but I'm daily agrowing."

"And when he was sixteen, he was dead, so have a care, *Master Tony.*" She surveyed Jennie coolly in the mirror; her china blue eyes were both round and oblique, like a kitten's.

"Will you come upstairs, Mrs. Glenroy?" Tony asked. In the next instant he'd twitched Hannah's apron untied and left her spitting maledictions.

"These are excellent for sliding down," he remarked, running his hand along the glossy rail.

"I should think so." Jennie agreed.

"Just you wait, young *sir!*" Hannah threatened behind them.

They walked around the balcony to the front of the house. The center door opened, and a cadaverous man in tobacco brown came out, carrying a doctor's satchel.

"Well, Tony," he said in a deep voice, "how do you fare these days?"

"Very well, sir," Tony said gruffly. "This is Dr. Amyas Waite, Mrs. Glenroy."

"How do you do, Dr. Waite?" Jennie said.

His face, which seemed to have only a thin layer of skin over the skull, corrugated into a cordial grimace. "Satisfactory, ma'am. Satisfactory. This is indeed a pleasure. Welcome to Maddox, Mrs. Glenroy." He took up his hat from the little taboret table beside the door and went away at a sort of lope.

Tony bowed Jennie into Mrs. MacKenzie's presence. Venetian blinds dimmed the large bedchamber to a clear amber shade, and Mrs. MacKenzie lay on a chaise longue among abundant draperies of East Indian splendor. Jennie thought it must be rather like meeting the principal wife in a seraglio. A very pregnant principal wife. That hadn't been so obvious yesterday.

"Make yourself comfortable, Mrs. Glenroy." She waved a large pale hand at a chair. Bangles on her wrist, musically jingling, added to the Oriental flavor, and so did the scent wafted about by her movements. "Where are the girls, Tony?"

"Probably in the paddock by now, riding their ponies bareback."

"*And* astride, with their frocks rucked up around their middles, the little savages. Before you go to the wharf, Tony, bring them to the house. It's a dreadful nuisance, Tom Bisbee taking ill this morning."

"Inconsiderate of him," Tony agreed. She gave him a sharp look.

"Eliza is a good, capable girl, but her father is of no earthly use whatever. If he would have the civility to die in one of these fits, she could move into this house and simplify her own life as well as mine. For heaven's sake, *go*, Tony! And send them directly to me."

"Your servant, ma'am," he said sedately. The instant the door latched behind him he began to whistle a jig.

Six

"INSOLENT BOY," said Mrs. MacKenzie, more bored than cross. "He's not mine, you know. He and his sister are the issue of the General's first marriage."

"Where is his sister?" Jennie asked politely.

"She married at seventeen, the little baggage. She had her heart set on that pretty boy Royall Tyler, and of course, what Christian wants, her doting papa will agree to. I told her that sort of prettiness runs early to fat and becomes merely pigginess." She shook her head. "They live a good distance from here, which is a blessing."

"I like Tony very much," Jennie said. If she'd been summoned here simply to natter on about nothing when she was aching to be outdoors, it was all too depressingly reminiscent of Christabel. Mrs. MacKenzie was much younger, and a mother, but she had Position and she had Whims, and Jennie was one of the beggars who had no choices.

Well, not quite, *Eugenia,* she thought, and sat up straighter in her chair.

"Tony has the better disposition of the two," Mrs. MacKenzie was saying. "My girls adore him, and he seems not to resent them, which is a blessing." Complacently she stroked the mound under the draperies. "If this is another son for the General, it may be a different matter. But why am I boring you with all this?" Her change to a warm and hospitable manner abolished Christabel for the moment. If it wasn't genuine, she was a consummate actress. "There will be hot coffee presently."

Jennie cheered up even more.

"You've just met our doctor," Mrs. MacKenzie said. "A most immoral man."

"I am surprised that you call him."

"He is the only doctor we have, and a very good one. He doesn't hold with heroic bleeding and purging, which is licensed murder. He is excellent in childbirth and always immaculate in his person, if not in his character."

"What form does his immorality take?" Jennie asked. "Gambling? Drinking? Atheism?"

"It's too tiresome to go into now. And when I say *immoral*, I'm merely stating the public point of view. Now tell me about yourself," she said. "You must have given up so much to come to America with your husband. I'm sure your story is as enthralling as any novel could be."

The back of Jennie's neck grew damp. She willed herself not to fidget.

"Your own story must be fascinating, Mrs. MacKenzie," she said. "You're married to a great soldier who helped build a new nation. You live in this magnificent house. You're a member of the American aristocracy."

Mrs. MacKenzie agreed with becoming modesty.

"Of course, I had nothing to do with his military career, which is a pity; Désireé was of no earthly use as a high-ranking officer's wife. If I had met ' im twenty years ago, he might be President by now. We need another ' ew Englander in that office. Those Virginians think the nation is their own personal preserve. They pass it around amongst themselves. However"—she gave Jennie a coruscating smile—"I did have *much* to do with the planning of this house. I wanted the *ambience* to be appropriate to our position; after all, as you say, the General and I are comparable to your aristocracy, even if we don't have hundreds of years of titles behind us."

There was a tap at the door, followed by a demure Hannah with a tray, her bow returned to its former perkiness. She set the tray on a low table by the chaise longue and left, with a swift glance down at Jennie's brogues. Mrs. MacKenzie sat up to pour coffee from the silver pot. There were also warm croissants in a covered dish.

"One thing we don't have here is a servant class," she said. "Not in the true sense of the word, persons with service bred into them. Oh, in the South they have slaves, but slavery is abhorrent to us. And the

General refuses to have a large staff, so we make do. A New England tradition, I'm afraid." Her full bosom rose and fell in a sigh. "No sooner have I trained a girl than she's marrying and setting up housekeeping and thinking she's as good as anyone. It's my husband's fault. He's a radical. Our property combines his purchases and my father's and *was* as large as any of your great English estates, but he keeps whittling off bits of it for old soldiers or their sons and what he calls worthy men, instead of making them his tenants. And under the Constitution they're all entitled to their say at town meeting and may even run for public office. I call it disastrous; the General beams and claims it's the American way."

She lay back on her frilly pillows as if exhausted by the mere idea of her husband's radical excesses. "Now he has imported these Highlanders, who can barely speak the language and who are not accustomed to such dangerous freedom. Except you and your husband, of course," she said kindly. "Obviously you two are in a class apart, even though you dress like the others. Very gracious it is of you, too, not to make them uncomfortable. *Noblesse oblige.*"

Jennie looked into her empty cup. "May I have more coffee, Mrs. MacKenzie?"

"Of course, my dear, and please have another croissant. You're a little too thin."

"The coffee will be sufficient," said Jennie. "I haven't tasted anything so ambrosial since a cup of tea I drank in Fort William before we sailed." *If you knew about that journey through the mountains, you would be struck dumb with consternation, Mrs. MacKenzie. You little reck what manner of woman sits before you, delicately stirring cream into her coffee. The story of my brogues alone would have your eyes bulged out like a lobster's.*

"Come, tell me more about your husband and how you met," Mrs. MacKenzie coaxed.

"It's very simple. My husband is in the position of a landless and penniless younger son. And because I chose him, I have nothing either. We were just able to gather our passage money. If I tell you nothing more, it is because we wish to forget forever the Old World."

Mrs. MacKenzie said with a spark of humor, "Before you forget it forever, will you talk to me about London? I've been starved for civilized conversation. What are the new hair fashions like? What are the colors they're all mad about?"

"I can't tell you," Jennie said regretfully. "I have been to London only once in my life, and that was some time ago."

The older woman raised her eyebrows. "That's very hard to believe."

"But it's true. I did have dresses that were made for me in London, but I left them all. We had no room for anything but the absolute necessities. I shall have other things to wear as I earn them."

"You mean as your husband earns."

"I intend to work, too. There must be something I can do. I wasn't reared to sit on a cushion and sew a fine seam." She smiled. "I was never very good at fine seams."

"Boring." Mrs. MacKenzie agreed. "What do you wish to do?"

"Anything within my strength and abilities. Is there a dame school in the village? I could start one."

"Mrs. Hardy kept one for years, but when she died, an infants' class was started in the village school. Now all the children go to O'Dowda, from five or six to fourteen. Tony and Christian went—I could do nothing about *that*, though I wanted to send Tony to stay with my relatives in Boston, to attend the Latin School and be prepared for Harvard College." She shrugged her fine shoulders. "I must say O'Dowda has prepared him quite well in the necessary subjects over the past two years, much as I loathe giving that opportunist little Irishman credit for anything. The General did allow me to send Christian to Boston to be finished." She made a wry mouth. "For all the good it did. She turned down fine old Massachusetts Bay stock for a pretty hobbledehoy who sits a horse like a sack of dirty laundry. Well, that's neither here nor there. Have you ever taught children, or do you merely have some romantic idea about it?"

"Hardly romantic," said Jennie. "As a favor to my aunt I took over my four cousins' education when their governess had to leave. Everyone was satisfied."

There were running feet in the hall, yips, giggles, stifled threats, a thud against the door. The children more or less fell in, followed by Oliver, on a pungent wave of pony sweat and damp dog. Mrs. MacKenzie fanned it away from her face. "Much as it pains me to confess it, these unsavory objects—the two-legged ones—are my daughters, Susanna and Frances. What have you been doing?"

"Jumping the ponies," said Susanna, the older girl. "Nixie went best."

"Only because Prince didn't feel like jumping," the little redhead said. Her hair was soggy around the ears from pony kisses. Jennie remembered how it was; Nelson hadn't been much for that, but Bertie had been a sloppy sentimentalist or else Jennie had tasted especially delicious.

"Who was watching you?" their mother asked.

"Mr. Frost. May I have one of those?" Susanna pointed at the tray.

"Not with such filthy hands. And I know just how Mr. Frost watched you. He was probably out of sight, grooming a horse or shoveling manure. If you try jumping ponies ever again without your brother or father there—" She paused ominously.

"Yes, Mama," they said in duet.

"Now go and wash yourselves thoroughly, and then come back. Can I trust you, or must I send for Hannah?"

"No Hannah, Mama," said the older girl firmly. "You may trust us."

"No water fight then?"

"No water fight, Mama."

"Very well. Change your shoes and stockings, and put on your blue checks and clean pinafores. You can brush each other's hair." Frances put up her face for a kiss, and her mother said, "Not until you have wiped off Prince. Now go. You too, Oliver."

When they were gone, the last wraith of Christabel had wavered out of existence.

"Now," said the General's wife, "what did you teach your cousins?"

"Reading, writing, spelling, arithmetic, geography—the usual things. Oh, and music."

"No music," Mrs. MacKenzie said emphatically. "Did you also teach needlework?" Jennie shook her head. "No matter. It was the one thing in which I excelled at school, dull as it is. I shall be happy to supervise that if I am able to drop the other things. It's been a frightful effort. What do you say to sixty dollars the quarter, with housing found, your washing done, dairy products and garden stuff supplied?"

Jennie knew she looked stupid with astonishment, but she couldn't help it; she was having all she could do to believe this was really happening.

"It will be a tremendous relief to have the girls instructed by a lady, and my husband will have no reason to send them to his precious village school. My dear, when I think what they could bring home from there!"

Her shudder, her vivid mask of horror belonged behind flaring footlights. In the next instant she was back to business.

"Lessons in the morning only; I prefer them to spend the afternoon out of doors as long as the weather permits. Eliza Bisbee will be in charge then. Of course, you may move lessons outside whenever you like. Do my terms suit you?"

A refreshing shower of cool common sense restored Jennie's sense of balance. This woman needed her; there was a demand, practically a cry, for her services. *She had work.*

"They suit me very well," she said.

"I shall pay in advance; you will be needing something to wear now that there's no need for peasant dress. The Misses Applegate work quickly." She opened a drawer on her side of the table and took out a small japanned box. The sight of silver dollars being counted out beside the coffeepot was as heady as smelling salts. *Wait until I show Alick!* Jennie exulted within the shell of decorum.

"I haven't much money here, so I'll give you twenty on account, and the General will make up the rest. You have nothing to carry these in, have you?" Mrs. MacKenzie swung her large feet in scarlet kid slippers to the floor and rose with ease, considering the added weight of pregnancy. She moved across the room with a peculiar stately grace, trailing her draperies. She opened one of the small top drawers of a highboy and took out a reticule netted of black cord and lined with green silk.

"I shall return it tomorrow," Jennie said.

"Oh, keep it. If you've come with as little as you say, you'll need it. Consider it simply a token of our agreement. Can you start lessons tomorrow?"

"In *this?*" Jennie looked down at herself.

"Why not? It won't be for long if you see the Applegates this afternoon. You must be longing to shed those garments for good and stuff them into a ragbag. As for those articles on your feet—how could you have ever *endured* them?"

"They're tough, and comfortable, and light." Jennie felt as if she were defending a pair of old dogs someone wanted to put down now that they could no longer work.

"Well, doubtless they served their purpose," Mrs. MacKenzie said indulgently. "You'll find a shoemaker at the corner of Ship and Main streets, across from the Ark. That's the tenement house my husband built for his new pets." She sighed and stretched. "Now I must dress and go out and walk around and around the garden and orchard. Dr. Waite has been scolding me for not taking enough exercise."

She sat down before her dressing table and picked up a silver-backed hairbrush.

Jennie arose. "Thank you for the coffee; it was delicious."

"You never once said, 'I must ask my husband.' Are you always this independent?"

"I didn't give up my character when I became Mrs. Glenroy," said Jennie, "and he did not expect it of me. Do you disapprove?"

"Not at all! I'm enchanted! Your husband grows more intriguing by the moment. What will he choose to do here?"

"I can't speak for him," said Jennie. "I won't know until we meet again."

"My word, married life must be full of surprises for you two," said the General's wife, and turned back to her mirror.

Seven

JENNIE WALKED down the stairs with Quakerish propriety, proving she could contain her exhilaration, but only just. She stopped at the kitchen door, where a tea party of sorts was going on around the big table in the center. A blowsily handsome woman was suckling a small baby, held in one brawny red arm, and noisily supping from a bowl. She saw Jennie first and smiled and nodded, unembarrassed by her bare breast.

Hannah sat primly straight, holding a cup, her little finger daintily extended. The third woman had to be Mrs. Frost. She rose without haste; a square-built woman shrouded in a long-sleeved apron that covered her from neck to feet and wearing a cap that hid her hair and closely framed a knobby white face. Her black eyebrows were a surprise in all that pallor. She folded her hands across her middle. "Yes?" she inquired from colorless lips.

A bell jangled on a board by a door across the room, and Hannah said, "Oh, *drat* it!" She stood up, smoothing out her skirts and settling her cap, and flitted across the room toward the inner door, which opened to a flight of stairs.

"I'm Mrs. Glenroy," Jennie said. "You must be Mrs. Frost."

The cook's expression admitted the possibility. "I'll be teaching the children, beginning tomorrow morning," Jennie continued. "I am to have things from the dairy, but I don't know where it is. Will you tell me, please?"

"You come to me for anything you need. It's me that has the dairy, but my young ones do the work. What will you have now?" She was neither flinty nor grudging but had a plain economical, to-the-point manner which Jennie appreciated like a wind straight from Northumberland. And for the first time today she thought in so many words that home was within her reach.

She left the kitchen with a large basket over her arm, containing a covered jug of cream, a larger one of milk, a pound of butter, another pound of cheese, and a dozen brown eggs. Without varying her noncommittal expression or wasting speech, Mrs. Frost had added a slab of streaky bacon and what she called a junk of salt pork.

"You can keep the basket; you'll find use for it. Now there's lettuce and radishes up in the garden, and early spinach, and some beet and mustard greens. Don't touch the General's asparagus. He's mighty partic'lar about that."

"My father was the same way. We'd have demolished it all like a litter of rabbits if he hadn't laid down the law. The same with the first peas."

"The General, he's intendin' his first mess of peas on Independence Day," the laundress contributed.

"Ayuh, he's been threatening Frank and Sukey with battle, murder, and sudden death," said the cook.

"I *heard* him!" said the laundress merrily. "Him and his peas, the dear man!"

Mrs. Frost didn't smile, but there was the suggestion of a twinkle in the pebble gray eyes. "Now you have a good clean cold cellar under the cottage, where you can keep all this. Tight as a drum she is. All shipshape and Bristol fashion. But you'd best leave the doors open during the day, to dry out the timbers. And shut 'em at night to keep the varmints out. Those raccoons are mischievous as Satan."

She wanted to dance through the trees, singing. She had only to work out her quarter, saving every dollar she could, buying nothing that wasn't an absolute necessity, and she could sail home at the end of September. "Oh, the oak and the ash and the bonnie ellum tree, they're all a growing green in my own country!" she sang at last.

All at once she was visited by one of the two phenomena that always made her feel as if her brain were soaring and diving inside her skull. One was the sensation that whatever was happening had happened exactly this way before and she knew exactly what would be said or done next. The other one came to her today: the conviction that she was dreaming, that the past seven weeks had taken place in an hour, and that she didn't know where she would wake up. Only that she *would* wake up.

Once as a child she'd frightened herself sick by imagining, during a boring grammar lesson, that she was dreaming Pippin Grange and everyone in it; she might actually be some poor beggar child sleeping under a hedge and would soon awake to the wind blowing through her rags and the frost biting her bare feet. Or else she was freezing to death as she dreamed and would never again wake up to misery.

That is best, she had gallantly assured herself, but she didn't want to die, and sobs of self-pity rose in her throat and tears fell on her slate. Everybody thought she was sickening with a stomach distemper that was going around, and the prospect of being dosed for that knocked the other horror out of her mind.

The recollection had brought her back to the cottage. "You're no dream," she said to it. "You're here, no doubt about it, and I'm here. For now."

The cellar bulkhead was under the front kitchen windows. She laid back the two leaves, and the sun streamed down the fieldstone steps, and an earth-scented chill came up. Racks had been built against the whitewashed walls. She arranged her various jugs and pots on one of the shelves and on the cold floor, in one of the stoneware crocks Mrs. Frost had told her to look for under the dry sink in the pantry.

She was in no hurry now to do something about her dresses. She had more than two hours until noon, when presumably Alick would come back, and they could have bacon and eggs for their dinner. She combed her hair again before the bedroom mirror and put on one of Elspeth's caps. She'd hardly seen herself for a long time; she'd had no glass aboard the brig, and since yesterday she'd been swept along too fast for loitering at mirrors. She forced herself to stand still and see how she had appeared to Mrs. MacKenzie.

She'd thinned down past her natural slenderness, and there were hollows under her cheekbones. She knew how prominent her collarbones were and how easily countable her ribs. But her fingernails were pink, and the whites of her eyes were as clear as a child's. Her irises were of an odd shade she had hated until Papa called it tawny topaz, and because of it, she'd received her mother's topaz jewelry, the bracelet, pendant, and eardrops still locked in the marquetry keepsake box.

Whether she'd ever see them again she didn't know, but it didn't matter. She was going home.

She transferred ten dollars to the claret velvet bag and hung it around her neck. The rest she left in the reticule and put that in the top drawer of the pine chest. Then she put Elspeth's shawl around her shoulders and took her basket and set out with a sense of high adventure. Main Street in a young New England village was hardly Samarkand or the Hesperides, but it was America. Jennie Hawthorne, not dreaming, was walking in America, and she intended to make the most of the experience.

She took the path north out past the Necessary and came to the lane Alick had discovered last night. She let herself out through the gate that swung across the drive to the brick stables. Across the lane the rising wooded land she had seen from the brig climbed to a sky the blue of flax blossom.

Two men on horseback rode past the western end of the lane toward the shore, and she heard a wagon coming down behind them. She walked the few hundred yards out to the road. At its foot the horsemen were turning off past the seemingly haphazard arrangement of sheds crouched darkly against the azure sparkle of the river. The wagonload of empty new barrels drawn by a massive gray jolted noisily past her; the driver sagged on his board seat with his hat tilted over his eyes.

She turned right and up the hill. The woods continued with her on that side, a susurrus of restless leaves over her head, but across the road the land was cleared to green meadow enclosed by stone walls. Half a dozen cows of mixed ancestry were grazing there. Partway up the hill a tidy red-painted house stood at right angles to the road; the dooryard was fenced off with white pickets from the road and the surrounding meadowland. It had a succession of additions, each smaller than the last. The final one connected handily with a barn that loomed over all. The barn doors stood open, and hens wandered in and out. Out at one side a girl was teaching a calf to drink from a bucket. Her laughter carried across the road to Jennie, who wished she could go over and hang on the fence and watch, and laugh with this American girl, and let the calf greedily suck her fingers.

The intersection of Main and Ship streets approximated a village square; there was a horse trough in the center, and a wagon had stopped there now to let the horses drink. Two men leaned on the rim of the stone basin, chewing straws and arguing vigorously in a friendly way. Across Main Street a tall brick house, with a porch and columns across its front, had a large sign mounted below its second floor windows, reading ST. DAVID INN. A long wing and an adjoining stable extended behind it down a narrow side street that seemed to wander off into the countryside. On the opposite corner there was a shabby shop. M.F. BAIN, GEN'L MDSE, said the lettering across a dingy window.

On Jennie's side the shoemaker was to her right, and across Ship Street to her left stood the Ark. Outside stairs led up the gable end to the upper floors. The roof fairly bristled with chimneys, and there was a small mountain of firewood just off the road behind the building, where the land slanted down to the northern pasture wall; small children were attempting to climb it. Past the woodpile clotheslines were crowded with washing, and more laundry was spread out on the grass. The Highland women had been early up and at it and were still busy around the washhouse. It had three extra doors, narrow and closed: Necessaries, Jennie guessed.

The girls sat on the stone wall, combing their wet long hair, talking and laughing among themselves. Jennie was pleased to see that Mairi was smiling and too absorbed to notice Jennie across the road. A small barefoot adventurer in a kilt reached the top of the wooden mountain and crowed like a young cockerel. As faces turned toward him, Jennie went quickly around the corner and entered the shoemaker's shop, under a sign shaped like a boot. J. Barron was a wispy man with flyaway gray hair and magnifying spectacles. At sight of her his eyes squeezed up in alarm, and he said loudly, as if she were deaf, "I . . . don't . . . speak . . . that . . . language!"

"Neither do I, Mr. Barron," said Jennie, "except about twenty words, and none of those are useful in ordering a pair of shoes."

He rushed around the corner to set a chair for her, incoherently apologizing. When he had run down, he took a tremendous breath, placed the fingertips of both hands together before his chest, and said quite calmly, "Now, how may I help you?"

He showed her some shoes waiting to be collected, and she picked a serviceable walking shoe that did not look too heavy and clumsy. He said modestly, "That is my own design."

"It's very trim and stylish," she said. She was taking off the brogues so he could measure her feet, and she held one out to him. "Perhaps you'd be interested in another man's work. Most Highland men are their own shoemakers, and this man was better at it than most."

"They're well made." He turned them over in his hands and examined every detail. "Well worn, too."

"They've walked a good many miles," she said.

"May I wish you well in America, Mrs.—?"

"Mrs. Alick Glenroy. Thank you for your kind wishes. Shall I pay you now?"

"Not until you have tried the shoes on and are satisfied. They will be ready in two days."

She looked around at the boots and shoes awaiting repair and the work in progress. "The brownies must come in and work for you at night, Mr. Barron. I hope you leave out milk and biscuits for them."

He laughed outright like a delighted child. "They're so notional these days! It's raspberry shrub or nothing in the summer and cider all fall."

Main Street was exceptionally wide and, surprisingly, was served by wooden sidewalks raised above the dust of the road. The Misses Applegate, DRESSMAKERS AND MANTUA MAKERS, PURVEYORS OF FINE FABRICS AND LADIES' INTIMATE APPAREL, were three houses beyond the shoemaker. Jennie met other walkers and was frankly stared at, tentatively nodded to, and one young woman in a group of three smiled and seemed about to speak, but the others carried her on. Smothered exclamations and exasperated hushings bobbed in their wake.

"They can't even speak English!" someone said indignantly.

The Misses Applegate had their business rooms on the first floor of a square white house and lived on the second floor. They were delicate little middle-aged women, apprehensive like the shoemaker at first sight of her and then so relieved that they offered her a cup of tea, which she accepted. She wished that Sylvia and William could see her sitting in a Queen Anne chair, dressed in linsey-woolsey and a mutch, drinking tea from a translucent cup while the ladies showed her calico lengths as if they'd been India muslin.

She had explained that she had come to America with little more than what she stood in and would like something practical yet pretty, if possible. They had already heard that a young English lady had run away from Scotland with one of the General's wild mountain men, and they were enchanted to have her in their establishment. Romance was in their forget-me-not eyes, tinting their cheeks with pink, fluttering in their voices. They could hardly wait to get a look at *him*.

She picked two patterns of calico, and Miss Louisa tenderly suggested that one be made up with a white lawn neck frill and long sleeves for cool days, and one with short sleeves. She should have a change of fichus for that; nothing was nicer than that touch of snowy white with a bit of narrow ruffling to take away the severity. And what about caps? Miss Helena asked. Their own were confections of lace and mull. She said prettily that she must economize, so her two caps should be plain. They sighed for her. The apprentices in the workroom were silent as they listened.

She would need a cambric slip and two full holland aprons with bib fronts and deep pockets. The ladies' intimate apparel counter supplied two pairs of lisle stockings and a pair of knitted garters, so she could do away with Kirsty's, and two pairs of India cotton drawers and vests.

She'd have liked a light shawl, but she was reluctant to spend her money on one of the mohairs or Paisleys. Still, the prospect of wearing Elspeth's heavy wool tartan all summer made her itch. Penny-wise and pound-foolish, she thought, and asked for the most inexpensive shawl in stock. The Misses Applegate thought she was being terribly brave. They came up with a plain cream-colored wrap of fine, light wool. Her pleasure in it pleased them. Meanwhile, the apprentices listened in an enthralled hush.

"And now, Mrs. Glenroy," said Miss Louisa, "will you step into this dressing room so I may take your measurements in your, er, petticoat?"

"Certainly," said Jennie, and then thought, *Corset.* They'd be shocked to death; going without a corset, even if you had not a spare ounce on your bones, was immodest. She was about to be punished for allowing them to treat her as a heroine when she was nothing of the sort; she would have to go into corsets after weeks of immoral freedom.

"Do you also sell stays?" she asked grandly. "I was obliged to discard mine. They were quite beyond help."

Eight

WHEN SHE LEFT with her basket of parcels, Miss Helena pattered out to the gate with her, lacy cap just reaching Jennie's shoulder. "I know, my dear," she said confidentially, "that someone else, your maid perhaps, has always thought of these details for you. But if I may just remind you, you will need a hat or a bonnet for church, and Mrs. Loomis, just down the street there beyond the bank, is a milliner. It's the house with the locust trees in the dooryard."

She waved Jennie through the gate like an affectionate aunt.

Jennie had intended to inquire at the post office about sending mail to England and to buy some writing supplies, but by now all she could think of was getting back to the cottage and shedding the new corset. Who would have believed either one of those little women had the strength to lace so tightly?

"Jeannie Glenroy!" Anna Kate sang out from the second floor landing of the Ark. "Will you just be stepping up to see?"

There was no escape without hurting her feelings, and she had just begun to be happy again after losing her baby. Jennie crossed the road, waving to those who called to her from the back yard. The old men sat on a bench at the front of the house, smoking their pipes and watching the traffic; a traveling chaise and four horses had just pulled up at the inn.

Jennie had never in her life until today felt tired of climbing steps. Confounded corset! She should have done her own lacing. Anna Kate hurried her into the room allotted to her and Hector. "And will you be looking at all this?" she exclaimed. The window that let in so much light and could be pushed and held open with a stick; the camp beds; the way the fireplace drew. Her voice faded, returned, diminished again. Strength poured out of Jennie's body in a wave from her head to her feet, as if all the blood were leaving it. She found herself on the floor, blinking dazedly into Anna Kate's frightened face.

She tried to laugh. "I must have tripped on something." Anna Kate whispered exhortations and reassurances, helping her sit up and reach a chair. She brought water in a tin dipper. Jennie waved it away. She was giddy again, and she lowered her head to her knees and felt the corset's resistance.

"It's these damned stays!" she said angrily. "I've been without them for so long, they're strangling me!"

"Och, *mo chridh*, surely you are knowing—" The soft voice broke off.

"Knowing *what*?"

"The trouble that is at you." She laid her hand on her belly, then moved it out a little way and sketched in the air a rounding shape.

Jennie stared at her, her mouth open and drying. She wanted to shriek that it wasn't so, but all the tantrums in the world couldn't make it *not* so, any more than they could bring back the dead.

Her forehead was wet and cold. What *could* bring back the dead? Nigel had left his child in her.

The giddiness passed. She even smiled at Anna Kate, saying, "I know it's the corset."

Anna Kate politely agreed that no doubt it was the corset, just. She walked down the steps with her, holding her elbow, but Jennie's head was mercilessly clear now.

She returned to the cottage like a sleepwalker, seeing and hearing nothing but what was in her brain, yet knowing it was no dream. "We sleeping wake, and waking sleep." No chance of waking from this.

She went upstairs and took off all her clothes and put on her nightgown. She had to take out her passion on something; she rammed the stays into a drawer as if getting them out of sight would do away with the other appalling visitation. She got into bed and pulled the covers up over her head to shut out the heartless summer sky and leaves, and curled herself up, knees to chest.

Nigel had been revenged even if he couldn't know. If she survived, the child would be her manacles and leg irons until it was grown and her youth gone. *If* she survived. One could never abrogate that "if" where childbirth was concerned. She shook her head in paroxysms of horror as if death had come in at her window like a grinning skeleton in an old woodcut.

How fearless, how jaunty she'd been about an autumn sailing for England. That was the lithe, unencumbered Jennie. Jennie the fool. Jennie the lamb prancing innocently toward slaughter. A fall in her stateroom during a storm, and she could have a miscarriage. Some women hemorrhaged; Anna Kate had been lucky, but Jennie saw herself sewn into canvas and buried at sea.

Stifling with panic, she threw off the covers and sat up. Her teeth were shattering. *In the spring, Jennie, you'll go home in the spring!* she tried to tell herself. When it is over. . . . Over *how?* Fear tried to garrote her as it had done when she saw Nigel dead, when she ran from Jock Dallas, when she nearly drowned in the flooded corries, and when she thought that Alick had abandoned her. She had survived all that only to die giving birth to this child. If it was in the wrong position, she and the child both could die of exhaustion. She could bleed to death. She could die of childbed fever.

If the child lived, and if Alick repudiated it, who would get it to her sisters? It would go to the workhouse.

The child. Not hers, but a loathed and punishing responsibility, as if some agency had chosen her womb like a public conveyance to carry the creature.

Why couldn't she expel it now before it was anything? There must be something she could take; she'd heard enough about that at home. Herbal compounds to bring on the menses—that was the genteel way of putting it. There had to be an herbwoman here. How could she find out? Whom could she ask?

She'd pretend a scholarly interest. She could even hear herself saying to some sympathetic face, "The lore of herbs has fascinated me all my life." If only she could meet Stephen Wells again. He would think nothing of her question; he knew she was full of odd quirks.

She lay back, hugging herself tightly. Against her closed lids she saw her gravestone. It would not carry her own name but this other one she'd assumed like the other woman's clothes. It stood in a windswept churchyard, and blowing snow heaped up in little drifts on the new-turned earth. *In the dead of winter I will die here,* she thought, *after a long agony, and be buried under someone else's name, someone who never existed. How could all this have happened to me? How could I become as dead as Tamsin and Nigel? Who would have dreamed the meeting in the park that day would end like this? Nigel there, and I here, our story ended before it was a year old.*

Tears ran from the corners of her eyes and down past her cheekbones to her ears. She forbade herself to weep aloud for fear of losing herself in a frenzy.

Think, Jennie. You can find the herbwoman. You must. If not today, tomorrow. Ask Mrs. Frost. You will be calmer tomorrow; you can bring it off. Look how you've brought everything else off. "Oh, God!" she groaned, her body twisting uncontrollably as if it were already in labor.

"*Jeannie!*"

Her eyes flew open. In her blurred vision Alick was an immense black shape leaning over her, as if the fantasy of death had become reality. "Have you not been up today then? Are you sick? What is it?"

"Nothing, nothing, just leave me alone," she entreated. "Go build the fire, and I will cook the dinner."

"No." He touched her wet cheek. There was a scent of new-sawn wood about him; his hand smelled of it. "What is this. Tears? Is it sick for home you are? We will have your fare before winter. I am beginning in the boatyard."

"Alick, I am carrying a child." She hadn't meant to say it like that or at all. She squeezed her eyes shut so as not to see his face. When he didn't speak, she said, "Nigel's child. We didn't leave him behind, you see. He is with us now, in this room."

"How long are you knowing this?"

"Anna Kate told me this morning. I am so stupid I never thought. . . Oh, yes, I've been up today, and I wish I hadn't been!" She grimaced in her effort to hold back, but the dam broke anyway. "I don't know what to do, and I am so alone and so afraid!" Her voice cracked into a whimper, and she grabbed at the bedclothes and pulled them over her face. "Go away! Please go away!"

"The fear is at you that you will die?" He sat on the edge of the bed, someone talking to a frantic child.

"Yes, yes!" she cried distractedly. "I will, I know I will!"

She felt herself gathered up, bedclothes and all, and strongly held.

Her cheek was pressed against the linen shirt smelling of sawdust and sweat, the hard flesh and bone beneath it, and his voice beginning there but coming out over her head.

"You are not alone, and you will not die. I am promising you."

"You can't promise that. No one can."

"You promised me a ship and a safe voyage. You promised me my life. Now I am promising you yours."

It was wrong; it was insane. No, it was the comfort given to that child frantic with night terrors. It would do until the next time or until the terrors became the permanent stuff of life. For this little while, it was someone to hold her, and she began to relax to the strong, regular beat of his heart under her ear. They sat like this for a long time.

After a while he asked, "When will this child be born?"

"Perhaps January," she said in a thick, tired voice. "I was going to be home by then, and you would be wherever you chose to be. *Free* anyway. Seeing the country before you settled down, the way we talked about it."

"Och, the waiting will do me no harm. I will be learning that much more here. In the spring you will be going home to your sisters with a bonny baby."

If I live, she thought. "I was going home a free woman," she said. "The world was almost as open to me as it is to you. It's true that 'pride goeth before destruction, and a haughty spirit before a fall.' I believed I could do anything, and I have been brought down."

"Not by your God, surely. He is the one who is not caring, remember."

"Well, then, but their God. Taking His revenge."

"That one is having enough to do to look after His own. Och, Jeannie, you are not sounding yourself, so meek and poor-spirited. Shall I be bringing you ashes to put on your head and sackcloth to wear?"

She forced a little sound, not quite a chuckle, but he deserved a reward for trying so hard. "I don't want this child," she said. "There are certain medicines, certain herbs, and there is always a woman who knows about them. There must be one here, and I am going to find her."

"No." He didn't raise his voice, but his arms clamped harder around her. "You could die of some of their mixtures or not be killing the child but bringing it forth in its time a poor wee thing that lives on and on with no wits to it whatever."

"You mean an *idiot?*"

"Aye. Or be born with no arms or with its palate cleft. And there can be even worse. Would you be having the courage to put the helpless creature to death then because you failed once?"

Revolted, she pushed away from him, but he didn't release her. She knew what he meant; there'd been such a child born in the village at home. Its deformities were blamed on incest between brother and sister. But it was well known that the mother had swallowed down one fearful concoction after another, trying to abort.

It was one of the few things not talked over with Papa because they weren't supposed to know about it. Otherwise, he might have told her what Alick was trying to tell her now. Both parents had been strong, handsome people, and so should the baby have been, incest or not.

"All right, Alick," she said drearily. "I'll dress now and prepare your dinner. You'll have bacon and eggs. I cannot eat."

"You will not be starving it under the same roof with me." He set her back against the pillows and stood up. "I wish I could be bringing you a cup of strong hot tea."

"I haven't bought any yet. I was going to the shop this afternoon."

"And you will be going," he said. "Where is the food? I can be frying bacon as well as any man."

"It's in the cellar. Oh, Alick, I took that great stand about there being no man and woman talk between us, but look at us! Look at *me*. You are so good, and I have been a—a menace to you from the first."

"The subject is closed." He went downstairs.

She washed her face and dressed. Now that the decision had been made for her, she began to feel familiar with herself again. Terror had temporarily loosed its grip so she could breathe and think a little better. It was still there, but now it wouldn't come after her until night.

Combing her tangled hair—this time not before the mirror, she didn't want to see herself—she thought about the deformed baby. The brother came to market one day with red eyes, grumbling that the baby had died in its cradle in the night. There was talk, but the authorities, including Jennie's father, were too merciful to ask questions. Besides, it wasn't unknown for even a well-cared-for and seemingly healthy infant to be found dead in the cradle.

The woman had turned very odd, wandering the hills at all hours of the day and night. One night the thatched farmhouse burned with the sister and brother in it, leaving only the stone walls and chimneys. The cows and horses had been turned out into the pasture, the pigs and poultry were running free, and the dog and cat had been put out of the house; the woman had made sure that no innocent creature should go to death with the sinners.

Nine

ALICK OFFERED to boil eggs for her, but the smell of bacon frying
in an iron skillet was making her mouth water in spite of all her
ravings and lamentations. Where was the morning sickness that had
plagued Sylvia? She'd never had a trace of it, and that ridiculous swoon
in the Ark followed too soon after the corset to be a coincidence.

Alick pushed a mug of milk toward her. "Drink," he said.

I don't believe I'm expecting at all, she thought defiantly, *but the milk
will be good for me. A week of eggs and milk and meat, and the flow will come.*
She'd always considered the monthly cycle a particularly nasty conspiracy
against females, but now she'd have welcomed, if not a flood, a rivulet.

Alick was reassured by her appetite, she could tell, though he wasn't
one for extraneous talk. The poor man had just put in a bad hour with
a hysterical woman who had howled all over his shirt. She owed him so
much, but he would probably consider himself amply recompensed when
she had removed herself from his life.

"We need a sweet," she said. "I'll fetch it." They finished off their
meal with the rest of the Indian pudding doused in cream. She told him
about her situation as governess and their new wealth.

"And now tell me about your work," she said. "You mentioned the
shipyard, but I was as entangled in my troubles as a sheep in the bur-
docks."

He couldn't hide the softening around his dark gray eyes. "I was never
dreaming of a ship at Linnmore. Never was yearning to sail in one. But
I was driven to it, and now here I am, beginning to learn how to build
a ship, and Tormod is along with me. The man in charge is a Lowlander,

but he is a fair man. We will go from one part to another, till we are tasting it all and seeing what we do best. Tormod is beginning at the forge with the shipsmith."

"And you?"

"With the joiners. Was I telling you that I will be studying mathematics in the dominie's night class? There is much mathematics in shipbuilding."

She took her basket and money and went out with him. While they were walking along the lane, she saw he could think of nothing but the shipyard. Or almost nothing; when a stone rolled under her foot and made her lurch, he seized her arm. "Are you all right then?"

"Not even a twist!" She held out her foot and shook it. When he knew she wasn't pregnant, he could stop worrying about her. She tried to imagine Alick lighthearted, not distrusting, accepting good fortune as his due. She wanted it to happen before she left for England, so she could remember him like that.

They passed on their left the stone gateposts and archway marking the formal entrance to the grounds of Strathbuie House. The shipyard was at the foot of Ship Street, on the western side of the wharf promontory. There were two half-built vessels up on the stocks, one intended for the Russian trade, the other to be a coastal lime carrier. The General had had three of these in service, but one had been lost in the spring to a fire that couldn't be smothered, which was the only way to control a fire in the lime.

"But the big one, she'll be the beauty," Alick said. "Do you know, the General is not telling what her name will be?"

He pointed out the brickyard across the deep cove to the right of them. From the next point beyond that a long dock thrust out into the fast blue currents of the incoming tide. A bridge crossed the narrows to the west of the dock, and beyond the bridge the river came flowing between precipitous slopes on its way through the countryside from its birthplace.

The harbor, called the Pool, was comparatively empty today. A few fast little boats were skimming along under the eastern bank; but only three large vessels were at anchor, and the *Paul Revere* was not one of them. "Has she gone again this soon?" Jennie asked.

"She's ashore up the creek on the other side," Alick said. "They will be washing her down and soaping her hull for speed." Just since this

morning he handled these terms with ease. "She is bound for the West
Indies next. And I am bound for my work." Men were coming down
Ship Street and around by the shore road from both west and east. "It
wouldn't do for me to be late now, would it? The Lowlander has an eye
on him like an eagle, just waiting to drop on a mountain hare."

Tormod MacKenzie caught up with them, doffing his bonnet to her
and grinning and puffing, too out of breath to speak. He was a big
redhead, a great wrestler but no runner.

She left them at the gate and walked on toward the store. She wasn't
pregnant. She should know. It was her own body; it wasn't keeping any
secrets from her. With the tight stays, and Anna Kate putting the idea
into her head just because she wanted a child so much herself, her body
had become panic's victim. Now it was telling her there'd been no sane
reason for the panic.

The store was half on the wharf, half on the land; the front steps
and entrance were on the land side. As she reached them, two women
in shawls and straw bonnets came out. She stood back out of their way,
smiled, and said, "Good afternoon."

"Afternoon," one of them said brusquely. The other lowered her
head in either shyness or incivility and hurried down the steps.

Tony was keeping store. "You saved me!" He joyfully greeted her.
"I was about to crawl into the darkest corner of the storeroom and die
of boredom."

She looked around appreciatively at the goods on the shelves, the
number of barrels, bins, and chests, the net bags of oranges, lemons,
and limes hanging from the beams; a door stood open into a crowded
storeroom. "What wealth! I have not seen so much food all in one place
since I don't know when. And the way it *smells*! Delicious!"

"That must be because Mr. Dickenson isn't smoking his pipe," said
Tony. "Either his wife or his pig is farrowing today, I forget which; that
is why I am here. And my father is out of his office I know not where,
so I am all soul alone here. The most exciting moment of my day—until
you came—was when I put vinegar in Mrs. Eubanks's molasses jug and
vice versa."

"Ah, Tony, you have my sympathy," said Jennie. "As for me, I came
out without a list, and I don't know where to begin in this cavern of
riches."

"Allow me!" He brought a round-backed chair over from the fireplace and set it by the counter and provided her with a slate and chalk. Then he sat on the end of the counter nearest the windows and looked out at the sails on the river.

"For the sin of being the General's son," he said mournfully, "I am *here* and my boat is *there*, a prisoner on her mooring, her sail furled, while other souls less privileged than I squander hours tacking up and down the river with a perfect breeze on a perfect tide."

"I really do grieve for you, Tony." Jennie was rapidly filling up the slate.

"I'm like young what's his name in the Tower. 'The day is past, and yet I saw no sun;/And now I live, and now my life is done.'"

"I thought that you were headed for college, not the block. Please tell me that you have soap. I desperately desire soap."

He slid off the counter, ducked down to a low shelf, and came up with a thick, pale, rough-cut bar. It had a pleasing herbal scent, predominantly lavender.

"Mrs. Shenstone makes that. We buy honey from her, too, and dry thyme and sage and suchlike, if you should have a hankering. She grows everything and knows everything."

Lightning zigzagged across her midriff; in the next breath she thought, *That foolishness is past. I am not pregnant.*

"At home some people called our herbwoman a witch," she said.

He laughed. "Anyone would have a hard time making out Hat Shenstone to be a witch. They depend on her too much."

"Do you think she would mind if I visited her, or doesn't she welcome guests to her herb garden?" She was asking out of simple curiosity and an interest in North American herbs, that was all.

"She's a friendly soul, but she lives a far piece out of town, in a section we call the Wolf Den. They say the last wolves lived out there. It used to be said she *raised* the last wolf from a cub when his folks were killed, and it died of old age."

"I love the thought," said Jennie. "Is it true?"

"My sister and I loved it, too, but my father says it was a dog she had. We'd have rather it was a wolf."

"Does she have any big dogs now that would attack me?"

He shook his head. "Goats, cats, and an old donkey. You turn off Main Street by the church and follow the track till it ends in her dooryard. But it's four miles at least."

"I am a good walker. . . . There, I think my list is complete, but I shall have to make two trips."

Tony gallantly said that he would carry the heavy things around when he was released from involuntary servitude. He tried to sell her dry beans and invited her to try a strip off a slack-salted codfish. "If you are going to be a citizen of Maine, you'll have to learn how to bake beans, and fix codfish in ten different ways," he told her. "Cornmeal, too. And salt pork."

When he could detain her no longer, he put a little stoneware pot of marmalade in her basket. "From Scotland," he said. "A gift to a new customer. Mrs. Glenroy, where are they all?" It was a *cri de coeur*. "Bain carries only odds and ends, and they can't be living out of the baker shop! I thought those girls might come."

"The day isn't over yet," she said kindly, "and they were busy washing this morning."

He sagged back against the counter, disconsolate. "I know. But today feels like forever."

Ten

THE FIRST thing she did when she returned to the cottage was to build up the fire and put the kettle on. She made tea in the George Washington teapot and drank three cups, walking around inside and outside the cottage. If she sat down for a moment, she felt defenseless, as if something were waiting to catch her off guard. It was only the aftermath of this morning's shock, she knew, but she couldn't make herself be still.

She cut up a piece of fresh beef and started it browning in bacon fat in the skillet, while she peeled and sliced some authoritative onions that had her weeping and whispering, *"Damnation!"* She added the onions, a little water, salt, and pepper, covered the skillet, and left the beef to simmer. She scrubbed potatoes for boiling. She washed the dishes and then her underwear and stockings; the new soap made a satisfying lather, and afterward the onion scent had gone from her hands, and her skin felt smooth.

She laid her clothing to dry on the open grass between the house and the well. By now she was starved again; she sliced a roll in two, thickly buttered the pieces, and poured more tea. She was ready to sit down for a few minutes now and took her *strupak* out to the bench.

The robin was harvesting the lawn; he had a mouthful of worms hanging down on either side of his bill like a thick mustache. Feeding young. Baby birds, all open mouths. Cherished in their blue eggs and then pecking their way out, naked, weak, helpless, perpetually hungry. Prey of squirrels and predatory birds, as human babies were the prey of disease, ignorance, and abuse.

She found she had her hand on her flat abdomen, pushing it tightly in. There was nothing there but the normal set of vitals, she *knew* it. She jumped up and went for a walk through the orchard to find the vegetable garden, where she pulled up lettuce, young spinach, a few beet greens, and a handful of radishes.

Alick wasn't home by six, and she fell asleep in a rocking chair with her feet up on a windowsill. When she woke up, Alick was standing by her chair looking down at her. She'd been so deeply asleep, without dreaming, that at first she gazed up at him as if straining to recognize him through fog. She had the feeling he had been standing there for some time, wishing she could read his mind to save him from having to tell her something important.

She lowered her feet and sat up, sniffing. "The potatoes have burned on!"

"No, no, they're fine." He put out a restraining hand. "Don't be jumping up."

"If I'm light-headed, it's from hunger. Aren't you starved?" When he was satisfied that she wasn't giddy, he went outside to wash, and she set the table. He had drained the potatoes while she slept, and they were drying in the pot on the back of the stove. The rest of the supplies from the store were in the pantry; he must have brought them. She was disturbed at having slept so heavily that she'd heard nothing, but she supposed it was natural after such a day.

Alick came in smelling of soap and water now instead of sawdust. "I am late because I went to the shop with some of the others. They were wanting to buy food, but they were feeling a bit shy. It is not easy to accept credit. And they were not knowing the names of some things."

"Tony must have been disappointed. He was hoping the girls would come to shop, pretty maids all in a row."

"They will be kept close as the old hen's chicks," he said. "Tony is not the only lad with an eye for them, and don't be thinking the minister was missing *that*. He is sure to be praying over them already and shaking his finger under the parents' noses." He laughed. "He has work at a cooperage. It is just across the road from the Ark, so he can be keeping an eye on the comings and goings."

They soaked their dry rolls in the stew and had a salad of the young greens sharpened with thin-sliced radishes and dressed with vinegar, sugar, salt, and pepper. They finished off with coffee and the last of the rolls toasted on a stove lid and spread with marmalade.

"Have I prepared a feast?" she asked complacently.

"You have indeed. Now tell me how you are feeling. You look feverish."

"The kitchen is hot, even with everything open. I think we can let the fire go out now, don't you?" He sat with his chin on his hand, watching her, and now she did feel feverish, with nerves and embarrassment. "I am perfectly well! You don't need to mother-hen me. I would like to discuss something, please."

"I am listening."

"I want to share my wages with you, so if you want to have boots made, new breeches, a coat—anything at all—"

"You should be putting away everything you can spare toward your voyage home in the spring." He rebuked her. "It will be making the time pass easier for you, knowing you have it. My wage will be a dollar a day until I am trained. Then it will go up, I am not knowing how much. But my earnings would feed us even if we left this cottage."

"But why should we do that? Do you still want to?"

"No," he admitted, "because it is comfortable for you, and for me, too. I am not denying that. But what if you are not able to teach for the quarter after this one?"

She looked at him in seeming perplexity, playing with her apron, thinking, *Shall I tell him now that I know I'm not pregnant or wait until I have conclusive proof?* He surprised her by leaning across the table and giving her hand a little squeeze.

"I wasn't meaning to frighten you like some old cailleach. It's just that you look thin enough to snap like a twig in winter."

"Oh, I know I haven't the broad, sturdy back for carrying a creel of peats," she said teasingly, "but it's the lean horse that wins the race, you know. I may be thin, but I'm tough as harness leather."

"A *Dia*, I know how tough you are! The feet nearly walked off you, scared out of your wits, half-drowned, half-starved, and never a yelp out of you."

"It's because I was too weak with fear to yelp," she answered scoffingly.

There was the rap of a stick on the open front door. The General stood there, and Oliver was halfway into the hall, yearning at them and panting ardently.

"Good evening, good evening!" said the General.

Alick went out to meet him. "Will you be coming in, General MacKenzie?"

"I would like to if I am not imposing upon your privacy or interrupting the evening chapter." He limped into the kitchen. "Ah, you've made it feel quite homelike already. I knew you would take the curse off the place. A figure of speech only," he added hastily. He was bareheaded and wore a loose blue jacket and linen pantaloons, and the informality gave a comfortable effect.

He motioned the dog to stay behind, but Alick said, "Oliver is already a friend here." Oliver promptly collapsed, making the dishes rattle.

The clock struck half-past seven, and the General cocked his head at it. "Ah, yes, the elegant clock and the empty parlor, and thereby hangs a tale, as someone once said."

He brought a small canvas sack from one of his jacket pockets and dropped it on the table. It fell heavily with a musical clash of its contents.

"The rest of your quarterly stipend, Mrs. Glenroy. Forty dollars. May I sit?"

"Please," Jennie said.

He lowered himself into a rocking chair, keeping his lame leg extended before him. "I'm sure you'll not consider it an attack against you, Mrs. Glenroy, when I say I'd prefer my daughters to attend the village school rather than be educated at home. But your fortunate appearance here has ended a stalemate between my wife and me, so I'm very grateful."

"Thank you," said Jennie. "Will you have a cup of coffee?" She didn't want to pounce too greedily on the money.

"I *will* have a cup, please. My wife likes tea at night, but I love a good cup of coffee. Sit down, Alick Glenroy, and have a pipe with me, and tell me how the Highlanders and Lowlanders are getting along."

Alick was not overcome by the surprise visit. He was neither on the defensive nor overanxious to please. Jennie poured coffee for both men and sat down with her cup at the other end of the table. She listened dreamily to them while the room turned shadowy and the birds gradually ceased. Alick's voice with its Gaelic intonations and rhythm may have influenced the General, may have brought back early memories of such voices; he spoke as softly as Alick, with now and then a Gaelic word dropped into the gentle stream. She hardly noticed the sense of their talk, there was so much enjoyment in the sound of it.

"Well, Mrs. Glenroy," the General said suddenly. "You're very quiet. Are we putting you to sleep? Would you like to hear the story of the clock?"

"Yes, I would," she said.

"You must promise that you will never mention it to my wife. It was, and still is, very distressing to her." He himself sounded more amused than distressed. "The cottage was built for an English couple imported to give us some style up here in the wilderness. They were to be butler and lady's maid. Their recommendations were so exalted, sprinkled with titles like stars in the Milky Way, their desire to settle in America was so passionate, how could anything fail? Well, to abbreviate the tale, they lasted for about six months, tried my patience to the breaking point with their airs, insulted our local people, though Mrs. Frost, God bless her, refused to be budged; that woman is the Rock of Gibraltar! Then they decamped one summer night in a hired wagon, loaded with everything they could carry. The parlor furniture was very good—they were to have nothing but the best, Mrs. MacKenzie insisted, because they were used to the best. Why they overlooked the clock when they took the lamps, we'll never know. Perhaps something startled them."

"Where did they go?" Alick asked.

"To Canada. My wife was for sending troops of horse in all directions and dragging them back—preferably behind the horses—having them tried, flogged, tarred and feathered, drawn and quartered—" He was laughing so hard he had to wipe his eyes. "Oh, my, that was a scene. My poor Lydia! I paid the farmer for his wagon and team and called the whole circus cheap at the price. They probably sold their loot as soon as they were over the border, and God knows what they are doing now. But prospering, I'd swear to it."

Still laughing, he heaved himself out of his chair and held onto the table edge for a moment. "My nuisance of a leg stiffens up at the end of the day."

"I will be walking back with you," Alick said.

"I shan't turn that down. One stumble, and I'll be cast like a hog on ice. A great sight for the crows to discuss at daylight!" When he shook hands with Jennie at the door, he said, "We shall find you some furniture for that room. There's enough in the attic to hold an auction." He maneuvered himself off the step with obvious difficulty. "It's a souvenir of my service to the country, and as such I should cherish it, but somehow I do not. However, it's better than no leg at all, isn't it? Good night, Mrs. Glenroy."

She put the sack of money away in the chest in the parlor. It was satisfyingly heavy; silver dollars were as comforting as gold guineas.

It was too dusky in the pantry to wash dishes now, and there were clean bowls and spoons for the porridge. She rinsed the coffeepot at the back door and also cleaned her teeth there, where she could spit with impunity. She visited the Necessary. Remembering the beast at the door last night reminded her to shut the cellar doors, and she wished she could surprise a raccoon in this cool amethyst-blue twilight. That reminded her of the woman who lived at a place called the Wolf Den and the story of the last wolf. She wanted it to be true; why couldn't it have been true? It was the kind of story she and her sisters had loved and fiercely believed.

She undressed and put on her nightgown, looking out at the pale splotches of her forgotten laundry spread on the grass and now wet with dew. The fitful sparks of fireflies were beginning to appear. Yawning and lethargic, she got into bed, intending to call to Alick when he came in and tell him the plaid was folded on the chest in the parlor if he was sleeping rough again.

But she was sleeping within the next five minutes, not even knowing it was happening.

Eleven

SHE SAT UP in bed, her eyes shut and holding her head between her hands as if to keep it in place on her neck. Alick had come in so quietly that only the faint creak of a board gave him away, and a whiff of woodsmoke from his clothes where he'd been building the fire. She felt him waiting and wished he would go away. Finally he said softly, "Jeannie, are you all right? Are you having a pain?"

"No, no." It was unpleasant to shake her head. "Stupefied. It must be like a laudanum morning-after. Why is it that a heavy sleep leaves you feeling worse than a light one? Where did *you* sleep last night?"

"Across the hall."

"And I never even heard you come up or go down. You Highlanders are a light-stepping lot." She kneaded the back of her neck, gingerly tipped her head back, opened her eyes, and gazed blearily at the ceiling and then at Alick. She came wide-awake, blinking the detritus of sleep out of her eyes.

"Where is your *beard?*"

"Do you see the blood? Andrew Glenroy's razor is a deadly weapon. I'm thinking he did everything with it but shave."

"You're a different person! I could hardly remember what you looked like before—" A nasty little qualm convulsed her stomach. From the straight, hard line of his mouth he was remembering the same thing: The last day that he was clean-shaven was the day of the burning. She turned her head away and stared unseeingly at the windows.

"Och, it was time," he said. "I am too busy a man to be bothered

with birds nesting in my beard. I would always be worrying about breaking
the eggs."

The effort deserved at least a smile and got it.

When she came downstairs, he ladled hot porridge into the bowls.
He ate his in the Highland fashion, without sugar, and the milk in a
small bowl at the side; he dipped each spoonful of porridge into the milk.
Jennie scattered sugar lumps over hers and poured on a mixture of milk
and cream. She was halfway through her serving before she realized that
Alick was watching her.

"I like to see you eat," he said. "You put your whole heart into it."

"You make excellent porridge."

"Aye, not bad," he said dryly. When he was leaving, he wished her
good luck with the children.

"Thank you, I may need it," she said. He hesitated in the doorway.

"If you feel sick or faint, you should not be keeping on with it. By
spring we could have the money, even without yours."

"I am *not* going to be sick or faint. I'm healthy as a horse, now that
I have recovered from the shock of it." She waved him away. "Good
luck yourself. Don't lose a finger or drop a timber on your foot."

The teakettle sang like distant bagpipes on the stove, the warmth of
which was welcome before the sun rose over the trees and could pour
in through the windows. She washed the dishes and made the beds and
swept the kitchen floor. She had nothing to read and nothing to write
on, though she kept starting letters to Sylvia in her mind, so she walked
around to the stable in a cool, breezy, brilliant morning, loud with birds.
Male voices came from inside, where Benoni Frost and a son were working. The two ponies were racing deliriously around the meadow, their
flying hooves scattering diamonds from the wet grass. Three horses—the
two grays and a bay—stood together by the gate, watching like indulgent
adults. When they saw Jennie, they came to her, nuzzling, snuffling,
and prodding as Adam and Dora had done. She stroked their noses,
promising them treats next time.

Oliver lay on the cool bricks outside the back door of Strathbuie House.
He got up with an air of glad surprise and cavorted a bit in his massive
fashion, then escorted her indoors. There was no one about but Mrs.
Frost, who was kneading bread that gave off a promising yeasty scent

and singing to herself in a monotone, words undistinguishable. She
was not embarrassed by Jennie's sudden appearance. "Morning," she
said with a jerk of her chin; her strong hands never paused in their
rhythm. "You can leave those jugs on the stand by the door. Clean,
are they?"

"*And* scalded," said Jennie. "Good morning, Mrs. Frost. Where is
the schoolroom?"

"On the northwest corner, upstairs. Eliza Bisbee has them ready for
you. The missis don't rise and shine this early."

"Thank you."

Jennie turned to go, and Mrs. Frost said after her, "You tell that girl
I can use her in the kitchen. Please," she added.

"I'll tell her, Mrs. Frost." The cook's economy of speech didn't offend
her; it was too reminiscent of home. "The missis" indeed. No *madam*,
no instinctive change of voice and manner to reverence. The General's
wife's ideal servant class, with service bred into it for generations, was
a biological impossibility in this country, where everyone seemed to have
begun new with the birth of the Constitution.

Wishing she could share this discovery with Papa, Jennie mounted
the spiral staircase with Oliver. She, of course, would never slide ecstatically down its swooping curves, but she'd like to see Tony do it. She
met Hannah at the top and wondered if she'd innocently foiled an
adventurous descent; the girl's salutation was on the pert side.

Eliza Bisbee was the rawboned young woman whom Jennie had seen
at the feast. Her lavender print dress and apron were much more becoming than the flimsy sprigged lawn. Her large hands on the children's
heads pressed them down into their curtsies; her voice led off the chant.

"Good morning, Mrs. Glenroy!"

"Good morning, Eliza, Susanna, Frances." Jennie shook hands all
around. "Eliza, Mrs. Frost—"

"Ayuh," said Eliza glumly. "She can use me in the kitchen stoning
cherries, and I hate that worse 'n Tophet."

"Cherry pie is worth it, Liza," said young Frances gluttonously, rubbing her middle. Eliza sighed and departed, not on winged feet.

"The trouble with that girl," said Susanna waspishly, "is she's bone
lazy."

"*Susanna*," Jennie said.

"I was only being Mrs. Frost. I sounded just like her, didn't I, Frank?"

she asked her sister. With her black curls and rich coloring, in a few years she would be a budding damask rose. "Everyone calls me Sukey," she told Jennie, "and she's Frank. I'm nine, and she's seven."

"Why do we have to have lessons in summer?" The little redhead rolled out her lower lip. "I wouldn't mind if we could go to real school. Nabby goes, and she's learning *everything*. And they sing, and they have games in the schoolyard. Nabby teaches them to us, but we don't have enough people."

"Mr. O'Dowda went to the Ark yesterday and got all the Highland children," Sukey said resentfully.

"Well, I am honestly sorry for you." Jennie sat down at the school-room table. "But here we are, and we might as well make friends and do the best we can. We will take our work outdoors on some days, and we may have some pleasant times. We don't know yet, do we?"

They slid into the chairs opposite her. "You know all about *us*," Sukey said craftily, "but we don't know about you. Why are you dressed like that? What kind of shoes are those?"

"Where did you live when you were little?" asked Frank.

The questions pelted her like a storm of hard little green apples. At last she put her hands over her ears and said, "Enough, enough! We must save something for tomorrow, mustn't we? I'll make a treaty with you: Every day when lessons go well, at the end of the morning I'll tell you something about my sisters and me when we were small."

"Will you honor it?" Sukey demanded. "Papa says that not to honor a treaty is a sin."

"I will honor it," said Jennie. "Now bring me your books so I can see where you are."

The schoolroom was well equipped, and Mrs. MacKenzie had done better with the girls than Jennie had expected. There was an extra: their casually expert identification of the varied birdcalls outside the open windows. She turned this into a subject which they could teach *her*.

Sukey was a compendium of information, requested and otherwise. She wanted to go to Harvard College like Tony. "They don't allow girls, but my father is an important man," she said. "He will have the law changed when I am old enough to go. Mr. O'Dowda will teach me Latin and Greek and things first."

"What are you going to be?"

"I haven't decided yet. I'll learn everything there is to learn, and then I shall decide. They have millions of books at Harvard College, you know, and I will have to read most of them."

"Polishing up your long division will be an excellent start," said Jennie. Sukey agreed and set to work.

"I am going to be a postrider," said Frank. "Then I can ride Prince all day. I don't think I need arithmetic for that."

"You might rise to be postmaster in time," Jennie said, "and you'll certainly need arithmetic then."

Sukey thought out answers before she set them down on her slate. Frank was slapdash, rapidly filling the slate with untidy figures and wiping them out with a good deal of spit and the hem of her pinafore.

"Use your sponge, Frank," said Jennie.

"I keep forgetting. Do you know that I can spit farther than Billy Higham? We always have spitting contests when he comes with his mama."

"They are simply disgusting," said Sukey. Frank looked complacent.

An hour and a half had gone by when Eliza came exuberantly in with a tray. There were silver mugs of milk for the girls (christening gifts from Mr. Revere) and a sultana bun each. Jennie had coffee in a miniature pink-flowered pot, with a cup and saucer to match, and buttered thin toast sprinkled with cinnamon and fine sugar.

"How go the cherries?" Jennie asked.

"Praise the good Lord, Mrs. Frost's sister came in all set to tell the latest, and they didn't want me around or Hannah either, so Sapphira took over the cherries. I dunno, but I'd liefer work in the quarry than fuss with them picky things."

She seemed set for a good natter until the General came in, booming, "*Good* morning!"

"Well, this won't buy shoes for the baby, nor pay for the ones he's wearing," Eliza said breezily. "I'll go through their stockings." She went into the bedroom next door.

The General was dressed for business this morning. He flipped up his coattails and took a chair. The girls gave him milky kisses, which he wiped off good-naturedly with his handkerchief. The dog came to him, was greeted, and began cleaning up the girls' crumbs.

"How goes the battle, Mrs. Glenroy?" the General asked.

"Not a battle at all," she said.

"Drink your coffee, you must be parched by now. Have they had their American history yet?"

"No, I must study it myself first."

"The girls can tell you all about Independence Day. I take it you are not painfully sensitive on that subject?"

She smiled. "On the Fourth of July my father always said at breakfast, 'The United States have another birthday.' "

"And how we celebrate it! There's a bonfire out on Hospital Point the night before and sometimes, I'm afraid, a little too much celebration on the day itself. We have a simple service at the church, but this year we are stepping a mast at the corner for a flagpole, and we will have a flag-raising ceremony there. And the *other* grand thing I wanted to do—" He hitched his chair forward, comically resembling Frank when she couldn't wait to speak. "I wanted to have a dance in the new lime shed, and I was hoping to show our people here some Highland dancing. They were always great dancers in Strathbuie, my father told me. But Mr. MacArthur is against it, and I would not offend the old man for the world. Ah, well, the summer is young yet, and I hope to win him over in time." His blue eyes were as young with anticipation as Frank's. "Do you know how long it's been since I've *seen* an eightsome reel, let alone danced in one?"

"What is it, Papa?" Sukey asked.

"It's a grand dance, my dearie. When I was a lad in Boston, my parents met with other Highland immigrants each New Year's day for a ceilidh, with dancing and singing and piping. And that's where I first danced in an eightsome reel. I was a wee boy of eleven when I stood up with my mother."

"Can you do it now, Papa? I want to see you do it!" Frank cried.

He put his arm around her. "I almost think with Rory piping I could do it. That's the music that puts the leap upon the lame."

"Mama says it's not music," Sukey said.

"What do you think, *mo chridh?* The two of you were jigging around the wharf from the first skirl of pipes over the water, and when they came ashore, I thought you'd be flying over the shed like gulls if your brother didn't hang on to you."

"I don't know if it's real music," said Sukey judicially, "but it makes you want to jump."

"Mama doesn't like music," said Frank, "so how can she tell if it's music or not? *I* love it."

"And so you should, my darling; it's in your blood." He kissed her round forehead. "I have interrupted for too long." Bracing himself by the table, he stood up, and Sukey put his stick in his hand.

"Thank you, my little love." He kissed the top of her head. "Mrs. Glenroy, my library is open to you at any time, and you are free to borrow any books you choose. If you have any letters to send, simply leave them on my desk, and they will go in my mailbag. The Congress has granted me franking privileges in perpetuity, so you needn't worry about the fees. The European mail packet arrives in New York and leaves from there once a month. My captain puts my padlocked mailbag aboard the packet into trusted hands, and it is delivered to my agent in Liverpool. He sees that all mail goes to its destination without interference. The British postal service is notoriously *not* private and confidential. The government uses it to keep watch on enemies, suspected or genuine."

And she had planned to tell Sylvia and William everything! Her distress must have shown before she could hide it, because the General said quickly, "Any mail from my bag will be hand-delivered by absolutely trustworthy persons."

"Even to a country rectory in Northumberland?" she asked doubtfully. "Or to an inn in Fort William?"

"Even there. My own letters go everywhere. I give you my word, Mrs. Glenroy, that your letters will reach your correspondents exactly as they left your hands. And you may give them the name and address of my Liverpool agent for any return mail."

"That will mean the world to my sister, and to me," she said, almost tearful with hope.

"If she can find a means to get a letter to him by hand, so much the better."

"She will find a way," Jennie said. Leaning over the table, he wrote the name and address on a page of Sukey's notebook. "Can you read this? My wife claims that if the Army had depended on written orders from me, the whole course of the war would have been altered."

Jennie laughed, liking him very much. "I can read it. I'm very good at ciphers."

Twelve

MRS. FROST had milk and cream ready for her, a loaf of new bread, and half a dozen cherry tarts. "Goes with the cottage," she said laconically when Jennie thanked her.

It wasn't until Jennie was building the fire that she remembered that yesterday at this time she had been in what they called at home a rare old taking. She straightened up and looked fixedly at nothing, her hands going to her belly again. Of course, it wasn't as concave as when they'd reached Fort William! Since then she'd had adequate, if monotonous, food aboard the ship, and she had eaten extremely well in the last two days. Another few days should see her right.

Preoccupied with these reassurances, she didn't hear Alick coming. She'd forgotten that he had shaved and so was astonished all over again. He tossed his bonnet at the row of books by the entry door and said, "*Aha!*" when it caught on one.

"You're happy," she said. "You must have built an entire ship single-handed this morning."

"Aye, and launched her, too. The cheering was wonderful. How was your school going on?"

"They're nice little girls. Sukey desires to read all the books at Harvard College, and Frank wants to be a postrider. She can also spit farther than Billy Higham when he comes with his mama."

"She is already so accomplished, what need has she for anything more?"

"She asked that, too."

They finished the stew with slices of fresh bread and butter and ate the cherry tarts. "Either the ravens will supply Elijah with supper or I shall have to think of something between now and then," said Jennie. "I'd forgotten that aspect of housekeeping. The thinking."

"In this partnership we both will think," Alick said.

She laced herself into her stays as loosely as possible for her fittings. She would not allow a Miss Applegate to tighten them. "It is not healthful," she would say impressively.

The walk to the corner was different today, now that she knew what lay at either end. Once she had passed the Frost farmhouse, she had to force herself onward against the powerful temptation to go back rather than pass the Ark. Her hands turned cold, her clothes were too hot, and her insides seemed to be pulling themselves tightly together like a wool stocking that is being boiled and shrunk down to infant size.

There was an early-afternoon lull in the road traffic, and it was quiet around the Ark; but she kept expecting Anna Kate's voice to hail her from the landing. When she had got around the corner, a young woman was trying to coerce two small barefoot children into the shoemaker's shop, assuring them that Uncle Zeb had been lying when he said Mr. Barron would cut off their toes and make pickles of them to eat with his baked beans. Uncle Zeb deserved to have his tongue cut off, and that wasn't all, the way he went tomcatting around town.

Jennie continued on, but nobody in the immediate vicinity could miss hearing that God would pay Uncle Zeb. God knew how to punish liars and lechers. And if they didn't rampse themselves through that door, she would fetch their pa from the tanyard *this minute* to tan two more hides.

This cogent argument won, and Mr. Barron's door closed on their whimpers. Jennie exchanged smiles with a thin-faced, faded-looking woman coming toward her. "They'll soon be real comfortable with Mr. Barron," the woman said.

"Oh, yes!" Jennie agreed. The encounter was quickly over, but Jennie walked buoyantly on. The lung-squeezing constriction was quite gone. She was not pregnant, so why should she fear to face Anna Kate?

An obvious mother and daughter pair were just going into the dressmakers', so Jennie didn't stop. She looked particularly for the church, and there before her, north of Main Street, were the white belfry and steeple overlooking the intervening roofs and treetops; its weather vane was a brass codfish that spun and flashed in the erratic wind like a huge celestial goldfish.

On either side of Main Street there was a mixture of dwellings and shops and some houses that were two in one. This section thinned out to commodious residences on large lots. Most of them had carriage houses behind and flowers and shade trees on the front lawn. Small children watched her through gates, and once a pet terrier barked at her. An occasional horseman or a gig passed her on the road, which dipped east toward another crowded section of Main Street.

She crossed the thoroughfare and turned into the narrow side road that led past the church. On her right there was an open field, newly mown; on her left a row of maples along a rail fence made her feel comfortably invisible to the inhabitants of the roomy white house behind them. She heard a man cajoling a horse outside the carriage house, and between the trees she could see him tightening the saddle girths on a handsome dark animal, not a big horse, but a noble one, a horse for a monument. He stood like one as the man swung into the saddle. It was Stephen Wells. He rode along the driveway toward Main Street and disappeared from her view.

The white clapboarded meeting house was graceful in its austerity, perfectly proportioned and perfectly situated among mown fields like a becalmed green sea. The cemetery was on the far side, spreading northward up the gradual slope toward the saw-toothed rampart of spruce forest. The road ran between stone walls past the cemetery and into the woods. She stood by the silent church, following the road with her eyes and wondering how deep was the forest and how dark where the herb-woman lived. A gust of wind blew the hot, resinous scent of spruce toward her and pulled at her shawl; above her the bright codfish whirled, tossing off the sun.

She went back along the north side of Main Street. After the Wells house and several other spacious houses the first shop was the ironmonger's, and there in the window, sitting among pots, firedogs, hinges, and pokers like a princess among peasants, was a spirit lamp with its own little copper kettle. It was difficult to pull herself away. Oh, the rapture of boiling water in summer without building a fire! But unless Alick would use it after she was gone—and she doubted that—it would only take a sizable bite out of her savings.

She had it in mind to buy him a gift, something he *would* use, and when she came to the barber's, she knew what it would be. There was no male customer in the shop at present, so she went boldly in. Mr. Jason Whynot greeted her with the fervor of Dr. Faustus beholding Helen of Troy. Before he could inquire if this was the face that launched a thousand ships, she said, "I should like to buy one of your best razors for my husband."

"Of course, madam!" He set a chair for her. "It will give me the utmost pleasure to serve you!" He began at once to lay out a display of razors, explaining the superlative qualities of each. His accent was as refined as he was; she suspected that he put it on every morning with his hair oil. He was an unlikely character for a country barber, more the caricature of a dancing master. His hair was unnaturally dark and glossy in comparison with his wrinkles; it had a curl molded over each temple and was fragrantly oiled.

"I really don't understand about steel, Mr. Whynot," she said, "and since I am in straitened circumstances, I cannot afford your finest razor, but I should like a very good one."

"Dear Mrs. Glenroy, you may trust me implicitly. *This* is the one."

"How did you know my name?" she asked.

"Dear lady, half of Maddox knows your name," he said gleefully. "And the stories are as wonderful as they are varied. The fact that the General and Madam MacKenzie snatched you and your husband to their bosoms, so to speak, lends credence to most of the accounts."

"I'm afraid it's really a very simple story," said Jennie. "I think I will have that shaving mug with the Greek key pattern in gold, and a brush."

She took also a little pot of liquid shaving soap, which he said was his blend of the purest natural ingredients. She chose a hairbrush for herself, but shook her head at his colognes and hairdressings.

"I am also a ladies' hairdresser," he said. "I go to all the best houses. Someday, when you and Mr. Glenroy have been restored to your proper station, perhaps you will call on me."

"And perhaps my hair will be grown out by then," she said with a smile.

He threw up his hands and exclaimed, "But on you the effect is charming!"

The next stop was the milliner's shop. Mrs. Loomis was a stout, dour woman in black bombazine and a black satin apron. Her thick, swarthy fingers, with her wedding ring embedded deeply in the flesh, looked grotesque among the prismatic flowers, ribbons, and feathers, yet they could trim hats and bonnets with fresh, delicate touches. She accepted Jennie's choice of an unadorned chip bonnet as suitable to her present condition, whatever her former one had been, but suggested with melancholy interest that pale rose ribbon ties would be summery yet subdued.

On her way to the stationer's Jennie recognized Stephen Wells's distinctive horse tied outside the bank. She thought he had a most intelligent glance and would have liked to tell the owner so, but there was no sign of him.

The stationery shop was in the same house as the post office, and the postmaster was also the stationer. He was a puffy, tobacco-scented man who was preoccupied with the vehement political discussions going on outside among the people collected to await the postrider with the weekly Portland newspapers. Jennie bought a slate and chalk, two exercise books, two pencils, two goose quill pens, a crow quill pen for its fine line, a stick of red sealing wax, and a bottle of ink. The stationer showed more interest in that than he did in her. He swore the ink would not fade, it was his own mixture, and it was the iron filings that did it.

His indifference had been refreshing and restful compared to the Misses Applegate's attentions during her fitting. They purled and fluttered about her; it was like being trapped in a dovecote. The slip and one dress and a cap were finished. "We thought you would want them *at once*, dear." Would she like to wear them home? Would she have a cup of tea?

They were transparently stuffed with questions, and she didn't enjoy being so conspicuous. Yesterday it had been comic; today it made her feel insecure. She refused the tea with graceful regret and said she would not put on her new raiment until she had her new shoes.

At last she was free, or would be once she had passed the Ark again. Facing Anna Kate wouldn't hurt her, she reminded herself; it was just that she wasn't ready for it this afternoon.

Thirteen

ALICK CAME HOME carrying a string of fresh mackerel. Some boys who had been fishing down at the mouth of the river came to the shipyard landing with their wherry laden with the blue and silver fish, selling them twelve for a penny. When he had washed up, and she had the potatoes boiling, she gave him the razor. He looked at it without expression or words. At once she felt as if she didn't know him at all and had somehow trespassed. When the silence was too much for her, she said, "If you'd rather I hadn't—"

"It's just that I was not expecting a gift." He opened the razor. "Och, it would be a beautiful thing to cut a throat with. The man would never feel it."

"Mind you don't cut your own."

He looked directly at her then, and she was reminded of the first time this had happened, on the ridge above Loch na Mada. She had sensed accusation then, or worse: a subtle contempt. "Alick—" she began, not knowing what she'd say next.

"I thank you, Jeannie," he said. "I am not easy accepting gifts, but I thank you."

"You are welcome." She sounded stiff and was ashamed of herself. What had she expected? Transports of joy? Doubtless no one had made him a gift of anything in his adult life, and he could not be any different from what he was.

He rolled the mackerel in oatmeal like trout and broiled them while she made a salad. When they sat down to eat, there was a penny by her plate.

"For the blade," he said. She had heard of this at home. For any sharp or pointed object given you, you paid the donor a penny a blade or for each point, lest a friendship should be slashed or pierced.

"You aren't insulted, are you?" she asked. "I wanted to give you something. I was spending so much on myself."

"I am not insulted." To prove it, he shaved with it after supper and told her it had a caress like a butterfly's wing. "The brush and the soap are not so bad either, and the mug is bonny."

All this from Alick was the equivalent of a toast to their comradeship.

That night he took an exercise book and a pencil and went to the first session of his mathematics class. She walked with him a short distance eastward along the lane between the wooded rise and the Strathbuie meadow until the creek was in sight ahead of them and the lane took a bend toward the north and the schoolhouse; if one followed it all the way, one would arrive at the lower end of Main Street and a bridge crossing the creek to the opposite bank, known as the St. David side.

Walking back in the serene hush of early evening, after the day's wind had dropped, she wished she'd gone all the way with him; anything to put off writing the truth to Sylvia and William. It was not that she minded telling them the truth. It was just that she couldn't bear to relive it, yet she must.

Sitting at the kitchen table, she wrote in her exercise book at first, making so many false starts that she reminded herself of Frank breathing hard over her sums. Finally she began the actual letter on the new writing paper. The ink was encouragingly black; the crow point, enticingly fine.

"Dearest Sylvia and William," she wrote. "If you received my note from Fort William, you know that I was alive then. When you receive this, you will know I am safe in America, but not just where, and if you are asked, you will be able to say that truthfully. Perhaps they think I am dead; Nancy MacNichol in Fort William will never admit that she knew me. By now you know that Nigel is dead, and this is how it happened."

She described as briefly but as vividly as possible the revelation that had destroyed her marriage, then the burnings, the fury, and the anguish, and Nigel with his watch in his hand amid the smoke. She wrote how she had wanted to give some of her guineas to help the evicted and would have sent it by a stableboy, but he disappeared in the night, so she took it herself to the man who would distribute it.

Now she was back in the sunny hollow by the Pict's House, with the sounds of the bees and the little burn and the mare and the pony grazing. She had to get up and walk around before she could go on writing, trembling and wringing her fingers until they hurt. Then she lighted two candles to stave off the twilight and went on writing.

She used the initial N for Nigel, but even that evoked him too cruelly: his bright head, his blue eyes, his embraces, and his final rage. She wrote how he had attacked his cousin, a smaller man, and was strangling him when Alick was able to throw him off. Nigel was knocked down and either struck his head on a boulder or his neck was broken. Alick Gilchrist was convinced he would have no chance at all in the courts, and she was convinced no one would believe her story and they would be called conspirators in a murder. So she had fled into the mountains with him.

She had planned to make her way home from Fort William once Alick was safely away on a ship for America. Then they discovered that he could sail that very night only if he had a wife. The ship belonged to a man who offered land and opportunities, but he specified married couples only.

There was no way to be subtle about this:

I could not go away to safety, leaving him there to wait for a ship, when every instant was taking him closer to the gallows. He could have deserted me many times in the mountains, and I would have surely died there. My actions that Sunday morning had destroyed N, though I won't take all the blame; he began it himself when he lied to me before our marriage. Be that as it may, he was dead, and another man could hang for it. I had brought them together, and all I had meant to do was help the homeless.

He has already found work, and I am governess to two little girls. I have been paid for the quarter and will, of course, work it out before I sail for home in the autumn. Our housing is furnished us, fuel, candles, and some food. Alick thinks that with careful management his wages will keep us and I may save most of mine to pay my way home. He is a good man, a gentleman in the truest sense of the word.

He has always been a thorn in their flesh at Linnmore but could not be legally evicted because he is Archie's and N's cousin and protected in their grandfather's will. I am positive that Archie and his wife consider themselves lucky to be rid of him, and Christabel is happy to see the last of me. If we are believed lost in some quagmire or drowned in a mountain loch, so much the better.

Don't be anxious for me, my dears. I have crossed the Atlantic in a spanking new vessel, and I expect I'll reach my twenty-second birthday halfway across the Atlantic on my way home in October. And Ianthe thinks that crossing the Channel and seeing the Matterhorn are the *ne plus ultra* of existence!

By the time she finished all the special messages at the end, her hand and arm ached, her neck was stiff, her head throbbed, and the candle flames wore rainbows. She was too desolate for tears. She blew out one candle and left the other so Alick could see the letter and read it; he had a right to know what she was telling her family about their situation.

Reliving that day had left her floundering in emotional exhaustion. She dived into sleep as if to drown herself.

She was up before Alick and out to the Necessary in the cold dew, down to the cellar for the milk and cream, building the fire, making the porridge. Her letter was on the table, but not just as she'd left it. Alick came downstairs and went out the back door without speaking. When he came back he said, "Good morning," and nothing else. Clean-shaven, his face was as hard to read as when it was bearded.

When the silent ritual of the porridge was over, and she poured coffee for them, she said, "How did the class go?"

"Well enough. The dominie has no difficulty whatever with telling us whether the sums are right or wrong."

"No doubt he has a book with all the proper answers," she said haughtily.

"Like Mr. MacArthur," he said. "He has one of those books also."

She laughed, and Alick smiled. Taking advantage of this, she said, "Tell me if you have any objections to my posting my letter."

He looked thoughtfully at her, stirring his coffee. "Well?" she urged. "I hope you do not mind too much my writing about you. It was necessary."

"Och, yes, they should be knowing I am not a brigand," he said.

"But what I was thinking through most of the night, and why I overslept, is that you are very trusting of the mails."

"The General assured me that his mailbag is locked and protected all the way, and his agent in Liverpool sees that every letter is hand-delivered by trustworthy persons."

"How can we be sure of *anyone?*"

"I am sure of the General," she said stubbornly. "Are you not? He is a Highlander like yourself."

"Perhaps. But once the letter is out of that bag of his—"

"He swears it will be safe. Alick, I must tell them my side!" she exclaimed. "They may have already heard something from Archie and Christabel, I'm sure they have. If my note from Fort William reached them, they know I am alive, or was then, but—"

"And they will have been writing straight to Linnmore with that news," he said bitterly.

"I don't think so. They would know by my note that something was very wrong, and they would say nothing until they heard more from me. And after they read *this* letter they will say nothing at all about us to *anyone.*" His skeptical eyes angered her even while she understood. "I know them!" she insisted. "They will believe me beyond question."

"Very well," he said distantly. "You have the right. I am owing you too much already to be telling you what you must and must not be doing."

"Believe me, Alick, this letter will not lead anyone to you!"

He went out into the front hall and opened the front door, and stood in the opening with his back to her. "That day is never far from me," he said in a strained voice. "He was my kinsman, and he is dead by my hand. It is a fact which wakes me often with a shout."

"Then it's a silent shout, Alick," she said. "I've not heard it since the mountains; never aboard the ship, or since we landed here." She felt stronger for reassuring him. "It was an accident that killed him, not you. And if you must blame someone, blame me. I was the one, just as I wrote to my sister."

The erect dark head didn't move; he was too still, too stiff. *He is blaming me,* she thought, with ice in her stomach, *and he is still haunted by the gallows.*

"You told your sister the truth: he began it. Let him and Archie bear the blame." He faced her. "It was not only the letter and that day keeping me awake," he said coldly. "So, after all we were saying yesterday, you will be chancing yourself and the child on the ocean in the autumn gales."

"Oh, Alick," she exclaimed in a sudden, puzzling anger, "there is no child!"

"Oh?" His eyelids flickered from the impact of her shout. "Has something happened then?"

"No, nothing has happened, but it will! A woman should know if she has conceived, she should be sure, and I am sure it's *not* so. Anna Kate wants a child so much that she thinks any woman who has a dizzy turn because of tight stays must be carrying."

"I will be going to work now," he said. He went past her into the kitchen to pick up his bonnet.

"You think I'm wrong." She challenged him.

"Not at all," he said politely. "What have I to do with it? I am not the father."

"There is no child to be the father *of!*" she retorted, but he was going out the door.

Fourteen

S HE WALKED TO WORK in the new dress, a becoming small mosaic print in shades of brown, yellow, and orange, wearing the white lawn fichu and carrying her apron in her basket. She'd put on the cap, glared at herself in the mirror, taken it off and put it in the drawer with her corset. In her present mood she needed no more irritations. If Mrs. MacKenzie didn't object to the governess going capless, nobody else mattered.

Alick's doubts and fears had infected her, but not enough to make her burn her letter. There came a time when one must simply trust, and Sylvia and William had to be informed. But to know that Alick was worried about her letter was an unpleasant start to the day, a wound to their friendship. Yet she believed she was right.

She had just written a note to Nancy MacNichol at Fort William, which didn't mention Alick. Nancy must read between the lines, but she could truthfully say she knew nothing of Alick's whereabouts. Jennie assured her that all was going well after a smooth voyage, and that there was plenty of work to be had. She concluded with affectionate thanks for a valued friendship.

The letter to Sylvia and William obsessed her as she walked through the oval garden without seeing Truelove Adams or even smelling the roses, except to half-dream she was inhaling the fragrance of the rectory garden. To think that her letter would arrive there in little more than a month filled her with an agony of longing to walk through that door and into their arms. How could she bear to wait?

But wait she must, through tomorrow and tomorrow and tomorrow until the end of waiting came, not in the last syllable of recorded time, but with a beginning. There had to be another ending first, of course; Alick would surely be glad to see the last of her.

The children were eating breakfast in the kitchen, attended by Oliver, and Eliza was drinking a cup of tea. Hannah was setting a breakfast tray, and Mrs. Frost was cutting up fowls. "I'm early," Jennie called into them. "I'm going to the library."

The library was at the front of the house, across the hall from the drawing room. Morning flowed through the long windows and illumined a rich and fascinating clutter in which she could have spent hours of discovery. Manners forbade her to linger, handle, and examine minutely, but she greedily gathered everything with her eyes on her progress from the door to the massive mahogany desk. Walls of books, of course; a half-played chess game set up before the fireplace; the mantel strewn with bewitching objects she could only guess at. A huge oblong table held not only books and pamphlets but rolled charts or maps, a globe, and a microscope. A telescope on a tripod was arranged in the center window, aimed down the river. She did take a few moments to stand by that window and look out.

Across the driveway the flag hung limply from the mast. Out in the Pool the boats lay above their flawless reflections in the hot stillness. The tide was half-gone, and the wet flats under either bank reflected the sun like oil. The only motion in the scene was that of the gulls picking around the flats and on the weedy humps of exposed ledges off Hospital Point. Beyond the Pool a narrowing river wound like an avenue of blue-white mirror to the sea.

It was a dream landscape or an imaginary scene in a painting, and she had to resist its almost narcotic attraction. She put her letters on the desk blotter, resolutely ignoring still more intriguing articles, and went to the books. Here was an embarrassment of riches, and she knew she could dither and twitch around here for an hour without making up her mind unless she chose something quickly. She picked Robinson Crusoe for Alick to read and, new to her, Castle Rackrent, by Maria Edgeworth. Wordsworth's Poems in Two Volumes were next to William Blake's Songs of Innocence, and she took all three. The tall clock in the hall struck eight, and Oliver and the children were coming for her when she left the library.

Mrs. MacKenzie sent for her during the midmorning recess and gave her hot chocolate poured from a tall pot of Chinese porcelain. "And how do you like my children?" she asked.

"I like them very much. I hope they like me."

"Oh, they do! You are their new heroine!" Then she tried with good-humored persistence to find whom Jennie knew in England and Scotland.

"I know no great houses and families," Jennie said modestly. "I have always lived a very quiet life."

"Then how and where did you meet your husband?"

I am not going to answer this, Jennie thought. *If she is displeased, so be it.*

Mrs. MacKenzie said with a half smile, "Forgive my romantic tendencies. I know where Strathbuie is, but I understand your husband is not from there. My husband tells me that Glenroy is a place-name and not common as a surname. Is your husband from that place?"

Jennie lied calmly. "I don't know what the original name was. *Glenroy* was taken by the family for self-defense. The other is never mentioned. It might be that the family still fears retribution from some powerful enemy."

"My word!" Mrs. MacKenzie was impressed. "You don't suppose they were Campbells, do you?"

"I have no idea," said Jennie solemnly. "But the name makes no difference here, does it? And neither should the life we left behind us."

The General's wife knew when not to press. Jennie's adroit dismissal of the subject was proof of her station in life, not the impudence of an inferior. "Ah, well, we know he has MacKenzie connections, and that blesses him in my husband's eyes. No, don't get up quite yet. I told Eliza to take the children out to run around if you were late returning. I want to discuss church with you, a boring subject but necessary in a small town."

She poured more chocolate for Jennie. "I take it that you are Episcopalian?"

Jennie nodded, and Mrs. MacKenzie leaned back with a burlesque sigh of relief.

"So am I. But does your husband oblige you to attend Mr. MacArthur's services?"

"He obliges me to do nothing. Of that sort," she added.

"He grows more remarkable by the day. However, it will look better if you attend either the Presbyterian services or the Baptist variety. We have no other forms of worship except for one family of Quakers, who hold meetings in their own house. We have a few freethinkers, and

O'Dowda is a lapsed, *very* lapsed, Roman Catholic. It makes no difference to me if you and your husband both are atheists as long as you don't preach it. But church attendance by the Strathbuie household is important in a town where the leading citizen feels he must set a good example."

"Then I shall go," said Jennie equably, "but I cannot speak for Alick."

"Well, he's not exactly *of* the household, is he? You may have my place in the carriage. I have such a good excuse to stay at home these days. No one in my condition should be forced to sit through one of Elder Mayfield's sermons. Is there anything worse than a reformed rake? When he embraces virtue, he can't forget his old habits; he makes a whore of her."

Jennie was about to make her excuses and leave, but this stopped her. "*Really?* I'd have thought the town was too straitlaced for that."

"Oh, my word, it *would* be if he'd been a drunkard, a gambler, or a womanizer!" She rolled her eyes in mock horror. "But to my mind he was something far worse. He was a traitor during the war, and how he escaped being hanged I'll never know. In some places he would have been tarred and feathered at the very least. He saw the light one day while he was hoeing his turnips, when it was rather forcefully pointed out to him by some returned veterans that the sword of Damocles was hanging over his head and someone was about to cut that famous hair. He felt called to some distant point—to labor in the Lord's vineyard, he said—where he was comfortably unknown."

"But he came back."

"Back he came when the General had established himself here permanently. Everyone was much too busy to rouse up sleeping dogs, and besides, he carried a Bible in his hand everywhere and announced that he was twice saved. And such was the brazen bravado of the man that when he knew his life was safe, he challenged the then parson to a duel on salvation, split the church down the middle, and *won*."

"How could there be a duel on salvation between ministers?" Jennie asked.

"Oh, they both were *for* it, of course. But our reformed traitor swore that it was only for the few. Foreordained. So he really shouldn't rail at our local sinners; if they believe like him, they have no hope of heaven anyway, and never did. Young Mr. Ames was a Methodist and preached salvation free to anyone who works for it, but apparently our fine democratic citizens preferred to believe with Mayfield in an extremely elite minority, to which they all belong, of course—something like a heavenly version of the Society of the Cincinnati."

"I'm surprised the General supported him," Jennie said. "Or can sit through his sermons."

"He was in Washington when the vote was taken, and he was furious; but he believes in majority rule." She shrugged. "He says the man may be sincerely repentant. *I* say, 'Never trust a zealot.' A hundred and fifty years ago he'd have been burning witches. As for the General's enduring his sermons, he mesmerizes himself into another world."

"I hope I can do the same," said Jennie.

"My dear, it's the *only* way. But you should become pregnant as soon as possible, and then you'll have my excuse." She stretched with lazy pleasure. "Oh, how I used to dread Sunday! . . . Does your husband care for cards, Mrs. Glenroy? We might have an evening of whist soon. Or you and I could play backgammon while the men played billiards."

"I'm afraid Alick isn't a very social man. He's too busy improving his neglected education with Mr. O'Dowda."

Jennie went back to the schoolroom annoyed at being forced to attend Elder Mayfield's church, apprehensive about Mrs. MacKenzie's insistent curiosity, and amused by it, too; what if she'd known there was a genuine earl in Alick's background? Then her amusement was clouded by the new tension between her and Alick this morning; it had felt very like enmity.

Fifteen

B UT AT NOON the morning's bad humor had disappeared like the dew. Now that she wasn't a pregnant woman in need of his protection and moral support, Alick could concentrate on his studies and his work and was no doubt happy about it. He even laughed when she told him she was expected to go to church and sit through the sermons of Elder Mayfield.

"That's not kind." She reproached him. "Especially when you won't be going anywhere near the Gaelic services."

"But I will be cooking the dinner. How many other husbands will be doing that?"

Sunday came too soon. Jennie wore her second new dress, the tiny pink and white flower print with a white lawn yoke and frill, with her new shoes and lisle stockings and her new bonnet and shawl. She carried a few coins in the reticule Mrs. MacKenzie had given her, and rode in the barouche with the General and Tony. Benoni Frost drove them and then joined his family; the horses were tethered in a long, open-sided carriage shed behind the church.

The General's pew was so close to the pulpit that there was nowhere else to look but at Elder Mayfield. He was a portly man in a black broadcloth suit which suggested he appreciated good tailoring almost as much as good food. His balding crown reflected the light, and graying blond hair curled around his ears. Rosy jowls and extra chins billowed over his stock. From his expansive and unctuous smile one didn't expect hellfire, but that was what one got.

The General and his son earnestly fixed their eyes on his face as if it were as beauteous as an archangel's. Jennie did the same, and all three let their thoughts roam free.

When it was over, there was a half hour of sociability on the front steps. Jennie was introduced to Elder Mayfield and his wife and smiled until her face ached. She was genuinely happy to see again the officers and crew of the *Paul Revere*. Chet Mayfield, the new father, brought his wife to meet her. He was the preacher's son, but she wouldn't hold that against him. Stephen Wells asked her how she did.

"Very well," she said. "I saw you riding a few days ago. That's a superb horse."

His angular face lighted up. "Do you think so? He's a Morgan, and a true American breed. He's named Justin after his great ancestor, who was named for his owner, Justin Morgan. I could talk about that horse all day!"

"I had a word with him when I passed the bank."

"And what did he say?"

"Not much, but he *looked* volumes."

"Ah, that's Justin for you!"

"Meeting Stephen Wells was the best part of the occasion," she told Alick. "I am never going to church again while that man is in the pulpit. Well, perhaps not never." She relented. "Three months aren't forever; they only look that way from here. Now I want to think about my dinner. You boil a fine fowl, Mr. Glenroy."

"That I do," he agreed with no false modesty. The General had sent them asparagus and strawberries by the little girls, so their first Sunday dinner in America was a small banquet.

Three months were not forever, but seven months were when you were pregnant and hating it. On Monday morning she knew when she came swimming out of night into day that she could no longer deceive herself, and for the first time she wept for what Nigel had been to her at the time when she had conceived.

There would never be anything like it in her life again. Never a lover, never anyone like Nigel as he was then. Now it was as if her life had begun and ended all within two months. But she couldn't lie down and die, the animal instinct for survival had kept her moving, and all the time a new life was sprouting from the ruins like an aspen shooting up among charred timbers. The marvel of it stopped her muffled sobbing. She lay perfectly still, holding her breath, and her hand crept over her belly again.

It was in there. Very tiny but living. Growing. A little swimmer in the dark. In seven months it would be a full-sized infant. In *her*.

She'd been the same once; the wonder was that anything so minute could ever live to be five feet seven inches tall, nearly twenty-two years old, and carrying another minute life in its body.

She got out of bed, dropped off the full nightgown, and washed herself carefully from head to foot, shivering in the morning coolness of air and water. Looking down at herself, she thought that her breasts were already slightly larger; they felt so anyway. She smiled sadly, remembering how she'd worried first for fear she'd grow breasts, then worried because when they did start they weren't very perceptible. That was comfortable when you made long runs in cricket but humiliating when you attended your first dance looking like a very tall *little* girl in a grown-up party frock. They'd grown a bit since then, more apples than plums, but they'd have to fill out more now, wouldn't they? So she could feed the baby? Whom could she ask so she wouldn't worry about it? Oh, if only she could sail for home right now! Sylvia would tell her everything.

Her hair was long enough now to fasten into a small knot at the back of her head, leaving it loose and wavy around her face. She pinned on a cap; but it still seemed a symbol of submission, and she took it off. Time enough to start wearing it when she was showing; it would be appropriate then.

Alick was stirring the porridge. "It's true, Alick," she said matter-of-factly, tying on her apron.

"What is true?" He sounded absentminded.

"I *am* carrying. I knew it before I woke up this morning."

He accepted gravely this illogical statement. "And are you glad, or sorry, or afraid still?"

Bemused, she said, "I'm not glad, certainly. I could have done without this, and I know that childbirth is dangerous for at least half of all women. But I'm very calm, can't you tell? I'm not going to shatter again and leave you tiptoeing gingerly among the shards. But *please* don't tell me you knew I was wrong."

"I was not knowing." He turned from the stove, the spoon in his hand, and gave her the long characteristic look that allowed for no deviation with either the eyes or the truth. "You will not be sailing in October then."

"I would be afraid of having a miscarriage at sea." She whisked away before his dark gray eyes could see in her face that home had dissolved in her grasp, and the loss was too grievous even for tears.

In the afternoon, when the next day's lessons were prepared, she was sitting out on the bench, trying to divert herself with *Castle Rackrent*, when a wagonload of furniture arrived. Benoni Frost was driving a borrowed workhorse, a large, phlegmatic animal with hairy fetlocks. Benoni's sons, Thomas and Merrill, rode with their father. She felt as if she were in a dream as she told them where each piece should go, a dream that was a bad caricature of the day when her wedding gifts had arrived at Tigh nam Fuaran. Yet she sounded clearheaded and very sure of herself as she talked and joked with the Frosts.

One of the first things brought in was a chest far different from the Glenroy chests, which were roughly built and scarred with hard usage. This one was plain enough but made of polished cedar with brass hinges and fastenings. "You're to open that right away, missis," Benoni told her when they left.

She opened it and found curtains for the parlor windows, in heavy creamy linen printed with flowers and birds, hardly faded at all. There were ruffled white cotton curtains for the bedrooms and, underneath, changes of bed linen and two intricately pieced quilts.

She saw everything with dull eyes and brain. Of what use were these fripperies to her in her situation? *Things.* Each piece was another boulder piled against her prison door.

She sat before the fireplace on a small carved mahogany and satin-wood sofa upholstered in peacock blue, and looked resentfully around at her furnished parlor. A square of embroidered wool carpet was under her feet; she had two high-backed "lolling" chairs with seats to match the sofa, an inlaid and veneered secretary that dressed up an empty wall even though she had nothing to put on its shelves. Even a few pictures had been included, colorful if not distinguished art, and a narrow mirror the width of the mantel hung over it, with candle sconces at either end.

She sat with her hands in her lap and looked up at herself in the mirror, as forlorn as Rapunzel in her tower before she found out how useful all that long hair could be. Now besides an unwanted baby, she had all these *things* to dust, and she had always hated dusting.

And wouldn't it have been nice if Mrs. MacKenzie had included a spirit lamp? But if there was a spare one at Strathbuie House, it was probably lost in a dark corner of the attic. Now that there was no point in saving every cent toward an October sailing, she might just inquire the price of the one in the ironmonger's window. She deserved to pamper herself.

As if Alick had read her mind, that night he brought her home three oranges and a little packet of raisins. She was immediately ashamed of her ingratitude and irascibility. She asked Alick to help hang the parlor curtains, and she put candles in the sconces; at dusk she lighted them, so they could see how the room looked. They agreed that it was a most superior cave.

Sixteen

Now, on every good tide, boys ferried bonfire materials across the Pool to Hospital Point. In turns they were freed from school or work for an hour to do it because the bonfire was very nearly a sacred ritual. The structure began to show up across the water like a watchtower or a monument thrown together by a lunatic out on the tip end of the point. The only thing that would prevent the fire would be a drenching rain or strong onshore winds. Ordinarily they could expect a heavy dew at night, and everyone attending the bonfire would be prepared to watch out for flying sparks and debris.

Up at the corner volunteers dug the deep hole for the flagpole. On Saturday afternoon the mast, painted and rigged, was carried up Ship Street by a crew of men and every young boy who could find a place on the mast to put his hands. Setting it strongly and solidly in place was an engineering feat watched by everyone who could spare the time.

The schoolchildren were learning new songs for the flag raising; Nabby sang them for Sukey and Frank when she came to play, and they sang them for Jennie. They were bitter about Nabby's luck. One of her brothers would take her to the bonfire for a while; she wouldn't have to watch it from across the pool like an infant. And boys had all the luck, too; they could stay up most of the night and roast potatoes in the embers. Boys had everything. It wasn't fair. But if you couldn't be a boy, the next best thing was to be Nabby. Nobody treated *her* like a wax doll baby.

There was a minor outbreak of xenophobia, miscalled patriotism, because the town had its share of bullies and blusterers. At the boatyard Tormod, being called a dirty Britisher and invited obscenely to go back whence he had come, had grabbed up a sledgehammer and swung it around his head, shouting, "I'm no bloody Sassenach, and I'll be hurling this amongst the eyes of the next man to call me one!"

He had them dodging and running, and that ended the harassment before Mr. Dunlop got wind of it. At the quarry the superintendent put certain men on notice; they were to keep civil tongues in their heads or be discharged. They accused him of being partial to the Highlanders and Irishmen so as to toady to the General, but he had been through the war with the General and never in his life had toadied to anyone.

Mrs. Frost knew about it because she had a nephew in the quarry. "What that Zeb Pulsifer needs," she said, pounding down yeast dough, "is to be put through a war himself. Take him down quite a few pegs. I dunno how Joseph Pulsifer ever got a whelp like that one. Well, I *do* know, but I'm not going into that right now." It was the end of classes on a hot morning, and the children were washing doll clothes with their miniature tub and scrubboard in the shade outside the back door. They kept coming in to see if the gingerbread men were done yet.

Jennie said thoughtfully, "There was a young woman outside Mr. Barron's shop one day, telling her children that God was going to punish Uncle Zeb for a number of things."

"There's no other Zeb in Maddox, and he's one too many." She brought a fist down hard on a bulging lump of dough. "That would be his sister talking. There's no love lost between those two, and I know about *that*," she said ominously.

Jennie and Alick were invited to watch the bonfire from the roof of the mansion and to have a dish of ice cream afterward. Some other people had been asked; viewing the bonfire and then eating ice cream were part of the ritual.

"It will be an opportunity for you to meet what passes for society in Maddox," Mrs. MacKenzie said, "and for me to become better acquainted with Mr. Glenroy."

"I will speak to him about it," Jennie said. It was possible to imagine Mrs. MacKenzie trying to become better acquainted with Alick, but she didn't like to dwell on it. She handed on the invitation, got the expected terse response, and gave it to Mrs. MacKenzie with a few artistic touches.

"The other Highlanders will be going down to the wharf to watch the fire," she said. "My husband has been so busy with his work and his studies he wants to have this time with them."

Mrs. MacKenzie took it well. "It is to his credit he doesn't snub them, but I shall have him in this house eventually, I promise you!"

A Dia, *but it's a long wait you'll be having,* Jennie thought.

Hector and Anna Kate walked back to the cottage with them from the wharf, which was still crowded with watchers who didn't want the evening to end. The bonfire had been spectacular, and its reflection in the black, still water had been ravishing. Across the pool they could hear the loud snapping and crackling of the flames. A fountain of sparks soared up into the velvety dark; showers of sparks cascaded in glory. Black figures capered against the raging light, whooping like Indians in a war dance, and the high, wavering cries echoed weirdly over the water.

Jennie thought of the last time she had seen fire. But these were shouts of fun and joy, not of fury and anguish. She took Anna Kate's arm and said, "We'll make some tea and have our own celebration. The pot has a picture of George Washington on it, so it's appropriate, and Mrs. Frost gave us a Fourth of July pound cake."

While Alick was building the fire, she showed Anna Kate through the house by candlelight, all but the small bedroom; let her think what she wanted about the double bed, but separate rooms would cause questions even if Anna Kate would be too polite to ask them.

She admired everything generously and without obvious envy. But in the parlor she became silent. The room shimmered with changing colors in the unsteady light; the birds on the curtains looked alive, and the flowers trembled.

"It is beautiful, just," Anna Kate said at last.

"I didn't ask for it, Anna Kate," Jennie said.

"But why should you not be having it? You are working in the great house."

"The cottage is part of my wages," Jennie said. "It is important for you to know that I was not expecting this. We would have gone with you and the rest to the Ark and been thankful."

"I am knowing that," Anna Kate whispered, smiling and patting her arm. "And will you be listening to himself out there? We have our land, and he is hardly sleeping at night."

"Are you *that* happy, Anna Kate?"

"So much I am trembling sometimes like that flame, when the fear is at me."

"The fear of losing it," Jennie said. "Of its not being real."

Anna Kate nodded vehemently. "Like this." She touched her middle. *Like the lost baby.* For a moment she looked haggard, nearly ugly, but that changed when she said tenderly, "And you, *mo ghaoil?*"

She couldn't say she wasn't happy about her condition, not to Anna Kate, so she simply nodded and smiled.

Later Alick walked them out along the lane to Ship Street. She put the cups and spoons in the pantry and covered up the rest of the pound cake. She was drowning in tiredness; was this the way it would be for the rest of the time, only worse as she grew heavier? No lessons tomorrow, no work for Alick; if she were lucky, she would sleep and sleep.

Alick came back in with an armful of kindling for the morning. He was smiling. "Hector is so happy he gives it off like heat from the sun."

"They have land already, Anna Kate told me."

"Yes, and there is already a well and a cellar. The man's wife inherited property somewhere, and they went away. It was Benoni Frost put Hector in the way of it. One of his cows went over the wall and was wandering Main Street. Hector took her back and was so *beulach* about what a bonny beast she was that Benoni has talked to the General about the great farmer Hector would be. And now the grant is his. The others are choosing their grants, but Hector has the best, because of the well and the cellar. Those two will be living in their own log cabin before winter."

"Do you envy them?" she asked.

"No." He looked around at the candlelit kitchen. "I am learning my trade. I have no time to cut logs and plow up a garden." He laughed. "Och, you should have heard him! He is naming every hill in sight of his cellar for the mountains above Strathbuie. He's a great poet in the Gaelic, is our Eachann MacCoinnich!"

The whole town went to the flag raising on the morning of the Fourth and heard the schoolchildren sing in harmony "My Days Have Been So Wondrous Free" and then the rousing "Free America" to the tune of "The British Grenadier." The Highland children—all the boys in breeches now—may not have completely understood the words, but their voices greatly contributed. O'Dowda was a small man, dwarfed by some of his older students, but he was in such control that his hands drew music from his singers as if from a harp.

The innocent beauty of the children's voices in the summer air moved everyone, some to tears. Then the flag was raised by one of the General's old soldiers, and the Stars and Stripes streamed out on a wind that seemed to have arisen just for the occasion, and the roar and the hats went up.

"Man, man!" Hector exclaimed softly. "Does it not put the great lump in your throat to see her up there? That's the flag for me!"

"Well, Alick," Jennie said when they were walking home, "it is to be the flag for you, too, now. Are you satisfied?"

"Yes," he said. "Already it has done more for me than any other."

They dined on salmon and green peas, a gift from the General. In the afternoon there was an informal open house at the mansion, but Tony escaped and came to the cottage to invite them to go sailing with him. Alick refused so politely and pleasantly that one would never guess how the suggestion had appalled him. Jennie would have loved it, but she was a married woman in the eyes of the world, so the excursion would have been forbidden even if her husband did not believe that anyone who stepped aboard a boat was flirting with suicide.

"Oh, well, sometime," said Tony philosophically. Instead of hurrying off to make the most of his freedom, he sat down on the bench with Jennie; Alick was inside, studying at the kitchen table. "I saw Mairi MacKenzie watching the flag raising. I'd like to be taking her sailing, but I suppose that can never be. I cannot believe she's been a married woman! Are you *sure*? She looks exactly the same as any other girl her age. Only prettier," he said aggressively.

"She *is* the same," Jennie said.

"Well, not—I mean to say, how could—" He bumbled into a miserable silence, looking everywhere but at her. If she touched his earlobes, they'd burn her finger, she thought in pity. She wished there were a way to tell him Mairi was a virgin widow, but of course it was not possible. All at once he jumped up and walked off without a good-bye.

"Enjoy your sail, Tony," she called after him.

"I may sail on and on," he answered with dramatic melancholy, "and go where the wind takes me."

"Ah, Tony, I'll be sorely missing you," she said.

He scowled at her and then laughed. "I may come back as the Ancient Mariner!"

Seventeen

THEY SAT UP later than usual for the night before a workday, one in a kitchen rocker on either side of the kitchen table, each with a spendthrift pair of candles. She'd done well to choose *Robinson Crusoe* for Alick, but she'd turned against *Castle Rackrent* because of trying to read it on the day she had admitted her pregnancy. Now she was reading William Blake's *Songs of Innocence*. She was wishing she had a cup of chocolate when Alick slapped his book shut and stood up.

"Enough of that. It would be keeping me up all night if I'd let it."

"You must like it then."

"For some the first taste of reading must be like the first taste of whiskey; they can never stop sipping after that."

"But I've never heard of anyone's being disorderly in a public place or falling into a ditch or beating his wife because he was drunk with a book."

He laughed and went out. She got up, stretching and yawning, and began setting out the breakfast dishes. " 'He who shall hurt the little wren/Shall never be belov'd by men,' " she recited. " 'He who the ox to wrath has mov'd/Shall never be by woman lov'd.' "

"What are you saying?" Alick came in from the entry with an armful of kindling.

"It's from Blake. He was our favorite because he said things like 'A robin redbreast in a cage/Puts all Heaven in a rage.' "

"And so it should. Come out for a walk," he said.

She started to say she was tired, but surprisingly, he insisted. "You'll be sleeping better for a good drink of fresh air." He took Elspeth's shawl from the hook and put it over her shoulders. When they went out the front door, he stopped her. "Listen to the pipes."

Wee Rory (Ruari Beag) was playing in Strathbuie House tonight, and Ian Murdo MacKenzie was dancing, for some selected guests of the General's. She'd seen Ian Murdo dance aboard the *Paul Revere*, featherlight, his feet seeming hardly to brush the deck and then only seldom, and his kilt flying out in the turns like a rooster's tail. The crew had whistled, stamped, and cheered.

"Mrs. MacKenzie has probably retired with a headache and cotton wool in her ears," she said. "But the girls will be listening at their door or they're prancing all around the gallery. Do you know that tune?"

" 'Shean Trubhais.' It means 'ragged trousers' or 'despised trousers,' and Ian Murdo will be dancing that one with his heart. It comes from the time when the Highlanders were forbidden the kilt."

The pipes stopped. "Now they will be having a dram to wet their throats," Alick said. They walked out to the back gate. It wasn't black-dark, and the lane showed pallid in the starlight.

"Take my arm," Alick said. It now seemed quite natural to do so, and why not? In the mountains they had slept in each other's arms to keep away the ghosts and the nightmares.

They went eastward with the trees thick motionless clots of black on their left and the open spaces of the meadow on the right. They reached the place above the black star-reflecting creek where the lane swung northward. The schoolmaster's little house was dark, but someone in it was playing a violin. The melody of pensive, nostalgic beauty was like the meandering and wistful recollection of times past.

Knowing what it stirred in herself, Jennie wondered what it meant to Alick as they stood listening. When it ceased, she said, "Was that O'Dowda?"

"Yes." They spoke in low voices as if the hush were fragile enough to be destroyed by a word. "I have heard him begin before we are fifty steps away from his door. I think he reaches for the fiddle instead of the drink."

"He's a fine musician as well as a scholar. I've never heard of a village school chorus like his. I wonder what *his* story is. He can't be a dispossessed gentleman, or Mrs. MacKenzie would have said so."

"Or perhaps she thinks there are no gentlemen in Ireland," said Alick. He turned her onto the right branch of the fork, which passed around

the far end of the house meadow, above the place where the creek opened
into the Pool and the salt water came crowding in at high tide. On the
far bank a few scattered lights showed like motionless fireflies.
"The rope walk is just along here," Alick said. It was a long, low,
narrow building running parallel with the road on the water side. Next
came the fish flakes, where the big codfish and pollack, split and soaked
in brine, were laid out to dry. They weren't there now, being taken into
the nearby shed at night because of the animals, but there was a clean,
saline, deep-ocean scent about the place.

They passed the dark store and empty wharf and the shipyard, where
they stopped again. Something scampered among the sheds, and after
that the silence was broken by a quickly stifled guffaw from above them
on Ship Street.

"Someone is not wanting the holiday to end," Alick commented.

"Someone up by the arch," Jennie said. "Tony and some friends."
They strolled slowly under the Strathbuie trees toward the gateposts.
Jennie was hoping maternally that Tony hadn't been given wine somewhere and was going home in a disreputable condition, when a strong
voice spoke distinctly just inside the arch. "The little pricks are just
coming out the front door. Git around behind that gatepost."

"*That's* not Tony," she whispered. Alick's free hand went over her
mouth, while the arm she was holding clamped her hand so hard against
his side that she couldn't wriggle it free. They were no more than ten
feet from the nearest gatepost but shielded by a lilac bush, and the two
lying in wait were too busy arranging their ambush and snickering to
catch the movement as Alick pulled her deeper into the shadows.

They could hear Rory and Ian Murdo coming along the drive, laughing and talking, not uproariously; like most Highlanders, they were soft-
voiced. But they were exhilarated by their evening of music and dancing
and a few drams. Jennie could see nothing, but she heard a rustling as
the two came nearer and then the quick, indrawn breath of surprise, a
startled laugh.

"Well, what have we here?" someone said in a sarcastic drawl.

"A couple of Miss Mollies," the heavier voice said. "All pretty in
their party dresses. Been pointing their toes and twirling their skirts for
the General, like."

"Good evening, gentlemen," Rory said, sounding out of breath with
nervousness. Jennie strained against Alick's grip, but it was no use. She

found that she could see movement through a gap in the lilac bushes and pick out the Highlanders' white shirts.

"Goot evening, chentlemen!" The sarcastic one mimicked Rory.

"You will be letting us by, if you please," Murdo said.

"By all means, *chentlemen!*"

The attack happened with shocking suddenness; there was a grunt as somebody lost his wind and a shout of pain, and someone else was trying to crawl away, cursing between gasps. In Gaelic.

Rory was saying painfully, "Now . . . what is at you . . . to do that? What is he . . . ever . . . doing to *you?*"

The hateful snicker again. "Let's see him dance now, man! And let's kill that squealing pig of yours that's an insult to Christian men's ears!"

"You'll not be touching my pipes!" He must have thrown them; they landed somewhere with a clatter.

Then the other two, laughing, overpowered him and threw him down. "Do you wear petticoats under that skirt? What kind of drawers? Lace frills on 'em, like? Or no drawers? Let's have a look!"

Their demented laughter was hideous. Jennie was burning up in a fire of rage; she hated Alick for holding her there, for not rushing forward himself.

"It's a male after all! What say we make a girl out of him? He won't be losing much, not by the size of him! Let's see what else is here—"

Rory yelped in pain. In the next instant Jennie was alone, and Alick was gone. Through the gap in the bush she saw Rory on the ground, his body arching and bucking as if in an epileptic convulsion, trying to throw the weight off his legs; the other figure bent over him, laughing like a maniac. Alick came up behind them like a shadow.

"*Christ!*" There was a bellow, and the man on Rory's legs nearly fell over backward in his hurry to get away. He went sprawling at Alick's feet, croaking, "He's cut my throat, damn him. He's killed me!"

"Who has killed who?" someone shouted. The General and two men were coming along the drive with a lantern. Oliver rushed ahead of them, barking and growling. The man still on his feet turned to run and tripped headlong over something in the way; overwrought as she was, Jennie could still suspect Alick's foot. Oliver delightedly pinned him down. Rory sprang up like a cat, and she could hear his fast, shallow breathing.

"This damn heathen has struck me, General!" The roar dwindled off into a whine.

Alick jerked the man up by the armpits. "Show him," he said grimly. "Show him where the blood is pouring like a river."

"Who in hell are *you?*" the man snarled.

"Is that you, Alick Glenroy?" the General said, squinting into the dark beyond the lantern's range. "What is all this? What are you carrying on about, Zeb Pulsifer?"

"We was just strolling by, Corny and me, when this one sprang out of the gate at us like a damnation wildcat and drove his knife at my throat!" He blundered forward into the yellow glow. "Look at the blood!"

The General held up the lantern and peered at the exposed throat. "There's a scratch there. No blood. I do worse to myself with my razor every day. You'll live. Rory, is this true? Did you put a knife to his throat?"

"Aye," said Rory, standing at attention.

"Well, Rory, we cannot have this," the General said sadly. "I'll have the knife if you please. I take part of the blame. I shouldn't have given you that parting dram, you'd had enough to drink, but it grieves me to have our evening end so badly, to meet this when I walk my friends to the gate." Rory walked forward and laid the knife in his hand. He looked down at it and shook his head. "A *sgian dubh*. I mislike taking that from a Highlander, Ruari Beag, but I must if you cannot keep it where it belongs."

"Your dancer has been injured, Colin," one of his guests said, leaning over Ian Murdo.

"I'm glad you two were able to stand off one of your adversaries," the General said dryly. "Get onto your feet, Cornelius."

Oliver, thrust off, smelled Alick's legs, and then came bounding around the lilac bush to Jennie.

"Go home, both of you," the General said. "You stink of rum, and when did you last take a bath? Where are you hurt, Ian Murdo?"

"General," Alick said politely, "it was not quite as it was told you."

"Come back here!" the General thundered after Zeb and Corny, who were rapidly vanishing into the night. "Come back, or your work and your wages end at this minute! Now, Alick."

"I would rather be telling it in private."

"It must all be open and aboveboard. I am already accused of too much favoritism. Zebulon and Cornelius, appear in my house at eight tomorrow morning, with your fathers. Now go, and I would take it kindly if you were both sober *and* clean when you come."

His guests were Mr. Dunlop of the yard and Mr. Muir, the quarry superintendent, two Lowland Scots. The four held a meeting over Murdo. He had been kicked viciously in the right knee, and it was already badly swollen. Rory stood alone as if he were genuinely in disgrace. Jennie was sure he felt so; he had been so abused and humiliated and had had to give up his *sgian dubh*. She wanted to go to him, but it would have humiliated him even more, knowing a woman was witness to it all. She sat on the ground beside Oliver, leaning on him, and he stood there like a warm and obliging rock, his tail gently waving.

The younger man suggested that he and Rory could make a seat and carry Ian Murdo to the Ark while the older man carried the bagpipes. The General called after them, "Tell his wife to put on hot and cold compresses, and I'll send Waite around tomorrow to have a look. Rory, you are to bring Mr. MacArthur with you in the morning." He limped back to Alick. "Bad business, bad business. Gives Rory the name of troublemaker, and worse, a dangerous lunatic who could attack anywhere, without reason."

"General MacKenzie, if you please—"

"No, Alick Glenroy, I will *not* hear it tonight," he said crossly. "Not a word. We'll have it all out in the open tomorrow morning, with no special pleading. Tell Dunlop I want you at eight. Now where is that confounded dog?"

He whistled, and Oliver gave Jennie a lick on the cheek and left her. Alick stayed where he was, watching the lantern growing smaller in the black avenue under the trees; the orange light bobbed with the peculiar rhythm of the General's limp.

Jennie went out to him, and they walked on toward the lane. "So ends the Glorious Fourth," she said. "I wish Rory had spilled a few drops of that monster's blood. He should have the game as well as the name."

"Oh, there will be enough blood spilled. But whose?"

"The General will surely be severe with those two when he knows the truth, and if he has the power over their livelihood—"

"And they will be blaming Rory for whatever the General says to them, and when the rum is in, the wit is out. And Rory will not be happy with *me*," he said wryly, "because he has been shamed by them, and my telling it will shame him more. He would almost be glad to have it stand as Pulsifer told it."

"But it can't be left like that!" she said. "You wouldn't *not* let him know that Rory was provoked, would you?"

"I will be telling him." They turned into the lane, and nothing more was said until they went into the house, where one candle had been left burning.

"A terrible mischief was about to be done tonight, I think," Alick said. "Because those two were carried away beyond what little sense they have, and this was in Pulsifer's hand." He laid a knife on the table, about the size of a *sgian dubh*. The initials Z.P. were carved into the horn handle. Taking in the sense of his words, Jennie saw the knife as an adder ready to strike from a nest of heather.

"It was knocked out of his hand, with Rory hurling himself about like that, and flew to me like a bird when I came up behind him. I picked it up and would have been holding him by the hair and promising to slice off his ear, but Rory reached his own knife first."

His soft laughter was real. "Och, the surprise of it! Where did it come from? Pulsifer is not knowing where the Highlander carries his *sgian dubh*. So was it God or the devil putting it into Rory's hand?"

She tried to laugh, too, but she was too tired for the effort. Alick sobered at once. "Are you all right?"

"Oh, yes, except for being sick with the injustice of everything. I loathe bullies. I think they should be wiped off the planet. People can be hanged for stealing food or poaching a rabbit, but the truly wicked go on to inherit the earth."

"I am wondering what Mr. MacArthur would say to that. Is the answer in his book, do you think?"

She lighted her bedroom candle from the one on the table. "I'm sure he and Elder Mayfield would find one to suit them, if not us. Their God is a bully, too. Look at what He did to Job."

The homely comfort of the kitchen had been subtly changed by what had happened tonight. She concentrated on bed and forgetfulness. Alick came behind her to the foot of the stairs and took the candlestick from her hand.

"You are too tired to be trusted alone on the stairs," he told her. He put his arm around her waist, and she didn't object to the help; it was very welcome tonight, when she felt so far from home and everything had gone hideously askew.

When they reached her room, he set the candle on the chest of drawers. "I'll build up the fire and make you a cup of tea," he said.

"Oh, no, you won't! Not at this hour! But I thank you, Alick, very much." Her eyes filled with tears. "You'd better go," she said, "before I make an exhibition of myself and hate us both for it."

Eighteen

IT WAS A HOT MORNING, and Jennie planned to have lessons under the west side of the veranda. She went up to the schoolroom before eight, expecting to have the children out of the house and settled at their arithmetic before the men collected, but when they came out into the upstairs hall with their slates and books, the meeting was already convening in the hall below. One hint of the unexpected, and the girls were glued to the railing like limpets on a rock, and just as deaf to Jennie.

The men stood in little knots isolated from one another; even Zeb and Corny were separated by a good twelve feet. Each was flanked by his father. Zeb didn't resemble his parent, a man of medium height, with dark-tanned skin, thick white hair, and a military bearing; he had been the flag raiser. Zeb was tall with big, meaty shoulders and long arms. His clean shirt strained over his heavily muscled torso. He would have been good-looking in a rough-cut way if it hadn't been for his slouching carriage and his brooding, hangdog expression. His hair was light brown and overlong, giving his big head a shaggy, leonine look. His throat was bandaged.

Corny was shorter than Zeb, but as muscular. His dull blond hair was wetly plastered over his forehead, giving him a low-browed appearance; he was a young edition of his stout and grizzled father. Corny was openly nervous. His busy fingers wandered about his face, scratching an eyebrow, rubbing his nose, picking it until a nudge from his father stopped him. He fingered his mouth, and pulled at a hair on his chin. He darted sidewise glances at his father, who scowled back at him, making Corny more skittish than before.

Rory stood by the tall clock with Mr. MacArthur. His meager face was impassive, his eyes fixed on nothing. Mr. MacArthur's lips were so tight they were almost invisible, but his eyes were bright and busy, taking in every detail of the hall and the other men.

Alick waited by the front door, his arms folded. Tony lounged against the wall beside him, occasionally yawning. Oliver rambled from group to group, ignored by everyone but Tony.

"What are they all here for?" Sukey asked in a loud whisper.

"Is somebody *dead?*" asked Frank just as the General limped into the hall. "Well, if anybody's dead," she said happily, "it's not Papa!"

Jennie looked across the stairwell at the door of the master bedroom, willing Mrs. MacKenzie to appear and order the children out, but it remained obdurately closed.

"Good morning!" said the General brusquely. "Everyone here? Good. We'll proceed to business."

"A chair, Papa?" Tony asked him.

His father shook his head impatiently. He took a stand before the console table, Oliver beside him. "Zebulon, I'll hear your story again."

Zebulon gave it in a way that suggested earlier rehearsals. He described plaintively his amazement and horror at being attacked out of the dark. "Like bein' leapt on by a catamount." He tried to wrestle the man to the ground and get the knife away, but he had a lunatic's strength. "He tried to cut my throat! You saw, General!" He touched the bandage. "I could've bled to death right there on the ground."

Corny's story was more halting, and his fingers were very agitated in his hair and around his ears and the back of his neck; but it agreed with Zeb's. His father spoke up. "I don't hold with this young one lallygagging around town when he should be home in bed. Makes him look like he's up to deviltry, even if he ain't. But that man"—he pointed at Rory— "if you can call the critter a man, should be locked up somewhere or not be here at all. He ain't safe. Having them around is as bad as Injuns."

"Joseph, what's your opinion?" the General asked Zeb's father.

"*Sir!* I opine that these folks come from a savage country and don't know civilized ways, don't know our lingo, don't know our laws, and this is no place for 'em. Begging your pardon, but I come up against 'em once in the war, and I know whereof I speak. They fight like devils from hell."

"That savage country was mine, Sergeant Pulsifer."

"And I beg your pardon, sir! But you was brought to America in a state of innocence, and you grew up an American. You ain't no more one of them than I am."

"I'll take that as I think it was intended. Well, Rory?"

"I am having nothing to say," said Rory.

"Has he talked with you about it, Mr. MacArthur?"

"No, he has not," the minister said curtly. "And I was not wishing for him and Ian Murdo to come to this house last night. It would lead to evil, I was telling them, and was I not right?"

"Perhaps," said the General politely. "How is Ian Murdo today?"

"The swelling is not so big."

"Good! Now if only his dancing has not been ruined." He gave Zeb and Corny a hard look from under his eyebrows. "I should not take that well at all."

"He brought it on himself!" Zeb flashed back at him. "The fancy little—" His father's hand fell on his arm.

"Rory MacKenzie," the General said, "if you cannot control yourself in the future, there is no room for you here. If a man knows he is likely to go wild when he has drink taken, the responsibility is his."

Rory never changed expression, but the dark red ran up his throat and into his hair. Alick unfolded his arms, and the movement attracted the General's eyes.

"Oh yes, Alick!" he said cordially. "You had something to say to me."

"Could I not be saying it in private!"

"No, no, I told you last night, this must all be open and aboveboard, with no special pleading. You may say it now for everyone to hear or not say it at all."

"Very well then." Alick walked to where the General stood. "I will be making it brief and simple so the gentlemen can understand. Ruari Beag said, 'Good evening, gentlemen,' when they stopped him and Murdo coming out the gate. He was mistaken, I think, calling them that."

Something like a growl began in Zeb, but his father's hand was still restraining him. Corny's head itched violently.

" 'You will be letting us by, please,' Ian Murdo said, and at once the two were at him and Rory. Murdo was early out of it, kicked in the knee. 'Let's see him dance now,' they said. Rory was thrown down and his kilt was thrown up. There was another knife drawn before he could reach his, and they were saying they would make a lass of him."

"I never had no knife!" Zeb bawled.

Alick was icily composed. "Who was it said, 'The little pricks are coming now; get behind the gatepost'? Or was someone else there who called them Miss Mollies in party dresses and was asking if they wore petticoats, and drawers with lace on them, or no drawers at all? Who was sitting on a man's legs and handling and hurting his private parts?" He turned to the General. "You understand why Rory cannot be telling this himself. Here is the other knife." Alick handed it to the General, who read aloud the initials on the haft.

"It's his word against theirs!" cried Sayers senior. "He's one of them foreigners!"

The General held up the knife. "There's this. And a man who won't speak up for himself because he has been so shamed. Is there any other witness? Ian Murdo should remember."

"I don't know what he heard; he was groaning with the pain in his knee," said Alick. "But my wife was there."

"Good God, man, your wife heard all *that*?"

For answer Alick looked up at the balcony, and so did the others. The children were dumbstruck without understanding anything. "Is your husband's story true, Mrs. Glenroy?" the General called up to her.

"In every detail," she answered.

She didn't remain to hear what the General said after that. She took each child by a shoulder and turned them relentlessly toward the back stairs. "Pick up your books," she commanded. If they said she was hurting them, she didn't care; she wanted only to get out. But she met with no resistance because they were obsessed with one earth-shattering question, and the instant they were out the back door, it came.

"What did Mr. Glenroy mean?" Frank demanded. "How could anyone make a lass out of a man? I know a lass is a girl. Papa calls us lassies all the time. Mama hates it."

Sukey laughed contemptuously at her younger sister's ignorance. "It's easy! If I put on boy's clothes and had a boy's name, then I'd be a boy!"

"Boys are different," Frank insisted. "Don't you know that little statue on the mantel in the library? That boy with no clothes on that Mr.

Somers brought from Rome? It's supposed to be David getting ready to throw a rock at Goliath."

"That is not a *boy*," said Sukey. "That is a *statue*. You can stick all kinds of things onto statues. Wings and tails and everything. It's like making up tales. If you write them in a book, they are stories; if you tell them to your papa, they are *lies*."

Frank was dogmatic. "We saw Mrs. Higham's little baby having his bath once. Don't you remember that tiny little thing?"

"But we all have one of those when the angels bring us, and then it dries up and falls off some of us, and then we're girls."

Frank appealed to Jennie. "Mrs. Glenroy, can it happen after you're grown up? Or—" She faltered. "They kept talking about knives. And *blood*." She put her fingers to her lips.

Sukey, pale around the mouth, implored, "Mrs. Glenroy, *please!*"

"Nobody was going to hurt anybody, except in their feelings. It was all a bad joke, teasing Rory about his kilt. Saying he was dressed like a girl so he must be one."

"But he wasn't dressed like a girl," said Sukey. "Highlanders are very brave men; Papa said so. Zeb Pulsifer is as numb as a turd."

"*Susanna!*" Jennie exclaimed. "What an expression!"

"We know a lot more," said Frank.

"I'm sure you do." And their mother was afraid of their learning to say "Good morning" in Gaelic! "Where did you gather this picturesque vocabulary?" They looked at her with the innocence of kittens.

"All right," said Jennie. "All I ask is that you remember there are some places where you must never, *never* use those words." She saw herself trotting out a particularly vivid phrase at the dinner table and her father nearly choking on his food.

"We will remember," they solemnly promised.

"Mrs. Glenroy, I can't remember when mine dropped off," Frank said. "But you were a little boy when you were as old as Sukey and me, weren't you? When you wore boys' clothes."

"No, Frances, I was always a little girl, and I wore pantaloons to save my frocks. Your papa would not turn into a lady if he put on one of your mother's gowns."

The two fell against each other laughing until they were weak.

Nineteen

ALICK TOLD HER at noon he'd gotten a few nods and some outright grins from men who had until now paid little attention to him; Tony came to the yard on an errand for his father and must have passed the word around. The man Clements, who was training him, had even slapped him on the shoulder and said it was time somebody hooped Zeb's barrel. The expression entertained Alick; he repeated it with a smile. "Let us hope it stays hooped," he said.

"I'd like to stuff him in it and take him out to sea and drop him overboard," she said passionately. "What did the General say?"

"Och, I couldn't be repeating it; he is a great man for strong language, the General. But he gave Rory his *sgian dubh*. Joseph Pulsifer went out looking like the north face of Ben Cheathaich, and Sayers like a marsh in a spring flood."

"How did Zeb and Corny look?"

"Their heads were hanging so low I could not be seeing. But it was not from shame. The fathers were shamed, but not the sons. The fear was at Corny, and Zeb was smoldering like a fire in a peat bog. They are on—what is the word?"

"Probation?"

"That is it. If there is anything else, they will be losing their work and be turned over to the law."

In spite of his forebodings the night before, he behaved as if the incident were already far behind them. Jennie tried to believe it was her new condition that made her so apprehensive. Anything could worry her now that she was so vulnerable. Exposed to death in the Highlands, exposed to death on the ocean, exposed to death by childbirth. "Third time never fails!" the Hawthornes used to say to encourage each other. But it could work the other way, too.

When Alick left, she lay down on her bed, thinking she'd fall asleep, after her late night and early waking, but she couldn't drop off. Nothing, not even either of the two Williams, Blake and Wordsworth, would offer escape from the nasty little threat, "Third time never fails."

She yearned for an hour alone with the untouched pianoforte in the drawing room of Strathbuie House. Well, that was forbidden, because of Mrs. MacKenzie's irrational aversion to music, but not the library. She took Maria Edgeworth and walked to the mansion. A strong, chilly sea wind was blowing up the river and turning the leaves inside out. She went around the garden in case Mrs. MacKenzie should be strolling there, and she liked the oceany smell of the wind and the boisterous gusts that swept through the grounds.

The General and Tony would be at the shore, and Eliza had taken the girls to Quarry Hill to look for late wild strawberries; if they were lucky, some other children would be there. Oliver slept on his back in the shade by the door. He rolled over and politely heaved himself onto his feet at sight of her, then sagged and sighed into sleep again.

The kitchen was tidied up, and Mrs. Frost and Benoni sat at the unnaturally bare table, drinking tea from large cups and sharing the newspaper spread before them.

"I don't intend to interrupt," Jennie said apologetically. "May I go into the library?"

Mrs. Frost shrugged. "Dunno what's to stop it. Help yourself."

She still wouldn't touch the telescope, but she stopped for the view. The river was peacock blue overlaid with silver by the wind, the distances silvered with the haze of what the sailors called a smoky sou'wester. In the Pool, where the wood coasters waited for the turn of the tide, the *Paul Revere* lay at her anchorage. So she was to go to Liverpool next. Liverpool, coaches across England, and *home*.

Aboard the *Paul Revere* what could happen to her? Blue skies and fair winds went with the brig where she sailed; she was the most blessed of ships. "Oh, God," she whispered, "to *be* there. To have Sylvia tell me I will be safe."

Such agonizing could bring her nothing but grief. She turned from the window and went to the books. The novels were to the right of the fireplace. Earlier she'd been punctilious about ignoring everything but books, but today she couldn't miss the little David on the mantel. He stood defiantly nude between a blown-glass galleon and an engraved brass snuffbox.

She had to smile at the sight of him. She'd wager that Sukey and Frank would be in here before the day was out to take another look, if they hadn't managed it already.

Upstairs a door burst open, and the General's voice reverberated across the stair well. "You are *not* going to Boston, and that is the final word on the subject! I'll hear no more!"

"I am going to Boston when *Lady Lydia* sails tomorrow." Mrs. MacKenzie had apparently followed him out of the room which until now had contained their argument. Her voice was as commanding in its contralto strength as his basso was. "I shall be aboard, make no mistake about that!"

"Hannah!" her husband roared. "Unpack Mrs. MacKenzie's trunks!"

"Hannah, if you value your life, do not remove one garment. Run on home and do your own packing."

There was a pause while Hannah ran down the stairs. Jennie heard a starchy rustling and agitated breathing in the hall and a scamper down the passage. Perspiring, she looked around for her own escape route. The MacKenzies sounded as if they were just at the head of the stairs.

"Colin," the General's wife said, "I am going away until you recover from your infatuation with these people. It's outrageous! Or would be if it weren't so ridiculous. Using their words. Whistling their tunes. And I nearly went mad when that—that *piper* was here last night. And good God, you're even acquiring an *accent*! I don't know what I'm married to! If you suddenly took to playing with toy soldiers, it would be more bearable."

"Lydia," he said warningly, but she overrode him.

"You are creating ill feeling in the town. A few years ago there wasn't enough that you could do for your old comrades, as you called them, even the lowest. And now, in the first squabble that comes up, you side with the foreigners."

"I side only with justice. Zeb Pulsifer and Cornelius Sayers were the offenders, and their fathers know it. And while you're scoffing at foreigners, my love, do not forget that our people came as foreigners. The only true Americans are the Indians."

"Ha!" his wife jeered. "I suppose I should be thankful that I'm spared your redskin friends while you're so besotted with your Highlanders. What will it be next, Colin? Will you be importing Italians or Greeks? That should wake up the town!"

"Lydia, *will you be silent?*"

Oh, why hadn't they put a door between the library and the dining room? Jennie blindly seized a book and skimmed about the room from window to window like a captive bee.

"I've had a boring winter and a boring spring, Colin. I'm going to save my summer and my sanity by going to Massachusetts, and unless you throw me down and bind me hand and foot, I shall board the vessel tomorrow morning. I intend to bear this child in my old home."

"If you won't consider the children and your husband, consider the infant. You'll be risking its life. A summer in Boston could kill it."

"That's what you're really concerned about, isn't it? The baby! I'm simply a broodmare. Well, this broodmare desires some congenial company, and she'll find it under her brother's roof in Quincy, which has as pure air as this place, and no salt fish drying across the road from the front gate!"

"Very well," the General said frigidly. "Go if you must. I shall have no peace otherwise. But I forbid you to take the girls."

"Never fear. It's hell enough to be *enceinte* for the first time in eight years, just so you can have another son."

"Son or daughter, it will be equally precious. And need I remind you, my dove, that you were hardly coerced?" he asked sardonically.

There was a pause during which Jennie, feeling sick, expected to be caught in the next minute or so. And then she saw that one of the side windows was really a pair of French doors. Rejoicing, she tried the latch; it was very stiff. Truelove Adams was riding the mower across the lawn. He looked asleep, letting the horse do all the thinking. He might not see her, or think anything of it if he did; but she was afraid the latch would spring open with a loud snap, and they'd surely hear it up on the stairs.

Lydia MacKenzie said lazily, "What a blizzard that night, eh? We must incorporate it into his name somehow. As one of the begetters."

Her low laugh and his chuckle blended together in suggestive intimacy, and the following silence made Jennie feel like a voyeur, because it was the silence of lovers.

"Just the same, Colin, I am going," Lydia said after a while. "My heart is set on it."

"Not on me?"

"I have my heart set on having you all to myself someday, if we live that long. Or some night . . . In the meantime, we are no good to each other where it matters—in bed. The very sight of you affects me as the first sight did, but there is nothing we can do about it while I'm carrying this enormous child like a bass drum I cannot put down."

"Oh, go!" he said. "But when you come back—beware!" There was a surprised—and young—squawk from Lydia. Jennie snapped the latch and ran out. She went down the steps to the lawn and ducked under the piazza. Truelove was jogging toward the foot of the lawn.

She was running now not from the fear of being caught committing the awful sin of eavesdropping, but from her own bereavement. As she had faced the fact that there could never be another lover like Nigel, now she had to accept the truth that she would never experience the confidently sensuous intimacy of long-married lovers. Envy and resentment were like bile in her throat; she'd expected so much, believed so many promises, and all she had for them was exile and a child she didn't want.

Twenty

SHE HAULED UP a fresh pail of water, in defiance of Alick's new orders against her going to the well, and had a long drink of water. Then she put on her bonnet and light shawl and went out to the lane. At first she was aimless, wanting only to keep moving. She hadn't yet walked west on the shore road, past the brickyard and the long dock, to the toll bridge at the foot of Quarry Lane. But today the solitude of the seldom-traveled back lane appealed to her.

She stopped at the pasture, but the horses and ponies were all at the far side, watching Truelove Adams mow the lawn. She turned and leaned her back against the top rail and contemplated the grove across the lane, a mass of constantly changing greens silvered by the wind as the river was. A path led into it, an invitation she couldn't resist.

The path wound upward through fern and bracken, around granite outcroppings and an occasional erratic boulder that seemed to have been dropped there and forgotten by a giant child. Tall wild roses bloomed in one clearing, reaching for the light; raspberry bushes filled another. Still another was carpeted with green and silver mosses and scarlet lichens grew from a rotting tree trunk. A ground-covering plant had minutely perfect pink blossoms. It had been a long time since she had walked in a wood, and this stretch between the lane and the town was charming. The little black-capped tits which the Americans called chickadees, from their call, were fearlessly sociable all about her as she climbed the gradual slope.

There was no thinning out to warn her that Main Street was imminent until she came out almost opposite the church road. Apparently this land wasn't needed for building yet and had remained untouched. To the right and left of it the grove ended at the back boundaries of the properties along the south side of Main Street. She wondered how long these trees would stand and what would be built here. She laid her hand with affection and regret on the trunk of the nearest maple.

The street was quiet. Nothing stirred around the Wells household on the corner of the church road but a black cat, which jumped onto a gatepost and began to wash up. Elder Mayfield was just entering the gate of the property on the other side of the Wells house, and a dog was barking at him from inside. A black horse and a gig were coming from west Main Street at a fast clip, raising billows of dust.

In the shade a short distance to Jennie's left three women were standing by a granite milestone. They all were staring at her as if she were an apparition strayed out of a haunted forest.

I'll make it really interesting for them and vanish again, she thought. The gig came abreast of them; the driver was Dr. Waite. One of them gave him a perfunctory glance; the others still stared at Jennie. He lifted his hat as he passed her, and she bowed, thinking that his fast-trotting horse was more beautiful than he was.

She watched the gig going away down the hill to east Main Street. *When I am home, I am going to ride and ride,* she thought. *When I have at last put down the bass drum.* Being that big was so impossible to imagine that she could even smile as she thought it, no longer depressed by the conversation in which she had heard the simile.

She was still looking after the gig when the women moved on her. She hadn't heard them coming; they were suddenly *at* her, ripping off her bonnet and half strangling her with the ribbons, snatching at her shawl. She was held from behind by hands that dug into her flesh and wrenched at her shoulders, surrounded by faces too contorted to resemble anything human or animal, deafened by shrieking voices. Someone slapped her face first on one side and then the other till her head was ringing, and she thought her neck would snap. Words came clear in the cacophony. "Your man's the General's arse-licker, and you're his hoor! Everybody knows he's keepin' you because his wife's too big to do it and she picked you for the job. Everybody knows. Everybody knows!"

"Slummocks!" Jennie spit at them. She lashed out with her feet and got shins and toes, struck out with her fists, drove her elbows hard into breasts, and exulted in the grunts and squawks. A good backward kick, and the woman holding her shoulders let go with a groan, and Jennie heard her dress rip. Someone had her by the hair. She hit an eye with one fist and teeth with the other. She laughed aloud until an arm went across her windpipe from behind.

Now they will kill me, she thought in a tiny spot of calm deep within her brain. *What a disgusting way to die, torn apart by stinking Furies.* She'd keep fighting while she had breath, but she was losing it fast.

When she was suddenly released, she almost fell down, but someone steadied her and was putting a coat over her shoulders. Elder Mayfield had the biggest woman's arms pinioned behind her, and curses burst from her mouth like vomit. Stephen Wells held another woman by the wrists with one hand. She spit in his face, and he calmly slapped hers. "Mind your failings."

"I'll take you to law!" she shrieked at him.

"Indeed?" said the unseen man behind Jennie. "And where will you find a lawyer to take your case?"

"And you, Leah Pulsifer," said Elder Mayfield to his squirming and profane captive, "I will not release until you stop that vile tongue of yours. And then you are to go home and down on your knees, and ask God's forgiveness for taking his name in vain, besides brawling in the street and assaulting this defenseless woman."

"Not quite defenseless," said Stephen Wells. "You handled yourself very well, Mrs. Glenroy. Now, Judy, you'd better set a straight course for home the way your sister's done, and keep yourself inconspicuous from now on."

"Mrs. Glenroy," said the third man, "will have no difficulty finding an attorney and creditable witnesses."

"There'll be quite a storm on Mount Olympus when the General hears about all this," Stephen said loudly over Mrs. Pulsifer's obscenities.

Judy began to howl that she hadn't wanted to do it; *she* never had no reason; *she* never said none of them things. Her nose ran, and she was such a revolting object that Stephen let her go in distaste. She scuttled up Main Street, wailing.

"Are you prepared to stop this?" Elder Mayfield demanded of Mrs. Pulsifer. She grudgingly muttered something, and he released her arms. She rubbed them, glaring from under beetling brows. Then she tramped off. *"Pray!"* Elder Mayfield trumpeted after her.

"How are you feeling, Mrs. Glenroy?" Stephen Wells asked her.

"All in one piece, though I think they'd have dismembered me if you all hadn't come along. Thank you, Elder Mayfield, and Mr. Wells, and—?" She turned to the third man.

"Jonathan Dalrymple, Mrs. Glenroy." He bowed, a thin, slightly stooped man with bushy gray hair combed back from a widow's peak, and pointed gray eyebrows. His crimson waistcoat was startlingly vivid for staid middle age.

She gave him her hand. "Thank you for your coat. Now if I can find my shawl—"

"I'm afraid it's beyond wearing," Stephen Wells said. It had been trampled in horse manure. The elder picked up her tattered bonnet. Both the shawl and the bonnet looked so abused and so pathetic that she couldn't say anything. She held a rueful little smile at the corners of her mouth to keep it from trembling.

"I apologize on behalf of Maddox—" the Elder began as if from the pulpit, and Stephen said simultaneously, "If you'll just come across the road, my mother will—"

A light feminine voice somehow managed to prevail over them. "*Jonathan!* Mercy, don't keep the child *standing* there!"

Two women were crossing to them, the smaller, slighter one fairly skipping ahead, holding up her flowered cambric skirt and petticoat to keep them from the soil of the road. A frilly cap rested like sea-foam on gray curls. Her expectant, dimpled smile showed what a pretty girl she must have been. She swooped down on the shawl and picked it up by a clean corner. "*Well!* Leah Pulsifer washes for me, and I am sure she will launder this with diligence, if not with enthusiasm, if she wishes to continue her employment with us. Now you are to come straight home with me and have a cup of tea with brandy in it. You must be quite faint."

"My kettle is already boiling, Lucretia," said the larger woman serenely. She was plainly Stephen Wells's mother; she had the same craggy features and blue eyes. "You'll come, too, Lucretia."

"Mr. Dalrymple needs his coat back," said Jennie. A number of places were beginning to sting or to throb, or both. She wanted to run into the woods away from all the smothering concern. Back in the cottage, alone, perhaps she could think clearly enough to see the assault in its proper perspective, which might be even more frightening than the assault itself.

"I will give you something to wear," said Mrs. Wells, and Jennie was inexorably escorted across Main Street.

In Mrs. Wells's austere but well-furnished bedroom Jennie washed her face and combed her hair, then bundled herself into a large fleecy shawl to go downstairs and drink tea. She wouldn't take off her dress so that Mrs. Wells could mend the ripped seam; she had a feeling her shoulders were beginning to show a multitude of bruises from Mrs. Pulsifer's powerful fingers, and she didn't want to look at them or have anyone see. She was glad of the tea and couldn't seem to get enough of it; she felt chilled to her innermost parts. There was no brandy because Mrs. Wells said she didn't need it; Mrs. Dalrymple teased her for being so puritanical, but there was a sense of genuine affection between them.

From the way they treated Jennie, she was sure that they hadn't heard the filth the harridans had spewed out and knew nothing of it. She wished she dared ask, but even to put words to it would have been degrading.

They ate some little spice cakes called Aaron's Bundles; she hadn't been able to, at first, but after the first sip of tea she felt as if she could devour the whole plateful. She apologized for her thirst and appetite, and Mrs. Wells said placidly, "It's because you're so wrought up. Don't hold back. It will do you good."

"Leah Pulsifer is a harpy," said Mrs. Dalrymple, "and the Keane sisters are bewitched by her. She's been the most exciting thing in their lives since Joseph brought her here. Perhaps after today they'll have had enough. They'll be expecting complaints to be sworn out against them, and they'll blame her for that. Are you going to swear out complaints, my dear? Jonathan would gladly advise you. He is Maddox's one lawyer."

"I don't know," Jennie said, knowing full well. She was hoping the threat of action would keep the Pulsifer woman subdued; she was afraid the reality would send her shrieking her dirt all over town. "I shall have to discuss it with my husband."

"And the General," said Mrs. Wells. "A word from him in the right places is very efficacious."

"I believe that," said Jennie with feeling. She was sure that what had just happened was a direct result of the General's efficacious words in the morning. It was her testimony that had corroborated Alick's, and she was going to pay.

She convinced them that she felt very strong and able and could get home alone by the woods path in fifteen minutes, and enjoy it. Once she was inside the rustling green shelter of the trees, she found herself smiling at the picture of herself embattled. It must have been a surprise to those three, expecting her to be a namby-pamby and meeting a hard-hitting, hard-kicking windmill.

But should she tell Alick or not? She'd have liked to brag about her fighting ability, but there would be no point in passing on the names they had called him and her. Least said, soonest mended. She could say any visible scratches were from brambles in the woods.

She hid the ruined bonnet in the bottom of the pine wardrobe in her room until she could burn it, briefly mourning the pale rose ribbons. She then laid aside Mrs. Wells's shawl and took off the ripped dress; a sleeve had been pulled out, and she'd get needle and thread from Eliza or Mrs. Frost tomorrow. Her bruises *were* showing. She scrubbed herself until she smarted, twisting and reaching to wash the places on her back. There was a pull in one shoulder, and one of her ankles hurt, but she'd received no punches around the body. It had all been pulling, ripping, and scratching until that great arm had come against her throat. The woman must have been insane, and her followers mesmerized, to attack her on a public way; she hoped they all were sick to the gut and shaking in an ague of fear, waiting for the constable to come after them.

Her scalp was a little tender where someone had gotten hold of a good handful of hair; Jennie had paid for that by viciously pinching the creature's underarm.

"That will leave a magnificent bruise!" she said aloud.

She put on her Highland dress, but some of the scratches showed on her forearms and on her face. Alick asked her about them, and she told him she'd been exploring in the woods above the lane and had gotten into the brambles.

"You should not go there alone." He rebuked her. "You could fall, and who would know where to find you?"

"I'd be only up on the hill there. I could shout and be heard. Or do this." She put two fingers in her mouth and whistled. That made him jump and then laugh.

"You're in rare fine spirits tonight."

"And why not? What have I to gloom about? And shall I tell you the latest news? Madam is sailing to Boston tomorrow. She is bored."

Twenty-One

Alick had a class that night, and for the first time he was reluctant to go. He didn't say so, but she knew it and bluntly asked him why. He avoided her eyes, also for the first time. Usually she was the one who couldn't look away from him; he could make her feel like a butterfly pinned to a board.

"You had better answer me, Alick," she said. "The fire is doing very well without you fiddle-faddling with it."

He put the stove lid back in place. "You are limping, and you were fingering your shoulder. Are you being honest with me?" Now she was pinned, but he saved her himself by asking, "Did you fall in the woods?"

She laughed with the relief of it. "No, but I turned my ankle. I should have worn my brogues. I shall next time."

"There is to be no next time. Not alone. You have not explained about your shoulder."

"It's nothing! It's going away already. I simply caught at a tree to keep my balance." That made it worse; he was looking at her as if she were intentionally taking risks. This only exacerbated both her physical and emotional discomfort.

"Alick, it was *nothing*!" she insisted crossly. "Don't you think I *know*? I have *asked* you not to mother-hen me—"

"Yes, and you have asked me why I am not anxious to be leaving you alone tonight." He was ruthless. "I am requiring your word that you will not be going out for any twilight walk."

"May I go to the Necessary?" She was mocking-meek. "I don't intend to walk anywhere but there, but Alick, I cannot be a prisoner! It's bad

131

enough to be already the prisoner of this—this—oh, what shall I call it?"

"Child," he suggested without pity.

"How do I know it's a child? It is too soon for it to be *anything*," she said wildly. "We don't even know what is really in there. Perhaps it's something else. A g-growth." She stammered out the last word, which had evoked a fresh horror.

"No!" His voice extinguished hers. "And I am not going out tonight."

"Yes, you are," she insisted. "I'm not really frightened, Alick, but it is something one thinks of sometimes. Now it's gone, I promise you, and I apologize for being difficult, and I shall never forgive myself if you miss a class. *Please.*" She was out of breath, and her agitation was genuine; she felt as if she would fly apart if she weren't left alone for a time. "I will put my feet up and read, and you may be sure that's all I'll be doing."

He went at last. She was cold, even though the kitchen was still warm with the dying fire; her teeth were chattering, and all her sore places, even her scalp, were hurting. She went upstairs and took the plaid off Alick's bed and brought it down to wrap herself in while she read. She had washed it in cool suds early one morning, and it had dried all one hot day, so the colors were brighter, but it still seemed to hold for her the faint smokiness from their fires and the sad, remote, fragrance of the dried bracken on which they'd slept.

She lit the candles before she really needed them, taking a little comfort from them. The book she had seized and carried away with her from the library was called *Ormond, or The Secret Witness*, by a Charles Brockden Brown, and she was determined to concentrate her mind on it. What had happened this afternoon was in the past; the things they had screamed at her were no more than Macbeth's tales told by an idiot. She was an idiot herself if she let them leave bruises on her mind as well as on her flesh.

Between the story and the cheerful radiance of her candles, and the embrace of the plaid, she felt a blissful tranquillity taking possession. It was very quiet; the wind had gone down with the sun, and the clock's voice enhanced the stillness.

After a time she heard the soft call of an owl. It resembled one she had heard often at home, and she laid her head back against the chair, shut her eyes, listened, and drifted.

She was aroused by voices outside the front door and thought Alick was bringing someone home. She took her feet out of the opposite chair and wiggled her stiffened and bruised ankle to loosen it and stood up, automatically smoothing her hair.

There were curious thumps outside the front door, and Tony called to her. "Mrs. Glenroy, will you open the door? Don't be alarmed. *Please.*"

"Alarmed by you, Tony?" she called back, on her way. "Why in the world should I be?" She opened the door.

He was holding Alick up, with Alick's arm hanging loosely around his neck and his arm around Alick's waist.

"I am truly sorry," he said. A strong whiff of wine came at her, and she thought at first that Alick was drunk, especially when he stumbled on the threshold and almost fell headlong into the hall. Tony caught him around the middle with both arms.

Once into the candlelit kitchen, Alick reached for the edge of the table and worked himself around to a chair, with Tony hovering behind him. He fell into the chair and looked up at her through the blood and dirt on his face, and she knew he was sober.

"I am sorry about this, Jeannie," he said.

"*Sorry!*" she said harshly. "My God, I'm the one who made you go! What happened?" He shook his head and hunched over with his arms folded across his belly. She was very frightened but tried not to show it, for all their sakes. She tucked the plaid around him, fussily thorough because she had to be doing something with her hands to steady them.

"I found him on the road just this side of the schoolhouse," Tony said. The smell of wine came from him. His cheeks were scarlet, and his black eyes brilliant. "They must have ambushed him."

"*They?* How many? And who?"

"No matter," Alick said faintly. "I am still alive." She put her hand on his shoulder and kneaded it through the plaid. *What have we begun?* she thought, looking down on his bent head.

She went into the pantry for a basin of water. Tony followed and took the basin from her because her hands were shaking so. He was a child still, a worried child trying to fill a man's part and afraid she was about to go to pieces.

"I am not going to faint or have hysterics, Tony," she said.

"A *Dia*, that is what we can be doing without," said Alick. He wouldn't let her wash the mess off his face. He did it with no gentle touch, and she remembered how vigorously she had scrubbed herself that afternoon.

He had some cuts and scrapes on his face, nothing deep. She wanted to take off his shirt, but he wouldn't allow that. "I am in no great hurry to see for myself," he said with grim humor. "But I will be needing Tony's arm on the stairs."

Jennie's throat shut off for an instant. If Alick was really hurt, and it was all because they'd tried to help Rory— She picked up a candlestick to lead the way upstairs and felt like driving it through the nearest window and screaming, "I hate this world! It is terrible, terrible!"

But while she silently screamed it, she was going ahead, turning down Alick's bed, bringing in another pillow. She watched her shadow wavering on the wall while she listened to their feet on the stairs and Tony's manful encouragement. She envisioned Dr. Waite coming down those stairs to her in the hall and trying to be kind, saying, "There is always hope, but—"

Alick sat down on the side of the bed, winded, holding to a post while Tony pulled off his boots. "Now shall I help you with your—" Tony looked uncertainly at Jennie—"with your other garments?"

"You may say trousers in my presence, Tony," Jennie said. "Or pantaloons. Or breeches."

"I will be doing it later for myself," Alick said. "Thank you, Tony."

"Lie back," Jennie commanded him. Tony lifted his legs up onto the bed, and Jennie covered him, watching for signs of pain.

"No ribs broken," Alick said to her with the wraith of a smile. She left the candle with him and went downstairs with Tony.

"Was it Zeb Pulsifer?" she asked him in the kitchen.

"I reckon so, because of this morning. But they left him before I got there because they heard me coming; I was whistling. Alick was trying to get up. I hope he'll be all right." He was acutely uncomfortable. "Mrs. Glenroy, I'd be much obliged if you didn't—"

"Mention you to anyone? I won't. But I am awfully grateful."

"So am I! I'm glad I was able to help. But I am supposed to be asleep in my room by now."

"Then that's where you'd better go, very quickly."

"I'm not drunk! I had only one glass of wine." With his flushed cheekbones and luminous eyes, his black hair falling over his forehead, his open collar, he looked like a young poet; Sophie would have been enchanted by his romantic appearance. Darling Sophie. Someday she would embrace her young sister again, but if she left Alick dead, it would be a bitter homecoming indeed.

"I don't think you're drunk, Tony, and I thank you for happening along when you did. I hope you will not be caught."

"I know how to manage it. They're having people in for cards tonight, so I shall flit up the back stairs like a ghost."

They said good night, and she took the plaid and went back up to Alick. He was watching the door as if waiting for her and said at once, "Are you all right?" He sounded stronger, now that he had rested, and she took heart from that.

"How many times a day do you ask me that? Alick, I never could suffer in silence, so you will know when I am ailing." She put her hand on his forehead. He shut his eyes, and she thought she had hurt him and took her hand away.

"You're not feverish. Alick, just how bad is it? Can you tell if you are hurt inside?"

"Nothing is broken in me, I think. But I felt the belly was being torn out of me at the time. I left my supper back there on the road."

"Was it Zeb and Corny?"

"Yes, but I will be sparing your ears what they called me."

"I have a good idea of it," she said dryly. She spread the plaid over him. "I had it wrapped around me while I was reading. It reminds me of the good things, like the bliss of being alive after the flooded corrie, and that day on the shore by the Loch of the Speckled Trout. We were always in danger then, but now it seems like a safe time."

"We are safe, Jeannie." He shut his eyes again, looking drawn and exhausted. Had he ever looked this tired in the mountains? She couldn't remember it. But pain could do it to a man.

"I wish I could give you something," she said. "If only we had whiskey or wine in the house."

"The pain will pass. Go to bed, Jeannie."

"Shall I leave the candle?"

"No. Good night." It was the definitive dismissal. What else did she want from him? What could she obtain beyond the laconic "We are safe"? She didn't believe it.

Twenty-Two

SHE LAY AWAKE for a time, her body drumming with far more pulses than should have been there. She was so keyed up that she had to go out to the Necessary again; she listened at Alick's door on the way, and he was so quiet she was sure that he was awake and knew she was there. She felt her way downstairs and went out in her bare feet. The owl had gone, and the night had no charm for her in its stars or its scents or its fireflies. Zeb Pulsifer was either still rejoicing or sleeping the sleep supposedly reserved for the just but enjoyed more by the unjust. The just were either worrying or hurting too much to sleep.

When she went upstairs, she listened again, going into the room and standing by Alick's bed this time. It sounded like a genuine deep sleep, so by the time she had warmed up in her own bed she could fall asleep herself. She imagined crawling into one of the caves where they had slept on their journey, for preference the ones where they'd had the most to eat; she imagined the intense pleasure of stretching out tired legs and of going to sleep watching the primitive beauty of the fire at the cave mouth.

The spell remained with her, so that when she woke up, she felt as if Alick had just left her side. She kept her eyes shut as she'd done those mornings, trying to hold on to the night if it had been a safe night, free of ghosts and nightmares.

Then the town roosters began. The Frosts' Jack was nearest, loudest, and proudest. He was Nabby's pet, and the family pretended he was too tough to eat by now, so he would live till he died of natural causes. There was an antiphonal lowing of cows wanting to be milked and a

136

contagion of barking spreading through the town. She tried to stay in the cave, but a pair of sea gulls dipping low past the windows and calling to each other dragged her out into a gray cool morning on the coast of Maine.

With her first stretch she felt soreness in her shoulder and some other spots on her body that throbbed with a life of their own. Instantly she remembered everything that had happened. She sat up in bed, aghast. She'd slept so heavily he could have died and she wouldn't have known. There was a faint sound from below; he was down there then. He might have gone outside to vomit the blood. This was at once so possible, so probable, that she was sure of it. He had been horribly injured, but he hadn't wanted to frighten her. She leaped out of bed and went down the stairs in her nightgown and bare feet, thinking, *I will have to get someone. Benoni. The General.*

The scent of the wood fire met her halfway down. In the kitchen Alick was stirring the porridge. His hair was damp and roughly toweled, and he had changed his dirty, blood-spattered shirt for a clean one.

"You're all right then," she said, holding to each side of the door-frame. "I thought—oh, never mind what I thought." She heard a light, foolish laugh coming from her. "You're all right."

"I am." He didn't turn his head. "I'm sore, but I have known worse. It will work itself off. The porridge will be ready when you are."

She went across the room to get a better view of him. One cheekbone was turning blue around a bad scrape. He gave her a sidewise look past it. "Your bramble scratches are red this morning. It's luck we are not appearing in public together; they would be thinking we are very hard on each other."

She went back upstairs and dressed in the Highland clothes again, all but the thick stockings and the brogues. The homespun fabric felt warm and friendly to her in the chill. Like the plaid and the memory of the caves, it breathed reassurance.

This time when she came down he had tea for her, and she sat on the woodbox, holding the mug in both cold hands, while she sipped. "Alick, what are you going to do?" she asked him.

He appeared to be gravely measuring the consistency of the oatmeal while he stirred it and thinking of nothing else. Just when she had decided he wasn't going to answer, he said, "What I will not do is be running to the General, or anyone else, with every little thing."

"Do you call *this* a little thing?"

"Today I do. Perhaps they have had their revenge, and it is over."

"*Alick!*" she flared at him. "I'm beginning to think you led a very sheltered life out there on the moors. Bullies like that will never let anything rest! They have nothing to do but make trouble, and next time it could be worse. Much worse! If they left you dead, and no one saw, they would never have to answer for murder, no matter how many suspected them."

"What would you be having me do?" he asked evenly, watching the slow, thick bubbling in the pot. "I cannot prove anything, and last night I told Tony he wasn't to be speaking of it. Is that so unreasonable?"

"No, but what if we left this place now, while the weather is fine, instead of waiting until after the baby is born? We would be settled somewhere else before cold weather, and free of this—this vendetta." She hadn't thought it out; it had come spontaneously, and now that it was said, she liked the sound of it.

He set the pot off the flame, replaced the lid, and then gave her his full attention. "You would be giving back the General's silver dollars then," he said in that maddeningly level voice, "and I would be giving up my chance to learn a trade I love, and we would go on the road like tinkers with a handful of money between us, and you carrying, all to be satisfying a piece of offal too rank even for the crows to eat."

"We would not be doing it to satisfy him, but so we could live free of persecution! There are other shipyards all up and down the coast. I can find other children to teach."

"Jeannie, we are not going anywhere," he said. "I will attend to Zeb Pulsifer in my own good time if it is needed. Now will you be bringing out the porridge bowls, or will I?"

She walked with dignity into the pantry. She'd have liked to say something he couldn't answer, but she didn't think it was possible. If she asked him just how he would attend to Zeb, she'd get a reply that would leave her floundering in a swamp of *buts*.

They ate breakfast without conversation, and he took his bonnet and left for work, saying his usual pleasant good-bye. She flung an angry, speechless message after him. *I know you have the right to stay where you please, but you're in a den of vipers, you insufferably arrogant Gael! You'll attend to Zeb Pulsifer, will you? Well, we'll see who attends to whom the next time you're coming home alone in the dark! If you thought it was a ghost*

*wandering around out there in the dark, you'd not be so damnably sure of
yourself!*

A raw, depressing wind had sprung up when she left for the mansion.
On a whim she'd wrapped in the plaid instead of Elspeth's shawl.

"My, that's a handsome length of goods," Mrs. Frost said when she
went into the kitchen. "What do they call it?"

"The plaid. It serves as a blanket or a cloak or a tent or to do up
your possessions in. They tell about sleeping rough in the dead of winter;
a man would soak the plaid in water and lie down wrapped in it, and it
would freeze and no wind would get through it, and snow could pile up
against his back and never touch him."

Mrs. Frost was not impressed. "But his feet and ears would be cold,"
she pointed out. "Sit down and have some coffee. The young ones are
down to the wharf to see their mother off." She set two warm raisin
muffins before Jennie. "Here, put these away. They'll widen you out.
You're looking some pikkid this morning." Without any change in in-
tonation she said, "I heard about yesterday. That Leah Pulsifer is a she-
devil, and the Keane sisters were born foolish."

"How did the news reach you?" Jennie asked. Somehow she was not
surprised. She *was* surprised that the muffins and coffee could taste so
good while she was discussing such a sordid business.

"Mrs. Dalrymple's hired girl is my niece. She was out in the dooryard
when they jumped on you, and she give a holler, and Mr. Dalrymple
and Elder Mayfield came out of that house like they was shot from a
cannon." She grinned. "Never knew the elder could move that hulk of
his so fast. Stephen Wells was just coming out of his gate, and Minnie
swears his feet never touched the road."

"Well, I didn't start the battle," said Jennie, "and I've lost my only
bonnet, and my dress is ripped. Could I borrow needle and thread when
I'm through this morning?"

"Liza will get it for you in the sewing room. Use plenty of cream,
you need it."

"Will you tell Minnie I thank her with all my heart?" Jennie asked.

"Ayuh. She said you gave 'em a good tussle before Leah bid fair to
strangle you."

"I think I left a few marks." Jennie agreed.

"Lord, Lord, it was a sorry day for Maddox when Joe Pulsifer brought that one here! The day he was mustered out of the Army a whole new war begun for him, and it won't end until one or the other of 'em is laid in the grave."

"Where did he ever find her?"

"In Boston. My Ben was there, too; he knows the story. *She* was one of the trollops that'd lift her skirts for any soldier, Yankee or redcoat, if he had a penny in his pack. Joe was green as grass. When she told him he'd put her in the family way, he believed her, and nobody could convince him she had half a dozen fathers for the brat and maybe more. She warn't a bad-looking girl in those days, Ben says, and she could cry like her heart was broken." She poured more coffee from the tall pot. "It's Ben's belief that these strumpets were ordered by the authorities to leave Boston or go to jail, and she was already suspected of getting soldiers drunk and stealing their mustering-out pay. She knew Joe had land promised at a good safe distance from Boston, and he was that gullible and good she could make a fool of him and he'd never raise a hand to her, no matter what. So she picked him. I reckon they hadn't been here five minutes before she was hating it and him. They've had four young ones since Zeb, and the good Lord alone knows how many she's got rid of. It's a wonder the rest of them was born with all their wits and limbs about 'em."

"Are the others as bad as Zeb?" Jennie visualized a horde of ravening Pulsifers.

"Not yet. The youngest boy and girl go to school. It's the law, and that may be the saving of them. The middle boy, he'd be Zeb's shadow if he could, but Joe still has a firm hand over him. The girl that came after Zeb, she was looking to get married by hook or by crook, and who's to blame her for wanting to get out of that hooraw's nest, and away from Zeb." She squinted one eye. "Well, you know about country matters, even if you was raised a lady."

"Mm," said Jennie. "And she did get away."

"Yes, and Rick Lancaster's better than any daughter of Leah Pulsifer had a right to expect. Not that I begrudge the poor young one," she said more gently. "And she values him, I hear. She's more her father's daughter than Leah's."

"Why is Zeb such a scoundrel if Joseph Pulsifer raised him?"

"If you ask me, Joe gave up the first time he saw something in Zeb he knew never came from *him*. He might've even recognized where it come from. And then he'd know what Ben and the others was trying to tell him that time. But if he ever tried to put his foot down, Leah's as savage as a she-bear with her cub, though it's insulting a poor dumb animal to call her that." Mrs. Frost was actually agitated. "I wouldn't be surprised but what she's raised a murderer."

Twenty-Three

THE CHILDREN and Oliver noisily ran in, Oliver cavorting like an elephantine puppy and trying to see what was on the table. The girls raced each other down the passage and crashed through the kitchen door together, chanting, "First the wind and then the rain, let your flying kites remain! First the wind and—*raisin muffins!*" Frank shrieked. Their hooded woolen cloaks, cherry red for Sukey, kingfisher blue for Frank, were shed with unladylike abandon. One landed by accident on a chair; the other fell in a heap on the floor.

"Frank, pick that up," said Eliza behind them.

"Oh, dang the thing!" said Frank audaciously, and Sukey gave a theatrical gasp.

"Think you can say that again for your papa, do you?" Eliza asked. "He'd be some impressed." Frank swiftly picked up her cape and laid it on a bench.

Mrs. Frost put a buttered muffin each on plates for them, and they sat down to the table with the gusto of farm workers coming in from a day's threshing. After the first bite Frank tried to tell Jennie the meaning of the chant, but Eliza and Sukey told her simultaneously not to talk with her mouth full. Sukey explained, with kindly condescension for Jennie's ignorance.

"When the wind blows first, like now, and then it rains, it won't be a real storm, so you don't have to shorten sail. But even if it did blow hard, Mama never gets seasick. *Never.*"

Frank gulped down her food. "But Papa thought she might this time

142

because she has got so fat. So he made Mrs. Walpole go, too. He said Hannah would be no good at all if anything popped between here and there."

"Lord, give me strength," said Eliza, gazing at the ceiling.

"As if Hannah couldn't hold the basin for her to be sick into!" Sukey said scornfully.

"But it would probably make Hannah sick herself," Jennie suggested. "That must be what he meant."

"I reckon so." Sukey agreed. "I think Hannah's real afraid of being seasick. Yesterday she was all happy and singing, and this morning she wasn't."

"And with good reason," Mrs. Frost said to her cup. "Sara Walpole is her aunt, and her being along will take the wind out of that fast little cutter's sails."

"I wish I was going!" Frank said passionately. "I hate to see a ship sail away when I'm not on her. When may I go?" She appealed to the adults. "Mama said she had to go, to lose her fat. If *I* could get very fat—"

"You can get as fat as a tub of butter," said Eliza, "but you won't go anywhere until your papa says. Now here's Mrs. Glenroy waiting, and not looking too up-'n'-coming this morning, if I may say so."

"You may say so, because it's true," Jennie said. "But it is nothing that won't wear off."

"I heard about it," Eliza said with a meaningful nod.

"Heard about what?" Sukey's dark eyes flashed from Eliza to Jennie.

"Heard about how some folks misbehave in public, like two young misses I could mention, running around the wharf and screaming like gulls fighting over fish heads. I doubt you'll be able to spin a thread today," she said to Jennie. "If the morning don't end in tears, I'll be surprised."

Theirs or mine? Jennie thought cynically.

Upstairs the girls were short-tempered and shrill with each other, jumpy and distracted with Jennie, as they fought to hang on to their ebbing excitement.

Jennie had them march around the upstairs hall singing "Free America" and "Yankee Doodle" at the tops of their voices. In a half hour or so she could settle them down to their arithmetic. This freed her mind to go off on its own, along either of two tortuous paths, and she hated them both.

Except when she grazed one of her sore places or felt her clothing rub on a bruise or a scratch, she hardly thought about her own experience yesterday; revulsion had been driven out by last night's scare. Alick hadn't been seriously hurt this time, but surely there'd be a next.

The other theme was less horrifying. It didn't fill her stomach with cracked ice, but it was an anxiety. She would be showing by the time Mrs. MacKenzie came back, and she and the General might not want an obviously pregnant woman teaching two avidly observant little girls. They'd had no hint, no promise that the angels might be bringing them a baby, and all preparations must have been kept under lock and key. Their mother had gotten dreadfully fat, she would return without the fat, and if everything went well for her, she would bring back a baby. To the girls it would be the most wonderful of coincidences, that she'd sailed to Boston at exactly the right time; otherwise, someone else might have found the treasure.

The governess, even a married one, was a different matter. If the children saw nothing strange about her getting as fat as their mother had, their parents might think her very indelicate to want to teach in her condition. Disgusting word!

Looking out at the gulls chalk white against leaden clouds, she thought, *Papa, I am in a most monstrous tangle. I am like Chidiock Tichborne, whom Tony quotes: "My prime of youth is but a frost of cares."*

But you are not on the way to the headsman's block, she could almost hear him say. He was right, of course; compared to young Tichborne, she was very well off indeed. Alick would be safe in the boatyard, in the cottage, and about the grounds; the peril wouldn't come until he attended a class again, so they had time to think of something. As for herself, weeks would pass before Mrs. MacKenzie came home again, and it would be an exercise in futility to worry now about what would happen then.

"Mrs. Glenroy?" Sukey was holding out her slate. Her long division was greatly improved, Jennie told her, and Sukey bridled complacently. "I will probably do something very important with sums when I grow up," she said.

"I will be a sea captain," Frankie mumbled, crouched over her slate. She breathed hard and made her slate pencil squeak. Doing sums was always an intensely physical activity for Frank. She brought her completed work to Jennie with the delirious triumph of the winner in a steeplechase, and Jennie wanted to hug her but resisted.

"You should have used your sponge instead of spit and your hankie, Frank," Sukey said. "I saw you, even if Mrs. Glenroy didn't."

Frank was insouciant, Sukey was in a ferment of indignation and general dissatisfaction, and Jennie felt like the war-horse who smelleth the battle afar off.

"Wash your hands," she said, "and we will go down to see if the pianoforte is in tune." She should have asked the General if she could play, but it was too late now. If he rebuked her, she would tell him it had been necessary to quell the mutiny in the ranks.

Giggling now, the girls jostled each other at the washstand, two pairs of hands splashing in the basin. "Wash and wipe together, live and fight forever!" they recited, trying to yank the towel from each other.

The drawing room ran the length of the house. The tall windows at the back gave a good view of the oval garden, where Truelove was working now, but the cottage, carriage house, and stable were screened by a zone of trees.

The side windows opening onto the veranda looked over the orchard and to the maple-shaded drive leading past the south side of the orchard out to the formal entrance on Ship Street. The archway and Ship Street were invisible from the house. The General loved trees and had spared them wherever he could, and he had ordered a variety of saplings set out on the grounds as soon as the cellar of the mansion was excavated.

The front windows gave on the Pool; the river was pewter and pearl under the light wind and a white glare from a disappearing sun. The wood boats had left on the tide, and the *Paul Revere* lay alone among the fleet of small craft that would not go fishing today. She wondered how soon the brig would be leaving for Liverpool. A pair of ospreys glided on the mysterious currents of air above the river, occasionally lifting themselves to a higher level by an unhurried motion of the wings. It was the first time she had seen one since the day she had entered the river.

Even in today's ashen light the room felt sunny, with its cream walls and ivory white paneling. It was not cluttered with random objects like the drawing rooms of Brunswick Square and Linnmore, and the muted colors of the leaves and blossoms woven into the damask drapes were echoed through the room by odd cushions, furniture coverings, and pieces of porcelain in lime green, apricot, hyacinth blue, deep rose. The total effect was of luminous elegance, and if Mrs. MacKenzie was responsible for it, Jennie respected and admired her taste.

Over one white-paneled fireplace there was a portrait of Lydia MacKenzie, superb in crimson velvet, her strong throat and handsome shoulders gleaming with the flush of life through a diaphanous scarf. A younger General presided over the other fireplace: portrait of a soldier in his robust prime, wearing colonial buff and blue. At that time the hair had been the same glowing copper as Frank's.

"That's Papa, and there's Mama," Sukey said offhandedly, making a beeline for the pianoforte. She opened it, and Frank began at once to jab at the keys. Sukey slapped her hands away.

"Let Mrs. Glenroy do it! You might break something!" Frank grinned and moved out of the way.

Jennie limbered her fingers with a few scales, and the children stood very close, watching her hands. "It's in tune," she said. "I'm surprised."

"Mr. Walpole comes and tunes it, and Mama goes out for the afternoon," said Frank. "But we like to watch him. He plays for us afterward."

"That is the only time," said Sukey solemnly, "that it is *ever* played. It belonged to Tony and Christian's mother. Did you know, Mrs. Glenroy, that Tony has a different mama from us?"

"Her name was Désirée, and she was a beautiful French lady," Frank said. "Tony has a miniature of her. He will show it to you if you ask."

"But don't ask in front of Mama," said Sukey. "Play something, please."

"Does Nabby know this one? No, somehow I cannot imagine Mr. O'Dowda teaching it. So you will have one to surprise her with." She repeated "The Star," from the Misses Ann and Jane Taylor's *Original Poems for Infant Minds,* until they had it by heart, and she thought she could not bear to hear them sing "Twinkle, Twinkle, Little Star" ever again. She went on to nursery rhymes; they knew most of them but were enchanted to be singing the familiar words. When they were hoarse but still wanted more, she entertained them with the fox who went out one winter night and prayed for the moon to give him light. They seized hands and began dancing around the pianoforte.

Suddenly a flute joined them, high and sweet and merry, a pagan spirit invading the drawing room on a faun's capering hooves, or rather

Tony in his stocking feet with his shirttail half out of his trousers. He led the girls prancing, leaping, spinning, through the room, skipping in mad circles around the furniture, swinging into lightning reverses that had them crashing into each other while he went blithely on his way. They fell onto the floor at last, too winded now even to laugh, except for little spasmodic eruptions now and then. Tony halted by the mantel under his father's portrait. Jennie was watching him in entranced disbelief. He lifted an eyebrow at her, gave her a sly and faunish smile, and then he began to play.

It was an air which must have been written for the flute alone, that solitary voice which is the purest distillation of melody. The wonder was twofold: that he should play at all and that he should play so well.

She wanted the innocent beauty of it to flow on and on, washing away all the uglinesses, carrying her on its crystalline tide. The children lay silent. When the last immaculate note had drawn out to a silver line and then to nothing, there was a profound silence in the room. Tony looked down at the flute as if vaguely wondering how it had come into his hands. The children didn't move; it was as if they had been bewitched into sleep. Jennie breathed deeply for the first time since he had begun to play. She wished she could be transported from here, without speaking or being spoken to, into a green solitude for a little while.

The General spoke from the doorway. "That was beautiful, Tony," he said huskily. "Absolutely beautiful. Your mother would be proud. Thank you."

When Jennie turned toward him, he was just putting away his handkerchief. "Papa!" Frank cried, like someone waking from a spell. She and Sukey leaped up and ran to him.

"Thank *you*, Papa," Tony said. He was himself again; the mischievous grin said clearly to Jennie, *Surprised you, didn't I?*

"What was it, Tony?" she asked.

"*Nur eine kleine Mozart-musik,*" he said. "And now you know it's not drink or gambling that will be my downfall."

The General came to the pianoforte with the girls hanging on him. "Do you play, Mrs. Glenroy?"

"She plays simply heavenly," said Sukey.

"Oh, yes, she plays, Papa!" Tony said breezily. "And very well."

"You can't tell that on the basis of nursery rhymes," she protested.

"Ah, madame, you have ze touch!" He twirled an imaginary mustache.

The girls threw themselves at him, crying, "Talk French, Tony, talk French!"

"We must have more music," said the General. "We must have our fill while my wife is away. Music is hard on her, very hard. Tragic, really. Can't understand it myself, healthy as she is. Complains that it stabs her through the head. *Well!*" Regrets were briskly disposed of. "We shall have our musical friends in for some good evenings, eh, Tony? They go on, you know," he said to Jennie, "but in other houses. So we'll just have to fill what time we have with music pressed down and running over. You and Alick will come, won't you? It will be a great kindness to me if you would consent to play."

She said, "May I come in to practice? I haven't touched a keyboard for months."

"It is yours!" He flung his arms wide open, laughing. Frank jumped up on him and clung like a monkey.

"Oh, Papa, I am so happy, happy, happy," she crooned against his shoulder.

"Come, *ma petite*," Tony said to Sukey, and she wrapped her arms around his middle and leaned her head on his chest.

Twenty-Four

IT WAS SPITTING RAIN at noon, and she carried her basket under the plaid. She smelled smoke blowing down on the wind, which meant Alick was home before her; he had last night's stew already warming, and their places were set. She laid a loaf of fresh bread on the table, and a little pot of wild strawberry jam, and spread the plaid over the rocking chair nearest the stove, to dry the raindrops on it.

"Alick, do you ever feel as if you have suddenly waked up from a dream?" she asked. "And don't know how you came to be here?"

"No, because I am remembering very well how I came here, and it is no dream," he said. "Every step of the way and every mile of the ocean." He picked up the big knife and began cutting slices off the loaf. For a disintegrating moment he became Nigel cutting bread in the kitchen of Tigh nam Fuaran.

"What *is* it?" he said sharply, transfixed, the knife poised above the loaf.

"It wasn't a pain, it was just a thought, and it went as fast as it came."

"Are you talking with any other woman about yourself?" he asked. She ladled the stew into the bowls.

"This should be better today than it was last night," she said.

"You should be talking with another woman," he said stubbornly.

"Anna Kate," she said, to get him off the subject. He nodded, and went back to cutting bread. When they had been eating for a few minutes, she said, "Was anything said at the yard this morning?"

He shook his head.

149

"How did you explain that mark on your face? Did anyone ask about that?"

"Some looked twice at it, but only Clements was asking me. I fell on the road last night. It was a very dark night, was it not? And I am not yet certain of all the rocks." Tranquilly he ate stew. "This *is* better than it was last night, and this time I will not be leaving it in the road for the raccoons."

"Alick, you puzzle me," she said honestly. "You're a proud man, a Highlander, and there is none prouder. This scum attacked you in the night, you had no chance to defend yourself, and if they had not heard Tony whistling, they'd have done much worse to you." From his expression she could have been talking about the weather. "Aren't you burning with rage?" she demanded. "Aren't you bent on revenge?"

"Would I be less than a man to you if I am not revengeful?"

She felt rebuked. "No! I could never look down on you, Alick Glenroy! But I am allowed to be curious, am I not? And I am revengeful. I *hate* Zeb Pulsifer. I know you should hate the sin but love the sinner, but loving Zeb Pulsifer would be asking too much of a saint, which I am as far from being as anyone could be this side of hell."

He lifted his eyebrows in polite bewilderment, and she had to laugh. "Oh, don't try to sort that out; it's dreadful grammar. I mean that even a very good person would have difficulty in loving Zeb Pulsifer, and I'm not even a *moderately* good person. But you must be one."

"I am not knowing about that, but I do know that brambles do not leave marks like fingernails. I heard some words this morning, but not about myself."

She was stunned into muteness at first, and her face was very hot, the scratches afire. He wouldn't let her go. "Well, Jeannie?"

"It was disgusting!" she cried. "Debasing! They tore at me, screaming vile things about us both. I couldn't repeat them to you, Alick! What would it have served? I wanted to pretend it never happened. And then Tony brought you home like that, and I knew they will never leave us alone."

"And that is why you were saying we should take to the roads?" His face softened into a smile. It was never a wide smile, and it was not frequent, but she was always appreciative of it. "Do you know what Mr. Dunlop said to me? He heard that you are a bonny fighter."

She laughed weakly. "What a lovely way to put it, and yes, I *am* a bonny fighter."

"Tell me about it. You can be leaving out the dirt."

There was a relief and even satisfaction in telling it because he was such a good audience and she could put in all the details, down to Mr. Dalrymple's vivid waistcoat and Mrs. Wells's serene refusal to provide brandy. The shrieking women were reduced—almost—to grotesque cartoon characters like Hogarth's. "I don't fear them, Alick," she said. "I didn't then, I was so furious, until Leah Pulsifer clamped that arm across my throat. *Then* I was afraid, but I could still use my feet and my fists, and I wished I could have given her a good hard bite."

"Och, it would have killed you," he commented mildly.

"Lord, yes, she must have venom in her veins instead of blood. She tricked Joseph Pulsifer into marriage, according to Mrs. Frost, and she has been hating the world ever since. But I'm not afraid of her. I shan't walk where I am likely to meet her and her creatures with no one else about because that would be foolish, but it's for you I am fearful because you're out in the night."

"Oliver is going with me, and a stout stick. He will hear them before I do, and he is not liking violence, Tony tells me; when he takes hold in anger, he is not anxious to let go."

"Oh, Alick, that's marvelous!" She laughed and applauded. "And so simple!"

"Yes, it will do for now. But I *am* burning with rage, Jeannie. I want revenge for what has happened to us both. I was so murderous last night that it was making me sicker than the blows. This morning, when I heard about you, the sickness was worse."

She tried to speak, but he forbade it. "Hear me out, and then we will discuss it no more. I cannot touch the women for what they did to you, not with my hands." He held them up before her. "I cannot rid myself of him. *Yet.*" The last word came light as a breath, and the small hairs rose on the back of Jennie's head, a cold tightness spread over her scalp.

"Unlock your fingers, Jeannie," he said, "or you will not be holding a needle this afternoon."

She spread her cramped fingers wide. "I thought I knew you well, but I don't."

"Any more than I am knowing you."

"But even if we have our mysteries," she said, "we are friends in a way that is unique between man and woman."

"*Unique?*"

"It means rare, unusual, extraordinary, unequaled."

"How is it spelled?" He got up and brought her the slate, watched her print on it. When he sat down, he dipped enthusiastically into the strawberry jam, tasted it. "This conserve is unique," he announced. "Meaning, it is unequaled. Like our friendship. Like *us*." They both began to laugh.

They didn't mention the Pulsifers again. When they were finishing their meal, she said, "Sometimes when I wake up after I've been sleeping hard, I think I'm waking up in one of the caves. Never out in the open, *especially* never in the little glen we thought was so perfect and we woke up covered with frost and the goat trying to pull off the plaid. Do you ever dream of the caves?"

"Sometimes." He was noncommittal.

"Do you suppose Bonnie Prince Charlie ever slept in any of our caves?"

"I think it was a different way he went. But I know I have come to a better life than he went to. Who would want to waste his days longing for a lost crown when he could be learning how to build a ship?" He pushed away from the table. "I will be building a vessel of my own one day."

She laughed incredulously. "Alick, you mean *you* would go to sea? *You?*"

"No, but my ship would," he said with a smile. "I would have a partner to be her captain." He carried his dishes into the pantry. His face might have been bruised, and his ribs sore, but she had never seen him look so young. The guilt that had lived with her for so long perceptibly lightened.

It was really raining now, and Alick folded the plaid and put it over his shoulders. As he picked up his bonnet to go, she said, "I wish I could work at something as hard and demanding and creative as building a ship. Someday, when you begin to build your own—"

He was half through the entry. "Yes?"

"Oh, nothing. Only that you will be married then, and will you let your wife humbly hold something in place for you or even make a few passes with a plane or drive a nail?"

"If she is asking me," he said. "And if there is a wife."

When she heard the outer door shut, she stood up and walked back and forth, her arms folded across her breast. She had almost said, "When you begin to build your own boat, will you let me help?"

Coming without any forethought, as involuntary as a sneeze or a hiccup, it was disturbing. All she had been dreaming about and planning for was a return home. In the spring they would wish each other well, and that would be the end of it. Perhaps the reason why she couldn't actually imagine the end of it was that their relationship had been concentrated so intensely on their common situation. Their *unique* situation. She smiled, remembering Alick tasting the jam.

Partners in crime, she thought. *About to dissolve the partnership, and high time, too.* It couldn't happen too soon. If only she weren't carrying, she could feel so free, as free as the ospreys that floated over the river the way their cousins drifted above Loch Na Mada.

Twenty-Five

A LL AFTERNOON THE RAIN ran off the slates into the gutters and poured down the spouts into the water butts. Jennie spent the afternoon mending her dress, keeping the fire going while a shoulder of fresh pork simmered on the stove, and reading *Ormond* with her feet on the wood-box. She cosseted herself by making a pot of coffee and drinking two cups, golden brown with cream. The coffee beans had come from the West Indies on one of the General's ships and were ground to order in the store; the richest cream came from the Frosts' Columbine, the brown cow that habitually escaped and always headed for Main Street, where she wandered along the wooden sidewalks, looking in shop windows and pushing through unlatched gates to sample the most cherished shrubs and to leave free fertilizer on the walks.

"Don't ever confine her too closely," Jennie told Mrs. Frost, "or she'll dry herself up just for spite."

The rain had stopped by early evening. Jennie went to bed when the western sky was clearing to a flaming sunset, leaving Alick studying at the kitchen table. After the turmoil of the last few days she was glad to look forward to simple things that would make no demands on her emotions, like the girls' lessons and shopping for food. She was able to put aside Mrs. Pulsifer's accusations because they were so ridiculous. To brood on them would give the woman dominion over her.

In the morning the children began talking music at once. She told them that yesterday had been a holiday, and now they must work; but if classes went well, they would have a half hour at the end of the session.

The half hour became forty-five minutes, and then she closed the pianoforte while the children protested.

"Tomorrow," she said flatly. "If I let you have all you wanted now,
you would have nothing to look forward to." Secretly she intended to
come back when her errands were done and Eliza had taken the girls out,
and then she could have the drawing room to herself. She wished Mrs.
MacKenzie would stay away for months; all this music would meet with
sudden death the instant she returned, and so might Jennie's position here.

She walked down Ship Street with Alick when he went back to work
after dinner, and to the store for provisions. She was the only customer
this early in the afternoon. The storekeeper had just become the father
of twins. He was not a young man, and he was bemused, if not outright
confused, by the double gift from God. Jennie felt some sympathy for
him but more for his wife.

Going back with her full baskets, she took the shortcut through the
front gate and across the grounds. When she emerged from the trees in
sight of the cottage, a girl or young woman was sitting on the bench,
holding a baby on her knees. Jennie thought first that it was Mairi
MacKenzie, who had brought along one of the Highland babies, and
then she realized there was no baby of that age among the group, and
this girl's hair was brown and done up, not chestnut red and loose on
her shoulders. She didn't see Jennie coming; she was playing with the
baby's bare toes and tickling its stomach. The baby chuckled and crowed
and strongly kicked its legs. Jennie was quite close before the baby saw
her, and then it nearly bounced itself out of the young woman's arms.
She caught hold of its dress and sputtered, "Gemini!"

Jennie laughed, and so did the stranger. "He's Jared." She had a wide
mouth and teeth very white in her tanned triangular face. Her twinkling,
mirthful eyes were the silvery green of leaves blown inside out in a squall.
"And I'm Mrs. Harm Clements. Are you Mrs. Glenroy? Of course you
are! Who else could you be?"

She stood up, hoisting the heavy baby to her shoulder. She was
shorter than Jennie, with plump round breasts straining against her bod-
ice. "Will you hold him for me, please? I must visit the Necessary, and
I cannot manage him and myself at once." Automatically Jennie put
down her baskets and found her arms full of Jared while his mother
disappeared around the cottage, crying, "Thank you!"

"Well," said Jennie, "here we are." Jared smiled and put one arm cozily around her neck. He was dry, and both he and his short white dress smelled freshly washed. He fingered her nose, not roughly, frowning like a thinker, and then put his finger in his mouth and braced back against her arm. A small cloud of doubt obscured his sunshine.

"Mama will come back," Jennie told him. She hadn't held a baby since she'd last seen Sylvia's, and one forgot the apple-blossom texture of a healthy infant's skin, the pink, curved perfection of nostrils and ears, the eyelids delicately veined as petals, and eyelashes made of the best brown silk to match the hair. His eyes were the lustrous young green of very new leaves through which the sun shone, and his little chest rose and fell with his quick, shallow breathing.

"You are so beautiful," she said. His mouth began to pucker, and she said, "We will go to meet her." Motion suited Jared; he bounced on her arm and tightened his grip around her neck.

They met his mother coming back. "Oh, my, I was really suffering!" she called. "I rode into town behind Ki Bisset's oxen, and I'd have done it in half the time if I'd walked, even with my sugarplum on my back." She took the yearning Jared back into her arms.

"Now you are wondering why I am here. Well, my husband told me to come." She grinned. "Your husband works with him. Harmonious Clements. Isn't that a silly name? Especially when he couldn't carry a tune in a basket. But it's a family name, and so they keep it going instead of leaving it at rest with the first Harmonious."

"Will you come and sit down, Mrs. Clements?" Jennie said.

"Lucy," she said. "My mother-in-law is Mrs. Clements. I suppose I will be accustomed to it when I am a mother-in-law." She kissed Jared's head. "I cannot imagine my baby being old enough to marry."

"Then you'll have his children to cuddle. . . . Why did your husband tell you to come?"

"He told me all about how you and your husband foiled Zeb Pulsifer and that fool Corny and how Leah Pulsifer and the Keanes tried to do you in, and he said it was time I called on you. He said you put up a good scrap. I didn't know anything about you until now. I know more about your husband because Harm came home grousing one night because a Highlander would be put to work with him the next day and they didn't speak English. Then he came home the next night saying this

Alick Glenroy wasn't so bad after all. He had a feel for wood and handled tools with respect."

"And spoke English," said Jennie.

"*That* was a relief!" They both laughed. "So here I am, and I have brought you something." She uncovered her basket and took out two little earthenware pots and a paper packet. "Calendula salve for sores and burns and a lotion for your hands because they can get so sore and rough." She held up her own hands: square, tanned, strong-looking, but smooth. "My great-aunt makes these things. The chamomile tea, too. Don't store it in the paper. It should go into a tightly covered jar."

"I'll take proper care of it." Jennie was touched and pleased. "What a surprise this all is!" She took Jared's hand. "It's so kind of you to come, Jared, and Mrs.—Lucy."

"I know you're Jeannie, but I don't expect to call you by your first name if you don't care for it."

"Oh, but I do! But will you call me Jennie, please? No one has called me Jennie for a long time."

"Jennie it is." Jared squirmed and kicked violently, and she put him down on the ground. He rocked forward onto hands and knees and began to creep. She said proudly, "If I'd set him down fifteen minutes ago, he'd be at Strathbuie House by now. They get strength from the earth, you know."

He was heading rapidly westward, and they followed him and sat on the well curb while he explored the territory between them and the house. "Lord, this is beautiful!" Lucy said fervently. "I spent all morning baking in a kitchen hotter than Tophet. I feel as well done as my pies."

Even if Jennie had been unnaturally shy, there'd have been no difficulty making conversation with Lucy Clements. At first it was mostly about Jared, and then Lucy talked about herself with a breezy and humorous candor, apparently without expecting anything in return. Jennie hated to be on guard. She didn't want to be on guard, she was so appreciative, and it seemed safe to talk about her own life if she stopped short of her father's death, which would surely bring the inevitable question "And what happened *then?*"

Lucy sprang up occasionally to run after her son and change his direction. Witnessing the intimacy of their communication, Jennie was charmed, even moved, but it had no personal implications for her; even when she held Jared, it was as if she had forgotten her own pregnancy and was unconsciously thinking, *All this goes on in other women's lives, and it is pretty to watch, but it has nothing to do with me.*

Lucy came back with Jared tucked casually under her arm, sputtering and wriggling. She sat down on the well curb and opened the front of her dress. Jared stopped fighting and began to suck.

"Pull for the shore, sailor!" his mother said. She grinned at Jennie. "The longer you suckle them, the less likely you are to start another one too soon. Besides, it's best for getting them through their first summer. But you have none of those worries yet, have you? Lord, how I hated myself the last few months before he was born! But he's worth it all." Jared, sucking away, gazed up into her face. "Sometimes I can hardly believe that Harmonious Clements and I made something so beautiful."

"I am pregnant," Jennie said. She was as surprised as if someone else had said it, more surprised than Lucy, who glanced over at her clasped hands and said matter-of-factly, "And afraid."

Jennie did not remember clasping her hands. She unlaced them. "Yes, I am afraid," she said. She wasn't abject about it, as she had once been. She wanted only to deal with it. "And I have no one to talk to, no one who has been through it."

"Now you have me," said Lucy succinctly. "What would you like to know?"

"I don't know where to begin, what to ask!" Jennie admitted. "Or rather, there is so much that I can't put words to. I feel so simpleminded! *And* unstrung." She waggled limp hands, and Lucy laughed.

"Then I will begin." Her questions were brief and to the point. Was Jennie of a naturally strong constitution? Or did she have palpitations, female troubles, a family history of consumption or any other diseases?

"Yes, I am naturally strong," Jennie said, "and it's no to all the other things. And my oldest sister has her babies as easily as a cat having kittens."

"Then she is not too narrow through the hips. Are you?"

"I don't think so." Jennie was startled; she'd never thought of that possible complication. Instinctively she felt through her dress for her hipbones.

"There you are then," said Lucy breezily. "Exercise, eat properly, drink oceans of milk, and put your trust in Dr. Waite. He believes in

cleanliness, common sense, fresh air, and he never bleeds a patient. He
calls that a licensed aid to murder."

"It can't be as simple as you make it," Jennie objected.

"Well, of course, you grow more and more uncomfortable all the
time," Lucy said, "and you should put your feet up as much as you can.
Do you have one of those husbands who expect a slave in the kitchen?"

"He's far from that."

"*Good.* The only other thing I can think of right now—" She became
diffident for the first time. She sat Jared up and fastened her dress. Sated,
he lolled against her. "Do you *want* it?" she asked suddenly.

"I don't know. I wouldn't believe it at first. Then I was desperate to
find someone who would give me something to start my flow. Would
your great-aunt be an herbwoman?"

"Aunt Hat would never have given you anything. Those who swear
by pennyroyal or tansy or white cedar have to stew up their own con-
coctions; she will have nothing to do with it." She was perturbed. "You
aren't still considering—"

Jennie shook her head. "My husband put paid to that idea."

"He's a man of sense. Is he looking forward to the child?"

How can one tell lie after lie and then suddenly stick at another one,
like a horse refusing to jump? Her hesitation seemed to stretch endlessly
on. Finally she said, "We both are superstitious about counting chickens
before they hatch." She smiled weakly. "This particular chick."

"Mercy, only an imbecile wouldn't worry!" Lucy said vigorously. "We
all go through it! But if you're too fearful, have hysterics all the time,
and don't eat, you can hurt the baby, and yourself, too. I like Mr. Glenroy
without even meeting him, but is he as healthy as you are?"

For a giddy instant she thought, *Nigel?* But Lucy, stroking Jared's
head, hadn't noticed anything in her face. "No consumption that I know
of," she said hurriedly. "And great vitality."

"Then everything is in your favor," said Lucy. She put Jared down,
and he began to creep away from them. "Think ahead to a year from
now, when something of yours will be creeping across the grass after a
butterfly."

But it will be the grass of home, Jennie thought, and it might as well
be twelve years as twelve months until that day, the way she felt. She
leaned back against the wellbox and shut her eyes. *Still, when we walked*

into the mountains that day, Fort William could have been half the world away, but day followed day and night followed night—and I followed Alick— and all at once we were there.

"Everything good takes time," Lucy was saying. "Jared is my nine months' masterpiece. . . . Someone else is coming to call."

Anna Kate, Mairi, and a comely little pigeon of a girl who reminded Jennie of Aili, were coming across the lawn, the two girls shyly hanging back. Jared sat on his bottom and stared up at them, and they went down on their knees beside him, cooing in Gaelic. They all were wearing cotton frocks now instead of Highland dress, and Anna Kate carried a light shawl. She still wore a mutch tied under her chin, but the effect was not incongruous; she looked rather distinguished, with her erect carriage and her thin, high-bridged nose.

Jennie jumped up and took her by the hand and led her to meet Lucy, who was not at all bashful about her eagerness to meet a genuine Highland woman. The girls stayed with Jared, stroking him, exclaiming softly to each other. He looked from one to the other and their coaxing hands and chose Mairi, climbing into her lap and reaching up for the auburn hair falling to her shoulders.

"Even he thinks it is lovely hair," said Lucy. "Everyone must ask you this," she said to Anna Kate. "How do you like America? Are you homesick?"

"In sleep, for what is gone. But we are already feeling like Americans," she said proudly. "We have land for a farm."

"I wish you well," Lucy said. "And will you look at my son now?" He was trying to stand on Mairi's lap. She held him under the arms with his toes just touching her lap, and he danced in her clasp and clutched at her hair. Una leaned over and gently untangled his fingers, and he burst into a howl of grief and frustration. Before Lucy could rise from the well curb, Mairi looked into the angry, wet little face six inches from her own and began to sing.

It was so soft it was a wonder he could hear it through his noise, but something reached him, and the howls diminished to sobs and then suddenly stopped. He watched her the way he watched his mother while he fed. When she settled him down in her arms, he didn't object but kept his eyes on her face. The tune was simple and tender, and the girl's voice was as clear as spring water.

Jennie had heard Mairi sing aboard the *Paul Revere*, at the first of the voyage but not after Calum drowned, and she had forgotten how true and pure her voice was, like the flute, and as sweet and effortless on the higher notes.

Oliver galloped around the corner of the house, emanating rapture, but two hands caught him by the collar, and Tony came into view. He forced the dog to sit where he was, and he leaned his back against the house and watched Mairi. He looked stunned, his sallow skin grayish as if he were ill.

When the song had finished, Mairi put her face down to Jared's head, but Una saw Tony. She put her hand up to her mouth. Tony made a gesture to Oliver, who groaned and lay down, and Tony came across to the well curb, walking well out around the girls and rigidly ignoring them at the same time.

"Good afternoon, Mrs. MacKenzie." His eyes glistened oddly, and his lips were pale. "Mrs. Clements, Mrs. Glenroy."

"You're looking very handsome, Tony," Lucy said. "You're not a youngster anymore."

"Thank you," he said unsmilingly. "Mrs. Glenroy, I left a large haddock on a shelf in your cellar. One of the boats came in with a good load, and my father thought you might like one."

"I would," Jennie said. "Will you thank him for me, please, and thank you for bringing it. Do you remember Mairi and Una there?"

He turned stiffly and bowed to the girls. "Would you like—" he croaked, and then with a startling outburst of manly vigor and a voice to match, he said, "I am taking some sugar to the horses. Perhaps you would care to accompany me?"

Una was overwhelmed, but Mairi was quite poised. She looked over at Anna Kate, who nodded.

"We would be liking it fine," Mairi said to Tony.

He reached down and lifted Jared from her arms and carried him to Lucy. The girls stood up. Una kept smoothing her dress and twisting her head nervously around, but Mairi waited in graceful stillness.

Receiving Jared, Lucy was kind enough to make nothing of it. He walked back to the girls. As the three reached the house, Oliver rose to meet them, and they all went out of sight.

"Och, what's the harm?" Anna Kate asked. "Who would be objecting to the General's son?"

"Not a mother in town," said Lucy dryly.

Twenty-Six

ON SATURDAYS there was no school, and it was a free day for most laborers, especially those employed in the General's enterprises, so they would have time to work around their homes and gardens. Tony came to the cottage in the early afternoon and asked Alick if he would help him take two horses to the blacksmith. The smithy was at the western end of the town, beyond the Ark and the muster field and across the road from the limestone quarry. It was a faultless day for riding, with towering clouds white piled on white toward the zenith blue as larkspur, and a west wind that smelled of hot hayfields yet carried a refreshing edge of coolness. Jennie would have liked to be riding, and she would ride again when she was home. Now she was glad for Alick to go; the parting from the garron, coming all at once with no warning, must still wound him. He had seen Mata into the world, he had told her in the mountains; he had steadied the little foal on his feet for his first steps.

After he told her that, he had never mentioned Mata again, and neither had she.

When he had gone, she took the woods path up to Main Street. The first time she had been dazzled by her discovery; this time she had the joy of preliminary anticipation and the charm of rediscovery and with no braying and squealing termagants at the end of it. She had been disturbed in her mind the first time she entered the path, too; this time she was almost euphoric.

She would not have believed that finding a friend her own age could make so much difference to her. After Anna Kate and the girls had left yesterday—Tony walked back to the Ark with them—she had asked

Lucy every question she could think of about what changes to expect in her body as time went on, and while she was no happier about her pregnancy than before, she was less baffled and irritated by her ignorance. At least she was not in the dark, there were cracks of light to mark the door through which she would eventually escape, and Lucy's frank, earthy information had nearly convinced her that the escape would be into life, not death.

Nearly. Enough so that ever since Lucy had left her, she'd been having unexpected moments of blinding revelation, when the mere idea of her death was so preposterous it was as if until now she had been possessed by the cringing spirit of another girl who had died in childbirth.

It hadn't been so, of course; it had been her own self or one of the selves she'd have liked to do away with. She was compassionate, but she would henceforth offer the craven no houseroom. "Cowards die many times before their deaths; / The valiant never taste of death but once." Declaimed from the staircase of Pippin Grange, uttered now in silence and dead earnest. *Be valiant, Jennie Hawthorne,* she commanded. Today it was easy.

She heard the heavy Saturday traffic on Main Street before she saw it. Because of the recent rain, the hooves and iron-tired wheels did not raise much dust; ordinarily to cross the road when it was busy would be rather like plunging into a desert sandstorm.

The black cat sat on its perch watching the world go by, and Jennie spent a few sociable moments with it before she went through the Wells gate. She returned the shawl to Mrs. Wells with her thanks. All the Wells men were away from home today, and she was slightly disappointed; she wanted to find out if young Captain Wells was as austere on land as he was at sea, and she'd have liked to meet the paterfamilias who called his sons downeast chowderheads. And it was always agreeable to meet her first American again.

Mrs. Wells didn't detain her; she was preparing to go out herself. Mr. and Mrs. Dalrymple were away for the day, but the servant, Minnie, behaved as if she couldn't believe her luck in meeting a genuine heroine. "Just the same as out of a book," she said gloatingly. "A duke's daughter that ran away with a common man and give them bi—critters as good as they sent."

"I am not a duke's daughter," Jennie said politely, but Minnie refused to give up her romance.

Without showing surprise by even the twitch of an eyebrow, Mrs. Loomis brought out another plain straw bonnet. Jennie asked for rose-colored ribbons again, to match her Sunday dress, and Mrs. Loomis suggested a few silk carnations in harmonizing shades. Jennie agreed, wishing to express her new frame of mind; she wore the trimmed bonnet away from the shop instead of carrying it in a box, even if she was wearing her everyday calico.

In theory any children of an age to be useful were supposed to be just that on Saturdays, but they all seemed to be on Main Street, the girls loitering along the wooden sidewalks looking in the shopwindows or at other people, the boys dodging among the road traffic or watching the postrider arrive and the postmaster come out to take the saddlebags. Those who had been sent to fetch the family mail or a neighbor's walked pompously into the post office behind him, either the envy of the others or the target of mild abuse.

There was a dry goods shop next after the post office, and Jennie went in to buy the linen and notions to make shirts for Alick. She had tried that morning to persuade him to go to the tailor and the shoemaker, but he was adamant. "I have all the clothing I need to be going on with. And my boots were new the week before I was leaving Linnmore. They'll be lasting me awhile yet."

"Well, I can't force you to have trousers made, and a coat, but I can do something about shirts," she said. "Lucy is going to help me cut them out."

"I am glad you are finding a friend in Mrs. Clements, but would not the time be better spent sewing for the baby?"

"The baby can wait for six months," she retorted, "but the only reason you have not been caught shirtless is the good weather. One week with no drying days for the wash, and you will not enjoy your own company, and neither will anyone else."

"It's the great advocate you'd be, if they were letting a woman into the courts. Who could be answering that argument now? The judge himself would be beyond words."

"Not if he was born a Highlander! I've never yet known one to be beyond words."

Alick laughed. "Your friend is as good as a tonic for you. There is a new fire in your eye."

"I like her so much, Alick. She isn't like any one of my sisters, but being with her reminds me of being with them."

"It's glad I am for you, Jeannie." When he'd brought home his week's pay the night before, he'd left it on the mantelpiece, and now he put it all on the table before her. Eleven dollars. "Take what you need, not only for the linen but for your new bonnet. A present from me, like the razor that gives me a shave a king would be envying."

She had to wait her turn in the dry goods shop while a young woman chose gingham and calico patterns for three little girls who chattered and hopped like young birds. The shop, which would have been called a draper's shop at home, was roomy and well stocked. She moved around the tables where the bolts of cloth were shown, looking for men's shirtings. A display of white against the far wall caught her eye and she walked over to it; the long table was stacked with infant goods. She swerved away but sharply recoiled from the impulse; that reaction belonged to the other shrinking and denying spirit.

She and Lucy hadn't discussed clothing yesterday, there'd been too much else of immediate importance. All she knew was that babies required miles of flannel for napkins, petticoats, nightgowns, and wrappers. They also needed knitted vests, stockings, coatees, and shoes; dozens of dresses garnished with lace, feather stitching, and French knots; lawn petticoats as well as flannel ones; mantles, shawls, light caps and warm ones. And that was only for the first two years or so. There was no end to what children needed until they were old enough for the responsibility of clothing themselves. Then their mother, prematurely aged from the unremitting struggle to keep up with the awesome rate of growth, could burn her workbasket on a ceremonial pyre and totter to her rocking chair, put her feet up, and contemplate a peaceful old dotage in which she never sewed another stitch.

"May I help you?" someone inquired. The other customers had left while she'd been wandering in a white wilderness. Saved, she smiled into a female face with effulgent gratitude.

"I'd like something for a man's shirts. Enough for two. I expect you'd know how much I should have, and what else. I've neither needles nor tape measure nor shears—I had to leave my workbasket behind." She sounded sincerely regretful and got little clucks of sympathy.

She and the proprietor parted like friends, and she stepped down to the sidewalk with a sizable workbasket over her arm and the linen folded in it. The children had flashed away like a school of fish or a flock of birds while she was in the shop, and a blue-painted wagon with a piebald horse in the shafts had been left in front of the post office. It was such a fresh and exultant blue—as blue as bluebells—that at first she saw nothing else. It was decorated along the sides with a line of even white peaks like stylized wave crests in a Japanese print. She was so delighted with it that she wanted to cry out to someone, "Oh, see that!"

Then she realized there were people in the wagon, and she looked up, already smiling and ready to speak, straight into the eyes of the woman on the seat. They had been watching *her*, and they met her eyes with the impact of a shout, all the more shocking because they were so light-colored in their valleys of shadow that they appeared blind. But they were not, and they did not look away from Jennie.

She heard herself stammering, "Is something wrong? Are you ill? How can I . . ." The words died away. Nothing changed up there; it *was* blind, she thought in dismay, a statue's face. She'd only imagined an anguished appeal. The woman tipped her dark-covered head toward the shawl-wrapped baby sleeping against her breast, and Jennie felt an extraordinary sensation of release. With her face turned away, the woman became just a figure on a wagon seat. There were three children behind her, all as still as she was, all watching two barefoot boys chasing each other in and out of the traffic, darting under horses' heads and being threatened with shouts and raised whips.

A man left the post office and went to the wagon; he was ordinary in build, black-bearded, the rest of his face indistinct under the pulled-down brim of his hat. His glance brushed over her and dismissed her. No one in the wagon moved or spoke; it was as if an even deeper stillness had settled over them. He unhitched the horse from the rail, climbed up on the seat beside the motionless woman, spoke a word to the horse, and it started off. She watched the wagon pull out into the thoroughfare and until it turned at the horse trough and went south past the flagpole into Ship Street.

Behind her the post office door opened and closed again, and Stephen Wells said, "Mrs. Glenroy, how are you?" Albion Hardy was with him.

"Very well, thank you," she said. "Could you tell me who those people are in the blue wagon that was just here?"

"The Evanses," said the customs inspector. "They live on a farm off the river road. They're heading for the toll bridge now."

"The wagon took my eye, it was so bright and so immaculately done, but the people don't match."

"Hugh Evans is an odd stick," said Stephen Wells. "He does likenesses for a fair price, and he carves figureheads. He lays on enough colors to blind you, but I doubt if he'd let his wife wear a scarlet shawl."

"Or have a red flower on her bonnet, supposing she had one," said Albion Hardy. He looked rather pointedly over his spectacles at Jennie's bonnet.

"He's heard about yours," Stephen Wells said with a grin. "Everyone has. But not from me or my ma."

"I know," said Jennie. "Minnie. Oh, I understand what it is to live in a small place. I grew up in one. And I can't help wondering about those people in the wagon."

"And well you might," said Albion Hardy. "She's had an education, if you believe it. Her father was a parson over in New Hampshire, they say. She teaches the young ones at home, and the school board allows it because they're a good eight miles from town. Besides being all a bit—" he tapped his temple.

"That poor woman!" Jennie exclaimed. "Poor children, too. What will become of them? The man had the look of a brute." She'd heard of things like this at home, a whole family backward or diseased; it was the contrast of the brightly painted wagon which gave the encounter a macabre atmosphere that lingered like a stench.

"It's hard telling," Stephen Wells was saying. "They might surprise you. Or one of them could. I've known stranger things. We're sailing Monday morning, Mrs. Glenroy. If there are any letters you'd like me to post in Liverpool, just leave them with the General's mail, and I'll be happy to take care of them."

"Thank you," she said composedly. She was used to the stab by now; it was like an old familiar ache expected in damp weather. "Will you be bringing back more immigrants?"

"No, it's all merchandise this time. We are carrying orders from private citizens and two-thirds of the businesses in town. The autumn sales will be stupendous."

"They will be if his brig isn't boarded by a press gang and all the crew taken off and hurled into the British Navy," Albion Hardy said.

"It's not likely," the mate said. "They'd have a hard time proving any of us were deserters."

"They didn't bother to prove Jonah Bisset was a deserter when they took *him*."

Jennie realized that young Hardy was only half-joking. "Could this have happened when we were sailing from Scotland?" she asked.

"The orders-in-council had just been withdrawn," Stephen Wells said. "We had no reason to expect that any vessel flying the American ensign would be stopped for any purpose whatsoever."

"Which is no answer at all, if you take it apart," said the other man.

"Albion is one of the demon performers of the Debating Society," the mate said, "and you can see why." Both men lifted their hats to an elderly woman passing by. She bowed, including Jennie with a slight smile.

Jennie smiled back, all at once seeing herself from the outside. Not only had she won doubtful fame by the brawl, but she was behaving in what might be called a free and easy fashion with two young men in a public place.

"I must finish my errands," she said. "Mr. Wells, I wish you a pleasant voyage and a safe return. Good day, Mr. Hardy."

She left with what she hoped was a suitable young-matronly manner.

Two traveling coaches were pulling up at the inn amid the usual organized confusion, compounded by an audience of children. The road through Maddox was part of Benjamin Franklin's consolidated route from the southern state of Georgia to the upper reaches of Maine. The next inn was at Tenby, twenty miles to the northeast; but the food at the St. David Inn was better, and the beds cleaner, and travelers strolling about town to stretch their legs could hope to catch a glimpse of the General.

Across the intersection the Ark looked deserted. All those who had taken land went out to work on it on Saturdays, women and children, too, except for the very aged and the toddlers who were too small to walk the distance but too big to carry. They were watched over in the grassy yard by an old granny, who sat knitting in the sun; she had knit stockings all the way across the Atlantic. Neither she nor the children saw Jennie go by on the far side of Ship Street.

Twenty-Seven

A LICK AND TONY were not yet back from the blacksmith's. She laid off her bonnet and shawl and went to Strathbuie House. Eliza had taken the girls to her father's farm for the day, and the General had driven himself in the gig to visit friends on the Tenby road. She had an hour alone with the pianoforte. The two disturbing elements of the afternoon retreated to a harmless distance; but when she was closing the pianoforte, the wagon woman's face came up before her as if the woman had been lying in wait, and the sight of the river reminded her that the *Paul Revere* was going to England without her.

She asked Alick at supper if he knew Hugh Evans.

"I have seen the Welshman, yes. He has come to see Mr. Dunlop, but he does his work at home."

"Does he speak with anyone else? Does he have conversations like an ordinary person?"

"You think I am a quiet man, but beside that one I am as a tree of singing birds."

"That's a lovely phrase," she said. "I shall be expecting you to break out in leaf and blossom anytime now. Is he a Welshman straight from Wales?"

"So they say. Why are you so curious about this man?"

"He looks like a man who would beat his wife and children. They were so *still*, Alick, as if he had told them not to move even a finger while he was gone. And when he came back, they went even quieter, if that could be."

She traced an invisible design on the table with her spoon handle.

"His wife has strange eyes. The way she gazed at me, I found myself answering her, but what was I answering? I have this feeling that when they went out of sight, they were going to some hideous ending."

He said angrily, "You are not to be imagining such things! It is bad for you, bad for the child. You have a friend now to be laughing with. Go on with that, and don't be always looking for horrors."

"I'm not looking for horrors!" she objected. "I thought I could tell you about this peculiar occurrence because people interest me, but of course, if you are *offended*—"

"I am thinking only of your good," he said haughtily. "But if *you* are offended—"

"Alick, listen to us!" she exclaimed. "We're both offending our friendship. I apologize." She put out her hand. He looked oddly at it, and for a moment she thought he was going to refuse it. Then he took it in a brief hard clasp and let go.

"I am apologizing also." He pushed her mug closer to her plate. "Drink your milk."

"Yes, *sir*!" said Jennie, and they both laughed.

She rode to church with the General and Tony and tried to give Elder Mayfield her full attention, to thank him for being one of her rescuers. It was a hot morning, close inside the church even with all the windows open, and a woman fainted, enlivening the services considerably; her husband carried her out and all the family trooped happily after them. Mrs. MacKenzie had used her pregnancy to keep her home from church, and Jennie wondered how soon she could take advantage of her own condition.

Alick spent the morning at the stables. He said he'd offered to do some chores for Benoni and thus give him a full Sunday at home.

In the afternoon Jennie wrote to Sylvia and William. She could not bear to let the *Paul Revere* go to England without something from her. In any case they shouldn't be allowed to expect her return at any moment. She wanted to end their suspense without letting them know she was pregnant; that would be a tremendous worry to them.

She worked out several drafts on the slate before she was satisfied. "My dearest ones," she wrote at last, "you may have already received my first letter. I am healthy and enjoying my work, and I have decided to stay on through the autumn and winter. I will have that much more to tell you. I love you dearly."

When she arose to light a candle to melt the sealing wax, Alick had left the bench outside, where he had been reading. She took some sugar lumps and young carrots and walked through the pines, expecting to find him leaning on the pasture gate communing with the animals. But he wasn't there, and she heard a muted hammering from the loft of the carriage house.

"Alick, is that you?" she called up to the open window.

"I am just finishing!" He answered her from out of sight, and in a few minutes he came out through a small door at the side.

"What in the world were you doing?" she asked.

"I am just making some shelves for Ben. Good practice for me. What have you there?"

"Treats for the horses. And the ponies."

"Och, those two imps!" he said lightheartedly. "The heels are in the air as much as they are in the turf."

On Monday morning she left her letter on the General's desk to be franked and taken to the wharf with his mail. She was glad she would be teaching when the *Paul Revere* left; she didn't want to see the brig go down the river and out of sight.

"This Ship was nought to me, nor I to her," Wordsworth had written. "Yet I pursued her with a Lover's look;/This Ship to all the rest did I prefer;/When will she turn, and whither? She will brook/ No tarrying; where She comes the winds must stir."

It wasn't true that this ship was naught to her; this ship was everything to her.

Lucy walked into town in the afternoon, with Jared on her back in a canvas carrier she had designed. Her brother, who worked in the sail loft, had cut and sewn it for her. "The Indian women strap their papooses to boards," she told Jennie, "and wrap them up tightly, poor little things. Jared can kick his feet and wave his arms around."

She had brought the newspaper pattern she used for Harm's shirts. They fenced Jared into the kitchen by a chest pulled across the door into the hall and gave him a wooden bowl and spoon to play with.

"My, but that's elegant!" Lucy said of the parlor. "Small but refined, as one of my aunts by marriage would say. She lives in Portland and never stops reminding us that we're still rude frontier settlers up here. I lived with her for two years and attended a female seminary, and I love her for that, but my goodness, she *will* consider herself an aristocrat because she married a descendant of someone who came over in the 1600s. He was probably a cowherd, not one of the gentlemen."

"Like all the people who claim Norman descent," said Jennie. "It's always from the knights, never from any of the servants."

"Or the camp followers," said Lucy.

They spread the linen out on the kitchen table. Lucy did the cutting and told Jennie where to baste. When they were each settled down to work on a seam, Lucy said, "Jennie, tell me how you met your husband. It must be a romantic story."

"Wasn't yours?"

"Oh, *very!*" Lucy said mockingly. "I'd known Harm all my life, and I *knew* it couldn't be love because it wasn't a bit like the books. Then he went to the West Indies on his uncle's boat. The captain and half the men died of yellow fever, and the rest sailed home looking like cadavers. I still didn't feel like a lovelorn princess waiting to be rescued from her tower, especially by one with his eyes in black pits and his cheekbones as sharp as ax blades. *He* couldn't have climbed that tower and fought off the evil guardians. All I knew was that I didn't want him out of my sight; he wasn't ever going to disappear down that river again."

"I think," said Jennie judiciously, "that it could be called love."

Lucy hunched up her shoulders and squeezed her eyes almost shut in an endearingly ingenuous grimace. "Must be," she said. "Lucky for me, he was willing. He'd been so sick, and as terrified of pirates as of the yellow fever, that he never wanted to go again."

"What if Jared wants to go to sea in one of those ships his father helps build?"

"I have some twenty years not to worry about that. We would never let him go underage, and if we are very lucky, he will go to college." They both looked down at Jared. He was lying on his back on the folded plaid, sound asleep. "Why borrow trouble?" Lucy asked. "These are the precious days. You will discover that for yourself."

"Looking on the practical side of the precious days," said Jennie, "what must I have besides a great supply of napkins?"

"I'll write out a list of the absolute necessities. And I've already begun to piece a cradle quilt."

"A cradle!" Jennie was dismayed. "Where will I find a cradle? I shall have to hire it made."

"*Hire,* with your husband a joiner?" Lucy asked merrily. "He will be happy to make his child's cradle, and Harm can provide a pattern. Every father likes to build the cradle. At least most of them do."

This child's father is underground, Jennie was thinking. *This child, born at Tigh nam Fuaran, would have slept in a cradle padded with satin and draped in muslin, and his father certainly wouldn't have made it.* But she could see Nigel leaning over it. She knew that smile: tender; proud; possessive.

Twenty-Eight

"AN EXCEPTION," Lucy was saying, "would be the man who knows the baby is none of his own. . . . You look pale, Jennie. Are you faint?"

"*No*," said Jennie strongly. "It is the light in here. What do you think of the way I put in this gusset?"

"It's a work of art. You must be sure to point it out to your husband so he will truly appreciate your labor of love. And let us be thankful," she said piously, "that he doesn't require dress shirts. All those miles of cambric ruffles with rolled hems and invisible stitches! Harm's sisters made one for him to wear at our wedding. I told him it would have to last him, and it has. He's never worn it since. What do you suppose Zeb Pulsifer wore at *his* wedding? Chains and leg irons if *her* family had a choice."

Lucy always settled herself like a hen on the nest when she had a story to tell if it was one she relished. Grim or sad stories were something else. "This comes *straight* from the family," she assured Jennie, "so it's true. She's an Allbright, but not all bright." She giggled. "One of my uncles married one of her aunts, so that's how I know. Oh, she's entrusted herself to Zeb, all right, unless he's added rape to his other crimes, and when she couldn't hide it, her father and five brothers went to Zeb and offered him a choice of being married or shot. He had just turned twenty-one, so his mother couldn't save him. She carried on as if he were her husband instead of her son and had left her for another woman. Now she sits all day chewing one finger and staring into space and never saying a word. It must be restful for Joe and the young ones."

"Was the poor girl obliged to move in with them?"

"Oh, no! Aaron Allbright might have forced the marriage against his wife's wishes—she had some pity for the girl—but he saw that she'd have a home of her own. He gave them ten acres, and he and the boys put up a cabin in a week. Joe gave a cow and some chickens and a pig."

"I can't believe Zeb could be domesticated in the twinkling of an eye," said Jennie.

"Well, it wasn't quite as quick as *that*." Lucy fastened a seam and snapped off the thread. "But it happens, especially when the bride has a father in his prime and five brothers. I am sorry for stupid little Malvina, but she's done Maddox a kindness. Zeb Pulsifer has been worse than the plague for most of his life."

"Bless Malvina," Jennie murmured. "I feel as if I should send her a wedding gift. Not long ago I was so afraid of him I wanted us to run away."

"Oh, Lord, I'm glad you didn't!" said Lucy. "When I think what I would have missed! I haven't had a friend like you since Olivia Jarrell moved to Massachusetts, before I was married. And now I've told you about Harm and me, and the *terribly* romantic tale of Zeb and Malvina, you must tell me about you and Mr. Glenroy. Fair is fair. *Tell*, Jennie!"

"It's a very simple story," Jennie said. "I was visiting in the Highlands, and I met him on the moors one day. They had begun clearing for sheep and evicting the tenants, and he was concerned for them, and so was I. It drew us close." She was staggered by the ease with which she put truths together to present a complete falsehood. "When he couldn't do anything to stop the evictions, he left, and I went with him, with what we had on our backs, which included the plaid Jared is sleeping on, and a little money between us. In the port town we bought a change of clothing and some household gear and our passage. It was just luck that our ship was the *Paul Revere*."

"It was luck for me, too," Lucy said with fervor. Then her mouth curved into a wry little smile, and she fluttered her lashes very fast and said demurely, "I have a shocking confession to make."

"I can hardly wait," said Jennie.

"I saw you two come down the gangplank that day, and I'm afraid I passed over you in favor of your husband. Oh, I liked the cut of your jib, but *he* was the one who took my eye. He was so trim and spare and straight, and the cock of his bonnet said, 'I am who I am, and to the devil with anyone who doesn't like it!' So I know why he took *your* eye, Jennie."

Jennie hoped she looked modestly complacent and gave closer attention to her work.

"I hope your family will forgive you for eloping, so your life here needn't be clouded by sorrow," Lucy said.

"I am sure they have already forgiven me," Jennie said. "A letter should come soon." She looked over at the sleeping Jared. He was like a cherub in a painting, but wearing a frock instead of wings. At this time next year a child of her own, almost as old as Jared was now, would be sleeping like this under an English roof. She knew she loved Jared, but she could not believe in, or feel anything for, the foreign object which Alick and Lucy called her child.

Noticing her glance, Lucy said, "Have you written them about the baby?"

"No, they would only worry."

"Have you talked with Dr. Waite yet?"

"Should I?" Jennie asked in surprise.

"To let him know you'll be needing him, and when. So he can give you words of advice, which I've already given you." Lucy grinned. "It will do you good. He's such a kind man. And he *never* prescribes calomel."

"Why is he a most immoral man?" Jennie asked. "That was how Mrs. MacKenzie described him to me. But tongue in cheek, now that I recollect it."

Lucy laughed. "It's thought he beds his housekeeper and landlady. But she's forty-five, if she's a day, and if it is her free choice—well, he's not debauching a young girl, is he? Like the doctor we had once, who just missed being tarred and feathered and ridden out of town on a rail. He galloped away in the dark of night, like a highwayman."

The hen settled herself on the nest again, with a smoothing and tucking in of wings. "Amyas Waite is the only doctor we have, so no one discusses him and Mrs. Pritchard above a whisper. Every so often Elder Mayfield feels we all should be brought up with a round turn, so he preaches a sermon on sin in Maddox. He looks very hard at certain individuals, points a finger like a sword, and thunders about abominations and whoredoms that have the more refined ladies reaching for their smelling salts. But never, *never* has he ever looked in Mrs. Pritchard's direction."

"Or the doctor's?"

"Dr. Waite never goes to church, but Mrs. Pritchard never misses."

"But why in the world doesn't he marry her?" Jennie asked.

"Because she doesn't know if she's a widow or not! Captain Samuel Pritchard sailed to Savannah fourteen years ago. He was going ashore to visit an old friend, he told his first mate. He never came back, and no one ever turned up a trace of him. Murdered, some thought, but others wondered if the old friend was a lady. Perhaps Mrs. Pritchard wondered, too."

"How long has the doctor lived in her house?"

"Since the General brought him here from Boston, about nine years ago, just in time to bring Sukey MacKenzie into the world. He arranged for him to lodge at Mrs. Pritchard's; she was supporting herself by taking boarders. But he's been the only one for a long time. He has his surgery there and is very well looked after indeed." She gave Jennie a quizzical look. "In all respects. She and Samuel had no children; she must be safely barren, so there was no risk of a wood's colt. The poor little critter would be doubly disadvantaged, being both a come-by-chance and looking like its father. He's a dear man, but what a scarecrow! Rose of Sharon King, now, all five of her youngsters have different fathers, but land of love, they're beautiful children!"

"The baby is one of the prettiest I've even seen," said Jennie. "She lies in a laundry basket and plays with her toes. Sukey and Frank are mad about her, and even the General chucked her under the chin the other day."

Lucy's face contorted as if with intense pain, and her eyes filled with tears. "I'd forgotten," she said hoarsely. She threw her work onto the table and went and knelt beside Jared, touching his moist forehead with her fingertips. "All my foolish gossip. I'm so ashamed. The cholera infantum is showing here, and that little baby has it. She is very sick." She bowed over her sleeping child in a gesture of protection against some evil assault from above.

"That lovely, laughing baby who talks to her toes?" Jennie dropped her own work. The green and gold day outside the windows darkened as if Lucy's terror were swooping down on immense black wings.

"They almost always *die*." Lucy whispered the last word. "I don't take Jared where there are other small children, and we don't share a well with anyone. But neither does Rose of Sharon, out there on the western edge of town. And if it can strike *there*—"

Jared came awake, kicking and gurgling with pleasure at seeing his mother's face so close. "I should change his napkin, and feed him, and take him home," she said. Handling his strong little body, she was restored to her confident self. "What am I afraid of?" she asked him. He sucked loudly, fat fingers splayed on her breast, leaf green eyes on hers. "You're a great big boy. That other baby is so young and tiny yet." Jennie saw the gooseflesh rise on her arms. "I pray for her, Jennie, I really do. You pray, too. For all of them. Jared, too."

"Yes," said Jennie.

She would do as Lucy asked; whether she believed or not that there was an ear and an answer out there in the void made no difference.

They had finished one shirt for Alick, and another was well under way. She helped Lucy harness herself into the straps of Jared's carryall and kissed them both. "Thank you with all my heart, Lucy."

Lucy was buoyant again. "I love helping you. Now you'll be showing soon, and you will need more dresses. Pick out some goods, and I'll help you cut and sew them. No need to pay the Misses Applegate when you have a useful friend."

"I only hope I may be a useful friend to you one day."

"You are already, just by being here."

Twenty-Nine

M RS. MACKENZIE was spoken of with respect and affection while the
family settled happily down to do things they couldn't do when
she was at home. The girls were allowed to ride their ponies bareback
around the meadow, and Tony was given time to take them riding outside
the grounds.

Eliza took them at high tide to a little beach on the creek, where
they played with other children, paddling, sailing boats, and skimming
flat pebbles across the water in games of ducks and drakes. They had
been frantic to play with some Highland children ever since they'd seen
them arrive, and now they had permission to entertain at a picnic supper
in the orchard; Nabby passed on the invitation and brought three little
girls between six and ten in age. No one could be shy for long with
Sukey and Frank, and the experiment proved that with encouragement
Highland children could be as noisy as born Yankees. They learned Indian
war whoops in no time at all.

Tony went openly at night to a house on the creek end of Main
Street, where he played duets with Mr. Porter, the tailor. The General
entertained certain old comrades of much lower rank, including Joseph
Pulsifer; they played cards, billiards, talked, drank rum punch, and ate
the hearty late suppers Mrs. Frost left for them. Between these sessions
the General dined at houses in and out of town where Lydia MacKenzie
never went.

He had intended to send the barouche to Tenby to bring back his
daughter Christian and his grandson for a visit, but with the outbreak

179

of cholera infantum in town, the idea had to be given up. The General was too busy being sociable to be disappointed for long.

Jennie practiced for the proposed musical evenings, though she wasn't sure that even one would take place. But she had a good excuse for playing. Once when Tony came home from riding with the girls while she was there, they played duets with melodies they both knew. The girls, Eliza, and Mrs. Frost were their audience, so he couldn't talk to Jennie about Mairi, but she knew he wanted to; he approached it when he played almost perfectly the song Mairi had sung to Jared. He had heard it only once.

"What is it?" he asked Jennie. "A lullaby, a farewell—*what*? I can't tell whether it is sad or hopeful."

"It can mean whatever you are feeling at the time perhaps," said Jennie. "We don't know the language, so it can mean anything." But she had recognized the words of endearment in it and knew they could have been equally for a child, a lover, or the memory of the dead. "It is most likely to be a lullaby," she said. "What else would she be singing to quiet a child?"

Alick went to the tailor, finally, because his breeches were wearing thin, and he consented to have two pairs made. Mr. and Mrs. Porter both did the tailoring, and they looked curiously alike. Choosing a good serviceable worsted should have been easy, but Alick's Olympian detachment made it awkward. At last the Porters tactfully removed themselves to the workroom.

"Alick, don't you have any preference at all?" Jennie asked.

"None whatever," he said loftily. "It is all the same to me."

"If you don't choose, they will think you are henpecked," she whispered.

When they came back, he said, "I will have this. Two pairs." He stalked off behind Mr. Porter to be measured. Mrs. Porter showed Jennie some fine cassimeres, kerseymeres, and broadcloths.

"Mr. Glenroy has a neat figure for pantaloons," she said wistfully. "My, but he would look elegant in these." She pointed out a fashion plate of an incredibly slim, long-legged man in snug trousers strapped under his boots, a tight-waisted long-tailed coat, and a ruffled shirt.

"Yes, he would," Jennie agreed. "But he has no occasion for such things."

"Ah, well," Mrs. Porter said comfortably, "the time will come when he will wear them, and wear them well."

Alick was not yet ready to have new boots made, but even he had to admit that the barber could trim his hair better than she could; her attempts with the new shears disquieted him.

"Och, I was doing better cutting your hair with my dirk," he had protested. "And *your* ears were safe."

"Whatever did you do with my hair?" she had asked.

"I don't remember," he said irritably. He went outside to take off his shirt and shake the loose hairs off.

They walked up the hill from the tailor shop to the center of town, and she left him at the striped barber pole and went on to the stationer's for more paper and pens. She spent a little while looking over the bookshelves and was mightily tempted by the price of some secondhand books, but there was nothing she really wanted, even at two or three cents the copy.

While the stationer was counting out her change, the blue wagon stopped outside, and the man Evans climbed down, tied the piebald horse, and went into the post office across the hall. The stationer said, "Good day," to her, and became the postmaster.

Jennie went quickly outside. It was the same as the other time, except that the woman's head was turned away. She still sat like a wooden image on the wagon seat, the baby in her arms, the three behind her watching the town children as if they were trying to gulp everything down before it was snatched away from them.

Alick came along the sidewalk. He passed the wagon, and when he reached the piebald horse, he stopped and stroked its nose and spoke to it. The woman turned that pale stare on him and then at Jennie, who smiled and said, "Good afternoon, Mrs. Evans."

The children's heads swiveled like those of young owls, their eyes almost as round. The infant stirred languidly and fussed in a tired way. An ammoniac reek came from it, and its cheeks were so red they looked scorched. Hugh Evans came out of the post office, and Alick took Jennie's elbow and walked her across the street in a gap between passing wagons.

"That baby is very sick," she said.

"Yes. I was not wanting you to be near it."

"I won't sleep tonight, thinking of that sick baby with no proper care and that man beating them."

"You are not sure that the baby has no proper care. You are not knowing that Hugh Evans beats them. The horse is well cared for, and the children are not looking underfed."

"But they are so *frightened!* I have known of men who were kind to their animals and cruel to their children and worse to their wives."

"He brings them with him, does he not, when he could be leaving them all at home?"

"Probably he thinks they all would run away when his back was turned."

"There is nothing you can be doing about them," he said, "and you have your own child to be thinking about."

She didn't like his reminding her of that, which was not his business anyway, and she did not wish to be told not to worry about what worried her. So she didn't bring up the Evanses again. There was no one she could ask about the baby, because the family didn't come often to town, and apparently nobody went to them.

Jared was still burstingly healthy. Two small babies had died, but Rose of Sharon's infant still gripped life by the thumbs. Lucy swore that the others died because they were so undernourished and had no resistance to fight the cholera infantum; their mothers ate the wrong foods, so their milk was no good.

Marriage and the combined weight of his wife's male relatives seemed to have sunk Zeb without a trace. His wife wanted him home with her at night in their new cabin, and her family saw to it that he was there. It was almost laughable now to have been so frightened of a hulk who could be so quickly defeated, first by the thought of Oliver's teeth and then by a determined girl backed up by five brothers and a father.

Oliver still went to school twice a week with Alick. "I couldn't be disappointing him," Alick said. "He loves the sociability of it." He always saw the dog safe inside the back door of Strathbuie House before he returned to the cottage. As the moon approached the full, there was a series of flawless nights, and Alick would stop at the cottage first, where Jennie would be waiting up; she walked with him and the dog to the mansion, and then they would come back through the sleeping garden, where moths fluttered about the white nicotiana that perfumed the wind-less air.

The spell of fine weather ended with a southeasterly storm on the day of the full moon. The *Lady Lydia*, returning from her weekly run to Boston and back, had to beat her way upriver through quick, savage squalls and hard bursts of rain. Each week the captain had carried a letter from Mrs. MacKenzie; this time the letter informed the General that he was the father of a healthy son.

He treated the crew and every other adult male on the wharf to a drink from his private stock of the best West Indian rum, which he kept in his office at the store. Even Tony was allowed a few mouthfuls. The General had been profoundly depressed by the deaths of two-year-old twin boys, the sons of a man who worked in the ropewalk; earlier that stormy day he had stood with the father in the churchyard, watching the rain beat down on the small coffin that held both children.

Now he rebounded with the vitality of a boy. He came to the cottage himself earlier that evening, when the rain was tapering off, to ask Alick and Jennie to Strathbuie House the next evening.

"Tonight is for the children and myself," he said. "Gaining a brother is every bit as momentous as gaining a son. But tomorrow night I'd like to rejoice with music."

"I have no objection to my wife going," Alick said, "but I have not the clothes for such an occasion."

"I wouldn't go without you, Alick," Jennie said in a wifely manner which she hoped he appreciated.

"Nonsense, man!" The General would hear no objections. "It will be completely informal, I promise you. And it's a Friday, so you'll be able to sleep late the next morning." He lifted himself up from his chair. "Oh, it's a great feeling when the baby is here safe and sound and their mother has come through it like an army with banners! I knew she would, you know. I *knew*, yet there's always that niggling little fear— Oh, forget that!" He put his hand on Alick's shoulder and gave him a little shake. "You'll be knowing all about it yourself one day, and forget what I said about the worry. You two are strong, and you will bring strong children into the world. Strong little Americans, eh?"

He laughed and went out, saying, "There's nothing like it. Nothing in the world."

Thirty

WHEN ALICK came home from work the next night, he took his boots to the stable and polished them with the compound Benoni used on the harness and saddles. He had his new breeches and new shirt, and Jennie put on her Sunday dress.

"I think you might enjoy this evening, Alick," she said when they were crossing the garden. "You like music, don't you? Besides the pipes?"

"I am not objecting," he said amiably. "Why would I not be willing to drink a toast to the General's son? It is a courtesy due him."

Oliver met them at the back door and escorted them past the empty kitchen and out to the hall. The notes of the flute danced out to them like a flock of goldfinches over a meadow, dipping, rising, dropping lower and soaring higher. The clarinet notes were the shadows skimming the grass below.

The long drawing room was filled with a pale apricot glow from the west, which invested the people in it with the auras of figures in a painting. Tony and Mrs. Porter stood at a music stand in the center window, rehearsing a difficult cadenza; Sukey and Frank, wearing pink muslin frocks and sashes, sat on a sofa with Eliza, being a respectful audience. Mrs. Porter occupied an armchair, doing embroidery in hoops.

O'Dowda and the General were standing before a cold hearth below the General's portrait. The teacher's violin was under his arm, and he was waving his bow to emphasize the strong points of his discourse. The General stood with his hands behind his back, giving the little man his full attention. He was informally dressed, as he had promised, and so were the teacher and Tony. Mr. Porter was a distinguished sample of his own work in snug buff kerseymere pantaloons strapped under his boots and a double-breasted olive green coat.

Alick lifted Jennie's shawl off her shoulders and laid it over the back of a chair. Tony rolled his eyes at him over the flute, and Alick nodded. He bowed slightly to Eliza and to the girls, who had obviously been cautioned to sit still, but their faces radiated bliss.

"Ah, here are the Glenroys!" the General said. "Come along, Liam, and be presented to Mrs. Glenroy." His large gestures embraced them all. He poured wine, and they drank a toast to Mrs. MacKenzie and the new son; O'Dowda proposed it in a captivating Dublin lilt. He had lank graying hair, hollow cheeks, and large, faintly bloodshot Celtic gray eyes. A few missing teeth did not detract from the smiling courtliness of his manner toward Jennie and Mrs. Porter.

Jennie congratulated O'Dowda on the children's chorus. "The new scholars have added immeasurably," he said. "Good voices seem to be a MacKenzie trait."

"There's a sweet-voiced lass too old for your school, Liam," the General said. "I haven't heard her, but I've heard of her."

"Mairi MacKenzie," said the schoolteacher. "The younger ones brag about her to me. 'Och, Mr. O'Dowda, it's the larks and the blackbirds who are hiding their heads with shame when they are hearing her!' "

The others laughed. "I've asked the MacArthurs to bring her tonight to sing a few of the dear old Gaelic songs for us," the General said. "Her parents are too shy. I think they are here now."

A bell sounded through the hall, and he went with outstretched hands to meet the MacArthurs, two white-headed red-cheeked little persons; their good, if threadbare, blacks set off by his snowy linen and her cap and fichu. Mairi stood diffidently behind them. Someone must have quickly made her a new dress for the occasion, a sprigged cambric with a round neck and puffed sleeves and a green ribbon sash. A narrower ribbon held her auburn hair back from her face.

She looked completely charming and completely terrified. The General took her hand in both of his and spoke to her as he spoke to his daughters; her diffident smile came and went. Tony, who must have been responsible for her presence, was struck mute and immobile by it, as usual. Mr. Porter had returned to his clarinet and sat in a corner softly playing it as if alone on a hillside, an aging shepherd lad in kerseymere and broadcloth.

The General led Mairi to Jennie. "Oh, Mrs. Glenroy!" she whispered. "With my heart in my throat how can I be singing?"

"It will be easy, because you will be giving such pleasure," Jennie assured her. "Come and see Sukey and Frank and Eliza." She led her toward the sofa, where the children were now unable to contain themselves.

"You are *beautiful*," said Frank solemnly.

Mairi put her hand to her cheek and looked sidewise at Jennie.

Eliza said heartily, "It's nothing to be ashamed of. They always say praise to the face is open disgrace, but I can't see the harm in a little honest sweet'ning."

Mrs. Porter was taking Mrs. MacArthur around the room, chattering away and pointing out objects of interest.

"I am understanding you are a lapsed papist, Dominie," the minister said to O'Dowda. "But I am satisfied that you are educating the children well. And I am liking their music fine as long as you are not teaching them with that." He nodded at the violin lying on the table. "She is the Devil's Daughter."

"But she sings like an angel, Mr. MacArthur. In the right hands, of course. In the wrong ones she sings with the devil's voice, right enough." He smiled and patted the minister's shoulder. "I need no fiddle with the children. Thank God my voice is still true, if it croaks a bit at times, and I have scholars who can pick up a tune the first time around."

Tony had come up on the other side of Mairi. "My sisters would like to show you the garden," he said. The little girls were surprised by joy; they slid off the sofa, and each took one of Mairi's hands. She wanted to go; she was at ease with the children. She looked anxiously over her shoulder at the widely separated MacArthurs.

"Oh, run along for a few minutes," Jennie said. The children towed her toward the door, and Tony moved so fast that he was out of the room before they were. Eliza winked at Jennie.

"Now that you have left the Whore of Babylon," the minister said to the schoolteacher, "will you not be coming over to us?"

"And isn't Elder Mayfield forever asking me the same thing? Faith, I am the most sought-after man in Maddox besides the doctor and the General! Now I have a question for *you*: Will you remain tonight after the girl sings and listen to the Devil's Daughter and her cousins playing noble music written by men who loved God?"

"The devil can quote Scripture!" Mr. MacArthur retorted.

"Do you not believe that God put the music into the composers' heads and gave them the gift of expression? And gave the makers of instruments the gift of building such lovely things?" O'Dowda picked up his fiddle and ran his hand over its back in a lover's caress. "Just as he gave young Mairi the gift of a sweet voice?"

Mr. MacArthur put two fingers inside his neckcloth as if it were too tight. "Where is the lass?" His voice went shrill, and his color darkened dangerously.

"She's only gone with the little girls to see the garden," Jennie said.

"Yes, it is beautiful in this light," the General said. "My wife's pride and joy. Will you have some wine, Mr. MacArthur?"

"The lad is not here!" the minister said accusingly.

"He must have gone with them," the General said with a broad, casual gesture which inflamed the minister even more.

His wife hurried to him and stroked his rigid shoulder, murmuring, and Alick spoke to him in Gaelic; but they could not reassure the minister, who suspected a conspiracy and was outraged.

"I'll go and fetch them," Jennie said.

"And I, too," said O'Dowda quickly. "I need the air. Unless Glenroy objects?"

Glenroy flicked a dismissive hand at them. When they were out in the hall, O'Dowda said, "I hear that either your husband gave up a title or you did. Looking at each of you tonight, I can't tell which. He dresses like an artisan but carries himself like something quite different."

"It is neither of us," Jennie said. "But this is America, where an artisan or a laborer can also be a gentleman, isn't that so? As well as an Irish schoolmaster."

"Touché!" They passed the foot of the spiral staircase and turned into the passage. "The little minister is in a rare old taking about the ewe lamb. Is she his granddaughter, perhaps?"

"No, but that ewe lamb is the flower of the flock, and he is the shepherd, and he takes his responsibility seriously."

Ahead of them Eliza cried out, "Oh, my God, Aldric! No!"

They broke into a run, and O'Dowda reached the kitchen first. Eliza was leaning across the table, staring at a disheveled young man in work clothes that smelled of fish. His head was bare, and his face bruised, striped down one cheek with dried blood. He turned wild eyes on Jennie and O'Dowda. "I must see the General," he said hoarsely. "They've stolen Roddie MacKenzie."

Jennie's first thought was that Zeb Pulsifer was on the prowl again, but O'Dowda snarled, "God damn their bloody English souls to hell! You come with me, Aldric Frost!" He seized the young man by the arm and marched him out of the kitchen. Eliza pulled a handkerchief from her bosom and began to cry. The little girls stood in the shadowy corner by the back stairs like two small ghosts with their pale faces and long light dresses. She went toward them, and Frank threw herself at her and Sukey was close behind her.

Eliza went into the pantry and bathed her face in cold water. "I'm sorry," she said in a muffled voice when she came out. "But it took me hard, coming so sudden. That boy's just the same as dead." She gave the children a sickly smile. "Time for chickabiddies to go to bed."

"Who is just the same as dead?" Sukey asked.

"We haven't heard any music yet!" Frank cried indignantly. "Just Tony! We want to hear Mairi sing!"

"Sweethearts, there may be no more music tonight," Eliza said. "We'll go upstairs, but if there is music, you can come down again." She opened the door to the back stairs and pushed them ahead of her. Over her shoulder she said to Jennie, "They were fishing in the bay, and a shaving mill shot out from behind Tucker's Rock and dragged the boy off for a deserter from their Navy."

"A *shaving mill?*" It was nightmare gibberish. Eliza shut the door behind her and the children, and Jennie ran back to the drawing room. Alick met her in the doorway.

"I was coming to look for you."

"I was with Eliza and the children. What has happened?"

"A press gang came down on them."

"The shaving mill?"

"It is a kind of boat they use with many men at the oars. It is very fast. They are saying there must be an English man-o'-war lying outside." Suddenly his control splintered. "A deserter? The bloody Sassenachs! That lad never set foot out of Strathbuie till he came to America!"

Thirty-One

T HE OTHER MEN, gray-faced, stood looking down at young Frost, who
slumped on a brocaded sofa.

"We was off the Tucker Rock bringing the cod in hand over fist,
and Roddie, he was laughing and singing. . . . They come up on us so
fast, with all them cussed long sweeps . . . come alongside and laid holt
of us. Jesus, how we fought the—" He lifted wretched eyes to the minister.
"I'm sorry, I warn't cussin'."

The minister nodded stonily. "What of Roddie?"

"He was fighting like a tiger when I—" He broke down into wrenching
sobs. Fragments of words squeezed out, not distinguishable.

O'Dowda sat down beside him and put his hand on Aldric's arm and
brought his head close to his, listening and nodding. He looked up at
the General and said, "They laid him out with something, he doesn't
know what. When he woke up, there was not a trace of Roddie. Except
his blood."

The General poured a glass of wine and took it to Aldric. "Drink it,
son," he said with such authority that the young man accepted it with
a shaking hand, slopping wine over his clothes.

"I will be going to Roddie's wife and his parents now," Mr. MacArthur
said.

"Tell them—Oh, dear God, what to tell them!" The General threw
up his hands. "I will see them tomorrow. Tonight I'll be writing letters
to the President, the secretary of state, and anyone else I can think of.
I shall be sailing for Boston to see my wife and son as soon as the vessel

is loaded, and I may go on to Washington. I'll be writing to England, too; I have friends there in high places. Assure Roddie's family of that."

"Why are they doing this?" Mr. Porter asked plaintively. "Must we go to war *again*?"

"I will not be leaving this house without Mairi," the minister said.

Jennie heard the rattle of Oliver's toenails behind her and Alick; she looked around and saw Tony and Mairi crossing the hall. They might have been still walking alone in the garden; Mairi carried a yellow rose and was dreamily sniffing at it. Tony gave Jennie a beatific smile.

The Newfoundland passed with a friendly glance and trotted to the knot of men in innocent anticipation of good fellowship. Before Jennie could warn the two in the hall, Mr. MacArthur was there. He picked up Mairi's shawl and thrust it at her. "Cover yourself," he commanded. She bit her lip and fumbled with the shawl; her hands were shaking, and Tony tried to help her.

"*No!*" the minister rapped out, and Tony jumped.

"Sir," he began, "we were only—"

"We will be leaving now," the minister said to Mairi. The General came out with Mrs. MacArthur, who was wiping her reddened eyes. She groped for her shawl without seeing it. Automatically Tony took it from a chair and held it for her. "I will be doing that!" Mr. MacArthur said, snatching the shawl from him.

The General went out through the front door with them. "Tomorrow," he said. "Tell them I will come tomorrow."

"What good will it be doing, General?" the minister said coldly. "You could be saving yourself the trouble."

The General came in, shaking his head despondently at Alick and Jennie. "The man is beside himself, knowing what he has to do. Come and have a glass of wine, though nothing can take off *this* chill."

"What's happening, Papa?" Tony asked. "All this can't be because I showed Mairi the garden!"

"No, son." He put his arm around Tony's shoulders, and they walked into the drawing room.

When Tony saw Aldric, he cried, "My God, has someone drowned?"

"I will walk home with Aldric now, Colin," O'Dowda said.

"We'll be going, too," Mr. Porter said. "Between Liam and ourselves we should be meeting our other musicians and tell them there'll be no music tonight."

"I'll see you out," the General said heavily. They were leaving by the back door, giving Tony a few minutes alone with Jennie and Alick, who told him what had happened. Tony folded into a chair, looking white and sick.

"Do you realize what it means?" he cried. "They took Jonah Bisset before I was born, and they knocked his brother so hard on the head it killed him! Jonah was seven years below decks, never setting foot on land, and they let him go only when he was no good to them, after his leg was shot off at Trafalgar!" He sprang up. "By God, this will mean war! So Britannia rules the waves, does she, the whore? We shall see!"

"Tony, guard your tongue!" said Alick quietly.

"I apologize, Mrs. Glenroy." He sounded anything but apologetic. "Do you know anyone influential over there?"

"No, and I am sorry."

"But my father does! He will never let this go by. *Never!*"

Alick and Jennie went home through the garden without speaking. They didn't bother to light candles; the house was shadowy with twilight but not really dark. They separated without a good-night, each locked into a personal isolation. Jennie undressed with hands that had no strength.

"Oh, you *God!*" The words suddenly erupted like vomit. "You—you monster! How can you expect anyone to love *you?* Half the world spends its life on its knees trying to appease you, and still you go on torturing and murdering the innocent!"

She fell over on her pillow and curled herself up like a threatened caterpillar. "I will not weep," she whispered. "I will not weep." It was torment not to give in; they were there before her eyes. Tamsin, the old people at Kilallan sitting all night by their dead cow; the drenched and shuddering children she had held in her arms; the woman who screamed like a dying soul as the thatch of her home went up in flames. The old man dead with the dirk in his hand.

The dreadful procession stopped short of Nigel, but he was there as he always was, a golden image just beyond the corner of her eye. Another of the dead.

This drove her off the bed. She had to talk to Alick or at least be with him, even if he did no more than listen or not listen. She hadn't heard him come upstairs, but he could move very quietly.

From his door she could just make out that his bed was undisturbed, and he was where she expected to find him, the place where he had slept on the first strange, troubled night in America. He sat on the plaid with his back against the wall under the parlor windows.

"May I sit with you?" she asked formally.

He shifted on the plaid, and she sat down and hugged her knees to her, and tucked the nightdress around her dew-chilled toes. The hem was wet and cold, too. Without a word he reached across and turned the corner of the plaid over her feet.

"Thank you," she said. "I have just repudiated God."

"What is that word?" he asked curiously.

"It means I have cast Him off."

"I thought you were doing that a long time ago."

"I wasn't so sure He heard me the first time." She rested her head on her knees.

He said in a voice so low she could hardly hear it, "I am hoping Roddie was killed by the blow that left his blood. I am hoping his body is floating somewhere in the sea, and it will be found."

"Then no matter how the family grieves, they will know he is beyond suffering," she agreed. "But it would still be murder, and the murderers are going free. My noble countrymen!"

"Hush," he said. "Hush. . . . If you let it possess you it will be sweeping you away like the flood in the corrie, and I could not be saving you by your hair then."

"I don't intend to let it carry me away. But a giant rage is as awful as a giant fear, isn't it?" She made a conscious effort to loosen her tight muscles and to breathe slowly. Gradually a normal weariness drugged her. She felt herself beginning to float, but the comfortable levitation was ruined when she fell against Alick's shoulder.

"You are going to your bed," he said decisively. He stood and pulled her up by both hands.

"Now I'll be all wide-awake with my horrible thoughts," she grumbled. "Why couldn't I have stayed where I was?"

"To wake up cold as a stepmother's breath, soaked with dew, and knotted with cramps." He was steering her toward the door. "You have a bed and a roof over it."

"So have you," she said petulantly, "but you'll stay out, won't you? Thank you for your assistance. I can find my own way upstairs." She stepped up into the front hall, and she felt the baby move.

She stood perfectly still. Could she have imagined it? It had been the slightest movement, more like a subdued flutter, but she had never felt anything like it before.

"It's too dark on the stairs now," Alick said. "I'll be lighting a candle for you."

"No. *Wait*." She braced her hand on the newel-post.

"What is it?" He stood close to her, his foreboding as palpable as a touch.

"It's all right," she said breathlessly. "Just wait."

It happened again. Now there was no doubt of a little human creature forming, as a chick formed inside the egg. Was it an arm or a leg that moved, or was it too early for limbs? Did it simply roll over or swim about like a tadpole?

"I felt it," she said, dazed with awe. "It *is* in there. It moved."

Thirty-Two

S HE INSISTED that she had not suddenly become a piece of china so fragile that stubbing her toe on the stairs could shatter her and that she didn't need a candle, but he waited at the foot.

"I have never lived with a pregnant woman before," he said. "You must be forgiving me."

"I am *thanking* you, even if it does not sound so," she answered. "But from the way you behaved while I was still strenuously denying everything, anyone would think you had been through it a dozen times."

"It is different now that the heart is beating. It gives me—it makes me—*Dia*, I haven't the words!" he said violently. "You are carrying a *life*."

"And *my* life is no longer my own. I don't own myself anymore. Good night, Alick."

She felt no instant rush of love and joy, only resignation. Her life and her body now belonged without a doubt to something unimaginably small but growing by the hour. All the possibilities remained but, as Lucy pointed out, there were more in her favor than against, so she was not so much frightened as dulled. She lay in bed curled up again like a caterpillar, but this time she was cocooned away from the tragedy of Roddie by this intimate phenomenon.

She woke in the morning with her hands laid on her belly, and her first conscious thoughts were questions. Was it waking or sleeping in the warm dark? Could it feel and respond to the heat of her hands? What did the word *consciousness* mean for it? Simply being and growing?

It was Saturday, and she was glad of that. She'd have liked to drift

all morning in this bemused state, but at breakfast she knew it wasn't
to be. It was as if Roddie MacKenzie sat at the table with them. Alick
looked as if he hadn't slept, and the night had put years on him.

"I will be going to see the family," he said. "You are not needing
to go."

"Of course, I shall go!" she heard herself protesting like a fool when
she could have stayed home away from the grief and read a book. But
she wouldn't back down; as long as she was playing the part of Alick's
wife, she would play it properly. She anticipated the visit with a disquiet
in her stomach that kept her from eating her porridge; she was harassed
by the memory of Roddie's and Ishbel's faces as they presented Paulina
Revere to the General. Much worse was what she could only imagine:
a sandy-haired boy fighting for his life, and outnumbered, and the only
thing left of him was his blood on the bottom of the boat.

Roddie's father worked in the quarry, and since Roddie had begun fishing
with Aldric Frost and doing well, the family had left the Ark and rented
a small house on the road that led off Main Street almost opposite Ship
Street; the inn was on the corner.

There was no one on the far side of them for some distance, so they
had plenty of pasture for two milch goats. Hens picked industriously
through the grass, and a young pig grunted and rooted about in the pen
they had built in a corner of the field.

When Alick and Jennie went there in early afternoon, the house
and yard were crowded with Highlanders. The men stood outdoors in
quiet groups. The children were there, but subdued, older ones taking
care of the little ones. Some went out to visit the goats, but there was
no racing around even out there in the pasture. They perched solemnly
on the granite outcroppings.

There was a scattering of Yankees among the men. One was leaning
on the gate talking with big Tormod MacKenzie, and Alick introduced
him to Jennie; he was Harmonious Clements. He was almost as brawny
as Tormod, fair and high-colored. Lucy was on the little porch talking
with Anna Kate and an American woman, and Jennie saw her with a
rush of gladness that briefly washed away her dread of what lay inside.

The men touched their bonnets or lifted them off as she went up the
walk with Alick; all the faces were drawn, with tired eyes. Hector talked
with Alick in near whispers, as if they were meeting beside Roddie's

coffin. Anna Kate ran down the steps and hugged Jennie. Her eyes and nose were red, and her voice was hoarse. "It's so terrible, Jeannie!"

Jennie felt as if she could neither speak nor swallow; she heard the weeping inside the house and wanted to break loose like a runaway horse. She and Lucy squeezed each other's cold hands and exchanged weak smiles.

"We drove in and left the wagon in the yard of the inn. I brought a big pot of beans," Lucy said. "Everyone's done well by them. They needn't cook for days."

"I didn't bring anything—I didn't think—"

"It's just a custom we have here when there's bad sickness or a death or a—when someone is lost at sea. But this is even worse. I almost wish Jonah had never come back to tell how it is." Inside the house the baby began to cry, and Lucy stiffened to listen. "I hope that baby isn't sickening. The dear little thing, with that soft black hair and eyes blue as forget-me-nots." The wailing stopped, and Lucy sighed. "She was hungry. I hope that's all."

"Bring Jared soon to see me," said Jennie. "Or I will walk out to your house. I want to walk for miles, Lucy, and let the wind blow all this away."

"Come out Monday, then, and don't forget your work. We'll make one of your dresses." They clasped hands again. Then Lucy went down the walk to Harmonious, and Jennie went into the house with Alick. The room was stifling with people, and no windows open to let in the reviving wind. The Highland women were all there. Two Yankee neighbors were trying to find room in the kitchen for the loaves and bowls they had brought, and Ishbel's mother was thanking them and sighing as she moved things ineffectually from one place to another. The young girls were all together, quietly weeping among themselves; the sight of each other's tears kept the fountains flowing. Mairi looked blindly at Jennie and away, as if they were strangers. It was the way she had looked for days after Calum had drowned. Roddie's parents and his wife sat in a row. The older faces were deeply rutted and gouged by grief. Ishbel was almost unrecognizable. Her eyes were swollen nearly shut, her lips raw from being bitten. She sat in a stupor, with the baby in her arms like a doll, as if with no comprehension of what had happened or what everyone was doing here.

Jennie felt like a child who had successfully played at being a grown-up until she was confronted by an adult ritual not of her choice. She wanted to run. She put her hand in Alick's arm, and they walked forward; Shonnie saw them and started to get up. His wife, Janet, smiled tearfully at Jennie, who forgot her revulsion and moved impulsively toward her. The minister must have been in another room, but now he appeared all at once before them like a little black genie out of a jar, thrusting himself between the men before they could shake hands. His eyes were like diamond points.

"You are not welcome here, Alick Glenroy, nor you, Mistress Glenroy."

"And why is that?" Alick asked in polite astonishment. The back of Jennie's neck prickled. Behind the minister the ravaged faces watched in bewilderment.

"You are having no business among us," Mr. MacArthur said. "You are a sinner. You are forsaking the faith of your fathers! They died for it, and you scoff at it. You are daring to mock God."

"I am never speaking of such things," Alick protested mildly.

"It is written in your face. Ah, laddie, listen to me," he said with a sudden change to tender pleading. "The Lord will forgive such pride if you are asking Him on your knees! He loves you; He is searching for the lost sheep; He will rejoice to be gathering you into the fold!" Tears sparkled in his eyes and ran down his cheeks. "Och, He would be weeping with joy! But *she*—" He pointed a finger at Jennie, and she jumped as if he had actually poked her with it. His voice rose and swelled. "*She* is the corrupter; *she* has led you out of the paths of righteousness!"

Shonnie pushed to his feet, and his wife reached out and took hold of the minister's coat. But he was in full cry, and there was no stopping him.

"A Sassenach woman she is, kin to the loathsome creatures who have stolen away a son, a husband, a father! And brazen she is, to be walking into this house of grief, and be defaming it by her presence. And Episcopal she is, kin of the papists who worship the Whore of Babylon. And—"

"And that will be enough," said Alick. "It is *you* who are defaming the house of grief. I will be hearing not one word more about my wife, or I will not be answering for the consequences."

Stopped in mid-crescendo, the minister was temporarily out of words, and Jennie said quickly, "Mr. MacArthur, what have I done that you should accuse me of such things? Surely you are not blaming me for what those criminals did. I *abominate* them."

"Och, it is happy I am to be telling you, Mistress Glenroy." The diamond points drilled deep, but the voice was velvet. *He's enjoying himself!* she thought, too amazed to feel insulted. "You wrought hard to corrupt a pure young widow; you were throwing her together with a sinful man."

"Tony MacKenzie a sinful man?" she asked incredulously. "That *boy*? And I certainly have *not* wrought hard to throw them together."

Alick took her around the waist and turned her toward the door. "We are leaving this place."

"He was ravening after her like a wolf after a lamb the day she first set foot on this land!" the minister shouted. "And it is you who have been urging him on in his lust!"

Alick spun around and spoke to the minister in Gaelic without raising his voice. He continued to speak at some length. It went on and on, musical as a brook, and it was only by the minister's aghast face and ashen pallor, and the gasps around the room, that she knew the content of Alick's speech was far from musical, unless it was very rough music indeed.

Alick finished. Still holding her, he walked her out of the little house. She felt touches on her free arm, on her back, and one hard squeeze of her elbow that made her look around. Anna Kate nodded vehemently at her. Jennie had time only for an unsteady little quirk of her lips before she was swept through the clustered men, who parted like the Red Sea. She heard Alick's name spoken, but he could have been both deaf and mute.

They kept the same rapid pace all the way up to Main Street. Placid amid the Saturday traffic, the cow Columbine drank from the horse trough. The sight of her was somehow comforting and restorative to Jennie, and she murmured, "Bless you, dear Columbine."

Alick hurried her across the intersection and well along Ship Street before he let her go. When he released her, he kept on walking as if he had forgotten her existence. She stood where she was, watching him go, straight as a soldier and marching to pipe music that only he could hear. Tunes of war, to be sure.

"Well, Jennie," she said, "you may as well sit down and rest your face and hands and continue home at your own pace." She found a little dip in the bank rising to the trees on her left and sat down among the oxeye daisies.

Before he reached the lane, he turned and came back to her, flushed, his eyes warmed with a very human and rueful embarrassment.

"I am sorry. Are you very tired? Shall I carry you?"

"Oh, I am perfectly well, Alick. But why were we hurrying? The devil isn't on our heels—or is he? Perhaps Mr. MacArthur had sent him after us to claim his own." She patted the turf beside her. "Sit here, and tell me what you said to him."

"I told him what he was needing to hear. But the great shame is that I said it in a house of mourning." He sat with his elbows on his knees, head and shoulders slumped forward. "I will be apologizing to them, but never to him. I am not forgiving him, ever."

She put her hand on his back and smoothed it. "He is only trying to be a good shepherd. He distrusts you because you refused to be enclosed in the fold, and he distrusts me because I am a different animal altogether. There is temptation all around in this place, and we may be the worst tempters."

He lifted his head and gave her an almost amused attention. "You are speaking very well for the wicked wee man."

"Ah, but we must be charitable, mustn't we? Even if he is not? If I were a Methodist, I could be a preacher. They allow women. Perhaps I should start a religion of my own. . . . Alick, can you see Tony as a ravening wolf?"

The spark of amusement shot out a small flare. "The poor lad would be flattered!"

Thirty-Three

JENNIE KEPT HER word to herself; she did not go to church the next day. Tom, the oldest Frost son, would be driving the barouche this Sunday, and she sent a message to him when Alick went over to help him harness the horses, to pass on to the General: Mrs. Glenroy would not be attending church this morning. Alick stayed at the stables after the carriage had left, and she prepared their dinner: beef browned and roasted in a heavy iron pot on top of the stove, with onions, slices of new turnip, and small carrots, and topped with little new potatoes for the last half hour.

It seemed indecent under the circumstances not only to be concerned with food but to be hungry while one was preparing it. The minister's attack was less than a mosquito bite in comparison with the agony inflicted on one innocent family. Remembering those faces could turn her stomach and take all the strength from her hands, and then that tiny movement would take her by surprise. A message: *I am here. Don't forget me.*

"As if I could," she once answered dolefully.

The kitchen was hot, and she stayed outdoors, going in only to tend the fire. She couldn't put her mind on her reading, and she observed the Sabbath to the extent of not sewing, so she took the wooden bowl and walked down to the orchard and gathered sweet yellow summer apples for their dessert.

The children's voices were blown to her like thistledown; they were reading Bible stories on the veranda with Eliza, who herself went to the evening church services. How peaceful it all was! A large company of orange and black butterflies hovered over the banks of goldenrod and the lavender clouds of Michaelmas daisies. Goldfinches and chickadees thronged the orchard.

God, if you are responsible for all this, I forgive you for some things, she said grandly. *But very few. If I made a list of all the crimes I do not forgive, this beauty would be of no more importance than a wisp of fog disappearing in the sun.*

Tony came to the cottage while she was setting the table and Alick was still at the stable. His face looked narrower than ever, and there were dark half-moons under his eyes. "My father sent me to see if you were well," he said grimly.

"Quite well, thank you, Tony. And thank your father. But when I arose this morning, I could not face the ordeal."

That evoked a joyless little smile. "You missed an awe-inspiring performance. The Elder was in top form. He had people who never knew Roddie MacKenzie existed until yesterday weeping and blowing their noses. Papa sat through it like a granite boulder. He has been writing letters since Friday night."

He walked around the kitchen and came to rest before the Simon Willard clock as if he'd never seen it before. He spoke to it, not to Jennie.

"I leave with my father tomorrow."

"So *soon?* I thought—"

"It was to be the week after next. But last night my father had a visitor." He ran a finger over the painted base, frowning. "Mr. MacArthur."

Ah, yes, thought Jennie. *To tell the General the Glenroys are a foulness.* "What did he have to say?"

"Papa took him into the library. I thought he wished to know if anything could be done to get Roddie back. But after he left, Papa came into the drawing room where I was playing for the girls and Eliza, and told me that I was to go with him tomorrow." His back was thin, straight, young, and vulnerable.

She was angrier with the man for this than for what he had called her. "Did he tell you what Mr. MacArthur said to him?"

"No, just that in the interests of peace and unity it would be better to go now. He was quite kind. He put his hand on my shoulder and said—" Tony's voice broke, and he pulled out his handkerchief. "He said he knew something about what I was feeling. He said such experiences were a part of growing up." He blew his nose, and Jennie felt the usual sympathetic prickle in her own nose.

Apparently Mr. MacArthur had discreetly stopped short of calling him a ravening wolf. "Well, Tony, your father is right about that," she said. "I'm sorry this had to happen, but it was bound to come. Perhaps in a few years they'll be less rigid and more trusting, and you'll be allowed to court Mairi."

"A few years! How can I think of a few years when I am not even to have five minutes alone with her to say good-bye?" He came back to the table, angrily scrubbing at his wet eyes. "I asked for it, and Papa said it was impossible. What could I do to her in five minutes? Debauch her? Get her with child?"

"We know it isn't fair, Tony," she said soothingly.

"That cruel little man, I can see him burning Roman Catholics to death or torturing harmless old women to prove they're witches!"

"I am so sorry, Tony," she said. "I wish I could make you a present of those five minutes, but I cannot."

"You can do *one* thing for me. You can give her this." He reached into the pocket of his Sunday waistcoat and brought out a red silk handkerchief. He opened the folds and took out a miniature of himself. "Will you give her this? It was done for last Christmas, and I've matured since then, I think, but it's still a good likeness. My stepmother had us all done as gifts for Papa."

She had seen the four miniatures—his sister Christian was included—on the desk in the library. "Your father will miss this."

"Then I shall tell him what happened to it."

"And your mama?"

"I will cross that bridge when I come to it. She is not likely to lower herself by making a scene and demanding it back."

"It is a good likeness," she said, "and very well done. Who painted it?"

"Hugh Evans. I wish I had one of *her*." He was cheering up. "I shall be home for Christmas unless there is absolutely no traveling on land *or* sea." He held up crossed fingers and then knocked on the table. "There, I've taken care of any evil spirits Mr. MacArthur may have hired to confound me."

"I thought people made nothing of Christmas here," Jennie said.

"Nor in Boston either," he said blithely. "Never within those harsh Puritan walls. But Mama does, and for that alone I love the woman."

She and the children saw the *Lady Lydia* off the next morning. The vessel was loaded with dried fish, early potatoes and other garden stuff, and eggs and cheeses. The children hugged their father again and again, sending embraces to their mother and the new baby, reminding him of the list of names they were sending with him. Tony was in work clothes; he was allowed to be one of the crew on the trip, but he would disembark in Boston looking like a young gentleman. He kept giving Jennie significant glances and sighing, but he seemed to be looking forward to the voyage.

No small boats were going downriver in company with the *Lady Lydia*. The shaving mill had put an end to fishing in the bay, no matter how perfect the weather was, and the fishermen on the wharf expressed their frustration in black looks or compulsive bursts of speech, saying the same thing over and over again, only the words differing. It was *their* bay, *their* codfish, *their* living, and thieves and murderers were roaming the waters like the pirates of the Caribbean. Where was the Holy Writ that said God gave the ocean to the British? Who'd won the war anyway?

"My boys, I shall do everything humanly possible," the General told them. "And so will our government."

"Meaning no disrespect to you, General," one man said, "but how can them old daddies living in high style down in Washington drive them cutthroats out of our dooryard? If *we* can't see 'em till they come at us, what's the President and the Congress aim to do from way down there?"

"By Godfrey!" said another one. "The British could send a warship up this river and put the whole town in irons, and they'd still be drinking wine and dancing at balls in Washington."

The General flushed ominously but kept his temper. "Perhaps the British will sail up the Potomac someday," he said lightly. He slapped a shoulder here, an arm there. "I know we cannot live with these conditions. And we *won't* put up with them! Trust me!"

"Good luck, General!" one man said, vigorously shaking his hand. "Might be you'll meet up with that hellish shaving mill out there today and leave 'em all good and dead."

"Well, we can always hope, can't we?" said the General. If the raider was still out there, with plenty of islets and ledges to hide behind, she'd be no threat to the *Lady Lydia* as long as the fair wind kept up to fill the coaster's sails. But if she should be becalmed, she was not helpless. She was carrying weapons today, and most of the male passengers as well as the crew could shoot.

"We'll be ready for anything!" Tony bragged to his little sisters and Jennie. She was glad to see him cheerful, if only for the moment, and she was too kind to ask him if he would be allowed a pistol.

She intended to get the miniature to Mairi as soon as possible. If she hadn't planned to see Lucy that afternoon, she'd have sought out Anna Kate, but she could do that tomorrow. She felt neither guilt nor satisfaction at outwitting the minister. It would be months before Tony was home again, and the miniature could not seduce Mairi in the meantime. By winter the romance would have doubtless passed away as painlessly as petals fell from a full-blown rose.

She had studied every precise and perfect detail of the miniature, and she could hardly believe that Hugh Evans had done this work. A figurehead was one thing. It was hewn larger than life out of a pine log, and color laid on thickly, gaudy enough to scorch the eyeballs. But this exquisite little portrait was a work of art, and it belonged to the General; someone like Alick could argue that Tony had no right to take it, and she should return it at once.

Oh, yes, Alick would disapprove of her being a go-between, even if he pitied Tony. And what if Mairi's mother found the miniature and dutifully took it to the minister? Then the fat would be in the fire. But it all came down to the promise she'd given Tony, and it was too late to take it back now without betraying him. She compromised; if she waited a few days, she might know better what to do.

Thirty-Four

J ENNIE HAD ALREADY gone once to the Clements farm, so she was
prepared for a nearly five-mile walk. The day was refreshingly cool,
bright, and dry; it brought a physical sense of well-being to alleviate the
aches and pains of the spirit. She went by Back Lane around past the
school and the master's house and up to east Main Street and the crowded
dwellings and businesses of the creek section. Across Main Street the
road to the farm led off between the Porters' establishment and the
saddler's shop and ran north along the high bank of the creek, which,
after it passed the millpond and the noisy sawmill, became Mill River,
born as a brook in the northeast distances toward the hyacinth purple
Tenby hills.

On Jennie's left the fenced and mown hayfields were turning green
again. They were divided by the track along which the oxteams came
from the woods with their loads of logs for the sawmill. Black-eyed Susans,
Queen Anne's lace, goldenrod with its attendant butterflies, and lavish
billows of mauve Michaelmas daisies bordered both the ox road and the
way to the farm.

On the right the bank dropped down through bracken and patches
of blossoming purple thistles to alders and willows. In their shade the
narrow stream was a lustrous olive green. It was bearing gradually east
of north toward its birthplace, and the road continued due north, as it
had been first cleared by an early Clements with an ax and a compass.
It ran through a grove of second-growth white pine, which seethed and
shimmered in the wind. A few old giants had been left, and a family of

crows called back and forth from their topmost branches when the alien entered their territory.

The first time Jennie had come, the pine wood seemed to go for miles, but this time she recognized individual granite outcroppings and a certain broad tree stump growing a miniature forest of its own; she knew when the next rise in the road would bring Harm Clements' house into view across the field where their animals grazed.

Their front door was flanked by the young bride-and-groom elms which had been set out when they took possession. The road led past the elms and on through orchard, cultivated fields, and woodlot to the old Clements homestead, where Harm's parents lived. They had given him a third of the farm when he married.

Jennie was thirsty but not tired, and her workbasket was no heavier than when she'd started. She hadn't felt the flutter for some time; it must have been enjoying the motion. She sometimes felt for it a resigned and whimsical indulgence, but except in surprise attacks of panic or dismay, she still saw herself and motherhood as an improbable combination.

She topped the last low rise, half expecting to see Lucy on the way to meet her with Jared on her shoulders or in the wheelbarrow, convoyed by the dog and at least one cat. Instead, she saw the doctor's gig coming at a fast clip. Anticipating her afternoon with Lucy, she didn't associate him with sickness; the black mare was a trotter best described as poetry in motion, and she waited at the side of the road to watch her go by.

Waite saw her and pulled up a little way past her. She walked back to the gig, and he lifted his hat and said solemnly, "Mrs. Glenroy."

"Good afternoon, Dr. Waite. I was admiring your mare. Is she a Morgan?"

"Yes." His gravity lightened. "Her name is Maisie." The mare pricked her ears and looked around at them.

"She knows her name, yes, she does," Jennie crooned, stroking Maisie's nose. "And a good deal more besides, I'm sure."

"Oh, yes, Maisie is a mare of great brain," he said. He fastened the reins and stepped down to the road. "Let me assist you into the seat, Mrs. Glenroy."

"But I am on my way to Lucy's," she said in surprise.

"I think you had better let me drive you home or to any place you prefer." He towered over her with a kind of paternal and immovable patience.

"Is Lucy well?" she asked sharply. He nodded. "Harmonious?"

"He's at work as usual."

Her throat had gone drier than mere thirst could make it. She had to swallow saliva before she could speak again. "Jared?"

"Jared is a little feverish," he said. "It could be teething. We will know more tomorrow."

A trembling began in her hands and legs. "Lucy must be frantic!"

"Lucy knows that children often run slight fevers for no dangerous reasons."

"I can be company for her, to help occupy her mind." Jennie turned away from the gig, but his hand closed on her elbow and gently detained her.

"Her mother is with her, Mrs. Glenroy. Let me welcome you aboard, as our seafaring men say."

To be thus turned back was both bewildering and alarming. She gripped the handles of her workbasket so hard that she saw her white knuckles, and she loosened and flexed her fingers. She had to keep licking her lips. There was no pleasure in riding behind the smooth trotter.

Without looking at her, the doctor said in his deep, slow voice, "You must not expect the worst, Mrs. Glenroy."

"But I do!" she blurted. "Because the worst is the most probable."

"It often seems that way," he agreed. They passed the loggers' road, and he waved to a man waiting at the intersection beside a team of oxen. "Ki Bisset and his brethren, Dandy and Davie," he said. "He looks like them, you know. The same full brown eyes and mild expression. The same brute strength and gentle nature."

"Dr. Waite, I am pregnant," she said. She hadn't meant to say it. He was not startled, but she was.

"How long?" he asked.

"About four months. I feel it now and then."

"You'll likely be delivering in January then. We should give ourselves some leeway, of course." His leisurely questions occupied them past the sawmill and out to Main Street. She would not have believed how eager she would be to answer them. She even admitted her fears, and he didn't insult her intelligence by brushing them off as childish or hysterical.

"But you have the advantage of good health, and you come from strong stock, and every year we discover more and more about saving lives. Your child's chances and yours are far greater than they would have been ten or fifteen years ago."

When they reached Main Street, she thanked him for his advice and the ride behind Maisie and said she would walk home from there. But when she had gotten past the school and was alone in the lane, she began worrying again, not about herself but about Jared. Of course, children had teething fevers and other small upsets; but why had the doctor kept her from going on? *We will know more tomorrow.* It sounded ominous, but there was already enough grief and woe around her without borrowing trouble. *Think about something else, Jennie,* she commanded. *For instance, the story you never even remembered all the while you were with him.*

Now she could see why this physically unprepossessing man could have won over a lonely, embittered woman without even meaning to. It would have taken time, but one day she must have realized that she couldn't do without him.

The afternoon still lay before Jennie. She took a drink of water and put the miniature, wrapped in the red silk handkerchief, in the reticule Mrs. MacKenzie had given her. Life being what it was, either Tony or Mairi could die in the next four months; why should either be cheated of the only romantic passage that might ever take place between them? And at second hand?

She went up Ship Street to the Ark. No one was outside today; the building was unnaturally quiet with the grief that was on it. Jennie mounted the steps which she had not climbed since the day Anna Kate told her she was pregnant.

Anna Kate met her with a hug. "It's glad I am to see you," she said fervently. "Your face is like a bright star in the black night of sorrow that is falling upon this place. I'll be making us some tea in my grand new American teapot." She held it up. "Is it not beautiful, just?"

"Yes, it is," said Jennie. Even with both windows open the room was very hot because a cock-a-leekie was simmering in the iron pot hung from the crane in the fireplace. But a fire also meant boiling water in the kettle on the hob, and she felt as if she could drink a gallon of tea.

"This Saturday we will be moving out to our land," Anna Kate said. "We have a tent of brush to shelter us. I will be happy to leave the mourning behind. Och, we will still be mourning," she said quickly, "but our eyes and ears will be filled with other things besides tears and the sound of woe." She set out mugs and oatcakes. "I made them this morning. With a bit of butter they are not bad," she said modestly. "Now, Jeannie, *mo chridh*, how are you? A *Dia*, the fear was at me last night about the little one! If you would be losing it, after the shock of the terrible things the minister was saying."

"Anna Kate, it is still there, and sometimes a busy little It," Jennie said.

"Och, the shame we were all having! The wee man is good, but all the young lambs must be where he can be seeing them every moment or the wolves will be at them." She couldn't resist a little grin. "Like the General's lad . . . And now the minister is not forgiving himself, with Roddie stolen away. He was encouraging Roddie to go with the fishing, you see."

"Then I am sorry for him," said Jennie, "but he had no right to attack either Alick or me."

"The grand man you have!" Anna Kate exulted. "What a hero! Mr. MacArthur was not having one word to say when you were gone. And it is not easy to stop the tongue of himself."

"Tell me what Alick said then," said Jennie. "I couldn't get it from him."

"He said he had no faith to lose until you gave it to him. Faith in himself you were giving him, which was what he was needing more than faith in Mr. MacArthur's God. He said you are a good woman who fought against the clearances, and you gave up riches and comfort, and you could corrupt nobody, least of all the children. He said he would not hear a word against you ever, and if he did, the great fear should be at the sayers, because next it would be his hands at their throats."

Jennie sank back in her chair. The sweat on her back had turned to chills delicately racing like feathers up and down her spine. Her thoughts swung in confusion between humility and pride. "Jeannie, you are white!" Anna Kate said in alarm.

"No, no, I am all right," Jennie protested. "But he does me too much honor. *He* has meant all that to me, and more, but he takes no credit."

"He would not, you see," said Anna Kate, "because it is just the way he *is*." She laughed and flung up her hands. "Will you listen to me, explaining to a woman about her man?"

He will be someone's man someday, Jennie thought. *Will she know how fortunate she is?* She took out the red silk handkerchief. "Anna Kate, will you give this to Mairi?" She showed her the miniature.

"It's the laddie himself!" Anna Kate exclaimed. "And isn't it beautiful? I am not ever seeing anything like it."

"Yes, and he wished Mairi to have it for a keepsake. Could you give it to her with no one knowing? Will she be able to keep it to herself?"

"She will be finding a way. Sheena and Donald are not always at her, and she has her own little box. What a lover he looks, with the bonny black eyes! He'll be growing into a man to break more hearts than his father ever did!" She wrapped the miniature tightly in the handkerchief and put it down her bosom. "Tonight she will be having it," she promised.

"After this," Jennie said, "I could be doing with one of your oatcakes."

Thirty-Five

SHE FELT HONORED by Alick's public defense and praise of her and proud because he believed she deserved it when she saw herself as a timorous, dithery creature. She went over and over the accolade in her mind. He couldn't know, of course; he'd have been more embarrassed than about his nightmares of the gallows and being afraid of the excise-man's ghost. Angry, too, at Anna Kate for telling her and at her for mentioning it to him. But she made up her mind to thank him when they parted and to say she would never forget it. And she would not. If he had told the truth about her—and who saw the truth with a colder clarity than Alick Glenroy?—he had given her the first sight of herself as a woman.

All week long she heard nothing about Jared, and twice she prepared to go out to the farm but lost her courage both times. The doctor had made her feel that she would be in the way. She couldn't believe Lucy would think so, but the doctor must have had his reasons. She wanted Alick to ask Harm for news of the baby, but each night he hadn't done so.

"Why?" she asked finally.

"We are not that familiar," he said maddeningly.

"Then tell me if he seems worried."

Alick shrugged. "He is as he always is." He consented to hand on a note for Harm to give to Lucy. She wrote that Dr. Waite had turned her away on Monday, but she would come as soon as Lucy gave the word. She hoped Jared's teeth were through by now.

There was no answer. But she kept expecting Lucy herself to show up at the door with Jared on her back.

On Saturday Alick spent the day helping Hector and Anna Kate to move out to their land and settle in. Eliza, who was sleeping at Strathbuie House while the family was away, took the girls to her father's farm again for the day. Expecting no interruptions, Jennie took a long bath in the wooden tub she'd excavated from that mine of treasures, the back entry. She sewed outside for a while, drying her hair in the strong late-summer sunshine. She went up on the hill and picked a bowlful of raspberries and early blackberries. Then she lay on her bed and read and napped, with the windows wide open to bring the day in. In late afternoon she went to the garden to get cucumbers and lettuce for a salad to go with a supper of cold ham and rolls, berries and cream.

When she returned to the cottage, Alick had just come back. He gave her one of his more distant nods and went out with his clean clothes, soap, and a towel. He liked to dip a bucket of water from one of the hogsheads and sluice down in the secluded angle made by the entry and house walls. She set the table, mixed a salad dressing of vinegar, olive oil, sugar, salt, and pepper, and was feeling mildly adventurous about adding sweet basil or chives when Alick came in again.

He was in a withdrawn mood, which reminded her of early days, when she thought he resented her so much that his only refuge was to shut her out.

"Is it anything you can tell me?" she asked. "Are you disapproving of the brushwood tent?"

He smiled at that. "Och, they will be snug as hares in a burrow. We built a log shelter around it with three sides and a roof."

"We must think up a housewarming present for them. What *is* at you, Alick? Mr. MacArthur again?"

"No . . . I will be winding the clock before I forget it."

"You've never forgotten it, and you wind it on Sunday morning, not Saturday afternoon," she said amiably.

He turned from the clock and faced her, looking oddly defenseless, his hands falling to his sides. She had seen that expression before, almost an entreaty for her to read in him what he could not easily say. But it lasted for only a breath or two, so she couldn't be sure she had seen it.

"You know the way to Hector's land goes out by the church," he said. "Well, when we were walking home, Wee Rory, Big Rory, Tormod and Donald and myself, there was a man digging in the churchyard. Wee

Rory has a dog now, and the young foolish thing was off into the graveyard to bark at the man, and Rory after him. He stayed to talk with the man, and he would be holding forth for an hour with the devil himself, so we went in to bring him out." His even tone suddenly jarred into a higher key. "There is no easy way to be telling you this, Jeannie! It was a very small grave he was digging."

"Oh, God, it's not Paulina Revere, is it? It can't be!"

"Jared," he said.

She frowned at him like a deaf person trying to read lips. But his expression told it all.

"No!" she shouted at him. "You heard wrong, or there's another Jared—I know there is." She glared across the room at him. "It's not our Jared. It can't be."

"Jared Arthur Clements," he said. "Ten months and twelve days."

Adding on the number of days was the worst; it summed up everything. Why did he have to say that? It was what the sexton must have told them would be on the stone. Jared had gone twelve days past his tenth month and spent five of those days in dying.

Alick moved swiftly around the table, but she dodged away and went across the hall to the parlor. She sat on the sofa before the fireplace with her hands in her lap. *Jared is dead,* she kept saying to herself. But repetition couldn't make it so, any more than it could make her see Lucy maimed by grief like Ishbel MacKenzie.

She heard Alick building a fire. *A good thing,* she thought absently. Her hands were so cold she rolled them up in her apron. They'd been cold the last time she'd seen Lucy, at the wake for Roddie. But was it a wake when there was no body? With Jared, now, it wouldn't be the same. He'd lie in the midst of it like a little sleeping prince, as he had lain sleeping on the plaid, his hands open like flowers. But he had been sick for five of his last twelve days on earth, so the small face would be different now.

Jared was dead. It came at her like a wave born of an earthquake and racing for the shore at a killing speed. She was driven deep down into chaos, blinded, deafened, and suffocated by it; whirling debris crashed against her body.

She fought her way up from the deadly smother and the spinning timbers from dead ships, and crawled clear. The next wave was in sight out there, but she wasn't waiting for it.

Alick met her in the hall with the plaid. He swathed her in it, and said, "I am making tea for you."

"Thank you. My stomach will appreciate something hot."

"I wish we had something stronger. We could be doing with a dram of whiskey distilled in the glens of Linnmore."

"Do you suppose Archie will ever have a licensed distillery?"

"He is a worse fool than I thought if he does not. The sheep will never be making his fortune. Come and warm your feet." He moved a rocking chair in front of the stove, and she sat down in it and put her feet on the oven hearth. The kettle was boiling noisily over the open flames. He removed it and replaced the stove lid.

Dry-eyed, she watched him warm the teapot. His hands were quick and neat in their movements. A cowlick stood up on his dark head when it was still damp from his nightly wash. He had two crowns, she'd discovered when she attempted to trim his hair.

He had an absorbed and studious expression as he measured tea from the caddy into the pot; there were marks like parentheses at either end of his mouth when he was preoccupied. His nose was like Nigel's and Archie's, therefore a Gilchrist nose. She had never noticed that before or the subtle family resemblance across the lower part of his face, which vanished when he moved only slightly.

He poured boiling water on the tea, and his lowered lids shuttered the entire face. Astonishing organs, the eyes. More astonishing was the power imputed to them. The windows of the soul and so forth. A squint marked a man as evil; eyes too small or too close together meant meanness, if not a criminal nature. But they could belong to a tender and greathearted woman, and steady and beautiful eyes could belong to accomplished liars. Green eyes were dangerous, but Jared's and Lucy's were green. There was a whole mythology of honor and truth about blue eyes, but Nigel had lied and lied.

She had no doubts of Alick's honesty from their first conversation on the ridge above Loch na Mada. But she had also no doubts of his secrecy. Well, if any man had a right to that, he did. Sometimes she wondered if he had reached the age of thirty without ever being in love; she doubted it because she knew he was passionate in his hatreds and loyalties. But she would never know. *I have left only graves,* he had said. His dark gray eyes told her nothing now.

Only small children and animals gazed at you with the transparent innocence which expressed exactly what lay behind it. Jared's eyes, new-birch-leaf green, fixed on his mother's face while he suckled. The small hand splayed on her breast.

"Poor Lucy," she said under her breath, and Alick said, "Poor Harmonious. He was having such pride and love for his son."

He brought her a mug of tea. "Taste it. I am not sure about the sugar and the milk."

She took a scalding sip. "It is just right, Alick. Thank you."

"When you have got half of that into you, we will eat a meal. You are needing your food."

As if in response, It moved. She said wryly, "So I am just reminded. I want to see Lucy. Will you go there with me tomorrow afternoon?"

He poured a mug of tea for himself. "The funeral is in the afternoon."

"In the morning then. . . . You know, we never wanted to make calls with my father when someone died, even someone we loved, but he always insisted upon it. He said it was our duty."

"Is it your duty now? She must be half-smothered with people; she will never miss you."

"It's a duty to friendship."

"Are you prepared to see Jared?"

She flung up her hands as if to stop a blow. "No! Please, I couldn't bear that! You're right, and I am a coward," she said.

"You are not a coward, Jeannie, and your friend would be the first to tell you to protect your own child. When it is over, that is when she will be needing you. Then you will be brave for a purpose."

"Not just for a gesture," she said. "Oh, you're right, Alick. And at this minute I'm tired enough to fall asleep in this chair. I could do it if I kept the plaid around me."

"You will not sleep before you eat," he said stubbornly. "Then you can be taking the plaid to bed with you."

"When I was homesick in London, I used to wrap up in my old robe made from Ebony's wool, and it smelled like home. The plaid smells of bracken and the hills. They seem very safe, viewed from here at this moment. No press gang, no cholera infantum."

Thirty-Six

I N THE MORNING the sun shone lividly through an oppressive ceiling of dingy cloud. There was no dew, and the wind was warm and enervating. Jennie knew she had slept heavily, yet she was still tired, and Alick looked the same. He went to the carriage house after breakfast. Benoni liked the shelves and wanted more, he said.

Soon after that Eliza came from Strathbuie House; she'd left the girls in the garden picking flowers under the grudging eye of Truelove Adams. He came on Sundays only when he suspected a robbery was about to happen. The General had been freely sending flowers to all the recent burials, for both old and young, and Truelove was on the *qui vive*.

"He'll do all right by the girls, but he won't give them any roses," Eliza said. "The General had to be real sharp with him to get a few; you'd think he was being asked to cut down his own children. Are you going to the funeral this afternoon, Jeannie?"

"No, I—you might as well know why, Eliza; it will be showing soon enough." She blushed, but Eliza's rawboned face mellowed with concern.

"If that's what you want, I am pleased for you, I reckon," she said doubtfully. "Always seems like a mighty risky business to me. Well, you shouldn't be squeezed into a crowded house, and in this weather, too. It's all a body can do to draw a decent breath. But would it be taking advantage if I left the girls with you while I go with the Frosts?"

"No, I would be happy to have them," Jennie said truthfully. She did not want to be alone while the funeral was going on.

Eliza brought Sukey and Frank to the cottage in the early afternoon. Their bouquets of sweet william, sweet peas, bachelor's buttons, pansies, and candytuft were frilled with white alyssum and tied up with their favorite sashes. Sukey's was salmon pink and Frank's was lavender. "They were frantic to give *something*," Eliza explained, "and I thought, *Why not?* They've enough ribbons and sashes to fit out every girl in Maddox five times over."

"Nabby's going to the funeral," Frank said bitterly. "And we can't."

"She'll be thinking she's a real grown-up and we are mere infants," said Sukey.

"Never mind Nabby," Eliza said. "You two mind your failings now, and don't make Mrs. Glenroy sorry she is giving up her Sunday afternoon to you." She was already blotched with the heat, her bony forehead shining with sweat, and her dark dress, black shawl, and gloves made her look hotter. She had taken the trimming off her bonnet and sewed on a black ribbon.

They all saw her off, carrying the bouquets, at the gate into the lane. Jennie wondered what to do with the girls; some quiet reading aloud seemed indicated in this smothering weather, but they were preoccupied with funerals and were not to be cheated. They had graves of their own to visit. There was a family pet cemetery fenced off at the far end of the pasture. "And *we* have been to funerals," Frank said belligerently. "When we buried Topaz and Baby Fluff." She added in a whisper, "And Jet. She was Oliver's mama." Both girls looked guiltily at Oliver, who lay on his back, cooling his belly.

"We can go there and show you," Sukey said, "but we have to go by the land and climb over the wall because Oliver can't go through the pasture. Prince and Nixie kick him." The pet cemetery was a secluded little enclave where the lane made a sharp curve to become the street that led down around the waterfront. There was no sense of a roadway outside the wall; the spot was surrounded by spruces and resembled a miniature alpine meadow. Getting Oliver inside was accomplished by telling him to put his front paws on the wall; then the three humans hoisted up his hindquarters. He jumped down on the other side and crawled into the slightly cooler gloom under the spruces. The girls pulled up their dresses and scrambled over. Jennie sat on the wall and lithely swung her legs from the outside to the inside.

The stones were small slabs of slate, with names and ages neatly scratched in by Tony. "Tony does *beautiful*," Frank said. "There's Topaz; she was Mama's cat, and she didn't like children."

"And there's Tyke." Sukey picked it up. "He was a little dog Tony and Christian had. And there's—" A quick glance at the oblivious Oliver, and another whisper. "The tall stone is for Jet."

"And here," said Frank tremulously, "is Baby Fluff." Baby Fluff had died only this spring. Frank wiped her eyes on her pinafore, and Sukey used her handkerchief.

She put it back in her pocket, sniffed a few times, and said, "Now we will put new flowers on."

They scurried cheerfully around, picking late-summer wild flowers, which Jennie tied into nosegays with long strands of grass. The interlude was surprisingly peaceful, laying the balm of memory on her sore spirit. She and her sisters had been exactly like this, decorating their pets' graves.

Sukey was arranging Queen Anne's lace at the base of Jet's stone. Frank climbed up on the wall beside Jennie and looked up at the sky, squinting against the difficult light. Then she said thoughtfully, "Jared's really up there now, isn't he? With all the other babies?"

"Yes," Jennie said.

Sukey sat back on her heels. "Liza says it's not fair, and she is glad now she never got married and had young ones. She says being an old maid has saved her a mort of trouble. She says the first summer is a murderer. *We* got by it all right, but we were lucky, she says."

"It strikes the rich *and* the poor," Frank said in a rush to share center stage. "And God sends it. He really does."

"I don't call that being a Loving Father," said Sukey. "Mrs. Glenroy, did you know that God doesn't answer all prayers?"

"Well, how could He?" Frank demanded. "When you think how many prayers are flying up there all the time, like millions of snowflakes falling up instead of down, and He can't hear more than one at a time, can He, Mrs. Glenroy?"

"Well—"

"Then, if He can't hear everybody's prayers, what did He make so many people for?" asked Sukey.

"I don't know how to answer that, Sukey," Jennie said.

"Maybe that's what God thinks sometimes?" Sukey's dark eyes begged for hope.

"I'm sure He does," Jennie answered. "I'm sure He does the best He can."

"Which is all anyone can do," said Sukey virtuously.

Jennie wondered if the funeral was over yet; she ached for it to be over, but for whom? Each hour that took Lucy and Harm farther away from the time when Jared was alive must be worse than the preceding one. It was not the business of closing a book and beginning a new one. Too much of themselves was going into the ground with Jared.

"Are you sad, Mrs. Glenroy?" Frank put a grimy hand on her knee.

"Yes, I am sad, Frank," Jennie said.

Frank's eyes filled with tears. "I am, too, for all the little babies. It's like the time when Baby Fluff died. He was so tiny; he had never even had much fun yet!" The last word came out in a wail, and she bunted her head against Jennie's arm. Jennie stroked her coppery hair.

"But he had love, didn't he? All his little life, he was loved."

"Yes, we loved him," Sukey said aggressively. "But he died. And we prayed like everything. I could have told God how to answer us if He'd only listened. But He never heard."

"And Mama said the way we carried on and made ourselves sick, we couldn't have another one until we're older. But now we have a little brother," Frank said, "and he has hair just like mine and Papa's, and he is *very* healthy."

"So I hear," said Jennie. "Well, I am ready for milk and cake. Is anyone else?" Oliver sprang clumsily to attention and made them all laugh.

Eliza had left a Boston Favorite cake when she brought the girls. They wanted to fetch Alick from the stables to have some with them, but Jennie saved him from that by saying he was too busy to be disturbed. "Sukey just *adores* the way he bowed to us," Frank said, "the night when everybody came for music, but there wasn't any except Mr. Porter and Tony practicing."

"You liked it, too!" Sukey retorted. "And Eliza says anybody can tell Mr. Glenroy is a gentleman."

"He will be pleased to hear that," said Jennie. "I'll tell him someday when he is feeling low in spirits."

Eliza came in carrying her shawl and fanning herself with her bonnet. Her dress was wet under the arms and between her shoulder blades, and her face more blotched than before, with crying and the heat. Her nose was raw around the nostrils from being blown so much.

She asked to wash her face and hands, and when she came to the table, she looked both cooler and calmer. She had a cup of cold milk and a slice of cake while the children pelted her with questions she refused to answer.

"Yes, they know the flowers are from you, and that's all I'm going to tell you," she said flatly. "It's over. For the rest of us anyway. Not for them, poor souls."

"Did Nabby like it?" Sukey pestered, and Eliza recoiled with such horror that Sukey was abashed.

"*Like* it! It was not a lawn party or a picnic! Nabby wished she never went. She cried so hard at the grave her mother had to take her away. She's in bed now with an upset stomach and a blinding headache. And I will *not* have any more questions."

Thunder growled and prowled in the west, promising a long, slow approach and an attack at midnight. The children were looking forward to it. Only the adults tacitly shared the thought of a cloudburst's savaging the flowers on a new small grave.

Eliza and the children left, and when their voices died away, Strathbuie House could have been far across the river. In the motionless air and the usual Sabbath hush the village might not have existed, except for a distant dog and the Frost cows wanting to be milked. Columbine's voice had a peculiar timbre all its own.

Jennie walked to the stables in an oppressively gray light that bore down on the head and eyelids like a burden. The birds were quiet. Alick was whistling in the loft of the carriage house, the absentminded and desultory music of a man content with what he was doing. She let herself in the side door and went around the barouche, the gig, and the sleigh, to the ladder that led up to the loft. She waited at the foot, reluctant to surprise him in this zone of privacy he had made for himself; it didn't seem quite right. She compromised.

"Alick, I am coming up!" she called. "Or don't you want me to?"

Absolute silence. *He is probably cursing to himself,* she thought. She wanted to slink away without another word, but the incident had to be properly ended. "No, I shan't come up," she called. "I'm just out for a walk. Forget I was here."

"No, wait!" She heard him cross the floor to the opening. He dropped to his heels and looked down at her. "Do you need help on the ladder?"

"Good heavens, no. Do you mean I am welcome, or have I boxed you in?"

"It is six of one and a half dozen of the other," he said resignedly. He took her arm and helped her out onto the floor of the loft. One side was given over to the usual spare tackle and gear appropriate to a carriage house. On the other side a long workbench ran under the eaves. The first thing she saw on it was a cradle.

She went slowly to it and ran her hands over the hood and the sides. The maple had been smoothed to the feel of satin inside and out and underneath, nowhere slighted. She looked around at Alick, and he colored deeply as if he'd been caught at something.

"You were not to be seeing it until it is finished." He almost stammered.

"Oh, Alick, I need to be seeing it *now*! It is so beautiful. I have never seen anything so beautiful." She couldn't stop stroking it, and her touch set it to rocking. "The balance is perfect. You are an artist."

He reached out and stopped the motion. "Never be rocking an empty cradle," he said. She went so cold she knew she must have gone white. Dismay slashed across his face.

"It was a bad thing to say at this time, but it doesn't mean what you are thinking."

"What does it mean then?"

"Only that the old folk believed the fairies would be tempted by a cradle rocking before the baby is born and put one of their own weans in it. Now, what is bad about that?" he asked, smiling.

"What would anyone do with a fairy's wean?" she asked, to do her part.

"Take it out to the nearest fairy hill and leave it in the heather; they would come for it as soon as your back was turned."

"I suppose," she said, "that anyone who attempted to raise a fairy child would be asking for trouble." She smiled and turned back to the cradle again. Lucy had begun piecing a cradle quilt when Jennie didn't know where the cradle would come from. *The father is always glad to build the cradle,* Lucy had said, on what was in retrospect an idyllic day. *This baby's father is dead,* Jennie had silently answered.

She doubled over the workbench and wept for the first time since Jared died. Alick put his arms around her. "Jeannie, I am sorry," he kept whispering.

She backed off and glared at him through tears. "Why? Because you made such a handsome cradle? I love the cradle, Alick! But suddenly everything came down on me. . . . I must look a fright. What can I blow my nose on?" She looked distractedly around her. She saw a stained linen smock dropped over some spare wheels and snatched it up and wiped her face and blew her nose.

"There," she said defiantly. "I'm nothing if not dainty."

He laughed outright. "I was never accusing you of that!"

"The storm's over." She grinned weakly. "The one out there is still to come." She nodded at the plum-dark west. "But mine is over and gone."

"No rage at God this time?"

"What is the sense of that? What happens happens, whether it's good or evil. I was sure of that a long time ago, and today Frank corroborated me. Though she says God is too busy. I call it indifference, and I like it much better than seeing His hand in everything." She touched the cradle with a finger. "Lucy was piecing a cradle quilt for me. But something happened. Who is to blame this time? No one! It makes life simpler. At least I will not be complicating my natural anxieties by wondering what next to expect from God."

"Are these anxieties having to do with the child?" he asked.

"Oh, Alick, it's a fearsome thing to become a mother," she said ruefully. "I shall be anxious from the moment it draws its first breath. But when I'm at home and close to my sister, I will be much braver. She's been through it three times. Besides, I have such a powerful belief that home is safer than anywhere else, I can almost feel that my faith in it will be my armor." She smiled as if to ridicule herself, but he left the bench and stood looking out the open window, his hands braced on either side of the frame.

"Is it starting to rain?" she asked. He shook his head.

"It's time to think of supper. Are you coming now?"

"No, I have a little more work to do here. I will see you down the ladder first." He came away from the window and went past her to the head of the ladder, his face and manner impersonally polite. "I will be going down just ahead of you."

"You needn't. I have been up and down ladders all my life."

"Just the same, I am preferring this way," he said stiffly. His cool distance baffled but didn't disturb; it was Alick being Alick.

Thirty-Seven

JENNIE WROTE a note to Lucy that night, to send by Harm. It was a short, affectionate message, not draped with condolences like black crepe, but asking if she could come out to the farm. Lucy needn't trouble herself to write back; Harm could tell Alick whether it was yes or no. Harm simply shook his head at Alick the next morning.

Jennie waited a week and tried again. The answer was the same. Harm said nothing these days except what was necessary at work. He was a painstaking craftsman who had always seemed to love what he touched, but now, even though he was as meticulous as ever, he went through the days like a clockwork man, wound up and set in motion. This was Alick's figure of speech. It came to him when he was winding the clock.

"He is wearing the flesh off his bones, and when the spring breaks, no one will be ever winding him again."

"Alick, that's gruesome," Jennie objected.

"You should be seeing him! The woman is killing him with her sorrow."

"Lucy carried that child for nine months; she bore him; she fed him from her breast—"

"Is it only *her* grief? Has his father no right to mourn with her?"

"Yes, of course he has, but how can you tell they aren't grieving together?" Jennie asked.

"Because it would be different," Alick said stubbornly. "He would not be wearing away before our eyes. *A Dia*, it takes the heart out of

223

you to be seeing it day after day. The man's *alone*, Jeannie. He is lonelier than I ever was."

His fiery compassion touched her. "I have a mind to go out there someday soon, invited or not," she said.

"It's a long distance to go to be turned away at the door," Alick commented. "You'd better be taking a *strupak* with you."

Eliza helped her finish one of her new dresses; the first two were too snug for her now. She had half-boots made for the colder weather ahead, and the Misses Applegate made her a rust woolen cloak with a hood. The first frosty mornings in September convinced Alick he should have a coat, but it was a workman's coat, made for service, not for style.

The Applegates treated her like a favorite niece who had been traveling around the world for a year. Without an outright mention of pregnancy they managed to convey with the utmost delicacy that they were accustomed to dressing ladies attractively through the ninth month.

"Caps are the secret, my dear Mrs. Glenroy," said Miss Helena. "The prettier the better, and dainty scarves and frills about the neck. They take the attention, you see."

Miss Louisa showed her bolts of merino and warm but light broadcloth. If nothing suited her, they were expecting more goods when the *Paul Revere* returned. Perhaps she'd step in then and have a cup of tea and view the selection.

"Perhaps," Jennie agreed. "But I must be honest with you, I cannot afford a large wardrobe." She did buy some lambs' wool underwear that would expand with her; she remembered Aunt Higham putting lambs' wool drawers in the top of her trunk, saying she would need them the instant she arrived in Scotland. These recollections were not so poignant now; too much had happened to dull the edges. She didn't allow herself to dwell on Nigel as the child's father; this lively and growing creature seemed to have nothing to do with him, or her either. It hadn't asked to be conceived, and she had a duty toward it, but she didn't think she had any of the proper maternal feelings and tender anticipations which made the difference between emotional motherhood and the purely biological process.

The General, wife, and new son were expected home on a Saturday in late September, when the *Lady Lydia* returned from her weekly Boston run. Jennie and Eliza took the children down to the wharf to meet them.

It was a pretty day, entirely suitable for the ceremonial arrival. The only sour faces around the wharf belonged to the fishermen who had not been able to go out in the bay for fear of the shaving mill, and that was where the big schools of codfish swam.

Wee Rory in kilt, sporran, and plaid piped the new baby ashore to a tune composed and named in his honor: "Allan MacKenzie's Reel." After the first congratulations were over, and the barouche had taken Mrs. MacKenzie and the baby home, the General announced to the disgruntled fishermen that a private cutter with a cannon mounted in her bows had blown a shaving mill to hell in Muscongus Bay. A body had washed up on a beach later and answered to Aldric Frost's description of the leader of the press gang: a man wearing one of the old-style pigtails and with a white scar like a lightning flash across his forehead.

On Monday they could go out into their own bay again; given a half-decent fall without too many gales, the stocks of dried fish would rise before winter set in.

It was too early to hear from any of his letters yet, but the General was keeping up the barrage. Powers in Washington were writing, and in England even Members of Parliament were demanding satisfaction from the Admiralty; the press gangs were harassing not only Americans but British fishermen and seamen as well.

Jennie and Alick stayed at the wharf long enough to hear this and then left to eat their delayed dinner. Jennie thought she was safe from confrontation until Monday, but as she and Alick were coming up by the store, Hannah called to them from the front gate of the mansion grounds. She was still wearing her Boston bonnet, with a curly white plume that thrashed madly in the wind and a stylish new coral red pelisse, and she had a new manner to match. She came saucily across the road, looking them up and down as if she were in the hiring business but found the material very poor.

"Madam wishes you to come to her *at once*," she said saucily to Jennie, and went back to the gate with a pronounced and impudent swing of the derrière.

"Is this not your free day?" Alick asked.

"It's not an ordinary occasion," Jennie said. "Mrs. MacKenzie must have received the news the instant she entered the house. So we'll have the business quickly over and done with." She put her arm through his. "Come, take the shortcut through the grounds."

He held her hand for a moment at the back door. "You are not worrying?"

"No! I only wish that *we* had a nice cozy little brush house to move into." She laughed. "Eat without me if you want to be going on to Hector's."

The girls were having their dinner in the kitchen, babbling ecstatically about Allan Robert's tiny fingernails, long eyelashes, and his white cloak and hood edged with swansdown. Upstairs Mrs. MacKenzie was giving Allan Robert *his* dinner. She half lay on the chaise longue, wearing a new peignoir of thin Florence satin in her favorite capucine color, against which the baby's hair paled to gilt. She seemed to bask in a new complacency and satisfaction. She smiled lazily at Jennie but didn't speak until she had finished feeding her baby and handed him over to Hannah. "Put him in a nest of pillows on Tony's bed," she told the girl.

"I thought the girls' cradle would do," she said to Jennie, "but my father insisted on supplying a wonderful creation for his newest grandson. No royal baby has anything better. They haven't brought it up from the boat yet." She walked around the room, touching one thing and another in the pleasure of reunion; when she came to her cheval glass, she admired herself with candid enjoyment, turning sidewise and running her hands over her flat abdomen. "I feel positively reedlike. It seems as if I carried that enormous child for *years*. I have a whole new wardrobe, and no Society to admire it. . . . Please lay off your cloak, Mrs. Glenroy; it's very warm in here. I don't intend to keep you long, but I'd like a quick report on the children, and I have a book for you."

She was talking to Jennie's reflection in the mirror as she contemplated herself. Jennie dropped off her cloak and stood waiting, until Mrs. MacKenzie's voice stopped in midflow.

"*This* I didn't know," she drawled. She turned to face Jennie. "One would expect—but no, Colin would not notice until you were out to *here* and about to deliver on the drawing-room carpet. When will it be?"

"In January."

"Well, sit down, sit down!" She sank into the familiar pose on the chaise longue. "Congratulations, I suppose. Did you know this before I left? Don't you think that your employer had the right to know?"

"I knew there was something wrong," Jennie said. "But I thought it was because of the strain of the sea voyage, the whole dislocation of my life. I kept thinking that good food and being settled in one place would correct the trouble."

Mrs. MacKenzie watched her from under her lids. "That could have been it, of course." She sounded distant.

"Would you like me to continue until the end of the quarter?" Jennie asked. "There is a week left. The children haven't noticed anything yet, but if they do, I can say I am growing fat. That's what they thought about you."

"Oh, Lord!" Mrs. MacKenzie threw back her head and laughed. "Between the village school and a pregnant governess there is no contest, as long as she is a *married* pregnant governess. Are you well enough to teach the next quarter? That takes us till Christmas, and then we shall see."

"I'm very well," Jennie said, knocking on wood.

"You look it. Pregnancy becomes you. The General will pay you at the end of this month, then, for the next quarter. Now tell me, what do you have ready?"

"Not much. Lucy Clements and I were to make things together, but I don't see her since—"

Mrs. MacKenzie broke in. "Yes, yes, I know. Dreadful tragedy. They all are! Now, there is no need of your putting out money on infants' things. I will have plenty for you. Allan Robert is already growing out of his first dresses, and by the time your child is born you'll have enough for its first six months. I shall have the girls' cradle brought down for you."

"I have a cradle," Jennie said. "My husband has made one."

"How nice," the General's wife said benignly. "I suppose he is expecting a son?"

"We will be satisfied with whatever comes."

"That is what they all say, my dear, but a man thinks his manhood is incomplete if he doesn't father a son. Well, I have done my duty, I have produced a son, and that's the end of it. I loathe being pregnant, and I shan't become so again. But neither do I intend leaving my husband's bed." She lay back, stretching and smiling. "There are ways, my dear, and I don't mean drinking some foul brew concocted by a witch or an Indian. When you wish to know, come to me. . . . Now, about dresses. If you are not too proud, some of mine can be altered to fit you.

Eliza does well at that. It's a bad enough time, the last few months, without having to wear the same dreary dresses over and over."

"I'm not too proud," said Jennie. "Thank you very much." Now she wanted to rush to the cottage and tell Alick they were safe. "The children are doing very well. I think you'll be pleased."

"So Colin tells me. I've brought them some new books, among other things. One is *Tales from Shakespeare* by Charles and Mary Ann Lamb. And here is yours. It might amuse you this weekend, and then you can tell me if it's interesting or not." She handed it across to Jennie: *Coelebs in Search of a Wife*, by Hannah More. "I've brought my husband a new edition of that vulgar favorite of his, Robert Burns. I expect I shall be quoted to death for weeks to come."

"Thank you for my book; I can hardly wait to get to it," Jennie said. She stood up and put on her cloak. "How is Tony liking college?"

"Scholastically he is still afloat. Socially—" She chuckled. "My nieces are keeping him very well entertained. He has never been so surrounded by girls in his life. There are times when he looks as if he wants to cut and run, but in a year the country bumpkin will be quite the young blade."

Alick had heated the clam chowder but had waited for her. Mrs. Frost had given her a loaf of gingerbread when she left, and they finished off with that. There was an air of quiet celebration about the meal. "With so many horrible things going on," Jennie said, "I hadn't had much time to worry about Mrs. MacKenzie, but it was there just the same. She was an unknown quantity to me."

"At the first I was thinking the lady a second Christabel," said Alick.

"She is too down-to-earth for that, for all her oddities, and she is thinking you are a mysterious aristocrat," said Jennie mischievously.

Alick went with some of the other men to help Hector again, and Jennie went to Main Street to collect her new shoes; she met Mrs. Dalrymple in the shoemaker's shop and gracefully fended off an invitation to tea with a promise that she surely would come before the snow flew. When she returned to the cottage, a thick letter waited on the kitchen table, propped against her stoneware jug of Michaelmas daisies and small branches of wild rose with wine red leaves and orange red hips.

The letter was addressed to her in care of Philip Musgrave, the General's agent in New York. The sender was Mrs. William Farrar.

Sylvia's handwriting. Jennie kissed it, and her eyes filled with tears but only for that moment. She put the letter down and built the fire and pushed the teakettle over the flames. She hung up her cloak and set her new shoes on the stairs. Then she sat down in one rocking chair and propped her feet up in the other and read her letter.

They had received both her letters. The assurances came first, so she would know at once that they loved her and believed her and knew that one day soon they all would be talking together, and everything would be made clear to them.

There has been no word from Scotland. Your two trunks arrived by carter early in June, padlocked. They will be put away safe and dry until you arrive. What a strange woman Mrs. Archie Gilchrist is! She has written nothing. What are we meant to *think?* Needless to say, we shall let sleeping dogs lie.

Sad news from the Highams. They have had to give up Brunswick Square and move out to Uncle Higham's old home in Sussex, because one of the partners has defrauded the other two and decamped with a fortune and his mistress to Virginia. The firm may recover, but it will be a dreadfully slow convalescence, and meanwhile, they must make every penny do the work of five. I must say that Aunt Higham will know how to do it if anyone can. They have been too distraught to notice that you haven't written; all our news of them comes in Charlotte's letters to Sophie, and *she* thinks you are too busy and happy and in love to write. She told Sophie that old Lady Clarke died of a stroke some time ago, and Nigel's mother went back to the country a few days after the wedding, so the Highams have not had even indirect contact with the Gilchrists. If they know nothing of what has happened, no one here will tell them.

I feel a great sorrow for Lady Geoffrey. I hope you are recovering from yours. You are young, and it was such a short period in your life, though a tragic one. We believe in you, my darling Jennie, and we are proud that you are holding your head up. I have written to Ianthe and sworn Sophie to secrecy. I am afraid she thinks it is all very romantic and envies you your

adventures. Now she intends to be a novelist and weave you into
a story. William has provided her with a thick new notebook, a
bottle of his own ink, and a supply of pens. As long as she is
writing about it, she won't be tempted to talk about it to the
other Hawthornes.

William wrote:

Dearest Jennie,

I advise you to keep a journal. It would be healthful for you
to concentrate on recording the new scenes about you, and in
years to come you will be glad of it. Observe and sketch the
American birds and plants; your father would not want you to
ignore this rich opportunity, after his initial distress at the cause
of it. I am assuming that you are able to obtain watercolors. Local
customs and idioms would interest me very much. You are wise
to make the most of this situation into which circumstances have
thrust you.

Your courage, generosity, and strong sense of responsibility
for this man's safety are a credit to the family and, I may add,
typical of you. We pray for your safe return to us when your errand
is accomplished.

He ended with news of each of the children, the dogs, and the horses,
and with all their love.

She was gulping with sobs by the time she had finished. She could
hear them; she could see them. She wanted Sylvia's soft, abundant
motherliness and William's hard tobacco-scented chest, and it didn't
seem as if she could wait.

She had done what had to be done; they saw and trusted her reasons
for it. Now she was to look forward, not back, and make meticulous
records of her surroundings. Who but William would say this? Unless it
was Papa. He'd have exhorted Lucifer to observe all the constellations
and planets during the plunge to hell which lasted seven days and seven
nights. Papa would call it a God-given opportunity that shouldn't be
wasted.

*Lucifer. Nigel. "How thou are fallen from heaven, O Lucifer, son of the
morning!"*

All signs of tears were gone when Alick came home. She was inordinately proud of William and Sylvia when she read the letter to him. "You have a very loving family," he said. "And a loyal one. It is no wonder that you are missing them."

"But I am done with whining," she said. "I will be seeing them soon enough, and I don't intend to wail and gnash my teeth from now until then."

Thirty-Eight

JARED WAS THE LAST child to die of the cholera infantum; the invisible Moloch was finally satisfied.

The General had brought Paulina Revere a silver mug and porringer from Mr. Revere, and he gave her family his promise that neither he nor the government in Washington would give up attacking the lords commissioners of the British Admiralty until they would think they were caught in a swarm of furious bees and would be forced in self-defense to take action.

There were only a few families left in the Ark now, spreading out comfortably into more rooms. Mr. MacArthur held services there, and the General was promising land for a church and a parsonage as soon as there should be an administrative body to hold the deed. Mr. MacArthur was reluctant to organize a church.

"The wee man likes it fine the way it is," Alick commented. "He is having them all under his thumb."

But Mairi had the miniature from Anna Kate, and Mr. MacArthur didn't know about it.

The evenings were drawing in, though there were days of summer heat. Jennie basked in these, but she looked forward to night, when she would put her feet up and read or sew by candlelight while Alick studied. Sometimes they read aloud to each other; he was becoming good at it, and the Highland cadences of his voice were pleasing to her.

She bought a pack of playing cards at the stationer's and taught him all the two-handed games she knew; he hadn't grown up with cards, which his grandmother called the Devil's Prayerbook. She borrowed the

General's cribbage board for him to copy, and he made one from a piece of maple left over from the cradle.

He was now studying penmanship and composition in addition to mathematics and history. Oliver had stopped going with him; the new baby required most of the dog's attention. On the nights when Jennie was alone, with the fire and the clock for company, an increasingly active child, and a persistent owl outside, it was hard to imagine that ten minutes away Strathbuie House was full of light, and the General and his wife were entertaining after the summer hiatus.

It was nearly impossible to believe that the town was teeming with the Male and Female Debating societies, the Temperance Society, and the Male Glee Club, conducted by Liam O'Dowda. Later the Singing School for both sexes would enliven the winter evenings. There were weekly prayer meetings with Elder Mayfield, the Female Reading and Uplift Club, and two rival sewing circles. The annual chess tournament began. The group that met all year round to play music commenced a season of Bach.

Some of the young married couples, headed by Albion Hardy, were organizing a dramatic society. Lucy had told Jennie that after New Year's a dancing master always came and boarded with Mrs. Loomis; the young people (and some light-footed older ones) would learn the newest steps and polish up what they already knew. The bachelors liked to get up dances and suppers; they hired the ballroom on the third floor of the inn.

Sometimes she imagined Maddox at night spinning around her in a sparkling whirlpool of singing, argument, exhortation, and laughter; but when she walked in moonlight or starlight to the Necessary, she heard only the owl and the scurry of something running away. This didn't frighten her, now that she'd actually seen raccoons. But otherwise, the cottage could have been alone on a Northumberland hillside or in a Highland glen.

She was not troubled by superficial yearnings for a lively social life; in her situation it was impossible anyway. But the thought of the dancing disturbed her like a sensitive tooth, which doesn't bother if only you can keep your tongue away from it. She had always loved to dance, and the heavier she grew, the more she danced in her head to music she hummed or sang. With remembered partners she danced the Lancers, a Roger de Coverley, a schottische, the new and daring *valse*. Her partner was never Nigel.

She did it because she couldn't help it, but she would be quickly weighed down with a leaden depression. Lucy loved to dance, as she did, and had pranced the length of the room with her shears in her hand, showing her how the Portland Fancy went. She'd talked about coaxing Harm and Alick to a dance, and Jennie said she'd never seen Alick dance. Perhaps he didn't know how.

"But you can teach him!" Lucy believed anything was possible; most Americans did. "After the baby is born, by March you could go. Promise me, Jennie! They always have a St. Patrick's dance, but it's really to celebrate the time Washington scared the British away from Boston."

"I can't promise for Alick!" Jennie had protested, laughing.

"But promise me you won't forget we talked about it. You won't know about him until you try. He may be a jim-dandy John Rogers dancer!"

Afterward Jennie had thought with a very real sadness that when she was able to dance, she would be able to travel; the sadness was for deserting Lucy, who thought she had made a friend with whom she would knit stockings for their grandchildren.

Now Lucy had deserted *her*, so she could walk away without feeling like a traitor. But she couldn't stop missing her. There was no one but Lucy to whom she could talk about her pregnancy the way she needed to; she wanted Lucy to see the cradle; she wanted to hear Lucy's gossip and hear her giggles. Selfish wishes, but as real as hunger. And then there was the very real deprivation of not being allowed to mourn with Lucy.

While she was darning one of Alick's stockings one night, and he was reading aloud from Hannah More's novel, she made up her mind that she would see Lucy. She would have a good topic to break the ice: Alick needed new stockings before winter, and she had never knit a man's stockings in her life. She could buy yarn at the dry goods shop; she'd seen some hanks of white worsted there the day she bought flannel for napkins; it was spun by a woman who had a small sheep farm on the River Road.

"Are you *really* liking this book?" Alick asked, startling her.

"You needn't suffer with it anymore," she said. "I must finish it because it was given to me, but I'll skim."

The next afternoon she went up to Main Street to buy the yarn, and while she was in the shop she saw Zeb Pulsifer ride by on horseback. It was an unpleasant surprise; she had hardly thought of him for weeks.

"Somehow I thought he'd never escape from under all those in-laws," she told Alick that night.

"Mr. Muir let him go from the quarry a week ago," Alick said. "He was already giving him two warnings."

"Why didn't you tell me?"

"Why should I?" he asked reasonably. "You would only be upsetting yourself. You are now, from the sight of him riding by."

"And with good cause. He'll be up to his deviltry again. Why was he discharged?"

"He struck a lad in the quarry for making a joke about him going home to his mother. His wife had a girl, and the man was in such a rage he stayed away from her for three days. Two of his brothers-in-law dragged him away from his father's farm, with the bodach pushing him from behind and the cailleach all the while drumming her heels on the floor and screaming."

"It must have been an enchanting performance," said Jennie. "I thought you never listened to gossip."

"I was not listening, I was *hearing* while I worked. There is a difference, and it is not gossip when it is coming from the horse's mouth."

"And who is the horse?" Jennie asked.

"One of the brothers-in-law who is an outside planker at the yard. They are going to send Zeb to sea."

Jennie clasped her hands to her breast. "Oh, where is the press gang when we need it?"

Alick laughed. "It was being said they might put him in a wee boat and set him adrift at high tide one night, but that would break the wife's heart. The lass must be away with the fairies, to be breaking her heart over that one."

"Everyone to her taste, as the old lady said when she kissed the cow. How do they intend to send him to sea?"

"One of the brothers has a fishing boat. He is taking Zeb with him. He will be so tired when he comes home at night the wife will be having no trouble whatever with keeping him in."

That night she dreamed of home, and Alick woke her up because she was crying. He thought she was sick or afraid again. Surefooted on the stairs in the dark house, he brought her a cup of water and placed it carefully in her hands. She apologized formally for waking him.

"You cannot be helping what you dream. I dream, and they are not always good." He sat on the edge of the bed.

"But if you cry out, I've never heard you. You are polite even in your sleep. . . . Are they ever good dreams?"

"Och, yes. Linnmore was my home, and I loved it. It is there my dreams are often taking me."

"And is your mother alive in them?"

"Yes. And sometimes she is not."

"And you are looking for her. Or you see her in the distance and you are so glad to find her, but—" She was almost overcome; Papa's face had been so clear. "It's as if she were looking for you, too, but something came in between."

"What happened now?" he asked.

"My sisters were there, and Nelson, our pony, and we all were laughing, and I looked around and saw my father coming through the orchard. I can see the way the shadows moved over him, and he was smiling. And I thought everything else was all a dream, had never happened, and I was waking up at home. I ran to him, and he held out his arms—" Her voice broke. She scrubbed her sleeve across her eyes. "And he disappeared."

"Not all your dreams end in weeping. Sometimes I hear you call out, 'Sophie, come!' and you are laughing."

"Do I wake you up?" she asked. "You need your sleep. I shall shut my door."

"You don't disturb me," he said. "And if you cry out, you need to be wakened."

"It's been just a year since my father died, and that must be what made this dream. Regardless of William's words, I have no sure and certain hope of the resurrection, except in my dreams or if someone dreams of me after I'm dead. Alick, if I die having this baby, and it lives, Anna Kate would take care of it, I'm sure, but when it is strong enough, will you find a way to send it to Sylvia? The General will know someone who would be traveling to England and care for it on the way."

He stood up. "You will be carrying your own child back to England." His voice had no expression. "You will be living to a great old age, and all this will become a dream you hardly remember."

"No," she answered. "If I do live, Alick, until the end of my life I will always have one dream to wake me in tears. For the best and closest friend I can never see again."

"Lucy."

"No. Alick Gilchrist."

He left the room without speaking. She heard the creak of one particular step and then the quiet closing of a door. She thought he had gone out to the Necessary, but she fell asleep before he came back, and when she went downstairs in the morning, the breakfast was ready, and he had eaten and gone.

She suspected that he had not gone back to bed again, and she thought it was because she had broken his night's sleep and he hadn't been able to go back to it.

Thirty-Nine

THE OCTOBER DAY was a return to summer; Jennie saw it as a good omen, a mantle of hot sunshine flung over the tawny and fiery maples and yellow-leaved elms. There were still Michaelmas daisies along the Clements farm road, and the bracken was still green on the river side. The mountain ash fruits, or rowanberries, hung in thick orange-red clusters where the birds had not yet eaten them. The air was pierced by the cheeky calls of blue jays and the smaller, more endearing voices of the chickadees among the alders along the riverbank. The crows were still the raucous guardians of the white pines and let her know they'd seen her and would be watching her every step of the way through the grove.

Her skin tightened with gooseflesh when she went into the shade, not because of the abrupt change from the heat, but with her involuntary expectation of meeting the doctor's gig like some phantom equipage forever traveling this road.

She met nothing except a red squirrel, which ran across the road and up the first pine he came to and swore at her in his native tongue. From the last rise everything looked the same, except for the autumn colors. Sheets had been spread out to dry and bleach on the grass at the western side of the house. A small black figure walked among them; it had to be Lucy, wearing the dark clothing she'd always hated. "Mourning is abominable!" she'd said when Jennie told her Papa had told them never to go into black for him.

Her dog made the rounds with her. He was a medium-sized, rough-coated black-and-white mongrel about whose intelligence she used to

brag, and Jennie wondered if she talked to him, if not to her husband.
The way he kept step with her and stopped when she did made it probable.
They went on beyond the sheets and into the apple orchard, moving in
and out of shadow.

Jennie took a long breath and exhaled slowly, watching the two
faraway figures. Then she went forward.

Seen close, the house gave off desolation; Lucy's flower beds were
sorry ruins. Jennie was picking her way around the sheets when the dog
saw her from the edge of the orchard and set up his view halloo. He
came like a black-and-white streak and pulled up short about twenty feet
from her, huffing and bristling.

"Henry, Henry," she reproached him. "Don't you know me?"

His ears lay back, and his eyes almost closed. He danced at her, and
she bent down and let him kiss the tip of her nose. When she straightened
up, Lucy faced her across the sheets, with her arms folded defensively.

She would not speak, and Jennie could not. The change staggered
her. Lucy had always been on the plump side, but now she was yellowish
skin and bones in an ugly high-necked black dress. Her dulled hair was
ruthlessly pulled back from her face and pinned flat to her head. Her
once-round cheeks were shrunken, and her mouth was severely brack-
eted. The only color about her was in her eyes, but it was a dead green,
as if she'd even willed the moist luster away from them.

The dog looked up at her and back at Jennie, wagging his tail and
making faint sounds in his throat.

"*Jennie,*" she said. Her voice sounded dry and old. "What do you
want?"

"A drink of water," said Jennie, "and a rest for my feet."

Lucy walked around her and led the way to the house. The kitchen
was neater than ever before and cheerless as never before. Jennie had
braced herself for not glancing at Jared's penned-off corner, but she still
saw it, swept and empty, the railings gone.

Lucy's shoulder blades pushed out the black cloth, she was so thin.
Her hands were red-knuckled and rough; she used to keep them smooth
with her great-aunt's lotion, for Jared's baby skin. She dipped water from
the bucket by the sink, turned it into a mug, and handed it to Jennie,
staring past her. Jennie drank faster than she wanted to and wouldn't
have been surprised if the water had come straight up again.

When she set down the mug, Lucy was looking impassively at her

dress. "It's the one you and I started," Jennie said. "Eliza helped me with
the sleeves and turned up the hem." Or was she looking at Jennie's
increasing midriff? Jennie felt like pulling her shawl tight around her.

"Sit down," Lucy said in that indifferent, exhausted voice. She leaned
back against the sink and folded her arms again. Very hot and prickling,
Jennie opened her workbasket. "Lucy, I can't admit to anyone else that
I don't know how to knit a man's stockings," she began, too fast. "And
Alick will be needing them. I *do* know how to darn neatly, but there
comes a time when there's not much left to darn."

Lucy turned her head away. Jennie had a blind impulse to throw the
hank of yarn at her, scream, stamp her feet, anything to make Lucy show
some human reaction.

What if she suddenly cried, "Alick is not the father of my child!"
or "Glenroy is not our real name, and Alick is not my husband." Or
"My husband is dead, and Alick could have been hanged for it."

Any one of them should have made a crack in the shell, but she
couldn't make herself do it.

"Lucy, will you teach me?" she asked gently. "You took pity on me
once. Won't you do it again? I've missed my friend so much."

"I am nobody's friend. I hate this world and everyone in it."

"Everyone? I know why you might hate *me*—" Jennie looked down
at herself. "But do you hate Harmonious?"

"Him most of all." New color flamed under her eyes as if someone
had rubbed her cheekbones raw with a wood rasp. Her voice flooded
with vigor. "All he talks about is having a child!"

"He must be grieving, too," Jennie said diffidently.

Lucy ignored that. "I *have* a child, and I am waiting to go to him. I
tried to go once, but they stopped me, and Elder Mayfield told me I
would go to hell and never see my baby again. So I have to live out my
years. If I am lucky, there won't be many of them."

"Lucy, think of all the people who love you," Jennie pleaded. "Think
how they would feel if they lost you."

"What do I care about *them*? My mother and his, weeping and pawing
at me and saying, 'Why don't you cry? Tears heal. We know what it is
to lose a child.' But they don't know what it is to lose Jared. Only *I*
know that!" she said with savage pride.

"Lucy, remember all our fun together?" Then she wished she hadn't
said it. Jared had been an indissoluble part of that fun.

"I will not teach you how to knit stockings," Lucy said in a monotone. "I never want to see you again. I don't need a friend any more than I need a husband. Leave now, and never come back again."

"Very well, Lucy," Jennie said sadly. "I shan't come back until I am asked."

"There will be no asking."

Jennie had covered a long distance before the noise of the great wheel at the sawmill rescued her from the emotional tempest which had been driving her on like a ship under full sail. She was hurt and angry on her own account, though she felt this was selfish and tried to subdue it; she was appalled by what grief had done to Lucy, and now she understood what Alick meant when he said Lucy was killing Harm.

She was not ready to be alone with all this. When she reached Main Street, she turned right past the tailor shop and went up the hill. She wanted houses with front gardens, shops, people, and even Columbine, who always made her laugh. She wouldn't even have minded if Mrs. Dalrymple had seen her going by and sent Minnie out to bring her in for a cup of tea. After the lacerating session with Lucy she'd have basked in the solicitous attention like a cat in the sun.

But it didn't happen, and there was no Columbine coming through someone's gate with nasturtiums dangling from her mouth. She wondered if she would see the blue wagon outside the post office. She would surely speak to that woman today. She wanted to do *something* extraordinary and uncalled for, make a gesture all her own, to act, rather than react. Lucy had made her feel futile and worthless. She should have known how to crack the adamantine shell and reach the essential Lucy inside.

She bowed to Mr. Whynot, the hairdresser, who was taking the air on his front step; at the ironmonger's she considered recklessly buying the spirit lamp and kettle, but the vision of England and home in the spring stopped her. She couldn't squander money now for luxuries. But five or ten cents for a couple of secondhand books from the new lot in the stationer's window couldn't be an extravagance.

The blue wagon wasn't there, but the piebald horse was tied to the rail. While she was trying to read the book titles, Hugh Evans left the post office and rode away. She watched him through the scanty weekday traffic until he turned down Ship Street.

She bought *The Vicar of Wakefield*, which had been presented to a

Thomas James Hardy on his fifteenth birthday in 1773; Thomas couldn't have read it, for some of the leaves were uncut. There was a copy of Fielding's *Tom Jones*, which she and Ianthe had read in secret; it wouldn't do for reading aloud; Alick might be shocked. But she took it anyway.

Just as she reached the entrance to the lane, the barouche emerged from the gate below, carrying Mrs. MacKenzie, and Hannah sitting opposite her holding the baby. There was a large hamper on the box beside Benoni. Hannah was looking up Ship Street and must have mentioned Jennie because the General's wife said clearly, "Wait, Benoni!" and he pulled up the horses. She beckoned to Jennie. "Come for a drive!" she called.

They drove across the toll bridge at the narrows and onto the River Road. Jennie had not been in a carriage since the morning when she'd left Christabel at the home farm and walked back to Tigh nam Fuaran and the burning. She could rejoice that it all was so far behind her now, and in the pleasure of seeing new countryside and riding behind handsome and willing horses, her spirits rebounded upward.

Mrs. MacKenzie was impressive in an amber crepe dress and mantle and a brown velvet hat the flaring brim of which was lined with amber satin. Hannah's Boston bonnet and pelisse were too hot for the day, but she was complacent even if badly flushed. The baby slept in his white merino cape.

"And where have you been with your workbasket?" Mrs. MacKenzie asked.

"I went out to see Lucy Clements. I hoped that if I asked her to help me start stockings for my husband, it might help *her*."

"And did it work?" Mrs. MacKenzie asked skeptically.

Jennie shook her head.

"I could have told you it would be a waste of time. Some people cherish their grief as a substitute for what they have lost, and they will not be cheated out of it. Eliza, or even Hannah here, could teach you to turn a heel in no time. I'm afraid my skills don't run past fine embroidery."

After the mention of Lucy the conversation was limited, perhaps because of Hannah's presence. Jennie enjoyed the freedom to look around her. The road traveled the high ground above St. David's River, through fields and woodland, past infrequent farm buildings; even the shabbiest of these was gilded by the day's particular beauty. On the left the land rolled down to the river. The oaks which Jennie remembered from the sail up the river in June were now leaved in copper and bronze.

Benoni turned the horses off to the left, into a narrow road cut through a spruce wood. When they came out into the open, the turquoise water lay below them at the foot of a sunlit field stained red with blueberry. The first moving things Jennie saw were two ospreys flying in separate arcs above the river, and she heard their whistling calls. Then her eye was attracted by a motion below them. A boy was running across the end of the field, small against the blue backdrop of the river. He reached a stand of oaks and vanished within them.

The carriage rolled and bounced in a right-hand turn, scattering squawking poultry, toward a house with a barn behind it. The long, low dwelling was almost black with years of weathering and seemed to be slowly tilting into the earth. The carriage stopped behind it and before the ramshackle barn, higher than the house but just as black. Its doors hung dejectedly open on the bare minimum of hinges; the blue wagon was inside. This was the Hugh Evans place.

Forty

TWO CHILDREN came at a run around the end of the house. The smaller one stopped, but the taller one came on, a girl about ten, barefoot, her dress short and torn, her brown hair all a tangle down to her shoulders and over her eyes. She ran to the horses and reached up to pat their noses. "I can hold them!" she called up to Benoni.

"No, you cannot, missy," he said. "One toss of Major's head, and you'll be dancing on air." He descended, grunting, and tied up to the hitching post. "Tell you what. You can fetch me the wheelbarrow."

"Geraint!" she shouted at the stocky, little black-haired boy who looked like a gypsy. "Bring the wheelbarrow!" She came to the side of the barouche.

"Good day, Mrs. MacKenzie," she said, and, taking hold of her ragged skirts, curtsied.

"That is very nice, Gwynneth," Mrs. MacKenzie said. Gwynneth's grin blazed forth; her eyes sparkled through the snarled fringe. This was one of the mute, motionless children in the wagon, but when Father was absent, something else was present.

"Is anyone in your family sick?" the General's wife said. "Does anyone have a sore throat or a cold in the head? A bad chest? A cough? A *rash?*"

Still grinning, Gwynneth shook her head to everything. "These children are insanely healthy," Mrs. MacKenzie said to Jennie.

"But *dirty,*" Hannah said fastidiously, wrinkling her nose. "And verminous, too, I shouldn't wonder."

"Now, Gwynneth," said Mrs. MacKenzie, "you know what happens to liars."

"Yes, *ma'am*," said Gwynneth emphatically. "I am not lying, ma'am. Ever since the baby died, nobody had anything but a stone bruise on Dai's heel, and I don't reckon that's catching."

"Neither do I," said Mrs. MacKenzie. "I think it is safe for you to come in with me, Jennie. Hannah and Allan Robert will stay out here in the open air."

Geraint had arrived with the wheelbarrow. His upper lip was pulled down very long to hold in his lower lip. Benoni loaded the hamper onto the wheelbarrow, then came around to help the women step down.

"Just watch where you step," Mrs. MacKenzie advised Jennie dryly. "Their cow has free run of the place." Between the delightful incongruity of the General's wife in her sumptuous attire picking her way across the barnyard and knowing that she was about to speak with the wagon woman, Jennie gladly put Lucy out of mind.

"They aren't verminous," Mrs. MacKenzie observed in a low voice. "Mrs. Evans is very particular about some things, as far as she is able." Gwynneth was a little ahead of them, and Jennie could see that the tangled hair was clean, and so was the child's scalp and neck. The tattered and faded frock was of a good cotton. There didn't appear to be any bruises on her bare arms and legs; perhaps Alick was right when he said Evans might not beat the children. Gwynneth seemed to be perfectly self-possessed as she led the way.

She hopped up on the granite step and pushed open the ell door, shouting, "Here they are, Mam!"

Mrs. Evans was standing before the fireplace in a small, scrubbed, bare kitchen. She was a spare-fleshed woman in a respectable black dress, with no fichu or frill. Her hands were writhing around and around each other and making a dry, rasping sound. She gazed mutely at the two callers from her strange pale eyes. Thin light brown hair threaded with gray attempted to curl around a plain cap, like the last traces of her youth.

"Mam put her cap on for you," Gwynneth explained. "She hardly never does that."

"Gwynneth," her mother murmured, "your *grammar*." The stare left her eyes, and her long mouth shaped itself in the smile of a hostess.

"Mrs. MacKenzie," she said with a ghostly vivacity, "how nice of you to come!" She held out her hand, which Mrs. MacKenzie took with equanimity.

"Allow me to introduce my friend, Mrs. Glenroy," she said.

The rough hand was extended to Jennie in an archly genteel gesture. "This is so very pleasant!" she exclaimed. Her tone and manner placed them in a phantom parlor. Except for the color of her eyes, she was no more the immobile woman of the wagon than Jennie was.

"It is pleasant for me, too, Mrs. Evans," she said boldly. "I've seen you in the town and wanted so much to speak to you."

"Oh?" Mrs. Evans tilted her head quizzically. "When was that, I wonder? I don't seem to remember. Won't you be seated?" She waved her hand at what the kitchen provided: straight chairs, rudely homemade but sturdy enough. She sat down on a bench by the cold hearth, her back very straight, and folded her hands in her lap. "I am sorry I cannot offer you tea," she said, "but as you can see, the fire is out, and my lazy children have not yet filled the woodbox. Gwynneth, take Geraint and find David, and remind him of his chores."

Gwynneth left reluctantly. "Gwynneth," Mrs. MacKenzie called after her, "will you ask Mr. Frost to bring the hamper, please? Now, Mrs. Evans, I have brought some warm things for the children. The boys' garments are from my nephews in Massachusetts, and I think David and Geraint will be very well provided for." Benoni carried in the hamper.

He mumbled, "How do, Miz Evans," and stumped out, feeling in his pocket for his pipe.

Mrs. MacKenzie unpacked the clothing, unfolding and displaying each garment before adding it to the stack on the table. Then she took out a collection of schoolbooks, paper, pencils, two large new slates, and a copy of Lamb's *Tales from Shakespeare*. Mrs. Evans cooed and murmured throughout, without moving from the bench or unfolding her hands.

Jennie didn't know what she had expected, but she knew that this wasn't it; not this charade of genteel civility in an imaginary parlor, while the hens walked in and out. The hens were comfortably themselves, but she couldn't be sure about Mrs. Evans. The General's wife, that indolent, sardonic, and sometimes arrogant woman, was patient and courteous but firmly bringing the other woman back each time she went hazily rambling into the past. "My Dear Father" appeared with increasing regularity in these confusing reminiscences.

Jennie envied the hens' freedom. She planned excuses. *I feel I must retire for a few moments.* Or, *I should like to walk down to the water.* But each time she prepared to speak, Mrs. Evans's relentless smile would pin her to the chair like a captured butterfly. "Do you not think so, Mrs. Glenroy?"

"Oh, yes, indeed!" Jennie replied, not knowing to what she was agreeing. Gwynneth came to the door.

"Mrs. MacKenzie, ma'am, Miss Hannah says the baby is hungry."

"Thank you, Gwynneth. I shall attend to him." She arose and went out, leaving Jennie alone with a woman who was either mad or a fool, and she couldn't think of a word to say. If only Mrs. Evans would stop *smiling.* Her face must be aching by now unless she was too deranged to feel it. The nape of Jennie's neck felt wet, and her back was stiff, and her feet had pins and needles.

"I must beg your pardon, Mrs. Glenroy," Mrs. Evans said suddenly, "but I do remember you now. You came from the post office one day, and you made me think so much of someone I once knew; it was quite startling." Her smile was nearly extinguished. "You must have thought me very rude."

"Not at all," Jennie said eagerly. "I wish you had spoken."

"But we were two strangers, with no one to introduce us." The arch smile was back. "It would have been quite improper."

"The second time our husbands spoke. I hoped to be introduced then." Then she remembered the baby. *Since the baby died,* Gwynneth had said. And here the woman sat maundering on about etiquette.

Two bereaved mothers in one afternoon; it was too much. Jennie kneaded her aching and perspiring neck. She had to keep talking, as if a silence in the room would expand and devour her.

"I understand that you teach your children," she said desperately.

"Oh, yes! I was trained to teach. I had thought of opening a dame school if we had settled in the village, but Mr. Evans is devoted to his solitude. He is an artist, you know."

"This is a very picturesque location," Jennie said.

"Mr. Evans finds it so." "Mr. Evans" now replaced "My Dear Father" in the monologue.

When Mrs. MacKenzie returned, Jennie rose and murmured, "If you will please excuse me," and went out. She felt as if she had just escaped from a straitjacket and couldn't breathe deeply enough.

She went looking for the Necessary, which should have been near the barn. She found the hen house and a crudely boxed well beside it, and wondered if the family used the water. Hannah sat in the carriage, reading a novel over the baby's head. Benoni sat on an upturned bucket in the barn doorway, smoking his pipe amid companionable poultry. He pretended not to see Jennie, saving his having to stand up, and she collaborated. At the end of the barn most distant from the house she saw a small board-and-batten shed, and she headed for that, remembering to watch out for cow pats and hoping that if the cow was lurking nearby she wasn't hostile to strangers.

When she lifted the latch on the shed door, she smelled paint. Immense yellow eyes stared coldly at her; she yipped in surprise and dodged back, then looked again. She saw the massively carved and freshly painted white head and throat, the dark shoulders and breast, of a bald eagle. Of course! Evans might have done the exquisite miniatures, but he was also a carver of figureheads. If the paint hadn't been new, she would have traced the predatory hook of the great beak and the bas-relief of the feathers about the throat and over the breast.

"Iolaire," she said to it, remembering the golden eagle which had flown at their eye level over the flooded corrie. She shut the door on it and went past the west end of the house through old apple trees toward the shore. The ospreys had gone, but a flock of gulls were riding the air currents, their white wings shining as they came into the sun and disappearing when they drifted away from it.

There were paths running everywhere through the bay and juniper and raspberry bushes. She passed another well at the head of a narrow alder swamp stretching to the shore. There was a garden where the potatoes had been harvested, and there were still turnips, beets, and parsnips in the ground. A black-and-white cow was feeding at a safe distance near the oaks where the running boy had vanished.

Children's voices mixed with those of the gulls. At the place where she'd seen the running boy, she looked down into a little cove with a small beach of pebbles and sand. An old rowboat was driven up onto it, and Geraint was rowing with one broken oar and a pole; Gwynneth sat

in the stern beating time with her feet and singing, " 'Bobby Shaftoe's
gone to sea,/ Silver buckles on his knee;/ He'll come back and marry
me,/ Pretty Bobby Shaftoe!' "

She saw Jennie up on the bank and waved excitedly. Geraint looked
over his shoulder, scowling into the sun, then returned to his rowing.
Gwynneth jumped out of the boat and came up the path.

"Where is your brother David?" Jennie asked her.

"Hiding," said Gwynneth. "He hates it when the lady comes."

"Do *you*?"

"No!" Her pale gray eyes were thickly fringed and bright as rain.
"No! I like pretty dresses." She looked down at what she was wearing
and smoothed it. "This was pretty once, but Mam hates to mend. . . .
Are there some pretty dresses this time?"

"Yes, and warm things, too. Now tell me where the Necessary is, if
you please."

"We don't have one. Mam always wanted one, but Da says no need.
It would only have to be cleaned out, and we have all the fields and the
woods. But Mam keeps a chamber pot in the house," she offered proudly.
"It has blue flowers on it. There is a pitcher and bowl, too. I think they
are the prettiest things we have."

"They sound lovely," said Jennie. "Well, I had better find myself a
nice thicket."

"Up there is good," said Gwynneth judiciously, pointing. "There is
plenty of nice soft moss."

Jennie climbed a granite whaleback where burgundy red blueberry
plants grew in the crevices, toward a coppice of alders and poplars; bare
now, their smooth gray trunks were gold-washed in the sun.

"Mind where you step!" Gwynneth shouted after her, just in time;
this must have been a popular spot. She found one for herself behind
some alders.

The chickadees picking at the alder cones were unconcerned by her
presence. When she left, she stopped on the whaleback to look around.
Southward each island seemed to lie just above the water, outlined in a
light of its own. The vivid blue of the bay vibrated in her vision and
made her eyes feel hot and staring. She looked northward to the house,
and then she knew it was the one which she had seen from the *Paul
Revere* on that June Sunday when she was so tired and wanted only to
know where she would sleep that night.

Gwynneth had gone back to her brother and the boat, and her strong little voice followed Jennie up the path.

" 'Bobby Shaftoe's fat and fair,/ Combing out his yellow hair—' "

Mrs. MacKenzie was ready to leave. "There is one more thing, Mrs. Evans," she said. "Has Mr. Evans had the children measured for their winter boots yet? The General will be very displeased if the children do not have boots by the first of December at the *latest.*"

"Mr. Evans will surely attend to it soon," said Mrs. Evans.

"And what about your own winter shoes?"

"Mr. Evans has never allowed me to go without the necessities of life," said Mrs. Evans with gracious assurance. "Mrs. Glenroy, may I offer you a cup of cold water before you go?"

"Thank you, but no," Jennie said hurriedly. Mrs. MacKenzie was already out the door. "I'm not thirsty."

Fingers pressed into her upper arm and detained her. She met again the voracious eyes of the woman on the wagon seat. "Shall I tell you who it was you reminded me of?" Mrs. Evans whispered. "The person I always wanted to be."

She released Jennie's arm and commenced again her inane smiling and nodding. "It was such a great pleasure to meet you, Mrs. Glenroy. Do come again!" She didn't need an answer. She babbled all the way out to the barouche and waved them out of the barnyard, fluting good-byes.

When they jolted into the wood road, Hannah said in agitation, "Mrs. MacKenzie, I'm *real* distressed!"

"Stop, Benoni!" the General's wife called. She took the placid baby, and Hannah jumped down without help and whisked off into the woods. The horses, anxious to go home to supper, were restive, and Benoni went around to their heads to talk to them.

"What will the General do if the boots are not provided?" Jennie asked.

"Hugh Evans should receive his deed next year. He won't want anything to delay that."

"And once he has it, who will remind him to shoe the foal and the colts, not to mention their dam?"

The way Lydia MacKenzie shrugged was her own inimitable gesture of indifference. "Who knows? He can well afford to clothe those children, you know, but he won't. I think her clothes are what she brought with her. Oh, I daresay he has allowed her enough during the years to cover her nakedness, but no more than that. I've tried to pass things on to her, but she turned them down, even something as small as a bright-colored kerchief or a cap with lace. 'Mr. Evans doesn't allow it.' The man's a monstrous tyrant! He is also too gifted to be hacking out figureheads."

Jennie wondered if she'd missed the miniature yet. "Gwynneth tells me they have one chamber pot in the house and matching jug and basin, the prettiest things they possess."

"And about all, I should think. I wonder what he does with his wages."

"Does she adore him as much as she seems to, do you know? He seems to be interchangeable with 'My Dear Father.' "

Lydia gave her a sardonic look. "He rescued her from 'My Dear Father.' He saved her from the hell of forever being a spinster daughter of a New Hampshire parsonage. He made her a wife and a mother when she thought it would never happen."

"Did she tell you all this?" Jennie asked.

"Oh, yes. A few years ago Colin heard that the children were running about half-naked in cold weather, and he asked me to make a call, just in case it was malicious gossip put about by men who don't like Evans—and that means most of Maddox. Well, it wasn't gossip, and the poor woman was starved for female conversation and told me all in the first half hour. I've heard it again and again. And never a word against *him*. He doesn't beat them, thank God. He simply ignores them.

"He was a journeyman painter, and her father engaged him to paint his portrait. He boarded at the parsonage, and swept Adelina off her feet. She had a little legacy from her mother, which must have helped. It was doubtless the last time he ever put himself out for her, but she behaves as if he has given her the world."

Hannah's coral red pelisse showed among the tree trunks. "We can keep an eye on the children until they're old enough to dree their own weird, as Colin puts it. It's a bore really," she said in the familiar languid way, "but one doesn't know how to stop what one has started. Sometimes I wish they'd move away."

Hannah was almost there, daintily picking her way among plants and roots. "Just the same," Lydia murmured, "I think I shall give them two new chamber pots. *Pretty* ones. Even Hugh Evans must realize what a fool he'd look, going into a rage about chamber pots."

Forty-One

T HE PERSON I *always wanted to be.*
  That fey whisper stayed with Jennie and echoed in her ears louder than anything else she had heard during the visit.

"She made me feel like a ghost," she told Alick. "It made my skin crawl."

"What was she meaning, do you know?"

"Mrs. MacKenzie told me something about her. She must have always been kept down; in a small town everyone watches the minister's daughter. Perhaps I looked free, lively, in control of my own life." She patted her belly. "Little did she guess who is really in command. The imperial It."

"Is it always It with you? Never him or her?"

"Always It, like a little plant I am nurturing. I simply cannot imagine the day when It is a son or a daughter."

"You are still not wanting it," he said thoughtfully.

"Alick, there is no question now of wanting or not wanting. It didn't ask for life, but It is alive, and I have a duty toward It."

She expected her birthday to go unnoticed and woke up resolved not to be sorry for herself; then Alick brought home the spirit lamp and kettle and a stone jug of spirits to fuel it. She was so astonished and so moved that she had to restrain herself from hugging him and tried to be as offhand as he was. "I know people are supposed to say, 'Oh, you shouldn't have,' but I'm so glad you did. Thank you, Alick. How did you ever think of the date?"

"Because I have never forgotten since the night we were talking about our birthdays." It had come up in one of those campfire conversations. He had been born in December; she remembered it now, a little ashamed to have forgotten. She insisted on his lighting the spirit lamp now, and she brewed a ceremonial pot of tea, and they drank a toast to their future.

"And to the future of It, too," said Alick.

"Tell me truly, Alick. Do *you* think of It as a boy or a girl?"

"It is not for me to think either way," he said austerely.

As the world of Maddox turned toward winter, a man was crushed to death under a load of rock in a quarry accident, and a woman and child died when their cabin burned down. Two very old people died in the natural way, he with grateful ease, she in a rage while she had the breath for it. When Elder Mayfield came to her bedside, she called him a carrion crow; the next Sunday he preached a sermon on the awful consequences of the sin of pride when committed on one's deathbed.

A collection was taken through the town for the family of the quarry worker, and there was a bee to raise a new cabin for the widowed man and his surviving children. Household goods were donated to furnish it.

One of the Highland women remaining in the Ark died of a stroke, leaving four young children. She'd been a shy woman who had kept to herself, and her death was as quick and silent as she was. Alick went to the funeral in defiance of Mr. MacArthur, so as to stand with the other Highlanders at the grave of the first of them to be buried so far from home.

Elder Mayfield had another good theme for a fire-and-brimstone sermon when the Society for the Investigation of Purported Ghosts was begun as a disreputable offshoot of the Male Debating Society. It caused panic for some who believed ancient evils were about to be unleashed, and gave the rest of the citizens a refreshing and stimulating week at a drab time of year. The church was crowded at both services, and believers and unbelievers agreed that the Elder had given a dynamic performance both times. Until the town had a dramatic society, the Elder would always be the star turn.

The weather stayed moderately calm for enough days of the week so that the fishermen could go out often. To sail down the river with the tide and return on it meant at least a twelve-hour day, which sometimes began long before daylight; Zeb Pulsifer's waking hours were well occupied. He was seasick at first and hoped his brothers-in-law would be forced to release him, but they threatened to force him to swallow a slice of salt pork on a string, the traditional cure, and this jolted him back onto an even keel. After that they kept his stomach tranquilized with nips of rum. The hard work in the cold air aboard a heaving boat saved him from getting drunk. When he was ashore, he was kept busy around his home place. One night he sneaked over to Priam Barrett's tavern on the St. David side of the river, where he was spotted by a brace of his wife's cousins, who escorted him home. He never went near his mother these days. She was quiet and docile but had to be watched for fear she'd do away with herself.

The *Paul Revere* returned, loaded with salt, coal, dry goods, hardware, and a miscellany of orders for business and private citizens. She was hauled out at the creek to be scrubbed and tallowed for the Caribbean, where she would spend the winter in trading ventures.

Jennie received a letter from Tony, asking for news of Mairi. His college classes were exacting, but O'Dowda had prepared him well; his cousins were most hospitable; and he had made friends with whom he could play music. To be honest, he was too busy to be homesick, except for Mairi. She answered that she hadn't seen Mairi to speak to, but the miniature was in her possession now. She didn't add that no one at Strathbuie House seemed to have noticed it was missing; it would have made her feel like a conspirator. She was one, she supposed, but as long as it wasn't written down, it was a moot question. *You're becoming a little too expert at hairsplitting, Jennie*, she thought.

Alick had an accident at the yard when his chisel slipped and gouged the palm of his left hand. Mr. Dunlop plastered the wound with the black salve that was his specific for all injuries except broken limbs and severed arteries, bandaged it, and sent him home. Alick said it was nothing and would be only tender in the morning. But Jennie knew he was up and down in the night, and in the morning his hand was swollen and throbbing.

"You can't go to work," she insisted, but he was adamant.

"There is much I can do with the one hand. I could be holding something in place for another man. Working is the best thing I can do for myself."

She returned to the cottage at noon to find him pacing the floor, cradling his hand. He would not eat, but she insisted on his drinking a mug of tea. "I am going to send for Dr. Waite," she said.

"You are *not!*" He sprang up from his chair, wincing with the jolt of the sudden motion. "I have been hurt far worse in my life, but I heal quickly. I am needing sleep, that is all. No doctor."

"No doctor." She agreed. He went up to his room. She followed in a little while and looked in on him. He was deeply asleep, breathing heavily, and he looked unrelenting even in unconsciousness.

Late in the afternoon he hadn't come down, and she went up again. He was still sleeping, but restlessly. She walked around the foot of his bed to look at his left arm in the light from the window. It lay out from his body, the bandaged palm upward; the fingers were thick and red. His sleeve was rolled almost to his elbow, exposing the underside of his forearm, and red streaks showed where the veins ran.

She held onto the foot of the bed for balance, unable to look away. She squeezed her eyes shut, made herself breathe calmly, and look again. The poisonous road was still there. "Oh, my God," she whispered.

He roused up as if she'd touched him and looked straight at her. "You'll not be taking it off!" he said thickly. "I will be dying with it. Leave me alone." He fell back, and she knew he had not recognized her.

Everything was up to her now. Moving very cautiously so as not to disturb him again, avoiding the places that creaked on the stairs, she went down to the kitchen and put on her cloak. She went over to the stables, where Benoni and his son Tom were grooming the horses, and asked Tom to saddle up and go for Dr. Waite. Mrs. Pritchard's house was away from the village, on the same road where Roddie's family lived but farther out.

"Anything I can do, missis?" Benoni asked her. He was a man of few words, so this was a surprise. "You want I should send the wife or Liza around?"

"Thank you, but there's nothing anyone but the doctor can do." She thought she could control her panic alone. She would have run back to the cottage, but It was going into its seventh month and it was like carrying a cannonball about with her.

From halfway up the stairs she could hear Alick's noisy and irregular breathing, as if he were fighting an uneven battle just beneath the surface of unconsciousness. She wanted to see if the red lines were still there, irrationally hoping they'd been an illusion, but she knew better.

The doctor was there in a half hour by the Simon Willard clock. She told him in a low-key, decorous manner what had happened and that he could go up to Alick's room alone. "He forbade me to call you, but he will be polite to you under his roof," she said. "He is a Highlander."

"Then will you be sure that teakettle has enough hot water in it? Thank you." He gave her an encouraging smile. "Your composure will be a great help through this, Mrs. Glenroy."

"My composure is a bowl of eggs balanced on the top of my head," she told him. "I could step on a twig and create havoc."

"Then for the sake of your husband, your child, and yourself, avoid twigs."

She listened on the stairway while he was up there. Alick was already half-delirious with fever, but in his clear intervals he was polite with his protests. "There was no need to be calling you away from folk who are needing you."

"It so happened I was driving this way," Dr. Waite said, "and I thought I would see how your wife was feeling. While I am here, why not let me take a look at your hand? It hasn't put me out in the least, I assure you."

She heard Alick's grunt of pain, and then he spoke in broken Gaelic phrases, to either himself or someone visible only to him. It reminded Jennie of his nightmares, but she had always been able to wake him up from them. Now she knew in her bones that this would be a long nightmare for them both, and she was afraid one of them would not wake up from it.

The doctor washed off Dunlop's black salve and put on a clean loose dressing. He got Alick out of his clothes but left him in his shirt in lieu of a nightshirt. He gave Jennie a packet of herbs to make into an infusion for Alick to drink twice a day.

"Viper's bugloss. It sounds evil, but it purifies the blood. Hat Shenstone puts these things up for me. Fresh would be better, but there is none at this time of year." Lucy's great-aunt Hat, the herbwoman. They'd planned to walk to the Wolf's Den long before this. But now that was a reminiscence of another country. "Now this," Waite's deep voice was saying, "is a laudanum mixture. The dosage is printed clearly on the label. Don't exceed it, but don't skimp on it. I shall give it to him before I leave, and he may not need any more before morning; but if he comes wide-awake, give it to him in a half cup of warm water or milk or broth."

The word *laudanum* had bad implications for her; it meant that people dying slowly and painfully could finish out their days in a drugged peace. She hated to take the brown bottle from the doctor's hand, and he saw that.

"We want to keep him as quiet as possible to give the body a chance to effect its own cure." He smiled. "Sleep does more than 'knit up the raveled sleave of care.' "

"Can his body cure this infection?"

"Your husband is one of the strong, wiry sort. He is not a heavy drinker, he doesn't overeat, so his system isn't clogged with fat, making the heart exhaust itself driving the blood through the body."

"But if it doesn't work, and the infection keeps moving, would you—" Her teeth began to chatter. "Will you have to take the arm?"

"To save his life, yes."

"He'll never permit that. He has already told me he would rather die."

"So he told me. But if it comes to that time, he won't be able to say aye, yes, or no. His wife will have to give the consent." His face and manner were kindly, but she backed off in revulsion from the facts.

"I can't ever do that! I can't speak for him. I have no right."

"You have every right—and the duty to save his life. But, my dear child, we are discussing something that may never happen." He patted her shoulder. "Now, if you'll give me a half cup of warm water." She moved on legs that felt like sticks. He measured the drops into the cup and took it upstairs. She heard his deep, unhurried voice but not what he was saying.

"There," he said when he came down. "He may sleep all night now. Try to sleep yourself, and make yourself eat. You have someone else to think of besides your husband and yourself, remember?" He was pulling on his greatcoat. "Do you have it all clear? His mouth will be dry when he wakes up. Give him the tea then, and try to make him drink a cupful. Then, when he has carried out his natural functions, and eats something if he wants it, give him the laudanum to put him to sleep again." He picked up his hat and his satchel.

"Thank you, Doctor," she said. Her lips felt as wooden as her legs.

"I've tried to make it clear to him that he must drink everything you give him. I shall be here in the morning."

Forty-Two

SHE SAW HIM walk by the windows on his way to the stable and his gig and experienced a pang when he went out of sight. Even when he was telling her that Alick could lose his arm, there had been a stability in his presence. He had treated her as a woman competent to carry on sensibly in this crisis, and that put her on her mettle.

She knew part of her light-headedness was due to hunger. She'd eaten only a few mouthfuls of dinner, and she knew that if she didn't make herself eat, she would be taking the risk of turning dizzy and falling on the stairs. The plates of cold food sat on the counter in the pantry. She put more wood in the fire, pushed the teakettle over the hottest cover, and emptied the tea and leaves from the pot out the back door. She picked the untouched slices of lamb off the plates and put them on a clean one and cut a slice of bread and buttered it. Before she sat down to eat, she went up the stairs again.

Alick was quietly asleep. The room smelled faintly of laudanum. The day was dimming now, and she couldn't tell if he was still as flushed with fever or if the red streaks had moved any nearer to the bend of his elbow, but perhaps the process had already begun to reverse itself. She went back downstairs, inwardly tremulous; the original discovery of the red streaks had already become a memory with frightful associations.

She lit two candles in the kitchen, made a pot of tea, and ate and drank solemnly, as if performing a ritual. So much to be got through, nothing neglected. If you did everything perfectly, the gods would be pleased. Then she would go up to bed and read *The Vicar of Wakefield* until she was sleepy; it should take her back to the happy time when she had first read it. With Alick bound to sleep all night, there was no reason why she couldn't sleep, too, and in the morning all the pain and fright would be past.

There was a soft knock at the front door and, taking a candle, she went to open it. It was the General. The smoke-scented November dusk came in with him. "I've just heard," he said in a low voice, looking up the dark stairwell.

"He's asleep," Jennie said. They went into the kitchen and she put the candle down on the table. The General wore evening dress under his military cape. His ruddy face was furrowed with concern. "Benoni told us something was very wrong here, and Tom went for the doctor. What is it?"

"Blood poisoning in his arm," she said tightly. "It may not go too far." Having to talk about it menaced her precarious balance. She could feel it swaying. She said in a formal tone, "Will you sit down, General?"

"No, no! You are tired, you don't need a caller; I wish only to know what I can do."

"No one can do anything but wait. Dr. Waite is giving him laudanum to keep him quiet."

"But, my dear girl, you shouldn't be alone here, and in your situation, too." He actually blushed, and that steadied her.

"He'll likely sleep all night, and the doctor will be back in the morning. I'm quite all right, General. We're very hopeful that the night will bring a change for the better."

"It happened devilish quick, didn't it? Well, I've known it to happen that way with battle wounds." He cleared his throat, and she guessed he was thinking about amputation.

Her words jetted out as if from a punctured artery. "I can't let him lose his arm! He is learning a trade he loves; he is good at it. Whoever heard of a one-armed shipbuilder?"

"My dear lass," he said in sincere distress, "it may never come to that. Don't be troubling your mind with it tonight; you need your rest. Lydia sends you her kindest regards and says you are not even to think of coming tomorrow; you are not to give the girls a thought until Alick is on his feet again."

She thanked him numbly, knowing that he considered amputation a strong possibility. She went to bed in all her clothes, trying to warm herself up. Who would have ever dreamed two days ago that such a ghastly choice would be forced upon her?

She couldn't read. She thought she heard Alick speak and went to him, but he was still sleeping. She leaned over him and felt the heat emanating from his skin. He hadn't begun to cool down; if anything, he was hotter. She knew she was dangerously close to panic, and then she remembered hearing someone say once that high fevers burned out impurities. Perhaps that was going on now.

She slept, finally, because she was too tired to do anything else.

In the morning he was still sleeping, but restless and talking to himself. She tried to look at his arm in the desolate gray light of a cloudy November day, but she was afraid of waking him completely and not knowing what to do with him; she hadn't made the herbal infusion yet, and there was the business of performing natural functions; if she brought him a chamber pot, he would be embarrassed forever. If he lived.

She was holding a mug of coffee to her mouth with both hands, her elbows braced for support on the table, when the doctor came again. She had made the infusion in a saucepan and had milk ready to warm for the laudanum. She was washed, dressed, brushed, and wearing an apron; It was lively, and she was not. When Dr. Waite came in, she felt like bursting into tears but didn't.

"He slept all night," she said.

"Fine, fine." The doctor warmed his hands over the stove. "And you?"

"After a time."

"And were awake before cockcrow? Well, drink your coffee and eat something solid with it, even if you have to force it down."

Alick was awake when he went up to him and insisted on getting dressed and coming downstairs. The doctor humored him, improvised a sling to support his arm, and helped him down the stairs, while Jennie waited in rigid suspense in the pantry, expecting them both to plunge down the full flight.

"Where is Jeannie?" Alick asked thickly when they came into the kitchen.

"Oh, she's about somewhere," the doctor said.

"I am not wanting her to see me like this."

By the time he had been out to the Necessary and back he was exhausted and drunkenly bewildered and apologetic about it. Jennie had run up to his room and put fresh linen on the bed. She made it up with the plaid, as a sort of token or talisman. Then she huddled on the stairs, listening to Alick's labored voice.

"A *Dia*, I was thinking once I had my legs under me . . . Man, I am not knowing what it is with me; it came at me so fast—"

"Sit there and rest," the doctor said. "Are you in a mood to eat?"

"Only to be drinking." His voice nearly faded out.

"Drink this then. It tastes vile, but it will do you good." That would be the herbal infusion.

After a moment Alick said, "Vile it *is*. It can't help curing."

"Drink it all, man," Waite said.

"Will it cool down the fire that is raging at me? My hand is shaking like a drunkard's."

"I'll hold the cup for you."

"Jeannie must be away early to her teaching," Alick said as if to himself. Then the blurred voice suddenly came into focus. "Will you be trying to take my arm?"

"Will you be finishing this drink?" the doctor said good-naturedly. "We don't leap to conclusions. We go from minute to minute, hour to hour, doing what has to be done. Let us sponge off your face and neck to cool you a bit and then another drink, and we'll get you back to bed again. Sleep is what you need."

"I can be washing my own face." Apparently he tried to push himself from the chair but fell back into it.

"*Christ!*" he said breathlessly. "How can this arm be paining so much and not be killing me? But it *is* killing me, is it not? Unless the fever is doing the job first." He laughed weakly. "The minister will be very well satisfied. He promised me this."

On the stairs Jennie hunched up her shoulders and doubled her fists. *If that man comes here, I'll throw the teakettle at him!* she threatened wildly.

"I think," the doctor said meditatively, "we will get you up the stairs *before* the drink."

Jennie went into her room and swung the door almost shut. Alick could grip the railing with his right hand; but his grip was weak, and so were his legs. He was trying to hold on to his pride as well as the railing; but he was humiliated and frightened by his condition, and she could not bear this for him.

We go from minute to minute, Dr. Waite had said. She slipped out and down the stairs and began warming the milk for the laudanum. When the doctor came down, she said, "Will you have a cup of coffee, Dr. Waite?"

"No, I have urgent calls this morning." He measured the laudanum tincture into the warm milk. "You're a level-headed girl."

"I am really feeling like a very *in*firm jelly."

"I know, I know. But if you keep it from him, you will be doing more than your wifely duty."

She braced herself to ask the crucial question. "How does his arm look?"

He stirred the laudanum into the milk as if it took close attention and skill. "It is doing what is expected in a case like this."

"You mean the infection is still moving. Has it gone past his elbow yet?"

"Yes, but not much. It could slow to a stop at any time."

But it won't, she thought. "Has Alick seen it?"

"I'm afraid so. But this will help him not to think of it." He went upstairs.

She heard the low rumble of his voice and Alick's voice lifted for a moment and then subsiding.

"What shall I do for him today?" she asked the doctor when he left. "Should I keep cold compresses on his head?"

"If it makes *you* feel better," he said dryly. "To be honest, it will make little difference to him or the infection. He will be sleeping. The infection has to take its own course." Halfway into his coat he stopped and said, "Perhaps you should have someone with you."

"Who?" she asked bluntly. "Anna Kate MacKenzie is too far away now, and Lucy Clements is too far away in another sense."

"That poor young couple," he said with a sigh. "Well, I shall be in later."

As soon as he had gone past the windows on his way to the stable, she went upstairs. Alick hadn't drowsed off yet, and his flushed face was turned toward the door. It was shadowed by two days' beard, and his eyes seemed to have sunk deep since yesterday. They glittered under heavy lids; when he saw her, they opened wide.

She felt herself assuming the approved mask of good cheer and es-chewed it as an insult to his intelligence.

"I wanted to let you know that I am here, and I shall be here all the time, so you are not alone," she said.

He lifted up on his good elbow. "I was not wanting you to be burdened with this." He fell back, panting. "Och, this damned weakness, my blood is turning to water, and my wits are in a fog."

She sat down in the chair by the bed. "You are tired, that's all it is."

"Aye, and I have drunk his concoction." He was fighting the laudanum. "Jeannie, have you *seen* the arm?" he asked. "Are you knowing what is going on with it? It is beating as if it had such a strong heart of its own nothing could kill it."

"And it is very painful," she said.

He nodded. "But it is living." He tried to smile. "When it is paining no longer, it will be dead. Or gone."

"Think of sleep, Alick. I put the plaid on your bed. It will make you dream of the moors."

"I cannot be sleeping," he said, trying to lift himself again. "The doctor will be taking my arm when I am asleep, Jeannie. Swear you won't be letting him take it."

At least she could safely promise it for today. "I swear it," she said. From minute to minute, we do what has to be done, and now that meant putting him to sleep.

"*Beannachd leat, mo coraid,*" he said drowsily. "Blessings on you, my friend."

"Ah, Alick," she said softly, "the day we were in Fort William and you left me to find a ship, I saw one sailing and I thought you were aboard and gone without even a good-bye. I said that then."

He was already asleep.

Forty-Three

SHE KNEW ALREADY how one day could stretch out to half a lifetime, so that by night you were surprised to see in the mirror the same reflection which was there in the morning; you have not turned gray, wrinkled, bent, and toothless. You only *feel* old.

People came and went downstairs, and Alick slept on upstairs, like a man dying serenely oblivious of the gathering mourners; he is already far out of their reach. Eliza and Mrs. Frost brought food from the house: a rich beef broth for Alick; hearty food for Jennie, fresh milk and cream, an apple pie. At noon men came during their dinner hour: Harm Clements and Tormod from the yard, and Wee Rory, all asking what they could do. She thanked them and shook her head. Someone could bring in two buckets of well water; that was all.

"The doctor keeps him sleeping; he says it is best. The doctor will be back later on and settle him for the night."

She knew they were too tactful to ask about his arm; besides, they knew too well what could happen. "And how are you keeping, Mistress Glenroy?" Wee Rory asked her with a delicacy which implied he was aware of her condition without appearing to see it.

"*Tha mi gu math*, Ruari Beag," she told him. Her use of the Gaelic tickled him. He vaulted from gloom to exuberance.

"I should be bringing the pipes and give the lad a tune that'll drive the devil out of him and back to hell."

"But not until he's awake to hear it," she said.

"Och, it's not I who'd be disturbing his sleep!"

During the afternoon Benoni and his son came to the door. Eliza stopped on her way home and admired Jennie's courage at staying alone. "I can go home and speak to my father and then come back," she offered, but Jennie refused with thanks. She hadn't been able to relax all day and was looking forward to going to bed as soon as the doctor had come and gone.

Tormod had offered to walk out to tell Hector and Anna Kate, but she asked him to wait; she hardly expected them to come into town at night, but everything was so wildly out of the ordinary today, she wouldn't have been surprised.

The doctor came at what would have been suppertime. Alick was emerging from his drugged sleep like a man whose bad dreams are pursuing him into consciousness. She had been up several times to speak to him, but she couldn't reach him, even when she wiped his face with a cold wet cloth or held his good hand. He had gone so far from her since this morning that she was positive the question of amputation would never arise now. And there was nothing she could do, no libation to pour out on the ground, no sacrifices to make. *Seeing that death, a necessary end,/ Will come when it will come.* That was how the verse ended which began, *Cowards die many times before their deaths.* That was how everything ended.

An obdurate pride kept her from showing defeat or resignation to the doctor. Tonight he called down the stairs to ask if she had a chamber; Alick was too weak to get up. After he had taken it outside to empty and rinse it, he took up a basin of tepid water and bathed Alick and put him into a fresh shirt. He left without any comment except that he would be back in the morning.

On the night of the third day he took the time to sit down at the table across from Jennie and accepted a cup of coffee and a piece of apple pie. He was so long stirring his coffee she felt her inner organs seemingly bunching themselves into a tight knot which would presently explode into crippling cramps, diarrhea, or uncontrollable nausea. When he did speak, it was cruelly slow.

"I gave up trying to get tea into him. He believes that he will die when he is unconscious or that I will cut off his arm. I forced him to take the laudanum by lying, but it was necessary."

"What did you tell him?"

"That he was improving and should start taking food; the beef broth was to begin with."

"*Is* he improving?"

"I think tomorrow we may have to make some decisions, Mrs. Glenroy."
She shut her eyes for a moment and folded her arms on the edge of
the table. Then she opened her eyes and looked at him without flinching.
It passed through her mind that he thought she had been praying. Well,
she *had* been: to herself.

"I promised him that nobody would take his arm." She measured out
the syllables like pennies laid in an even row.

"If we don't take it, Mrs. Glenroy, he will die in torment. Unless,
of course, we can keep him heavily drugged until his heart stops. But if
he could think clearly, he might not appreciate having that decision
made for him."

"Why not?" she asked. "He can't think clearly now; he is already
brought low by pain and fever. Of what value would consciousness be
to him when the end is certain anyway?"

"I have not said it was certain, Mrs. Glenroy." He chided her. "And
if the arm is amputated, he might very well be glad to wake up alive,
even without it. He'd have his right arm, his wife, his child. Men have
survived and done well with less."

"But the operation itself is sometimes fatal, is it not?"

"I'll not lie to you about that. But sometimes it's the only road open
to us. If things keep on the way they are going, by tomorrow the only
choice will be between that road or none."

He got up to go. "Thank you, Dr. Waite," she said automatically.

"Fix yourself a decent meal now," he ordered her. "There is nothing
more you can do for him tonight. I'll stop in and report to the General.
He didn't wish to disturb you by coming here when you might be resting."

She was glad of that. She was grateful because people came, showed
solicitude, were anxious to help, but they undermined her attempt to
maintain poise and dignity in her own eyes. Their sympathy was deadly.
Even with the doctor she was now feeling the treacherous and degrading
temptation to let go.

Alone with Alick; that was the way it should be. Alone as they had
been all those days and nights in the Highlands, each other's sole comfort,
shield, and buckler. She ate a meal without tasting, for the sake of It.
Mrs. Frost had sent a chicken pot pie by Eliza, and she knew it was
delicious; but it was just something in her mouth to be chewed and
swallowed like medicine.

She went out to the Necessary. The November night was quiet, the stars were thick and close, and there would be frost in the morning. *In the morning.*

She left one candle burning on the kitchen table, in case she needed to come downstairs for anything, and took the other one upstairs. Alick slept on his back, and the inflamed arm, hidden by the covers, was stretched out on a pillow. She did not want to see it; she felt a personal loathing for it and for the laudanum on his breath and the scent and heat of fever.

She went to her own room and got into her nightgown. She took out Elspeth's Bible and began to read, not for a message but for the poetry of verses memorized for Papa in an innocent time. David's lamentation for Saul and Jonathan; certain psalms; Paul's message to the Corinthians: "Though I speak with the tongues of men and of angels. . . ." Singing like harp strings or as poignant as Tony's flute, the old music surrounded her. She leaned back and shut her eyes, and the candlelight became the sunlight on the orchard walls.

She woke suddenly, aware of having traveled a long distance in what must have been a long time. Someone had called her. *Alick?* She was out of bed so fast that her head was reeling as she reached the door, and she staggered against the frame and knocked her elbow hard. That brought her completely awake, and she went back for the candle.

She set it on the chest of drawers across the room from his bed and sat down beside him. If he'd called, it had been in his sleep. He was so quiet she had to lean close to his face to know he was breathing. She couldn't find any pulse in his neck and put her hand under the covers and laid it on his chest. Her own heart was beating so hard she couldn't distinguish his for a moment. By taking long, deliberate breaths she slowed her pulse, and then she could feel the halting rhythm of his.

He is dying, she thought. *Like this, and he doesn't even know it.* His skin was chilly with sweat; it glistened on his face. The expression *the cold dew of death* came to her. This must be it.

She wished she had said good night to him, but at least she wouldn't leave him to die alone. She took his good hand from under the covers and held it in both of hers, warming it. It had always been a hard-skinned, strong hand, but now it bore the new calluses and healed blisters of his trade. She examined it, the long thumb with the supple backward arch, the square-tipped fingers with the little coppices of fine dark hair between the knuckles, the strong sinews fanning out from the wrist.

What a marvel the human hand was, capable of both violence and tenderness, crudeness or delicacy; how eloquent and expressive. This one lay unresisting in hers, and she felt as if she were taking advantage of his helplessness, as much as if she were prying into that leather sack of his, the only personal possession he had brought from Scotland besides his clothing, the plaid, and his dirk. It was in a chest across the room, and she thought, *I will never look into it; I will bury it with him.*

Dimly she heard light steps on the stairs. Dr. Waite could move easily, for all his bony height and the size of his feet. He must have been expecting something like this when he left earlier, but he hadn't wanted to alarm her. Someone came into the room, and unconsciously she missed the usual aroma of tobacco and a faintly medicinal tang. Without looking around she whispered, "He is dying."

Lucy leaned past her and put her hand on Alick's forehead. "Oh, I think not," she said. "He is cool."

Somehow her being there was not that much of a shock, after all the others she had taken.

"He is *icy*," she protested.

"You think that because you are so warm yourself. You're so tired you may well be feverish." She removed his hand from Jennie's, held it for a moment, and then put it under the covers. "The plaid," she murmured.

"I think he rests better under it," Jennie whispered.

"Now come downstairs," Lucy said, "and we'll build up the fire. He doesn't need you to help him sleep."

"I could hardly feel his heart; it is going slower and slower."

"Because it is not racing and raging with a high fever. It's steady, believe me. Jennie, I'm thirsty and starved. Come downstairs. He isn't dying. I *know*."

She carried the candlestick and kept her free arm around Jennie's waist on the stairs.

"Let's not take any foolish risks. This is no time for a broken leg."

"My legs feel like yarn, and poor yarn at that," Jennie admitted.

"My, but you're grown around the middle. You may have twins in there."

"Sometimes it feels like a cricket match. Lucy, am I dreaming you?" she asked weakly.

Lucy gave her a small pinch over the ribs. "Are you dreaming *this?*"

They smothered absurd juvenile giggles with an effort that made their ribs ache and forced out small snorts and gurgles and hiccups. The candle flame fluttered frantically and sent their shadows into a weird dance on the walls and ceiling.

"No time to set ourselves afire either," Lucy said, placing the candle on the kitchen table beside the other one. She set about reviving the fire, and Jennie took the teakettle into the pantry to fill it. She slopped cold drops from the dipper onto her bare toes and rejoiced in the sensation. Alick was not dying; Lucy was here. It was too tremendous a happening for mere bliss; it was comparable to the instant when she knew that Alick had escaped Jock Dallas and the time when they had rested above the flooded corrie.

When she came back to the kitchen, Lucy took the kettle, scolding, "Look at you, running around in your bare feet! And your eyes are like two burned holes in a blanket. You'll have to take to your bed next, and that man of yours can be no nurse to you for a while yet. Sit down and bundle up." She pulled Jennie's cloak off the hook and tossed it to her. Jennie put it around her and sat down in a rocking chair, obediently putting up her feet. Lucy wrapped them in a shawl.

"Now, miss, stay put while I make us some tea. What is there to eat?"

"Look in the pantry and take your choice. They have brought us all kinds of things."

"How much of it have you eaten? Never mind, I haven't been eating very well myself, but for some reason I could do with a meal of vittles tonight."

The clock began to strike ten; for Jennie the strokes could have come from Kilmeny's harp of the sky. They had been tolling a knell for the last three days.

Neither moved until the tenth stroke died away. "I've been hating the sound of a clock striking," Lucy said.

"So have I." She put her head back and watched Lucy moving between kitchen and pantry. She was still in dark clothes—she who had always loved bright things—and her cheeks were still hollowed; but she moved with the familiar, positive energy, and her eyes were alive again.

"I'm bringing out everything, Jennie, and we shall have us a feast. Look at *this*." She set a half bottle of Madeira in the middle of the table between the candlesticks.

"Lucy, tell me how you came here tonight," Jennie said.

"How?" Lucy tilted her head sidewise and then moved one candlestick an inch toward the wine. "I roused my long-suffering husband to saddle up Jack for me. I've put him in a loose box over in the stable. Jack, not Harm."

"He let you come alone at night?"

"Why not? He trusts us both. Jack's like a cat in the dark. Besides, the stars are so bright it's not black-dark." She poured boiling water into the teapot. "Harm said he would come, but I wouldn't let him. And he was so happy because I wanted to *do* something he wouldn't have argued, no matter what."

"But what decided you? What made you wake Harm?"

"Let us eat. I am so hungry I cannot believe it."

She wasn't going to tell then. But she needn't; she was here, and that was enough. "I suppose we'd better not drink the wine," she said. "The state we're in, we could get either very sick or very drunk."

"And could you imagine poor Dr. Waite walking in on *that?*" Jennie asked.

Lucy sputtered into her teacup. "I have not even smiled for so long, Jennie, I shall have a lame face tomorrow. Why did I come? Perhaps because it was time. What I have put my poor Harm through! Another man would have given up long ago and begun avoiding me like a plague ship." She rested her chin in her hands. "Night after night he would tell me all he'd seen and heard that day, and I went on giving him stones for bread. When he told me Alick was bad and might die, it was like words in a newspaper about things happening far from here, to strangers. But tonight I woke up quick thinking, *Jennie needs me.* It was as simple as that. And the way I woke up Harm, the poor man thought the house was afire."

"If you hadn't come," Jennie said, "I would still be thinking I was sitting by his deathbed."

"And catching your death of cold while you waited." Jennie started to stand up, and Lucy said, "Where are you going?"

"I want to look at him again. Just to be sure."

"I'm not wrong, but let me do the looking." She took a candle and went up. When she came back, she said, "I hope we sleep as well." She poured hot tea for herself and cut a wedge of pumpkin pie.

"When I was jogging along with old Jack, looking up at the stars and hearing the owls, I thought about Harm. I thought about him all the way. I wondered how I would feel if *he* was dying of a septic arm. I imagined it all, I spared myself no detail, and it took me by the throat. Then I knew I hadn't died when—" She gave Jennie an angry, wet-eyed nod. "I can't say it yet. But tonight I knew there was leftover life in me, and I had better use it." She held up her cup. "To life."

"To life," Jennie repeated solemnly. They touched cups and drank.

They took a final look at Alick. His hair was wet, and the pillow slip and his shirt were damp. They managed to put a dry towel on the pillow without waking him but did nothing else. "He won't catch cold if he's well covered," Lucy said. "We shouldn't disturb him."

"He would never forgive me," said Jennie. "Dr. Waite has bathed him morning and night, and that was hard enough on his modesty."

She tucked the plaid around his shoulders, and they went across the hall to her room. Lucy had brought a nightgown with her. They talked drowsily for a little while and fell asleep.

Jennie awoke later and visited Alick to see to his covers. He stirred, and she whispered, "It's all right. Go back to sleep."

He mumbled some words and then said clearly, *"Mo graidh,"* and then nothing else.

Jennie had heard the phrase before, in a song of farewell and exile which Mairi had sung aboard the ship, only once because the simple minor melody expressed such an ineffable longing that it had most of the passengers in tears; even Jennie, who hadn't understood the words.

Anna Kate told her that *mo graidh* meant "my beloved," and she supposed the words referred to the beloved land; Alick must be dreaming of home.

Forty-Four

J ENNIE WENT BACK to teaching, but Alick could not go back to work until the infection had completely gone and he had regained the strength leached away by the high fever. He was to drink a good deal and not to push himself. The General paid a call to tell him his wages would go on; he allowed sick pay in all his businesses.

Alick did not talk about his experience after that first morning when he awoke and looked lucidly into Jennie's eyes and said, "I am back." There was a difference in him which she couldn't define. He had once told her that he couldn't remember ever being seriously ill, and now he had almost lost his arm or died, or both. He was either shaken by these intimations of his mortality or somberly rejoicing in his luck. She wondered if he remembered making her promise to save his arm; she wasn't about to remind him of it, and she herself didn't dwell on the hours she had sat by him thinking he was dying.

What mattered was that he was back, and Lucy was back; It was in good health, if its activity was any sign. On a cold, windy Saturday afternoon she was quite happily writing in what she called William's Book. Her first pot of beans was baking, and cranberries were softly popping in a saucepan on the back of the stove; Hector and Anna Kate had brought them. Alick had gone upstairs to read and sleep.

The day brightened and darkened under the rapid sweep of clouds, and in the heaviest gusts there was so much noise about the cottage that she didn't hear the knocking at first, until it became a hammering.

Mairi MacKenzie, swathed in a plaid, stood on the doorstep. She

looked wordlessly at Jennie, through tears. Jennie pulled her into the
kitchen, and the girl caught at her and held on as if she were drowning.
Jennie embraced and patted her.

"Mairi, what is wrong?"

Mairi shook her head, biting an already-raw lower lip, and the gentian
blue eyes overflowed. Jennie sat her down by the stove. "Catch your
breath," she said.

Mairi obeyed, but the effort was painful to see. "I ran away to tell
you," she said. "They are making me marry Ewan MacLean."

"But his wife is hardly cold!"

"But he is needing a housekeeper and someone to care for the children. I have been doing that, and I could be going on with it and never
be asking wages. But to wed him, to go into his b—b—" She couldn't
bring it out. "I cannot!" she wailed. "He is not even *young*!"

Jennie gave her a handkerchief and let her cry. She was so indignant
she had to warn herself to hold back. When Mairi had subsided into
weak sobs and a blind picking at the edge of the plaid, Jennie said, "Do
your father and mother want this? Or is it just Ewan?"

"They are wanting it," the girl said bitterly, "because Mr. MacArthur
says it is best. Jeannie, I *hate* him!"

"He is doing only what he thinks is his duty," Jennie said, despising
herself for a hypocrite.

"What am I to do?" Mairi cried. "If Tony were here, we would run
away, we would find gypsies and marry by jumping over the campfire!"

Thank God he isn't here, Jennie thought. It was just the sort of thing
he'd come up with.

Mairi had both her hands. "Please help me, Jeannie!"

She hadn't been able to quench Tamsin's fears or stop the evictions,
and she could do nothing here but hold Mairi in her arms until she'd
cried herself out.

"I have no authority, Mairi," she said. "You belong to your parents.
Have you told them how you feel?"

"Yes, and they say it is foolish, Ewan is a good man, and my head
is turned by the General's son. I said I loved him, and they said that
has nothing to do with it whatever. Love is something in songs, nothing
more. Jeannie, my father and mother together sing songs about love that
are breaking my heart. They taught me my songs! Why would anyone

be making songs about something that is not true? My father believes in the fairies. If I say there are no wee folk, he is angry. Why cannot I believe in love?"

"Mairi, you ask hard questions. All I can tell you is that my life took a dreadful turn, and I thought I wouldn't survive it, but I did."

"But everyone is knowing you and Alick Glenroy ran away because you were in love and your family was not allowing it. And you had a handfast marriage."

Oh, dear, Jennie thought, *how our lies do trip us up.* "We are much older than you."

Mairi didn't even hear it.

"If Tony and I could not be finding the gypsies, we could go to the Indians, and they would marry us. Tony *knows* Indians," she said proudly. "Some great chiefs are his father's friends. Jeannie, will you please write to Tony so he can be coming for me?"

"Mairi, love," Jennie said, "I cannot! If you were a lost kitten or a puppy or a foundling left in a basket at my door, I would care for you and not let anyone else have you. But you are somebody else's child and not a castoff. I can only be your friend, and I always shall be."

It was cold comfort, and the girl's anguish told her so. *Why am I being forced into this?* she thought. *I don't need it!*

Mairi was staring hopelessly past her toward the windows, and suddenly she gasped, "It's himself! He went by the glass!"

She was out of the chair and into the pantry just as the knock came at the front door. It was indeed the minister. He removed his hat and said silkily, "Good day to you, Mistress Glenroy."

"And good day to you, Mr. MacArthur. Won't you come in?" He brought with him the atmosphere of the Highland manse and the long walks across the moors and through the glens; he was worn thin with battle in the service of his God.

"And how is the sick man?"

"Much better," Jennie said. "He is sleeping now. Will you take a chair, Mr. MacArthur?"

He was looking about him with those bright eyes; for a Bible? she wondered. She thought he had passed over the crumpled plaid in the chair until his gaze came back to it and stayed. Then he lifted his sharp little chin. "Come here and face me, Mairi MacKenzie!" he rapped out.

The girl came out and stood there trembling like a cornered hare. Jennie put her arm around her.

"Mairi is my guest, Mr. MacArthur."

"She is a runaway on the road to Gehenna. She has lied."

"I did not lie!"

"But you deceived. You lied in silence. And for this." He put his hand into his coat pocket and brought out the miniature. Mairi caught her breath and made a lunge for it, but he pulled it away and put it back in his pocket.

"Your innocent little brother was finding it just now, and your mother brought it to me."

"I will never be forgiving them for this," Mairi said between her teeth.

"I was returning it to the General," said the minister, "but I stopped to see the sick man, and I find you here nestling in Gehenna like a bird returned to its nest."

"If this is Gehenna," Jennie said, rather exhilarated, "hadn't you better leave before you are singed by our flames?"

"They cannot touch me. I wear God's armor. I am doing God's work."

"Are you quite sure you know everything that is in God's mind?" Jennie asked.

"I know, and He knows, that you are a bad woman. You are setting this child against her parents and filling her ears with honeyed promises."

"That is not so!" Mairi defied him. "She was telling me I must obey my parents. Just when you were knocking at the door, she was telling me that."

"Och, Mairi, you have learned fine in this place how to tell lies."

"She is not lying, Mr. MacArthur," Jennie said, "and now that you have told me what you think of me, will you please leave?"

The minister held out the plaid to Mairi. "Wrap yourself, lass, and come with me."

"No! I will be walking back alone."

"You've wrought hard for punishment, Mairi MacKenzie."

"But it's not you who will be giving it to me!"

"No, your father will be the one—"

Alick spoke from the hallway. "Leave my house, Minister."

The three turned to him as if he were a speaking ghost, and he faced them impassively. The minister's arm struck out like a sword pointed at his heart. "Alick Glenroy! I prayed that you would be given a lesson that would save your soul. But God only scorched you with His wrath. He was merciful; He left you your arm. Take heed! The next time He will take your life."

Jennie said incredulously, "You prayed for him to lose his *arm?* Just who *is* your God?"

He spun light as a fencer, pointing the sword at her. "Have a care, woman! The angel of death is hovering over your own head and your child's!"

"Uilleam Torcall MacArthur," Alick said. It was not like the time in Roddie's house when he had spoken in anger. This time he could have been speaking poetry in rhythmic Ossianic cadences, like the rise and fall of surf on a long strand. He didn't thunder, but he went on and on. She caught the minister's name again, and familiar words, but not the context. The minister's arm dropped. Shock, outrage, and dismay crossed his face. He couldn't seem to look away from Alick, his mouth fell open, and he looked pitifully old. But life flamed into Alick's face as it left the minister's.

Mr. MacArthur walked like a dream-struck man to the front door and went out. Jennie watched from the doorstep in common concern; he seemed so fragile all at once. She waited in the cold wind until she saw him walking quite steadily along the path toward Strathbuie House. Alick had followed her out and put her cloak over her shoulders.

"You shouldn't be out in this cold wind," she said automatically.

"Nor should you!" They went back into the house, where Mairi was shrouding herself in the plaid with shaking hands. She kept glancing at Alick while he put more wood in the stove and then looked away, and back again.

"I will be going back now, Jeannie," she whispered.

Jennie kept an arm around her as they went into the hall. Away from Alick, Mairi still whispered. "Did you know what he was *saying?*"

"I caught only a word now and then."

"Och, it was that dreadful!" Jennie had a feeling that if Mairi had been a Roman Catholic, she'd have crossed herself. "How was he daring to say such things? And to the *minister?*"

"Honest rage, I suppose. The man wanted him to lose his arm and perhaps his life, as a lesson. You felt rage yourself, did you not, when

Mr. MacArthur showed you the miniature?" She kissed Mairi's cheek. "Remember, I am your friend."

She walked to the corner of the house with her, but Mairi was unresponsive. Jennie returned in a chill of depression.

Alick was slumped in the chair by the stove; exhausted, she thought, until he gave her a lively sidewise look that swept away her depression at one fell swoop.

She pulled up a chair beside him. "What did you say to him?"

"I cursed him," he said blandly.

"It was quite a long curse."

"It was not a simple curse, you understand. But a very ancient one. If his goat goes dry, and his oatmeal goes moldy, his fire will not light, and his hens begin to crow, he will be certain the curse is working."

"Did you actually threaten those things?" She was between dismay and delight.

"The curse is not listing the details. It is bad enough as it is. I spared his wife; the poor woman has enough to bear. And I did not curse God. I told him I know I am not one of the elected, and so I am free to do and say as I please. God has not given me up; He never chose me. So He is not waiting to pounce on me like a great cat."

"I think we both need a strengthener," said Jennie. She brought out the rest of the General's wine and divided it between them. "Is there more?"

"A wee bit. I told him he was the devil's get, and the devil will be having his own. I promised him that all the fiddles he had smashed and burned in the name of God would be made whole on the day of resurrection and fiddle him into hell."

"It *was* poetry after all!"

"Poetry?" he repeated politely. "He is forever calling down the wrath of God upon the helpless. I was only calling down the wrath of Satan upon him."

"And you are proud of yourself." They both burst out laughing. "Oh, Alick, it was shameful," she said. "If he has a stroke tonight, you will be sorry."

"Perhaps." His tone said he doubted it. "And he will be wondering if it is a judgment of God or Satan. He had no right to say what he did."

"About praying for you to lose your arm, to humble you? That was unforgivable. I could have struck him in the face for that."

"No, it was what he said to you, about the Angel of Death. He should be thankful I struck with a curse and not my fist. But I was respecting his age and his white hair, the wicked bodach."

"Alick, he didn't frighten me. Those days are past."

"Just the same, I was not liking it, and I was not having it." He drank down the rest of his wine, and when he set the glass on the table, it rattled as if his hand were unsteady. His manner defied her to mention it. They'd waked him up, she thought repentantly, and he was still weaker than he wanted to admit.

Forty-Five

LYDIA MACKENZIE told Jennie about the return of the miniature. "This means, of course, that Tony shan't be able to come home at Christmas. It is too bad because we keep Christmas, and our celebration is one thing for which Tony and Christian have always given me credit. But Colin's right, of course. The boy would see himself and her as Romeo and Juliet, and the silly children might elope, if they didn't kill themselves. The sooner the girl is married, the better for all."

"Except for Mairi," said Jennie.

"She's not being walled up in a convent. She's not going to the headsman's block, like those wretched girls Henry the Eighth married."

It was heartless coming from a woman who had made a love match and was still reveling in it, from the looks of her and the General these days. "Poor Tony," she added indulgently. "There's no anguish like young love. It stabs so deep, but it heals with hardly a scar."

"But poor little Mairi," Jennie objected, "to be given over to a man she doesn't love."

"The first night doesn't bear thinking about, does it?" Lydia said cheerfully. She poured more coffee for them. "Ah, well, if the man is kindly and uses some delicacy—and Colin swears these Highlanders are capable of it and not just in their songs—she will be so grateful she will begin to love him, you'll see."

The *Paul Revere* sailed for the West Indies, carrying potatoes, dried salt fish, new barrels, hogsheads, and spruce shakes. The Debating Society invited the public to attend an open session; the resolution was that the United States should go to war to protect its right to the freedom

281

of the seas. The debate blossomed into a riot when the audience became passionately involved, the president broke his gavel, and the town clerk and the first selectman had to be forcibly restrained from striking each other. This made for more spirited conversation along Main Street than the subject of the debate, which was never formally resolved.

There was a confrontation about Columbine. Usually she was tolerated, but a lady took exception to fresh manure on her front walk the day she entertained the sewing circle, and had her impounded. The pound was behind the tannery, and Nabby was in hysterics, thinking Columbine was to be slaughtered. Sukey and Frank joined in the lamentations. Benoni had to pay a dollar to get Columbine back, and the General told him to take a day at home to rebuild his fences. Bets were laid on how soon she'd be through or over it.

It did not like Jennie to lie on her back in bed, making restless nights for them both. Lucy had asked her what names she favored, and she wondered if there was something strange about her because she had no lists of male and female names. She still thought of the baby as a sexless little swimmer in the dark, attached to her by a magic cord.

Lucy was coming once a week, finishing the cradle quilt while Jennie either hemmed napkins or knit Alick's stockings. They made tea on the spirit lamp just for the fun of it, though the big teakettle was steaming on the stove.

"Alick gave it to me for my birthday," she said.

"Oh, Lord," Lucy was dismayed. "I clean forgot."

"You're here. Every time you come it's a gift."

"That works both ways, you know," Lucy said. "I needed you as much as you needed me." She laid down her work. "Jennie, if you could have had whatever you wanted for your birthday, besides a spirit lamp and me, what would it be?"

A safe birth and a safe homecoming. "Let me put on my thinking cap," she said mincingly with a finger to her chin.

Lucy grinned. "You must be a contented woman if you can't name off ten things at once."

"I'm trying to choose among them, and I cannot."

"I know what I want," Lucy said. "And I know what I can't have. Jared." Tears hung on her lashes, and she blinked but didn't look away. "This is an anniversary for me, Jennie. The first day I've said his name aloud. Up till now I've been screaming it or wailing it silently, day and night."

"I'm honored that you said it to me," Jennie said.

"I *am* going to become pregnant again. I shall be terrified for the baby from the moment it's born, but if my mother or Harm's had given in to their terrors, neither of us would be here. The children before each of us died. Oh, Jennie, we will have young ones yet to rear together," she said staunchly. "And we won't be like these old hens trying to marry them off to each other. But wouldn't it be a wonderful thing to share grandchildren?"

"Yes, it would be." She could be honest about that because it would have been wonderful if she'd stayed in Maddox. "Lucy, I'll piece a cradle quilt for you this winter," she said. "I haven't many scraps, but they sell them by the pound at the dry goods store."

Jennie had not seen Mairi since the affair of the miniature. Anna Kate walked into town whenever the weather permitted and usually came to the cottage; she was disgusted with Mairi's parents and wouldn't have stopped at the Ark at all except to give the girl some silent sympathy.

"It's bad enough to be going there for the Sabbath service when I am not thinking very good thoughts. Mr. MacArthur has gone too far. They could keep Mairi from the lad without all *this*. How Sheena and Donald can look at her every day without being heart-scalded! I would never be believing. *Never*. And does the poor laddie know?"

"He knows there was trouble about the miniature and that is why he can't come home at Christmas. But they won't tell him about the marriage until it's over."

"Poor young things. Ewan's a good man, but och, he's twice her age, and his teeth are going. He never *was* bonny, even when he was young. He is not believing his luck; he will treat her like a princess. But we all are knowing who the prince is."

She had other news. A few days ago a traveler on horseback, putting up at the inn, took a walk out toward the muster field and the quarry to stretch his legs after a day in the saddle. When he was passing the Ark, the children just home from school were chasing each other around the house shrieking like Indians, and Old Dougal called to them in the Gaelic to watch out for the gentleman before they knocked him off his feet. The stranger stopped in his tracks and answered in the Gaelic, "The gentleman will be watching out for *them*."

Well! The tongues and the hearts were leaping in the Ark that night, with the joy that was at them all from hearing their language spoken by a stranger. Of course, in ten minutes he was no longer a stranger. He was a prosperous-looking man, on his way back to Canada after a stay in Boston, and he was telling them of the settlements in Nova Scotia where only the Gaelic was spoken, and from the looks of the land you would think you were back in Scotland. The old ways were kept, except that every man had a chance of becoming his own laird, as in Maddox.

"Mr. MacArthur could not be getting enough of it," said Anna Kate. "Old Dougal joked that the minister would have hidden himself away in this Ian Fraser's saddlebags if he could only be squeezing the rest of us in, too."

On a warm, silvery day at the end of November Jennie walked up Ship Street for the first time in weeks, to buy a pound of scraps for Lucy's quilt. She had enough of everything for It. Allan Robert's first dresses, slips, shirts, stockings, and caps were folded away in the chest with everything else she and Lucy had sewed, and knitted sacks, shoes, and two blankets from Eliza and Mrs. Frost. Lucy wasn't pregnant yet, but she would be; Jennie was obsessed with the idea of leaving her a completed cradle quilt when she left for home. She didn't dwell on the actual hour of departure; she concentrated on the quilt. Her fine seams were improving, and she wanted it to be a work of art which Lucy would always cherish in memory of her.

On this dreamlike day when the smell of woodsmoke from the lime kilns hung motionlessly over the town, Jennie saw the blue wagon again, outside the shoemaker's shop. So the children were getting their boots, at the very last minute. Apparently they'd already got them because they were in the wagon, and their mother sat on the seat, wearing a drab-colored cloak with the edge of the hood drawn out nearly to obscure her face. Evans was inside the shop, taking coins from a purse. Mr. Barron saw Jennie through the window and waved and smiled, but Evans didn't look up from his counting.

"How do you do, Mrs. Evans?" Jennie called. She thought there was a slight response from the depths of the hood, but she couldn't be sure. "Well, Gwynneth, it is nice to see you again," she said to the little girl.

"And Geraint, too." Gwynneth's small face was impassive. How could this be the same child who had scampered and sang? Geraint merely looked excruciatingly shy, but the older boy watched her like a cat poised to leap away at her first move.

The bell over the shop jangled, but she would have known Evans was coming out, even without the bell, by the way the children's eyes shifted past her. They seemed to hold their breaths. It infuriated her enough so she thought that she couldn't look at the man without showing it. She went behind the wagon and across the street to the dry goods shop. When she left there, the blue wagon had gone.

"Do you know Hugh Evans any better?" she asked Alick when she was getting supper.

"Who could be knowing him? He is still only talking to the General or Mr. Dunlop. He will be putting the letters on the ship when the time comes, but until then he works at home."

"What is her name to be?"

"If anyone knows, he is not telling," Alick answered. "The General is allowed his secrets."

"*Eagle!*" said Jennie triumphantly. "That figurehead I saw down there, like a heathen god in its temple—that must surely be for the new ship."

"*Eagle* is not much to keep secret. There is already one *Eagle* in the Pool."

"The difference will be in what other word he puts with it. Gallant, brave, valiant, American. Or perhaps he'll call her *Aquila.* That's the Latin word." She realized he wasn't listening to her; he had something heavy on his mind. It felt like the time when he knew Jared was dead and she didn't.

"Are you feeling good?" she asked sharply. "How is your arm?"

"The arm is fine. But bad news has come up the coast from the south. A wood boat brought word from Boston this afternoon. It is about the *Paul Revere.*"

"Oh, God!" She was setting the table, and the plates slid out of her weakened hands onto the wood. "Is it so bad that the town will be in mourning tomorrow?"

"She was last seen by a North Carolina vessel, one mast gone, and drifting in a hurricane in the Caribbean, west of the Leeward Islands. She was too far away, even if they could be putting boats overboard, and the other ship was having her own troubles at the time. But no small boats could have lived in that sea, they said. A *Dia*, it is hard thinking about her!" he said violently.

Neither ate much supper, and they made no pretense of keeping up a conversation.

Lying awake that night, she watched the now-familiar parade of the lost and the bereaved; her year had been full of such processions. Mrs. Wells's face became Lady Geoffrey's and then Lucy's. She saw Chet Mayfield when he first heard of his son and when he joked with Roddie and Ishbel that they must make a match between his boy and Paulina Revere. Both young fathers were gone now. Mrs. Wells came again, stoical as the legendary Roman matron, with two sons dead, the austere young captain and Stephen Wells, Jennie's first American; he was there most of the night, in and out of her waking and dreaming, from their first meeting at the top of the ladder in Loch Linnhe to their last, when he had been so affectionately proud of his Morgan horse. How long would the horse Justin look for him to come back? Would he always retain some memory of a certain voice, a certain touch?

That made her cry, and the other vision crowded in, the one she had been trying to hold at bay, and she knew that across the hall Alick was fighting to do the same.

Last seen with one mast gone and drifting in a hurricane.

Forty-Six

L OST, THE MEN of the *Paul Revere* became everyone's sons, and the handsome brig had been the town's pride as well as the General's. It had taken the wood boat's skipper perhaps ten minutes to tell the General all he knew about her fate, but he had left a picture which could never be erased.

In that ten minutes the ambience of Strathbuie House suffered a change as palpable when one stepped through the door as if a coffin lay in the drawing room. Even Oliver was affected because the General had become so quiet. Only Allan Robert was untouched, and when Oliver was in the house, he stayed in the nursery.

"Papa doesn't laugh and tease us anymore," Frank said. "Everyone is cross. Liza's cried so much she sounds as if she had a cold in her head. She isn't fun anymore."

"Because it's so *awful.*" Sukey rebuked her. "All those people are *drowned!* They're deep in the ocean, and nobody knows *where.* They will never come home *again!* Don't you *realize?*"

"Of course I do!" Frank shrieked. She flew at her sister and pounded her with her fists.. They both burst into loud crying. Jennie hugged a child to her with each arm. She hadn't cried and didn't expect to. It would be like the too facile, too temporary, relief of drunkenness. The violent death of the *Paul Revere* was an intimate loss for her. She had come to see the brig as a charmed ship: nothing could happen to her. She was like Wordsworth's ship; she would brook no tarrying.

She had become inextricably involved with Jennie's existence from the moment they'd bought their passage; her very name always sounded in Jennie's consciousness with the resonance of the church bell which the man Paul Revere had forged as a gift to the General.

And now, with common sense telling her the disaster was the sort of random accident that is always possible at sea, all her fears of childbirth were back like a horde of gibbering goblins. She was too ashamed to tell Alick or confide in Lucy, whose own emotions were still in a fragile state. She kept everything buried by day, but at night they would come when sleep had destroyed her defenses and tell her, "The *Paul Revere* died, and so will you."

When she was reluctant to go to bed even though she was half-sick with weariness, Alick said the stairs were getting too much for her. He and Tom Frost moved the narrow bed down into the parlor. "I will bring you anything you are wanting from up there," he told her. "I told you once I could be setting up as a lady's maid."

"Och, you are only wanting to have my big bed," she said teasingly. She missed his being just across the hall, but conversely his absence helped hold off the goblins because it reminded her how much lonelier she would be now if he had been the second Highlander to be buried in Maddox churchyard.

When she thought the children had wept long enough, she sent them to wash their faces. They came back refreshed and cheerful. Having leaned against her bigness (it was a wonder they hadn't felt It kicking at them, she thought) they wanted to discuss it.

"Mrs. Glenroy, will you go to Boston like Mama to get over being so fat?" Frank asked her. "If you do, *you* could find a little baby to buy. They have a lot of them in Boston."

"You could bring home a little girl," Sukey said, "and when she grows up, she can marry Allan Robert. We'll save our clothes for her, so it won't cost you much to raise her."

"That's a splendid idea," Jennie said. "I shall have to think about it."

Mrs. MacKenzie went on with her Christmas plans. "It is more important this year than ever before," she told Jennie over midmorning chocolate. "I can't cheat the children; this house is grim enough for them. The baby is too young to know it is his first Christmas, but it means a good deal to the rest of us. I hope it will cheer Colin up. If he is to take every loss like this, he had better get out of the ship business. This vessel for the Russian trade is another one; he has already hung his heart from her bowsprit. God knows what will happen to *her*, and we shall be going through all this again. And *again*."

The fruit cakes made from Mrs. George Washington's recipe had been baked in November, and venison mincemeat was ripening in a stoneware crock. An elderly couple far out in the country at the edge of the bog always made wreaths for her and evergreen garlands to festoon the banisters and doorways; the house was scented with pine and fir. In a town where the majority considered Christmas a pagan/papist ritual (the two words were interchangeable) there could be only a few guests for dinner. Liam O'Dowda was always one of them. Lydia had to admit that he ate and drank like a gentleman; she suspected good blood there, though she'd never been able to find out anything. He brought his fiddle, and they sang the old carols, the only sort of music she could tolerate, because it reminded her of Christmas at home.

There were usually two other couples; but this year one pair had gone to New York, and the other didn't think any sort of festivity, even in private, was appropriate; they did not wish to offend the bereaved families.

"I hope no one is brazen enough to accuse my husband of callous conduct," she said. "It would be the blackest calumny. They are perfectly free to attack *me*; I am accustomed to it." She was very grand about it, even impressive. She stopped short of implying that the loss of the *Paul Revere* was a personal inconvenience to her; she had written graceful letters of condolence to all the families; she had attended the memorial service.

"Exposing myself to lung fever and God knows what else. It was all very well to keep a cold church when they stored gunpowder in it, but there is no reason now why they cannot have proper fires in winter." She crumpled a letter in her hand and threw it across the room. "Royall and Christian won't be coming just when we need them most. Royall has always come only for love of Christian; to him our little celebration is the next thing to a Roman orgy. This year he has a perfect excuse; Christian has a bad cold. . . . We should have let Tony come home! If we could have trusted him," she added skeptically. "Did your family keep Christmas, Mrs. Glenroy?"

"Oh, yes," said Jennie softly. She pushed herself onto her feet. "It's time to go back to the girls."

"I wish you and your husband to dine with us on Christmas night."

"Mrs. MacKenzie, my husband has no dress clothes," Jennie said.

"I don't *care!*" she retorted passionately, sounding remarkably like her daughters. "He has a clean shirt, has he not? We must have someone else at the dinner table besides O'Dowda, or it will be like eating the funeral baked meats. I *beg* it of you, Jennie!" It was the first time she had ever used the name.

"I will do my best," Jennie said, but both the desire and the hope were very faint.

"I suppose it will not be harming me much," Alick said taking her aback.

"You mean you will *go?*"

"The woman sounds desperate. It would be only Christian, would it not?"

"Why do I suspect this?" she asked, and he laughed.

"I will go for you, Jeannie. You are needing a little cheer these days. I have survived worse than a dinner in Strathbuie House, and not too long ago."

Christmas was not new to Alick, although he had never participated in it. Archie's mother and Nigel's had kept the day in a discreet fashion, but Christabel, if she couldn't winter in London, liked to fill the house with guests daring enough to come to the Highlands in midwinter.

"Dr. Macleod was having the great difficulty with this," Alick said. "Linnmore House kept the manse in coal and firewood and himself in pheasant and venison and salmon. So what could he do, poor wee man? What would become of him if he was refusing to dine at Linnmore House on Christmas Day and ask the blessing? He was their tame minister, was he not? It was expected of him."

On Christmas Eve, Alick brought her oranges again and more raisins. "It is not a Christmas gift," he said sternly. "It is just something I have been intending to do."

She saw the fruit through a haze of unexpected tears. "Alick Gilchrist, you are a dear man," she said. "You surprise me again and again. You remember my birthday, and I let yours go by without a word; I was so taken up with myself, spoiled and selfish beast that I am." She couldn't find anything to cry on and used her sleeve. She heard him moving around, and presently a towel was put into her hands. "I don't know why I am doing this," she said, snuffling. "It not just because of your birthday, though it is bad enough to forget that."

"Jeannie, it was the day after the news came about the *Paul Revere*. Who would be remembering anything else? Not myself."

"But I should have remembered before," she insisted. "And now with the ship gone, I am afraid again. I am so ashamed, but I can't help it!" It all came out in a blubbering flood against his chest, and underneath the humiliation and the degrading joy of letting go there was the sweet relief of being held. It seemed to go on for a long time before her pride drearily asserted itself. She pushed away from his arms and hid her face in the towel. "I must look a horror. I *hate* weepy women," she said peevishly, "and all I do is howl all over you. You're a saint and a martyr."

"Far from that." The soft answer came from across the room.

"You see? You could hardly wait to escape my frantic clutches." She blew her nose on the towel. "I wish I could promise you this was the last time. Wouldn't that be a magnificent birthday present? But I have this birth to go through, and I know I will be perfectly awful. So when the time comes, you had better go for a very long walk. I don't want you to hear me disgracing myself."

He didn't answer. She lowered the towel and found she was alone in the room. He had taken his coat and his bonnet and gone out.

"I don't blame you," she said aloud. "I would run away from me if I could. If I could go into a desert somewhere and be a hermit, I would not allow me past the door."

When Alick came back, he brought her a little bell. "If anything frightens you," he said, "you are to be ringing this." He would hear no apology from her; he was aloof again, civilly discouraging all overtures.

Whether it was because of the bell or the catharsis of confession, she slept well that night between the baby's bouts of strenuous activity. When she was awake, she heard a southwesterly wind blowing about the corners of the house; it felt more like March than December. Having been temporarily purged of her terrors, she used one of these interludes to compose in her mind a letter to Sylvia, to be mailed in the event of her death. She tried to decide if she should tell Alick about it beforehand or leave it where he would find it afterward.

Beforehand was best, if she could discuss it rationally as she was thinking about it right now. She would write it in the morning before the fatigue and depression of the day could chip away at her endurance.

They were finishing a silent breakfast when a tentative knock came at the front door. Alick went to open it; Frank and Sukey stood on the doorstep in their blue and red cloaks. Oliver crowded in past them.

"Will you please be stepping in, young ladies?" Alick asked.

Holding hands, their faces preternaturally solemn, they came into the kitchen. "Papa sent us," Sukey said, "to sing you a song." And they began to sing; they commenced on different notes, and Sukey jerked Frank's hand hard. "I will start the song," she hissed. Frank's lower lip came out. Then Jennie caught her eye and winked and Frank grinned.

"We saw a ship—" Sukey began, and Frank opened her mouth and came in on tune. "Come sailing in, sailing in, sailing in,/ We saw a ship come sailing in,/ On Christmas Day in the morning!"

Jennie glanced at Alick, who lifted an eyebrow at her. The children sang on:

"And what do you think they called the ship? called the ship? called the ship?/ And what do you think they called the ship?/ On Christmas Day in the morning?" They were so near to exploding with laughter they had a hard time getting into the next verse.

"They called the ship the *Paul Revere*, the *Paul Revere*, the—"

"She's back!" Jennie cried. "*Is* she back? Really?"

"*Really!*" Frank superseded Sukey in speed and lung power. "Papa looked out this morning, and she was coming up the river. He woke us up to come see, and he woke Mama, and she wasn't cross, and then he rushed down to the wharf, and—and—"

Sukey took over. "And when he came back, he said, 'It's a miracle.' And he said we should come over and sing, 'I saw three ships,' only to sing it the way he told us."

"Are they all back?" Alick asked. "The captain and the first mate? Everyone?"

"*Everyone!* That is why it is a miracle! Happy Christmas!" They ran off, shouting the song at the tops of their voices.

Forty-Seven

THEY WERE BURNING COAL NOW; that meant they could keep a fire all night, so there was no need for Alick to come down several times a night to see to it. But he began doing so after her ignominious confession, even after he had given her the bell. She told him he shouldn't break his sleep for her.

"That is not the case," he said imperturbably. "A man may be wakeful on his own account."

She heard him only if she was awake; she was sleeping better now, between the baby's spells of jumping about. It was literally growing by leaps and bounds. *It can hardly wait to be born,* she thought, trying to shift herself into a position where she and It both would be comfortable. "It hates lying on your backbone," Lucy told her. "When you're up and around, it's in a hammock, but when you lie down, it probably feels as if it's perched on a woodpile."

"Charming," said Jennie. "You have just taken away any delusion I ever had of being a moderately attractive female human being."

She finished out December with the children. It was understood that she would be back eventually, with the baby in a basket; Mrs. MacKenzie supplied the basket and had it repadded and lined with soft cambric. But Jennie refused to accept wages for the next quarter.

"We don't know when the quarter will begin," she said.

"Fiddlesticks! Colin pays for sick leave. Why shouldn't I?"

"We have Alick's wages coming in. I would rather not be paid until I am actually earning it."

"Stubborn girl. You understand that I will stoop to anything to get you back, even bribery."

Jennie smiled. "I will be back." *Only until spring*, she finished to herself. *The girls will go to O'Douda yet.*

The first week of January was interminable. New Year's Day was wiped out in a blizzard, and for days foot travel was so poor that neither Anna Kate nor Lucy could walk into town to see her; Harm was going back and forth on the horse Jack. Jennie felt enormous and out of balance. Her nights were broken; she slept the soundest when she could nap in the daytime, tipped back in a rocker with her feet up on another chair. It was ready to nap then, too. The paradox was that she could be so peaceful, and all because the *Paul Revere* was back with every man safe. It was as if she had brought Jennie's life back with her.

Superstition, she thought lazily, *but a pregnant woman is entitled to humor herself. And how much of it is superstition? How much do we really know?* The General called it a miracle, and there was no one in Maddox who would dispute him.

The *Paul Revere* had ridden out the hurricane without losing a man overboard and without jettisoning her cargo of coffee beans, mahogany logs, and molasses. As the mountainous seas subsided, the captain's navigation and a fair wind took them to Trinidad, where they stepped a new mainmast and sailed for home; for a mast of honest Maine pine, the captain said.

It was arranged that if Jennie's time came in the night, Alick would go to the Frosts' and Tom would ride for the doctor; Mrs. Frost would come back with Alick. During her days at home alone, one of the men working around the stable would look in once during the mornings, and Eliza did the same in the afternoon, when she was out with the girls. The cradle was in the parlor now and made up. Lucy had told her what she should have in the house for the birth and how to prepare her bed for it. Alick slept in his clothes or half slept, listening for the bell. A candle burned all night on the kitchen table.

Everything was ready. It was like the last breathless moment at the top of Tumbledown Hill before you gave your sledge the final nudge to send it plunging over the lip in that glorious, terrifying, ecstatic sweep.

But when it did happen, it was as if someone had pushed her before she was ready, and her startled and furious shout was thrust back into her mouth by the gale wind of her descent. A pain woke her one night and she thought it was indigestion; it couldn't be anything else. But it wouldn't go away as long as she lay in bed. She rolled over to the edge and pulled herself up by the bedpost.

She was alone a long time with her pains, not wanting to wake Alick for nothing. She walked around and around the kitchen, leaning on the table and the backs of chairs when the pains took her. It was nearly four in the morning and perfectly still outside; the snow seemed to have a phosphorescent glow in the light from the brilliant multitude of stars. Inside, Jennie's shadow, more monstrous than ever, kept her company on her tortuous progress around the room.

Finally she hobbled back across the hall, stopping to hang onto the newel-post till a spasm passed, and rang the bell. She heard Alick come out of bed over her head, and he ran downstairs in his stocking feet. He found her sitting on the edge of her bed, trying not to groan.

"Why were you not calling me sooner?" He felt her sweaty forehead and damp hair. "Never mind. Back into bed with you." He swung her legs up onto the bed and covered her.

"Alick, the bed isn't prepared yet, and—"

"When I come back," he said. He went out into the kitchen, and she heard him stamping down into his boots. "I will be quick, Jeannie," he called.

She was alone, except for It, who was striving mightily to be born. She was not frightened; the pains took up all her attention. Still, it seemed as if she had been alone for hours when she opened her eyes after a particularly excruciating spasm and saw candlelight in the room and Alick bending over her.

"Where is Mrs. Frost?" She was so out of breath she could hardly hear herself, but he heard her.

"She can't speak with a cold. Give me your hands." He unclamped her fingers from wadded-up bedding and rubbed them. "Now, hold on to mine. Nothing can sweep you away while you are holding fast."

When the next wave had gone by, she gasped, "Have I wrung them off at the wrist?"

He smiled. "You cannot be hurting me, Jeannie."

Her voice was strange, so light and shallow. "They are coming too fast, and we haven't made the bed properly!" Too fast, too fast! If you did not roll off the sledge in time, you would smash into the stone wall. "Alick, it is *happening*, and no one is here!"

"You and I are here." He held her hands against his chest and squeezed them hard. "We will do it. Are you afraid with me?"

"*No!*" She laughed at her own shout, with tears running from out of the corners of her eyes. He put her hands down on her breast and turned back the bedclothes.

"Don't be trying to be brave. Shout or cry, curse or pray. It will help."

"I . . . don't . . . pray." She set her teeth until the new wave subsided.

"So it is indeed just yourself and me and the wee It," Alick said. "I am very experienced, Jeannie. I brought Mata into the world."

"And *his* mother never cried or cursed—"

"She was always a quiet beast." His last word was drowned by another surge. She wanted to tell him this must be how it felt to be drawn and quartered, but she couldn't say it while she was screaming in the dark. As the agony ebbed away, she opened her eyes; ashamed of her noise, relieved to be still in one piece, she saw Alick's shadow bending over the room; then her wet eyes came down to his absorbed face.

"I am seeing the head," he said. "Can you be pushing a wee bit, Jeannie?"

She started to say, "Did you ask that of Mata's mother?" But it took all her strength to push, and all her breath; she was panting and there was a pounding in her ears like kettledrums. There couldn't be a worse pain than the last one, but there was. She heard herself calling out for it to be ended, for someone—for Alick—to end it. After that the baby came quickly into his hands.

"She is a lovely girl," he said. Jennie listened in disbelief to her child's first cry. That squall of helpless protest moved her to tears; It had never asked for life, and now It had been thrust brutally out of the warm dark. When Alick showed It to her, she wept at the sight of that angry, contorted little face streaked with blood and mucus. How could she not love It for its very defenselessness?

"It is over, Jeannie"—Alick soothed her, not understanding her tears—"and you both are safe." He cut the cord and tied it with yarn from her workbasket. "I will be washing her now and bringing her back to you."

"If I were Mata's dam, I could wash my own child," she said faintly. It was then that Dr. Waite and Mrs. Walpole arrived.

"I will never forget his face," the nurse told Jennie later that day, when Alick had gone to work. "I will never forget the smile he gave us when we came into the room. *Proud?* I've seen a parcel of fathers in my day, but not many of them as proud as him. Well, why shouldn't he be? He brought his child into the world. And one of the prettiest new babies I ever saw."

"She's a beauty," Dr. Waite said. "Sound of wind and limb like her parents."

Jennie thought she could never stop studying the small face at her breast. This little creature sucking so greedily, knowing exactly what to do, had already made her place in the world after her first furious objections to it. Blue eyes like a kitten's; could they see yet? Or was it all just a blur of light and dark to her? A thick, soft fluff of fair hair. Nigel's daughter and a long baby, they said; she'd be a tall one. Nigel's daughter, but only in the most impersonal sense. *She is all mine*, Jennie thought. *She has nothing to do with back there. I never knew about her until I set foot on America.*

They had no room to keep the nurse overnight. "I will be attending them at night," Alick stated. "Every woman does not have a nurse surely."

"But there is usually a female friend or a relative who comes in to help."

"My wife and I are not what you would be calling usual."

"You certainly are not," Mrs. Walpole said dryly.

When she had Jennie settled for the night and had given Alick instructions, which he received with Highland courtesy, she left, and Alick came to Jennie.

"What would you be liking, Jeannie?" he asked. There was a fire in the fireplace, and the light constantly brightened and darkened his face, as it had done by their campfires.

"To talk a bit," she said. "Sit down." He pulled a chair up to the bedside. He was politely attentive; rather like a visiting solicitor, she thought, coming to hear some old lady's instructions about her will.

"I have not thanked you yet," she said. "There was no time; they came in too soon." She wondered if he was embarrassed now that it was over; *she* was not, a wonder in itself. But then the fundamental facts of life and death leave very little room for embarrassment.

"You were so serene," she said. "If you had acted frightened, I would have been, not to have the doctor here. But you made it all so simple."

"*Serene?*" He grinned. "*Simple?* And me soaked with sweat from the skin out and praying like a madman. It was simple because everything was right, Jeannie. A *Dia*, I was fearing she'd be lying wrong." Sweat sprang out on his forehead. "Look at me," he said. "Just from thinking about it now."

"But the point is that when I knew it would be just us, it felt so natural." Smiling, she looked around the room. "Our elegant parlor we thought we'd never use turned out to be another cave last night."

Neither spoke for a few moments while they watched the flames. Then he touched the sleeping baby's cheek with a forefinger. "What will you be calling her?"

"Priscilla, for my mother. Priscilla Hawthorne."

"The hawthorne is the plant badge of our family," he said. He stood up. "Would you be drinking a cup of your herb tea?"

"I would be playing a game of cribbage," she said, "if you don't think you have done enough for me already."

Forty-Eight

ON THE FIRST DAY the inquiries and congratulations had been left at the door. The next day Lydia MacKenzie herself came, bringing a wine jelly for Jennie and an exquisitely embroidered cap for the baby; she had made it herself. The General had sent the baby's name and birthdate to the Reveres for the ritual mug and porringer, by land mail because the river was frozen. The girls sent their love and kisses and bibs, which they had embroidered and hemmed in their needlework lessons with their mother.

"They can hardly wait to see the baby," she said. "They cannot get over the wonder of it all, that you should find a beautiful baby in Maddox and in the wintertime. They tell me they advised you to go to Boston for the best choices."

She sat beside Jennie's bed in a ruby red merino dress, making the parlor look smaller than ever. Her brown velvet winter mantle, trimmed with chinchilla, lay over the back of the small sofa. Out in the kitchen Mrs. Walpole was preparing to roast a chicken Mrs. Frost had left that morning.

"So your husband was the midwife," Mrs. MacKenzie said. "Well, at our Christmas dinner I thought, *Here is a man who does not say much, but neither does he have the eyes of a simple man. He has unplumbed depths,*" she said ironically. "I wonder how else he will surprise you."

Lucy came into town and stayed half a day with her. Some of the Highland women visited, bringing socks and shawls they had knit for Priscilla. Mairi's mother didn't come, nor did Mairi. She was already married, Anna Kate told her, and Ewan had rented a house on Quarry

299

Lane, over beyond the Frost farm; Ewan worked in the quarry. Mairi was hardly seen away from the house, and she kept it and Ewan's children spotless. Anna Kate had gone down there to tell her Jennie had come safely through and had a bonny wee girl. Mairi had not smiled, but she sent her love.

"I wish she would come to see me," Jennie said. "But I suppose that the weight of her parents, her husband, and the minister would be too much."

Anna Kate shook her head. "It is mostly herself, I am thinking. She is having to forget everything that went before."

With unruffled poise Alick received congratulations on fatherhood and midwifery. Mrs. MacKenzie was right about unplumbed depths, Jennie thought. He couldn't help caring for the child he had helped to be born, but to play the father's part when they had left the father dead, and by his own admission he still sometimes dreamed of it—that must call for superhuman willpower.

She spoke to him about it when he brought Priscilla to her for a feeding in the middle of the night. "How can you do it so well? It must be very hard on you."

"They all would be finding it strange if I was not seeming pleased with myself. Is it stabbing at you?" he asked. "Because you are thinking of *him* and how it is a tragedy he cannot be knowing his own child?"

"*No!*" she exclaimed. "Or yes, it *was* a tragedy, but it is a long time ago. Time rushes us along like the flood in the corrie. I think sometimes about Lady Geoffrey," she admitted diffidently, "losing her son and not knowing her grandchild. But I don't dwell on it. I cannot."

"Then there is nothing to be said. We are so deep in this, Jeannie, we can only be doing what is to be done. If everyone sees me as the father, that is what I am." He carried the sleeping Priscilla back to the cradle. Jennie watched him leaning over it, arranging the coverings snugly about the child.

"You will be a great builder of ships," she murmured.

"Why do you say that?"

"Because you do everything so thoroughly. Like tending her. Like seeing us through the delivery."

"And shaking for hours afterward, with the remembering and hearing. Good night, Jeannie." He took the candle back to the kitchen and left her.

She was up in a week. "I'm too healthy to lie here like an invalid. I have read everything twice, and I want the pleasure of walking around feeling *thin*."

She did not have to cook much because they sent so much food from Strathbuie House, but she washed the dishes. Eliza was in love with Priscilla and came in every afternoon on her way home. "Allan Robert's a big rumbustious boy with the whole family at his feet when they aren't wound around his little finger. This one is a flower, like the first white violets." Poetry was not strange, coming from Eliza; it came from other unlikely sources in this New England village: Truelove Adams's garden; the ships on the stocks; the spoken admiration of good horses; Nabby's love (and everyone else's tolerance) of Columbine.

Eliza's poetry had a practical underside. She took home the baby's laundry each night, washed it and dried it by the fire in her farm kitchen, and left it off in the morning.

The real winter had set in now; the *Paul Revere* had left for the West Indies just before the river froze and put an end to all boat traffic. The beached fishermen would go to work in the woods for either themselves or the General. Zeb Pulsifer's in-laws had him cutting logs for an addition to his one-room cabin. His mother crept out one moonlit night and tried to throw herself into the farm pond, but it was frozen, and she had possibly cracked her skull. A week later she was still dazed.

"Though I don't know how they could tell," Lucy said. "She's been so queer for so long."

"It's dreadful," Jennie said honestly. "I hated her when she was tearing at me and trying to kill me—I believe she would have crushed my windpipe if the men hadn't come—but it is still awful to think of her becoming what she is."

Jennie went back to teaching in the middle of February. Alick carried the basket each day into Strathbuie House and up the stairs to the schoolroom and stopped at noon to carry it home. With two babies in the house Oliver and the girls were distracted. Jennie could settle the children down to their work, telling them Priscilla should be left to herself to sleep, but Oliver couldn't decide where his duty lay. He worked out his own compromise: He stayed by Priscilla while she was in the house and escorted the basket back to the cottage, and when he was not playing outdoors in the snow with the girls, he gave the rest of his time to Allan Robert.

The second son of the house was now seven months old, a strapping, boisterous baby who laughed as hard as he howled.

"Don't forget," Sukey said, "he is going to marry Priscilla when they grow up."

"He may not want to."

"Of course he will! She will be beautiful!" Sukey reproved her.

"She is beautiful now." Frank sighed over the basket. "Just like Baby Fluff."

There was good skating in February; Eliza took the girls out to her home to skate on the duck pond. The General's ice-cutting crew sawed great blocks of ice from his ponds outside the village. It would be stored away in the icehouse until it was shipped in the spring to the southern states.

Sleigh bells rang through blinding blue days and starry or moonlit nights; March came in like a lamb, and the ice left the river except for the rotting floes thrown up on the shores. Influenza struck the town after the first week. It was not as bad as in Tenby, where, Christian wrote, she was keeping herself and the baby immured like refugees from the Black Death.

In Maddox the selectmen agreed to postpone the opening of school until the worst had passed by. School was always suspended for the three winter months because so many of the children had so far to walk and it was a time when epidemics blossomed; one child with scarlet fever or measles could infect a roomful.

Two elderly persons didn't survive the influenza, and three younger ones with fragile lungs suffered relapses; for them the long, hard climb up March hill each year was a matter of two steps up and three steps back. In Boston and Cambridge the influenza was allied with an outbreak of putrid fever, and the college suspended classes. Tony could have stayed in Quincy with his stepmother's family, but without asking his father's consent he came home by mail coach as far as Wiscasset, and hired a horse there from one of his father's friends.

Jennie didn't know he had come until he knocked at the cottage door, and at first she thought it was a stranger standing there in a caped blue coat and wearing a high-crowned black hat. Then she embraced and kissed him as if he were a young brother, she was so glad to see him.

His shoulders had widened, and his face grown older and more determinate. He had begun to shave. But the long-lashed black eyes were those of young Tony, and she knew what they were asking before his mouth could say it.

"*Is it true?* Or are they just telling me that? Hannah is only making mischief, isn't that so?"

"No, it's true, Tony," she said. He looked as if he had taken a deathblow and knew it. Blindly he turned to go, and she held his arm.

"Please stay and have a cup of chocolate with me! You needn't look at Priscilla; admiring a new baby is the last thing you want to do, but—"

He pulled roughly free. "How could they do it to her? How could *she* do it? Why didn't she run away?"

"How could she run away, Tony? Where was she to go?"

"Did you know it before it happened?"

"I had heard something," she admitted.

"Why didn't you tell me? I would have come home and taken her away." There were tears in his eyes.

"Tony, will you please sit down?" she said sternly. He obeyed, looking very young and obstinate. "I know this has been a terrible discovery for you. But it is pointless to blame anyone, least of all *me*. You and Mairi both are children in the eyes of your parents and the law. I had no right even to offer an opinion, only my sympathy, and Mr. MacArthur questioned my right to that. I meddled enough when I passed on the miniature."

"Where is she?" he asked doggedly.

"In Ewan MacLean's house."

"But where is it?" He stood up.

"You cannot go there, Tony. If you care anything at all about Mairi, if you care more for her than you do about yourself, you will not go there."

"Will he beat her?"

"No. He's a good man. You will be the one to hurt her. She is trying to forget the past; it is all she can do. Leave her in peace."

"Don't tell *me* I shall ever get over this!" he said ferociously.

"You won't," she said. "No one ever does. But don't you suppose that the rest of us have been through it? Your father, your mother, myself, Alick? Everyone has! But not many people die of it, Tony, though sometimes they wish to."

Plainly he doubted that.

"Everything looks so sad to you now," she said, "but I can tell you from experience that you never know when your life will change in the twinkling of an eye, sometimes for the worse, sometimes for the better. Nothing ever stands still. Sometimes it goes too fast; sometimes it 'creeps in this petty pace from day to day,' as Macbeth says, but it never stands in one place. . . . Will you drink chocolate with me now?"

"No, thank you." He was polite, though distraught. "If you won't tell me, I will find out from someone where she lives."

She shrugged. "I cannot stop you."

He went out and then put his head back in the door. "I should have brought the baby a gift. If I go back, I shall find some pretty thing for her."

"*If?*"

He shut the door on that. She watched from the windows while he ran along the snowy path toward Strathbuie House. Hannah would gladly tell him where to find Mairi; the girl was a born mischief-maker. But whatever happened now had nothing to do with Jennie. Priscilla was stirring, and she lifted her from the cradle and sat down to feed her. The two of them were enclosed in a globe of intimacy as seamless and shimmering as a soap bubble. Priscilla now saw her face; she was sure of it.

Forty-Nine

THE NEXT DAY while she was having café au lait with Mrs. MacKenzie, Lydia told her Tony had come home without permission. Jennie said nothing of his visit to the cottage.

"He is so upset about the girl Colin didn't have the heart to give him the tongue-lashing he deserves. He did forbid him to go near her." She sighed. "Well, at least he has the news. I was dreading it. Now he will be able to put it all behind him. He knows he is to go back next week, by either land or sea. Quincy is the best place for him, and he can't be gloomy around my nieces; they won't allow it."

"Where is he now?"

"He has taken a dory and rowed downriver, to camp overnight on Spar Island. He may be running away to sea, but I doubt it, and I don't think he intends to do away with himself either. Mrs. Frost tells me he has taken enough food for half a regiment."

"It's a beautiful day," Jennie said. "The winds feel soft as spring, and the pussywillows are out. If anything can help a broken heart, this should be it."

"Not to mention enough physical exercise," said Mrs. MacKenzie, "to burn up all that young lust rising like the sap in the maple trees."

The gentle weather continued the next day. It was as Saturday, and Alick was home; he put in most of the morning working on his lessons for the next week, and Jennie did the baby's wash. The rainwater hogsheads had been set back under the spouts, and one good rain last week had filled them all halfway and soaked up the seams.

In the afternoon she went outdoors to take the dry things off the lines. After being washed in rainwater with Hat Shenstone's soap and blown dry in a mild wind, the baby's napkins were velvety to the touch. The sun came warmly through the silver gray maple boughs, and there was green grass close to the house; when she walked on it, it released a subtle scent like a whispered promise.

Alick went out to the well, whistling, and Tony came tramping up from the orchard through the last long rags of melting snow. He wore heavy woolen breeches and a jacket flapping open, and his cap was on the back of his head. His face was flushed, and his eyes looked watery. He ignored their greetings and sagged down on the front doorstep.

"I couldn't go into our house." He was shivering. "My mother is entertaining ladies at tea, and I didn't want to tell Liza and Mrs. Frost, and my father is having a meeting in the library."

"You're wet," Alick said. "Have you fallen overboard?"

"Quickly, come in to the fire," Jennie said. "I will make something hot for you."

He huddled close to the stove, his clothes steaming with a powerful odor of wet wool and salt water. His teeth were chattering. "I stayed on Spar Island last night. I made a bed of fir boughs and slept under the stars." He gave Jennie a sheepish little grin. "It almost convinced me that life was worth living. I dug clams and boiled them over my campfire, I saw a splendid moose, and this noon I set out for home with a mess of clams for my father. He is partial to Spar Island clams."

Jennie gave him a mug of fresh tea, and he held it with both hands. "You know where the Evans place is?" he said to Jennie. "Well, when I was rowing up past it, I saw two of the young ones out on the old dock, and the girl began waving her arms at me and jumping up and down and shouting, and pointing off the end of the wharf. I rowed in, wondering what she saw there, and—" His hands shook so hard he splashed hot tea over them, but he didn't seem to feel pain. "Oh, my God, I shall never be warm again, never!" The color had even left his lips.

Alick drew a chair up close to the fire. "Now, Tony, you must breathe deeply before you talk."

Obediently Tony took a few deep breaths. "Now drink some tea," Alick told him, and Tony took a scalding gulp that put tears in his eyes. After that he spoke carefully, looking past them as if describing the scene while it was happening.

"When I was almost at the wharf, she began screaming 'Be careful, be careful, she's *there!*' And she was. The water was flat calm and clear as crystal, and I saw her lying there looking up at me, and her hands were moving up and down, up and down, like this." He put out one arm and demonstrated. His hand floated lifelessly in invisible waters. "And her hair was moving all around her head. Very gently, like fronds of seaweed."

"Mrs. Evans?" Jennie's voice sounded peculiar to her; it was that light, shallow voice she'd heard during Priscilla's birth.

" '*Get* her, *get* her!' the girl kept screaming," Tony said. "But I couldn't reach her; I had nothing to use. I rowed to the beach, and I tried to make them come with me. I didn't want to leave them there with her, but the girl was beside herself; she couldn't endure to see her mother in the water. I said we would get someone to help." His anguished eyes appealed to them. "They saw her do it. The girl was talking so fast it was confused, but I think she filled an apron with rocks, and she tied up more in a scarf and tied it around her neck, and she jumped off the end of the wharf." His voice dropped to a whisper. "I think she wanted to drown them first, but they ran."

"There is an older boy," Jennie said.

"He wasn't there. No one. I ran up to the house, and Evans wasn't there. The wagon and the horse were gone. He must be in town somewhere. Somebody should tell him to get her before the tide goes out." He swallowed hard. "She'll be lying on the mud, and the gulls and crows will be at her."

"We'll be finding Evans," Alick said, "and somebody will go down there whether or not we find him."

Tony sprang up. "I'm going with you."

"No," Alick said gently.

"But don't you see, I cannot simply wait here and do nothing!" Tony shouted at him.

"You can if I am telling you," Alick said. "You will kindly be staying with my wife." Tony subsided.

"I will speak to Ben Frost," Alick said to Jennie. He took his bonnet and went out.

"Well, Tony," Jennie said, "we shall drink that chocolate now. I don't know why it is, but something rich and sweet always helped me when I was horribly upset. And I am now."

He was glad to be taken out of his own hands. The baby began to fuss a little, and he sat by the cradle and kept it gently rocking while Jennie made the chocolate.

"I tried to make them come with me," he said. "I had to leave when I did, or I couldn't have got out on the river. The tide was going, and I had to tell someone about her. I didn't want to leave them," he kept repeating.

"But now you have told someone. . . . Pris is asleep again. Come and drink your chocolate." She buttered thick slices of bread for him. The food and the sweet drink helped, as she had expected it would. He became more composed.

"It was the most terrible experience of my life," he said with a kind of awe. "I shall never forget the way she looked. She must have been insane if she tried to kill the children too."

"She is, or was, a strange woman," Jennie said. "Your mother knows a little of her history." She talked about seeing them in the wagon and how, if Evans was anywhere near, they all were turned to stone. "When he did the miniatures, what was he like?"

Explaining how the artist had executed the preliminary drawing for the miniatures, Tony sloughed off some of the day's morbid effects. "He didn't talk, except to say, 'Move your head this way,' or 'that.' He was completely absorbed. Christian said he had beautiful eyes, and she was going to make him smile. We had a wager on it. I won, and she became very angry because he ignored her blandishments." He grinned. "He had Sukey and Frank absolutely quenched. They hardly dared blink or breathe. So you see he must be a brother of the Medusa; he turns people to stone."

Then he looked guilty as if he'd been caught joking at a funeral and swallowed down the rest of his chocolate with an audible gulp.

Nabby Frost came to the door, a plain little girl who could be as stolidly economical with words as her father and as loud as Sukey and Frank when they played Indians in the orchard. "Mr. Glenroy said please to tell you he is going downriver with Pa and Tom and Mr. Parker." Mr. Parker was the constable.

"Thank you, Nabby," Jennie said.

The child's face was suddenly transfigured with happiness. "I'm going to play with Sukey and Frank and eat supper with them. We are having Brown Betty!"

"That's lovely, Nabby. Eat some extra for me."

"I will," said Nabby seriously. She went away in her little brown cape, every other step a skip.

"Now it is really somebody else's business, Tony," Jennie said. "You did your part. You needn't sit here with me any longer if you'd rather leave."

"He asked me to stay with you." He sounded sullen, but she knew him too well by now.

"I don't need taking care of. But if you would like to stay, you're welcome. We could play cribbage to pass the time."

"No, I will go home and change my clothes. Perhaps my father's meeting is over by now."

"Yes, he should be told"— Jennie gravely agreed— "and you are the proper one to tell him."

"That is what I've been thinking. . . . It doesn't sound as if they found Evans, does it? What will they do about the children?"

"If he doesn't come while they are there, they will bring the children back."

"Of course." He was trying to sound maturely objective; but the children had been on his mind, and now he could be openly relieved. He gave her a very young little smile. "Thank you for the chocolate and the company, Mrs. Glenroy." He hadn't mentioned Mairi once.

Alone at last. Well, not quite. She looked in at Priscilla, who was lying awake wiggling her fingers before her face and talking to them. When she saw her mother, she kicked her feet. "Rather outside than in," Jennie said to her. "My, the way you punched and kicked your poor mama before you popped out."

She had dropped her armful of baby laundry on the chest when they brought Tony in, and now she began arranging it on the backs of chairs around the stove to lose its last dampness. The parlor was still warm with late-afternoon sunshine, so she spread little dresses and shirts over the furniture in that room.

Priscilla was loudly hungry now, and she brought her into the parlor and sat down in the sun, in one of the little lolling chairs with her feet on a stool. Before the birth she used to wonder dispassionately if she could satisfy a baby, but from the moment when she had taken the baby to her breast before it was an hour old and felt its lips fasten on her nipple, she had known the milk would come and there would be enough.

Feeding Priscilla kept Mrs. Evans at a distance. She loved to look for the day-to-day changes in the baby's face. If she thought of Priscilla as Nigel's daughter, it was infrequently and distantly. The baby seemed absolutely her own. But in her length and her coloring, if it didn't change, there would always be reminders of Nigel, which her mother could not refute. Perhaps one day, a long time from now, she would tell Priscilla that she resembled her father and that he had been a handsome young man as well as a brave one, a soldier. She would be able to think of other true things to flesh him out for the child. A child deserved a father; even a dead one was better than none, if only she could picture him.

She had caught once that evanescent likeness which she had seen in Alick; it was both fantastic and comic to glimpse it in the baby features. She'd have thought she imagined it, but several persons had said, at first sight of Priscilla, "She looks like her father."

"She's too tiny to look like anyone," Jennie said, "except herself."

But Anna Kate had gone on about it, how clear it was—"Cannot you be *seeing* it?"—until Jennie was embarrassed for Alick's sake. But Alick hadn't turned a hair.

"It's the nose," he said blandly. Now Jennie found herself studying Priscilla's nose from different angles to see if it was indeed the Gilchrist nose. But she couldn't tell yet.

Fifty

ALICK DIDN'T RETURN until long after dark. He looked in the front door and said, "I'm back," then he sat down on the doorstep and took off his boots. When he came in, one glimpse of his face told her not to ask him anything. She made tea and ladled warm water into the pantry basin from the big pot kept on the back of the stove. He was in his stocking feet, and she saw traces of dried mud on his boots almost to the tops before he threw them into the entry as if he hated them. He looked morose and bone-tired.

While he was washing up, she gathered the baby's things and folded them with more than usual precision; she needed something to do with her hands.

Finally he came out, drying his head and ears. She poured tea into two mugs and added milk and sugar. "Here, drink this," she said. "I wish I had whiskey to put in it."

"That was never a favorite dram of mine," he said. "It is only spoiling good tea and good whiskey." He left the towel around his neck and took a cautious sip. "*Ah* . . . when it burns the gullet out of you, you cannot be thinking of anything else." He dropped into a rocking chair and leaned his head against the back of it and shut his eyes. She sipped her own tea, watching the play of the candlelight over his face. After a few moments he sat up and reached for his mug.

"The children are safe," he said.

"Thank God." One said it instinctively, and Alick gave her a wry look.

"Thank *me*. Himself was having nothing to do with it. I found them,

311

and we brought them back with us, Tom with the boy, and the girl rode with me. Parker was carrying their mother along in his wagon."

"Where are the children?"

"Ben said we should be leaving them with Rose of Sharon. She takes in all the orphans until the town is deciding what to do with them."

"She will be good to them and for them," Jennie said. "I am so relieved I am almost light-headed. Tell me how you found them."

"We could hear the cow bellowing before we turned off the road into the woods, it was that quiet down there. We were hearing the gulls and the crows shrieking down at the shore. That was a sound to be turning Tom's lips white, and mine, too, from the cold I felt." He took a long draft of the tea. " 'I'll be tending to the cow,' Ben says, with a stammer. Och, he was happy about having *that* to do. Tom and I walked to the shore, and Parker drove his wagon down. We had ropes and a boathook. The gulls were diving and screaming enough to send you mad, and the crows were swooping amongst them, as close to the water as they dared. When we walked out on the wharf, they all flew, but not far."

He stopped. Jennie took down a shawl to warm herself against the chills that ran over her body in arpeggios from her crown to her heels.

Alick was speaking with eyes shut. "And there *she* was, with only enough water to cover her. 'Jesus,' Tom said, 'but the water is running out like a brook, and we cannot be walking out there to get her; we will be sinking ourselves.' Parker came running—he is not a large man but strong—and we pushed the old boat down over the flats and into the water, with Tom praying aloud that it was sound. . . . And it was, though I am not convinced God did that for us in just five minutes. It is certain He did not give us another oar. But there was no depth for rowing. Tom poled us out with the one oar and around to the wharf where she was."

His eyes flew wide open then, as if he didn't want to see anything else. "All the time I am thinking, *They are watching. They have been watching by their mother all day, and they will not be leaving while she is here.* I could feel them watching."

"I can believe that," said Jennie hoarsely. She got up and filled their mugs again and then stayed hovering over the stove, rubbing her arms to drive away the gooseflesh.

"We were reaching her just in time. I will not be giving you the details of the rest of it, except to be saying it was not easy to kneel in a small boat and lift up a body weighted with rocks, and be trying not to look at her face. . . . And the arms and legs stiff as tree limbs. If we had toppled out, we could not drown in two feet of water, but the tide was running so fast we could have been stranded on the mud till the tide came again, Tom and myself and her." He added with black humor, "At least the birds would have quieted once it was dark. A *Dia*, how they were carrying on."

They had gotten away in time. The rowboat beached out a distance from the shore, and they dragged it up over the flats with her in it. Then they cut away the scarf and the apron in which she'd tied up the rocks, carried her up to the wagon, and wrapped her in a tarpaulin.

Tom lost everything he had eaten that day. He climbed up beside Parker, but Alick would not ride up to the house. He stayed behind, scraping the mud off his boots and listening. The gulls and the crows had flown off, so it was quiet again. Across the river the winter-brown fields were turned gold in the late sunshine, but here in the cove that shade was a cold blue. He went up onto the bank and looked around, and he knew they had to be watching from behind the granite slope to his right; the oak woods to the west were too far away.

He went up the granite ledge and sat at the top, wiping his boots with handfuls of moss. There was such a hush, he could hear the children trying to be stealthy behind him in the dead leaves.

"Come to me," he said, busy at his boots. "I am meaning you no harm. Your mother will be going away now, and you will not be wanting to stay here alone." They were perfectly still. "Or is your father coming back? Tell me this, please."

"And so," he said to Jennie, "they crept out to me, she holding tight to her wee brother's hand. With the eyes on them they put me in mind of the Dallas children. But these two were not playacting."

Their father would not be back, Gwynneth said, and the older boy had gone with him. "Da's shadow," she called him. Da had left a letter, and she had read it, while the mother was sitting there deaf and blind as one of Evans's figureheads. All at once the woman was away to the shore, and they followed after. She walked out to her middle in the cold water and tried to lure them to her, but they were afraid. They cried and begged her to come back, but she would not. Gwynneth wanted to run along the shore to the nearest neighbor, but the little boy was in such fear he lay on the ground and howled, and she was afraid to leave him for fear the mother would be drowning him. "You are bastards," she kept crying to them. "You are children of sin! You must die to be saved!"

"Don't go on," Jennie wanted to beg him, but she knew he could not leave it here.

"So they cuddled together up on the big ledge, just in the spot where she was telling me about it and watched her lay her apron on the wharf and go back and forth, carrying rocks to put on it. Then she tied it up in a bundle and fastened it around her waist, and the scarf around her neck, and jumped off the end of the wharf. They ran down there, Gwynneth dragging the little one, and they saw her drown; but there was nothing they could be doing to save her."

He leaned his head back again. This time, when he shut his eyes, the light caught on the wet glistening line below his eyelids.

After a time he sat forward. "The note was in the Bible, she said. Her mother put it there before she ran out of the house. And so it was. At the Song of Solomon," he said. "Do you know the one that has the words, 'Rise up, my love, my fair one, and come away'? It must have been what he was saying to woo her away from her father." He was grimly sardonic.

"He might have used it," Jennie said. "Somehow he talked her out of that parsonage."

"We were thinking he went away in the night and left the note for her to find. He slept in a room off the kitchen, and her bed was upstairs at the other end of the house, so he could be moving out all his painting gear without her knowing. Creeping out like a thief, taking the older boy. Do you know he delivered the figurehead yesterday and was paid? He must have had this planned."

"What did the note say?"

"It would be turning your stomach," he said in disgust. " 'Our marriage was false, so I owe you nothing!' You should have been hearing Benoni swear! 'I was already married, and my wife's still living. I am going to her.' So he has gone, like that!" He snapped his fingers.

"I could kill him with my own two hands!" Jennie said. "I knew he was a monster when I first laid eyes on him! He spent her money, forced three illegitimate children on her, turned her into a ghost, and walked out. He should be shot. No, hanged," she said with relish. "*Slowly*, the way they used to do it. Then drawn and quartered before he was dead."

"As to that, we all were in agreement."

"Where is the note now?"

"I took it to the General. He will be seeing to everything now."

Jennie sighed and stretched herself as if she'd been bound with ropes for an hour. "If it hadn't been for you, Alick, they would not be safe with Rose of Sharon tonight," she said.

"But they will be dreaming of it."

"But they will not be alone," she said firmly. "Come and eat, Alick. You have done all you could, and the poor soul's torment is over."

He stood up. "Not in these clothes. I should not even be wearing them into the same room with you and Priscilla."

He took a candle and went upstairs. When he came down, he threw the clothes into the entry after the boots. "I would be burning them if I could afford to," he said.

"Never mind, we will get them clean of all that." She knew he meant the touch of the corpse. She sliced bread on the wooden board and ladled the hearty stew into the bowls. "Come and eat."

Just as he sat down, Priscilla stirred and fussed. He pushed back his chair and went swiftly to the cradle and lifted her out, expertly supporting her head in the crook of his elbow while he wrapped a blanket around her. "We will be taking a wee walk, *mo chridh*," he told her. She liked being talked to and always responded in her own language, with her arms and feet in ecstatic motion. "Ah, you'll be jumping out of my hands one day like a lovely slippery trout," he said, "the way you came into them, the night you were born."

He walked back and forth through the rooms with her until she fell asleep again. Then he put her back into the cradle so deftly she didn't wake. When he finally sat down to eat, it was as if the time with the baby had washed his mind clean for a little while.

That night neither of them wanted to go to bed. They played cribbage until their eyes were burning and fogging and the spots danced on the cards. When Alick won the fourth game in a row, Jennie said, "I am finished. I am so sleepy I don't know how I could possibly lie awake and think about anything."

"Because it is over." He was putting the cards and the board on the mantelshelf. "You said it yourself."

Fifty-One

THE SLEEPINESS PASSED by the time they had settled down for the night, and she was wide-awake. If her body wanted to be quiescent, her mind refused to rest. She lay on her side looking through the hall at the candlelight in the kitchen, listening to the clock measuring off the night, so melancholy that the dead woman could have been lying out there in the kitchen with the light of the candle playing over her drowned face. Her mind scurried around and around as if it were literally a prisoner inside her skull. With a whole universe in which to rove, she was a mean, impoverished creature if she couldn't do better than shackle herself to a corpse.

She turned over on her back and folded her hands on her now-flat belly, but even that couldn't give her the usual sense of achievement and satisfaction. She thought of Dr. Johnson waking in the night thinking he had had a stroke and composing Latin verses to prove to himself that his mind wasn't affected. Jennie's Latin was weak; Ianthe had been the one to make Papa's eyes light up. But Jennie could memorize in English better than the rest, and now she went dredging for long-forgotten lines, the more obscure and complicated the better.

"Victorious men of earth, no more/ Proclaim how wide your empires are. . . ." The search for the next part woke her up even more. The owl was out there again, the voice as elusive as a cuckoo's. From across the room she heard the baby's light, quick breathing. Only hunger woke Priscilla, and she'd fed well before Jennie went to bed.

This would be a perfect time to light the spirit lamp and boil enough water for a cup of chamomile tea, which was supposed to settle the nerves. She sat up in bed, and when she did so, she heard, or rather sensed, other movement in the house. Alick was walking back and forth upstairs, probably in his bare feet and stepping lightly, but there was no mistaking it.

If she thought *she* was shackled to the dead woman, what about him, who had helped lift the body out of the mud? How could she have been so self-centered as to ignore what waited for him when he was alone in the dark?

Lord, she was as much of a monster of selfishness in her own way as Evans was in his. She got out of bed and went out into the hall and listened. He walked past the head of the stairs, a shadow moving among shadows, and she went up a few steps. When he came back, she said his name, just loud enough to reach him.

"What is it?" he asked.

"We both are wide-awake, so come down, and we will keep each other company for a bit."

He didn't move. "Please, Alick," she said. She went back down the few steps, and after a few moments he came. He was still dressed except for his shoes. When he reached the foot, it seemed as if she could feel the cold coming off him, the dreadful winter of an isolation which was almost as absolute as death. Without any conscious forethought she put her arms around him. "Come and warm up," she said. "We both are so cold."

She took his hand and led him to her bed. She was light-headed but very clear in her mind, aware that he walked with her like someone in a spell. She turned back the covers with one hand, still holding on to him, and got in.

"Come in with me, Alick," she said. "It wouldn't be the first time, would it? Except that this isn't a bed of fir or bracken, and the plaid isn't here."

"A *Dia*, Jeannie," he said in a low voice, "it is different now."

She answered unsteadily, "I want to warm you and comfort you. Is that so terrible?" She held up the covers, and he came into her bed. They lay on their backs side by side, not touching; like man-and-wife effigies on a tomb, she thought. Stone forever. "The grave's a fine and private place,/ But none, I think, do there embrace."

She turned toward him and into an embrace so close she could not tell whose heartbeat was the wildest.

"Jeannie, do you know what you are doing?" he whispered.

"I think so," she whispered back. *"Yes."*

He raised up on one elbow, trying to see her face, and she put her hand on his cheek. "I leave your bed now or not at all," he said. "Which is it to be?"

"You leave only long enough," she said, "to take off your clothes. I want nothing more to separate us."

There were no bolts of lightning, no stars falling in showers of gold; for them it was the long, leisurely creep of the tide as they were lifted up and powerfully borne on a broad, calm, moonlit current toward the moment of flood and their cries stifled against each other's mouths.

Afterward they kissed with almost as much passion as before. "Am I dreaming this?" he said.

"No," she said drowsily.

"You will not be leaving me, *mo graidh.*"

"No. Never." She kneaded his bare shoulder. "It will take me too long to learn all your bones."

"And I yours. But I am making a good beginning. I think there is not much of you I have not touched tonight." His hand stroked the smooth, soft skin on the inside of her thigh but made no demands now. "I am not believing this."

"Neither am I," Jennie said. "But if it is a dream, I never want to wake up."

"I have been loving you so long I was thinking sometimes it would kill me."

"I have loved you so long as my friend," she answered, "but I didn't know what else was happening to me. . . . I should have known the night I thought you were dying. Oh, I love you, Alick. I *love* you!"

And I thought it could never happen again, she rejoiced. She wanted to hold him in her arms forever.

They slept entwined, too drugged for either one to wake up cramped or numbed. When she half woke and realized he was leaving her, she reached out for him with her eyes still closed. "I am just bringing the baby to you," he whispered. He kissed her forehead and her cheek, and she turned her mouth to find his.

Across the room Priscilla burst into full cry. "Did I say something about wishing the dream to go on forever?" Jennie murmured. "I forgot the dawn chorus."

She felt rather than heard him laugh. In the dim room she could just make him out as he went to the cradle. He came back talking to Priscilla, who would have none of his Gaelic blandishments.

"What every woman needs to start the day," Jennie said as she took the child, "is to have her baby brought to her by a naked man."

Alick was not abashed. "I wrapped her well because she is wet. I would have brought her to you clean and dry, but she is so angry she would never be putting up with it."

"No, she would not. But I would never ask you to wash her, Alick, if I were able to do it myself. Men don't do such things."

"This man would." He leaned over and kissed her head and the baby's. Then he took his clothes from the sofa where he had thrown them last night and went out to the kitchen.

Listening to him stirring up the fire, going outdoors, coming back in again, she felt in her body a whole new set of exquisite responses, and she knew it was not *again* after all. There was no déjà vu with it; it was of itself. Her body was new-minted this morning, and so was her life.

She bathed the baby on the table while Alick was making the porridge. There had been just one moment, as she went into the kitchen, when she was shy of meeting him in the light of day. He was just coming in from the entry with an armful of dry kindling. They had looked across the kitchen at each other with exactly the same joyous and vulnerable surmise. He dropped the kindling and came to her, and they kissed over the baby's head.

"Jeannie, is it true?" he asked. "You are not counting the days until you sail?"

"If I write to Sylvia today, will you believe me?"

"Och, but it's hard," he admitted. "I believe you, but I cannot be taking anything for granted. It is so long I have been fighting it and thinking it could never be true for me."

"It *is* true, and we have all this Sunday to be saying so, and looking at each other, and *touching*. And going to bed," she added. He grinned.

"And everyone will be knocking at the door to be passing the time of day. No. We will be waiting for night."

"Do you think we can survive until then without burning to cinders?"

"If we can keep our hands off each other," he said. "Tony is here, don't forget. He will be coming in after church, if not before, and we will likely be having his company for half the afternoon if he is not getting the proper sympathy at home."

Jennie said, astonished, "I had completely forgotten what happened yesterday." It sobered them so that they ate breakfast without much conversation. The sun shone through the bare trees, and newly arrived song sparrows were singing. The springlike weather would hold for today at least. Jennie wondered how Gwynneth and Geraint had slept at Rose of Sharon's and felt a little guilty because her happiness was stronger than any other emotion this morning. She hoped that it was the same for Alick and that his brooding expression didn't mean he was slipping back too fast from the heights.

"We are not married," he said all at once.

She was not exactly shocked or appalled; *consternation* was the word that came to mind. She reached across the table to him. "What are we to do?" she asked unsteadily. "We cannot stay apart, Alick. Not after all this."

He took her hand and kissed it, then kept it lightly against his lips. "We could not be going to either of the ministers here, and I would not."

"Can you imagine what they would *think?*" She tried to laugh. "We have been passing as man and wife since Fort William, sleeping in the same cabin, living under the same roof, and now we have a baby. What are we to do? Find some gypsies or Indians, as poor little Mairi wanted to do?"

He lowered her hand and looked at it with his head on one side. *"Handfast,"* he said. "We have spoken of that handfast wedding of ours so many times I can almost believe it happened. What we will do, *mo chridh*, we will find a minister in another town, when we are knowing more about where to go, and we will tell him that under Scottish law we are wed; but the fear is at us that it is not legal in America, and now there is a child to consider." He kissed each finger separately, keeping his eyes on hers as he did so. *This man is a lover!* she thought in fresh delight.

"And the reason," he went on, "why we are not being married by a minister in our own town is to keep the talk from starting among people who would not understand that under Scottish law the child is legitimate."

There was an energetic scratching and one deep bark at the front door, and he sighed. "Our first Sabbath caller," he said. "What was I telling you?" He went to let the dog in. "At least you will not be repeating what you hear or see in this house," Alick said to him. Oliver pushed his big head under his hand and then Jennie's, and finally lay down beside the cradle.

"How many witnesses must there be for a handfast marriage?" Jennie asked.

"Two. Who were they?" Alick laughed. "I am not remembering that much."

"I *feel* married to you, Alick," Jennie said. "I have known you for so long, and we are bonded together by so much we have endured together I could not feel more married. But we have two witnesses here for a handfast ceremony, and we should do something to celebrate the wedding last night."

He looked around at the cradle and the dog, then cocked an eyebrow at her. "And why not? Neither of them will be telling."

They knelt on either side of the cradle. Oliver was briefly carried away by having their faces on a level with his, but he lay down at the foot when Alick told him to. Priscilla woke up, yawning and stretching, then smiling and kicking in her usual sociable response to attention when she wasn't furious with hunger.

Alick and Jennie joined their four hands over the lively coverlet. "I, Alexander Charles Gilchrist," he said soberly, "take you, Jeannie Hawthorne Gilchrist, for my wife."

"I, Jen—Jeannie Hawthorne Gilchrist," she said, "take you, Alexander Charles Gilchrist, for my husband. Until death do us part," she added.

They kissed solemnly above the cradle.

Fifty-Two

MRS. EVANS was to be buried on Monday afternoon. Her suicide following Evans's departure was now public knowledge, but the letter was not. The General had turned it over to Mr. Dalrymple for safekeeping. Alick, the Frosts, and Parker, the constable, had agreed not to mention the letter except to their wives, and then only if they could be sure of secrecy. No one else needed to know the extent of the woman's shame and the status of the children.

"Certainly not Elder Mayfield," Mrs. MacKenzie told Jennie in the morning. "There is no knowing what that man could say over her coffin if he was sufficiently carried away by his own eloquence. I might be forced to remind him that there is at least one little bastard in Maddox with the distinctive Mayfield ears." She smiled with dreamy pleasure. "How I would love to. . . . He did manage to provoke Colin to wrath. He mentioned the impropriety of burying a suicide in the churchyard, and Colin asked if he preferred to bury her at a crossroads with a stake driven through her heart. He suggested a spot between the flagpole and the horse trough. The Elder retreated in disorder, as they say in military circles, and the General came home swearing."

Monday was raw, gray, and damp after three fine days, with rain-filled clouds hanging low over the town, discouraging anyone who might go to the funeral simply for something to do on a sunny afternoon, in case the Elder outdid himself. Only a few responsible citizens attended: the General and his wife, the Dalrymples, the senior Wellses, and a handful of others who had always pitied the woman and felt some respect should be paid her if only by standing at her graveside in the cold. Tony

322

went, dreading it; but he had been the first to see the body, after her children, and he felt compelled to see her through to the end.

On the morning of the funeral Mr. Dalrymple and the General had asked for a meeting of the selectmen and overseers of the poor. The lawyer volunteered to act for the children as their guardian; he stated that they were not properly pauper-orphans since they had some property and their father might come back for them at any time. The town officers were glad to hand over the responsibility, especially with the General willing to pay for their keep and clothing. This would give both men the authority to protect the children from separation, and from adoption by persons who might promise a good home but be actually looking for trainable slave labor.

The lawyer sold the cow and the poultry to Nick Basto, the man on the next farm up the river, and put the proceeds in the bank under the children's names. This inspired more contributors, so within a week after their mother's death they had a small savings account. Their other property consisted of the famous flowered toilet set, the two colorful chamber pots Mrs. MacKenzie had promised, their clothing, their books and slates, their mother's few books from her past, her Bible, and her keepsake box of small pathetic relics. The lawyer and his wife drove to the farm themselves and packed everything up. The children's things were taken to Rose of Sharon's; the mother's little trunk, with the bedroom earthenware wrapped up in her few dresses, was stowed away in the Dalrymple attic until the day when the children might ask for them.

The General hired Nick Basto to repair the barn doors. He padlocked both house and barn and paid Basto to inspect the premises regularly.

Rose of Sharon's good-natured crew of youngsters tried to coax Gwynneth to go to school with them, but she would not be drawn away from the laundress's bosomy and unfailing warmth. She came with her to Strathbuie House on washday, shadowed by the grim Geraint and tending the baby with an anxious devotion, as if to prove how indispensable she was to her foster mother.

Mrs. MacKenzie tried to talk to her about school, but the child was too numbed by the splendor of the house to respond. She was a sprite only on her own ground. Lydia asked Jennie to try her luck, and took over the reading lesson while Jennie went out to where Gwynneth and Geraint were spreading pillow slips and towels on the bleaching green. The baby crept across the grass, stalking dandelions.

Gwynneth folded her hands before her and gave Jennie a tight, wary, little smile. She wore a new dress of blue and white calico and a long apron over it and shoes on her feet. Her light brown hair had been cut to just below her ears and lay like sleek feathers around her head. The snarl over her forehead had been trimmed to a neat fringe which revealed her silvery gray eyes. They had not her mother's bereft stare, but she reminded Jennie of a small, very reserved cat, if one could imagine a cat with silver eyes.

"You look so pretty, Gwynneth," Jennie said. "Geraint looks very nice, too." He wore brown calico trousers buttoned to a white blouse. Gwynneth glanced at him with a maternal pride, and Geraint scowled back at Jennie.

"If you went to school," Jennie said, "I'm sure you could take Geraint with you. I know you would not want to leave him behind."

Gwynneth pressed her lips together and looked at her shoes.

"Mr. O'Dowda would like to have a girl who reads as well as you," Jennie said.

Gwynneth didn't lift her head. With her thin little neck bared as if awaiting the ax, she was the picture of a child martyr. This did not deceive Jennie.

"Are you afraid of the other children? The Kings will take care of you."

Gwynneth shook her head without raising it.

"Well, Gwynneth, keep up your reading and writing," Jennie said, and left her.

"Perhaps she misses the older brother," she said to Mrs. MacKenzie. "Losing him as well as her mother and father could be the last straw."

"I suppose we might as well let her take her time," Lydia said.

Tony came to see Jennie the day before he sailed back to Boston on the *Lady Lydia*. She expected him to leave a message for Mairi, but he did not. "I didn't try to see her. I wouldn't even ride down Quarry Lane and chance seeing her. Jennie, I thought my life was over when I heard she was married, but when I saw that woman lying in the water, with her life *really* over, I saw what a petty brat I'd been, weeping in a tantrum because I couldn't have just what I wanted."

He didn't know that when he came home again Mairi would be gone from Quarry Lane, and thus she would always remain for him a memory of particular sweetness. A month or so from now, when the roads would be dry and the weather moderate, Mr. MacArthur would be leading his pilgrims to Nova Scotia. The General had talked to him and been told that he had become as ungodly as the rest of Maddox. It would not be a large group, only those few who had never gotten over their home-sickness. They had been putting their earnings into wagons and horses. Hector had argued for weeks, but the minister was more persuasive, describing a land that not only deserved the name New Scotland but kept the old ways. Old Dougal was going, against his will, because his daughter and her husband were taking their daughters away from the Yankee boys. Ewan MacLean was taking Mairi and the children, so her parents and the younger ones would go.

Young Ishbel, Paulina Revere's mother, took an unexpected stand when her parents and Roddie's wanted to make a new start away from the scene of such sadness.

"Go without me!" she flared at them. "The baby is an American, and Roddie was wanting that. Besides, if he ever comes back, it is *here* he will expect us to be."

In the end both sets of parents decided not to go.

There had been no St. Patrick's Day dance because some of the committee were still debilitated by the influenza and were saving their strength for the town meeting. This event was held in the church. It was a time of violent disputes and outright recriminations. There were still reverberations a week later, and a group of men at the yard had been forbidden by Mr. Dunlop to have any conversation whatever if they couldn't keep the peace about the recent elections.

Columbine made her first appearance of the year on Main Street after a winter spent in the barn. She was so frisky that she sailed over a wall like a hunter, according to Mr. Barron, and galloped to the corner, uttering a cow's version of glad cries.

April came, and the snowdrops had long gone by in the oval garden, followed by banks of crocus. Now there were pools of blue scilla, and white and yellow daffodils. New birds arrived every day from the south. The wild geese flew over in long skeins, their calls as exciting as bagpipes.

Four town boys rowed down the river one Saturday afternoon, os-tensibly to visit the ruins of an old fort on the property which was still called the Evans place, though it had reverted to the General. They meant no harm but were morbidly attracted by the site of a suicide. They had looked in the house windows and seen nothing, then had wandered through the woods, teasing each other about ghosts, jumping out at one another, yelling to hear their echoes. They overstayed so long that they were tide-nipped until after sundown, and it was then that they saw something in the house.

They were halfway between the house and the shore, and each of the four had a different version. There was a face at a window, or something white moving by it, something black, someone crying. Someone or something waving. The only agreement was that there had been *something*, and they were so badly frightened they had waded in mud up to their knees to push the dory overboard.

It was dark before they got home, and their families were beginning to be worried. Their stories averted thrashings in three cases; the fourth boy was trounced for having gone without permission when he was supposed to be whitewashing the henhouse. The news of a ghost in the Evans house was all over town in twenty-four hours. The General mentioned it during one of his early-evening calls on Alick and Jennie.

"It was bound to happen," he said ruefully, "with the suicide and the situation so isolated. The boys simply frightened themselves out of their wits, and now the place is tainted. I was hoping to have someone in it by summer. A house deteriorates when it is deserted, just as a person does." He rubbed his scar. "Poor soul, poor soul," he muttered. "Evans probably never gives her a thought; he hasn't the conscience for it. He took the boy who was big enough to be of some use to him and left the other two and their mother to dree their ain weird. No thanks to him that the children aren't dead along with the woman." He slapped his hands on his thighs. "Enough of *that* gloom! It's of no use to exhume the past, is it? The dead haunt us only when we won't leave them in peace. Which leads me to something else. The ghost hunters have been at me to let them have a try down there," he said. "I am tempted to tell them to go ahead if they will guarantee to swear afterward that they've exorcised the ghosts for good. . . . Well, I must go. I always enjoy coming here, you know. From the very first there was a certain atmosphere about you two." He smiled winningly at Jennie. "And now that you have your little girl with eyes the color of Scottish bluebells, there is even more charm under this roof."

He reached for his stick and shoved himself up. Oliver arose with a groan. "Thank you for the coffee and the tart, Mrs. Glenroy. Oh—

something you might find interesting! The name for the Russian trader. Can you guess it?"

"From the figurehead everyone is thinking *Eagle*," said Alick, "but there is already one here."

"*Aquila!*" said Jennie triumphantly.

He shook his head, smiling. "Have you never thought of a Gaelic eagle? She will be *Iolaire*, and I've asked Rory for a tune to pipe her down the ways. We may even have a dance the night after the launching, you know. Mr. MacArthur will be gone." He winked merrily at them. "I thank God he can't persuade our piper to go with him. Now, I think it is a great pity that I haven't yet seen an eightsome reel danced when Rory composed a reel named for my son. Do you think we will have enough Highlanders left to do it?"

"Och, I believe so," Alick said.

"Will you be dancing in it?"

"Indeed, I will, and my wife, too. I will be teaching her."

"I didn't know you danced, Alick," Jennie said, laughing in surprise.

"Of course, he dances, my lass!" said the General. "He's a High-lander, isn't he? He hasn't yet given up his bonnet."

Fifty-Three

I N THE FIRST WEEKS following Priscilla's birth Jennie had put off writing the news to Sylvia. After months of suspense she felt lazy about doing anything which was not absolutely necessary at the moment; she seemed to be encapsulated in a new world, very small but holding within it all she wanted. She looked forward not in terms of months, or even weeks, but to Priscilla's next waking up, Alick's return from work, someone stopping by. Gradually her anticipations stretched out to cover a day, but never more than a week. She would think, *Tonight I must write Sylvia a long letter.* But by night she would be too sleepy. Well, there was no hurry. The longer she waited, the more she would have to write about Priscilla.

After the night with Alick and the ceremony over the cradle, she wrote that she had safely borne Nigel's child and explained that she had not mentioned her pregnancy because she didn't want them to worry:

> Now my life has changed in all ways. Alick and I have come to care for each other very much. We have now been quietly married, and I am going to stay in America. In time I think it will be perfectly safe for you to write to me in this place. I will see you all again someday, I am sure of it. I long for you to know Alick and Priscilla. I must tell you this: Priscilla came too soon, too fast, and Alick delivered her. I have never felt safer with anyone in my life since I left Pippin Grange. He loves Priscilla as if she were his own, and I am content for him to raise her as his own.

She promised to write often and in detail, and begged Sylvia to do the same. She would adore receiving a letter from Sophie, and she would like Ianthe's address.

Lucy walked into town often, picking her way along the grassy edges when the roads were a thick stew of mud. She had her brother make a canvas carrier like Jared's. By summer Priscilla would be ready for it. "Unless you intend to keep her swaddled in acres of petticoats and long dresses until she fights her way free of them!"

"She's fighting her way free of them now. No, I shall horrify everyone with my advanced notions," Jennie said.

Lucy thought she might be pregnant, but she wasn't sure. "Of course you are," said Jennie. "I know about these things. Haven't I made you a cradle quilt? That makes it certain." She remembered how fierce she'd been to finish the quilt and leave it as a memento of herself, and she tried to remember just when she had stopped looking forward to going to England; she did not call it "going home" anymore. Details were hazy, but she thought it dated from the night when she had realized it would be only Alick with her for the birth. She had not gone frantic with terror; she had been intent on doing the very best she could, because there was such a *rightness* to it; she and Alick had been each other's lifeline for too long.

Lying in bed, they talked about it. "Agreed, we saved each other from foundering," she said, "but when did you begin to love me?"

"The day we met on the ridge, and you asked me about the fairy hill and the Pict's House. I was so jealous of my cousin I was nearly blind and deaf with it."

"But you went on to tell me about the Year of the Sheep. Were you actually seething then about more than sheep?"

"A *Dia,* I was a volcano!"

They had moved upstairs to sleep in the big bed. He carried the cradle up, and during the days downstairs Priscilla lay in her basket or surrounded by pillows on the bed in the parlor. Sometimes at noon Alick and Jennie lay on that bed like young lovers out in the fields, kissing as if making up for a lifetime of deprivation. "I feel so immoral," she said luxuriously, "lolling lustfully about in broad daylight." Her fingers moved tenderly over his cheekbones and around his ears, fingering the rims and the lobes. "Did you know you have elegant ears? My hands cannot get enough of you."

"It is not just my hands that are not getting enough of *you*." He rolled off the bed and onto his feet. "Whenever a man is five minutes late back to the yard, do you know what they accuse him of?"

She held out her arms, laughing. "Come and have the game as well as the name!"

He looked down at her, shaking his head slowly and smiling. "Och, Jeannie, you make it all worth waiting for."

"And you, Alexander Charles, you can't tell me there was never anyone before me. You know too much."

"Could not a man be having a natural talent?" he retorted. She threw a pillow at him.

One Sunday afternoon, when rain and wind were thrashing through the red-budded maple boughs, they went upstairs. He built a fire in the little fireplace, and while she was undressing, he went across the hall to his old room. He came back with his hands cupped as if he were carrying something. He lowered them for her to see into them, and there was her hair curled up in the basket made by his fingers.

"I was thinking then it was all I would ever have of you, besides the remembering," he said. "And it would always be telling me that the memories were not dreams, just."

She took his face in her hands. "We have so much to make up for, so much living to do, and none of it will be dreams, just."

She slept more deeply with Alick than she had ever slept, but she always heard Priscilla's first little sounds and would be out of bed and attending to her before she could cry loudly and wake Alick. He had brought a rocking chair upstairs; sitting in it and feeding Priscilla, with the plaid around them both, she could just make out Alick's dark head on the pillow if it was starlight or see it clearly in moonlight. Sometimes his face was turned her way, untroubled and youthful in sleep, all defenses down now that he was no longer braced to endure loneliness.

She gazed at it while the baby fed. Their whole world was here in this room. If they could ask anything more, it was that their world should be under their own roof.

Again and again she saw the house looking out across the river mouth to the bay, not as she'd seen it with Mrs. Evans in it, but on that first day. There was something elemental about it. Rooted. It was an old house as houses went in America; poor Adelina Evans wandering in it, wringing her hands and weeping, which had now become the accepted ghost story, could not put a blemish on its essential character. The Evanses would have been simply a passing incident in its life, birds resting a moment on the granite whaleback and then flying on, leaving no footmark.

The property was eight miles from town and they would need a horse to take Alick back and forth, and a gig or a wagon if she were ever to see the village. But oh, to walk down through the field and taste the sea wind, and feel it blowing her hair back from her face and flattening her skirts against her legs and to hear the surf on the shore. It could never be the big surf with emerald-hearted combers towering eave-high before they crashed ashore, but enough to make a music in your ears all day long when the wind was pouring from the southwest across a seething green and silver bay. And when you woke in the night, you would hear it. For a woman who had grown up on the shore of the North Sea, she had been an unconscionable time away from the salt water. By this summer it would be two years since she'd had her feet in it.

It was still only a fantasy, belonging to these night sessions with Priscilla. But Alick had always expected to have his own home, and Hector was forever talking to him about the land adjoining his, to the northwest of the town and in sight of the Tenby hills. Locally they were called the mountains; for a Highlander they were better than nothing.

Ian Murdo MacKenzie, the dancer, who had limped for weeks after Zeb Pulsifer kicked his knee, was Hector's neighbor now, but he was going to Nova Scotia with the minister.

Alick agreed that the spot was bonny, but he would give Hector no satisfaction yet.

Jennie was just leaving the store on the following Saturday when the General came up from the wharf, where men were wheeling casks of lime from the shed and loading them aboard the St. David, bound for New York.

"Any mail for New York?" he called to her. "I shall be locking the mail pouch within the next few hours."

"No letters this time, but thank you."

He took off his hat and wiped his forehead. "Summer in April, isn't it? The New England spring makes the winters worth it, though this has been a better winter than most. I've known some to last into May, or so it felt."

They walked across the road together. "Have the ghost hunters been to the haunted house yet?" she asked. "I haven't heard that they've exorcised the ghost."

"Which haunted house?" he said quizzically. "To hear those lads talk—and our thoroughly respectable Albion Hardy is amongst them— you'd think Maddox offers quite a selection."

"The Evans place," she said.

"Oh." His amusement was erased as if by a cold, wet sponge. He was opening the gate for her, and he stopped with it half-open. "I let them have a key, and they spent one night there but saw and heard nothing but mice. I knew there'd be nothing. But I am really worried about that house. It should be lived in, and soon, or it may not see another year. Albion told me someone had already broken into the house, evidently by prying up a window. Nick Basto tells me there has been a fire in the kitchen fireplace. I should hate to board it up. Nothing kills a house faster."

He rubbed his hand hard over his scar in the familiar gesture. "The place could go up in flames some night when we've had a long dry spell, and so could the barn, with summer coming on and mischievous boys roaming the countryside and tramps on the roads. I don't know how they could get into the barn with every window boarded up, and too high anyway, but stranger things have happened, and there is a loft half-full of hay to catch fire if some half-wit lights up his pipe. I'd like to have Hugh Evans by the neck for more than one reason!"

His hand went up to his cheek again. "Drat that scar, it burns and itches as if the black flies had been at it! . . . There's a good bit of land and shorefront in the parcel, and plenty of wood, too. I'd never have believed that Zeb Pulsifer would be the only one after it."

"*Zeb!*" She thought she'd shouted it, but apparently not; the General merely nodded, abstractedly.

"His father has been talking to me. He thinks Zeb is straightening out now that he is a family man. He has taken so well to fishing for a living that he is buying his own boat and taking his next younger brother with him."

Jennie clamped her hand savagely over the wooden knob on the gatepost. "But he has a cabin and land." She just managed to keep her sense of personal outrage to herself.

"He can sell that easily enough. Now that he is a fisherman, he would like a saltwater farm, and he has been down there looking it over. The wharf could be extended out over the flats to the low waterline. Oh, it's all perfectly reasonable!" He did not look happy about it. "Nick Basto will not be charmed at having Zeb for a neighbor, but still, if he has turned over a new leaf—well, I was never one to make a dog carry a bad name once he stopped biting. . . . It must be sunburn inflaming that scar," he said irritably.

"General MacKenzie." Her voice sounded wavery to her, and she bore down on it. "Have you made a decision yet?"

"No, no!" He shook his head like a horse plagued by flies. "I told Joe I must think on it. I want to talk with Nick and with the man who owns the land across the road. I would not have them think I pulled a low trick on them." His face cleared; he looked like Frank when her sums came out right. "They might even join together and buy it! I hadn't thought of that. I'd make it easy for them."

"Sir," said Jennie, "would you please not see anyone else about it until you talk with Alick and me?" She could hardly believe her own temerity; still, she was not committing Alick to anything but a discussion.

"My dear Mrs. Glenroy!" The General was astounded. "Do you mean *you* have been considering it?"

"Only thinking," she said truthfully, leaving Alick out of it. "So I am rather surprised myself to be saying this, but the thought of Zeb Pulsifer knocked the words out of me. I love your cottage, and my greatest happiness has come to me under its roof, but this was never meant to be a permanent arrangement, if you remember. We have always looked forward to having our own home, and now that Priscilla is here, and we will doubtless have other children—"

Don't fall all over yourself, Jennie, she thought crossly.

"Of course, it's a natural thing." The General was kindly agreeing. "You'll need room with a growing family and so forth. My objections would all be for selfish reasons. It has been very pleasant for me, and for my wife, too. And she will be upset about the children."

Now that Jennie was halfway in, there was nothing to do but plunge on up to her neck. "But that was not to be permanent either. I love Sukey and Frank, General MacKenzie, but I am not equipped to go far with them. They are bright children, and before long they will need more than I can give them. Nabby Frost is having a far better education already. I know that from the things she has passed on to them. And their questions are becoming harder and harder to answer."

His face was burnished with pride. "Ah, I know how intelligent they are! But they will miss you."

"Not if they can go on to school. It is all they talk about. They really need to be with other children."

"You know, Mrs. Glenroy, when I encouraged Liam O'Dowda to remain here, I was thinking of my own children. Mrs. MacKenzie is not unreasonable." She suspected a twinkle in his eye but couldn't be sure. "And now that she has her boy to take up so much of her attention, and it's so devilish hard to find a governess with all the qualifications, I'm sure she will see the wisdom of putting the girls' education in O'Dowda's hands."

"And she can always send them to Boston to be finished," Jennie said demurely.

"Indeed, she can!" He laughed and impulsively seized her hand and pressed it in both of his. "You and Alick could make that place live again. You two—no, three—will exorcise the most persistent, most wretched ghost that ever was."

She felt both deceitful and exhilarated. It was a little like the suspenseful instant when she had decided they were to sail to America as the Glenroys. No one's life was at risk now, and she had still not committed Alick, but here she was poised at the top of Tumbledown Hill again, with a sort of Greek chorus chanting away at her, "Beware the ghost! Beware the ghost!"

"May we borrow the gig to drive down there this afternoon?" she asked.

"Yes, of course! Take Roy." He was radiant with relief. "The sooner this is settled, the happier I'll be. You will find the terms very easy. I shall make the property over to you at once, and it will be yours with all the time in the world to pay for it." He put his hand under her elbow and urged her through the gate. "Now come along, and I shall give you the keys."

How could she have done this? Trepidation set in with a shivery malaise like the onset of a bad cold. *Now, Jennie,* she lectured herself, *if Alick balks, it will not be the end of the world. You will survive if those other men buy the place. Or if it should go to Zeb Pulsifer, you can bear it; you have Alick. You will simply be extremely careful never to think of it again, because for the rest of your life Zeb Pulsifer's possession of it will set your teeth on edge.*

All this while they were strolling under the budding trees toward the house, and she heard not a word the General was saying. Suddenly they came in sight of the flagpole. The flag hung against the white mast, hardly moving. But one good breath of wind, and it would leap into life and snap its colors out against the April sky.

For the first time she realized that it was Priscilla's flag. Her child, like Paulina Revere, had been born an American citizen. *We shall have other children.* How confidently she had said that. They'd be Americans, all of them, before their parents were.

It was incredible.

Fifty-Four

A LICK WAS WALKING up and down the kitchen, carrying Priscilla and singing in time with his step. She gave her mother a ravishing smile over his shoulder. He went on walking and singing until the end of the verse. Jennie took off her shawl and put away her groceries. Alick came into the pantry, holding Priscilla's hand before she could put a finger in his eye.

"She is hungry," he said, "but music fed her soul."

"Kiss me," said Jennie, ducking her head around the baby's bobbing one. Then she washed her hands and took the baby out to the rocking chair to feed her.

"What was the song about?" she asked. "English it for me."

He sat on the corner of the table and tapped his foot and sang softly. "Horee, horo, my bonny wee girl,/ Horee, horo, my fair one!/ And will you go along with me,/ To be my own, my rare one?"

"Sing it to *me*, love, and I will follow you anywhere. May we talk, or are you about to fly off?"

"Talk," he said indulgently. "I am knowing that spark in your eye."

"That spark in my eye is a bee in my bonnet. Alick, are we agreed that we wish to sit under own our vine and fig tree as soon as possible?"

"Yes . . ." It was more interrogative than affirmative.

"And if you are to have your own yard, you need land on the shore."

"It helps," he said, "though it is possible to move a vessel to the water by ox teams. But my own yard is years from now, *mo chridh*."

"Let us forget the yard for a moment. If we could find the perfect

336

situation now and move there before summer, you would be all established when the time came."

"Where is this perfect situation?"

"You needn't be suspicious," she said. "I don't propose selling our souls to the devil for it. We could have forty acres of shore, fields, and woods, and we could get it very easily." Under his dark gray gaze the heat rose in her throat and into her face. He could always do that to her, she thought. Perhaps in time she'd learn how to control a blush.

"You are speaking of the Evans place." His tone was ominously flat. "Is this what you and the General have been discussing?"

He didn't add "Behind my back," but he might just as well have. She reached out to touch his knee. "Zeb Pulsifer wants it, Alick."

He stood up, ignoring her hand as if it were a dead leaf, and walked away from her. "I wish him luck with it and the ghost, then."

"That *damned* ghost! You know the boys made up a story to excuse their lateness, and the more they thought about it, the more real it became."

He stood at the windows with his back to her, a familiar rejection from the past. She wished she had never brought up the subject, but it was too late now.

"A woman killed herself there," he said.

"And she is gone forever, and at peace, we hope. She won't come back, any more than—" That was a mistake, and she couldn't erase it.

"The excise man?" He wheeled around. "Oh, yes, I am a superstitious fool! But the men who met him were not fools. And there are men here who have seen the ghosts down the river since the boys were telling about it."

"Anyone can see a ghost who has a mind to!" she retorted. "If I were looking for one, I would surely see *something* to freeze my marrow! Oh, Alick, come back here! I can't come to you, this child is fastened to me like a leech, and I swear she'll bite me if I move. But I can't apologize to you if we're not touching."

"Where are the teeth to bite with?"

"They're coming. Besides, she's very resourceful. I'm sure she'd do it with her gums."

He smiled and came back and leaned over her and the baby with his hands braced on the arms of the chair. His face was only a few inches from hers. "Why should you be apologizing?"

"Because we had our first quarrel about that dratted excise man. I wished it *had* been a ghost and scared Jock Dallas to death! I am sorry for what I said earlier, and I love you too much to want to offend you in any way. I will never mention the property again."

He kissed her hard on the last word and kept it up so she couldn't begin talking again. Priscilla went on feeding, her bemused eyes watching the incomprehensible motions above her face.

"Listen, my Jeannie," Alick said at last. "I am apologizing to you. At least I can be courteous enough to consider it."

"I should never have spoken about it to you, and not just because of the ghost. You had a dreadful experience there, and it must crowd out everything else for you. I should have remembered it."

"I have had a number of dreadful experiences in my life, and I am still here. I said I will consider it."

"Are you willing to drive down river this afternoon and consider on the spot?" she asked eagerly. "We can use the gig this afternoon, and I have the keys."

"I cannot be refusing you anything except to say I will gladly move in with a ghost."

"It's a heavenly afternoon, so the ghost can't be anywhere about," she said. "Alick, if it feels absolutely wrong to you when we get there, and you know beyond doubt you can never be happy there, then that will be the end of it. I promise."

"Can the General be serious about Zeb Pulsifer?"

"He doesn't wish to be. But he is afraid something will happen to the house if it's left alone, and Joseph Pulsifer tells him Zeb has turned over a new leaf. *And* no one else has come forward. The General thinks it is because of the suicide and the ghost stories."

"Well, we will drive down and look at it," he said gloomily.

Priscilla was fourteen weeks old now, and wearing her second set of Allan Robert's clothes. She had outgrown her basket, and Alick had built a box for her downstairs bed, large enough for a pen when she began to move round and try to pull herself up. At Strathbuie House she occupied the crib from which Allan Robert had graduated. When she wasn't sleeping, she talked to the small toys the children had tied to the rails.

She had been blessedly free of colic from birth and was almost always good-natured unless she was wet or hungry, or wanted Alick to take her for a walk around the house the instant he came in from work.

Overall she was a responsive, sociable child. Today she was placidly enjoying her first ride behind a fast-trotting horse. The air was warm and calm enough for them to travel with the top removed from the gig, and the occasion would have been pleasant enough for its own sake without a specific destination. They could, and probably would, pay for this balmy spell with a patch of cold weather, late frosts, or even a surprise snowstorm, but everyone accepted the blessing with a whole heart and didn't waste it.

The bay horse was glad to be out on the road, and Alick was glad to be driving him. Jennie thought that Alick was enjoying the drive even more than she was, because he was in no suspense about the result. He had already made up his mind and now he was humoring her. Well, she had given him her word, but she would continue to hope until she received his final No.

The first time she had been on the River Road, everything had been steeped in the old gold of autumn. Now the countryside was illumined by the unique light of April, the color of the clearest and palest white wine. Swallows patterned the air about the barns, red-winged blackbirds whistled and displayed their scarlet epaulets.

The tree toads sang piercingly in the alder swamps. Small children raced about like the young lambs while their mothers dug dandelion greens. The planting of corn and potatoes was going on, watched by crows that might—or might not—defer to the scarecrows. And every little pond was as blue as Priscilla's eyes.

They turned off the main road to drive through the spruce woods, then left its twilight for the heat and scent of green fields scattered with dandelions, and the river at high tide in alternating bands of aquamarine satin and sequins where random breaths of breeze touched it. Tears came into Jennie's eyes. *I will not mourn for it,* she swore to herself. Alick saw none of what she saw; for him there was only the road to the shore and a drowned woman at the end of it. How could she expect him to live with that? But it was too beautiful, and she wished they hadn't come. They drove into the barnyard and stopped by the repaired and padlocked double doors. Alick helped her down. "It is too hot for the horse here," he said. "I will just be tying him in the shade." He led Roy toward the apple trees at the far end of the house. It was so quiet here today she found herself straining for some other sound than that of birds and the bees around the flowering weeds. She loosened her bonnet strings and let the bonnet hang down her back. Holding Priscilla against her shoulder, she walked across to the workshop. It, too, had been locked.

Alick came back, wiping his forehead. "Man, but it's hot. Well, we are at the barn; we might as well be looking in there first."

"There is nothing to see but a loft half-full of hay," Jennie said.

"Never mind, I said I will consider." He took out the ring of keys. "So I will be considering everything." He could be blithe about it, having taken his stand; the ghosts would gain no ground with him.

He swung one of the doors back against the outside wall and took the baby from her. With the windows boarded on the outside, the barn was lighted only by what light came in with them, but it was enough. The cool dusk was scented with hay and past manure. The light from the door picked up a pair of sawhorses against the far wall, with some planks laid across them.

Two thick logs of seasoned pine, about six feet long and with the bark removed, were propped against the wall beside them. "He must have used these for his carving," Jennie said. "I wonder if he has really gone back to his wife, or if she really exists and if she'd take in his son by another woman."

Alick was looking back toward the door, listening, but not to her. She heard a sound too indistinct to describe except as something between a scratch and a scrape, and there was the impression of a footfall. She and Alick walked quickly across to the door.

Just as they reached it, there was a startled outburst of crows at the front of the house. The birds erupted into the air above the chimneys and went flapping off over the apple trees to the woods, calling all the way. Roy continued to graze without lifting his head.

"Whatever it was went around the house," Alick said, more thoughtful than perturbed.

"A raccoon," said Jennie. "Or a fox. I wish I could have seen it. Or maybe it was a cat, but all those animals are too small. I could have sworn it was something heavier. A deer?" she said hopefully. "Or even a moose. I'd love to see one of those."

"Perhaps," he said absently. "The moose is a slow-moving beast, they tell me. Hector has seen one."

From the front of the house there was nothing to see but the sunny field and the small winged lives that owned it, and the water beyond, shimmering in the waves of heat rising from the land. There were no gulls today, no fishing ospreys. A minor explosion of angry sparrows was taking place in the swampy thicket running from the well to the shore.

"I am disappointed," Jennie said.

"You will not live out your years in Maine without ever seeing a moose," he said, unlocking the ell door.

"Is that a promise?"

He smiled. "No. A probability."

They went into the kitchen, and she was relieved to find that Mrs. Evans had not left an indelible impression on it. It was just a shabby room with unpainted cupboards, smoke-grimed plaster, and an uneven floor of worn softwood planks. The table and chairs had been left, and a few odds and ends of dishes in the pantry, evidently not thought worth packing and saving. The only furniture in the other rooms consisted of rough unpainted bedsteads with old feather beds on them, and a couple of scarred chests of drawers. The house was full of sunlight, and flies buzzed against the hot panes.

There was a surprising amount of room in it, seven plastered rooms and five of them good-sized; there was also a large unfinished chamber over the ell kitchen, where the house's skeleton of timbers was exposed, and the pegs that joined its parts. It was well lighted by an easterly window in the gable, and a narrow flight of back stairs led down to the kitchen.

Silently and apart Jennie and Alick walked through the house, their footsteps echoing in the emptiness. With Priscilla sleeping on his shoulder, Alick lived up to his promise to consider everything. He studied the structure of the house as revealed in the open chamber; he examined the moldings and wainscoting and the condition of the bricks inside the fireplaces. The kitchen fireplace was larger than the others and took up most of a wall. It included an oven. Jennie caught herself thinking, *I shall just have to miss a stove until we can afford one.*

She sighed. It was depressing to inspect cupboards and closets like an optimistic housewife when it was only a charade. She could not bear to go to the windows; all those across the front of the house looked out the river mouth and down the bay.

She wished she had not come; she wished she had never spoken to the General about it in the first place.

Fifty-Five

S HE SAT DOWN at the kitchen table, wishing Alick would not be so damnably thorough in his considerations. It was rather cruel of him, now that she thought about it. He came out to the kitchen, saying, "I have found a door to the cellar under the front stairs, but it is dark as the pit down there." He sounded regretful. "This is a very well-put-together house."

"Can we go now?" Jennie asked.

He was surprised. "Will you not even be walking to the shore?"

"I have seen it," she said tersely, "and so have you." She went out and he came behind her.

"Is that all you have to say?"

She nodded and took the baby so he could fasten the padlock and walked away from him around the other end of the house. The instant she was out of his sight, she began to miss him, and when he caught up with her, she said cheerfully, "It hasn't all been wasted; we enjoyed the drive down, and we can enjoy the ride back."

"Tell me truthfully, Jeannie. Do you think you could be happy in this house?"

"Not if you were unhappy. There will be other houses."

They came abreast of the open barn door, and he swung it shut. He was just about to lock up when the sound of a cat crying startled them both. It came from inside the barn. Alick put the door back against the wall, and Jennie stepped over the threshold and called tenderly. She tried "Kitty," and she tried "Puss, puss"; she tried "Darling," but the cat didn't come. It went on crying either from the hayloft or below it.

Alick came in behind her. "They must have left her," she said sadly, "and the poor thing hasn't been able to get into the barn since. She might have had her kittens in the hayloft, and she was out when they locked it up, and she's never been able to get back to them." She was at the edge of tears; all the restrained emotion of the past hour was about to be undammed by the tragedy of dead kittens and their mother's bewildered, plaintive, questioning voice.

"We have time," Alick said, "and we will not be leaving until we have her out again. There is enough for her to eat outside, and once she knows the kittens are gone, she may be making her way to Basto's house."

She put the still-sleeping baby into his arms. "I think I can coax her down from the hayloft. She sounded so forlorn she will come to a loving voice." She left the swatch of light and walked into the dusk toward the ladder rising to the loft. "Don't speak," she said in a low voice. "She may be afraid of men, after a life with Hugh Evans."

She reached the ladder and looked up into the hay-scented dark. "Here, darling," she said seductively. "I'm waiting for you. Nobody will hurt you. Come, sweetheart, come."

She smelled something besides the hayloft and the stalls, something which hadn't been there earlier. She sniffed like a dog, trying to place it, and her scalp tightened. "Alick, do you notice anything?" she asked. Something enormous bolted past her with a great noise of feet and hoarse breathing. She heard Alick's shout, and then the barn door was slammed shut, and they were in the dark. Priscilla woke with a cry of rage.

"Jeannie?" Alick called through the blackness. "Did he touch you?"

"No. Stand where you are, and I will come to you. There is a crack of light under the doors." She reached him, and his free arm drew her to him. She stroked Priscilla, and he jogged the child lightly on his arm trying to quiet her. "Who was it?" she asked. "Did you see?"

"Zeb," said Alick. "He rushed straight for the door like a charging bull."

"He is what I smelled then," said Jennie. "Stale tobacco, rum, and the stink of fish from a week back. . . . Do you suppose he has gone now?"

Guided by the line of light, they went to the doors and tried them. They gave very slightly, but no more. "We are locked in," Alick said.

"He was the cat!" she said. "He did it to lure us in. If I hadn't been

so tenderhearted! What are we going to do?" She was rather proud of
her arctic tranquility, like a glacier beneath Priscilla's angry screams.

"First you will fill that hungry mouth," Alick said. "You can sit on
the planks, and I will use one of these logs for a battering ram to loosen
the hasp." They felt around for the sawhorses and planks, and she sat
down and began to feed Priscilla. When the screaming stopped and the
silence rushed back, the dark seemed blacker, and thick enough to choke
them with a hideously familiar pungence. A flare of red light irradiated
the rafters; the hay was on fire.

Alick pulled her up as she was, baby still at the breast, and hurried
her to the doors. "Sit on the floor," he commanded. He steadied her
and the baby until she was sitting with her back against the wall next
to the doors. Then he ran back to the logs; she could see him in the
leaping light from the flaming hayloft. He came back with one of the
logs as if it had been no heavier than a stick of firewood and ran it at
the door. The door rattled and shook but did not give, and he backed
off to try again. The fire gave off small, busy, secretive sounds as it licked
at the walls and reached for the beams.

Alick drove the log ahead again, and again. Again. Swearing in
whispers. She watched through the smoke while a beam caught fire. The
fire would go up through the roof next, and flaming timbers would fall
on them. They were going to die, horribly, before the walls collapsed.
If she kept her nipple in the baby's mouth, would it keep Priscilla pacified
until she died? With a little baby it should be very quick if the rafters
fell with enough force to kill outright. Smoke killed, too, and it was
getting thicker up there. But how fast would it be?

Alick dropped down beside her. He was panting. "I cannot do it.
Jeannie, lie down with your nose to the crack." He kept pushing her
into place. She lay on her side with the baby against her, her face to
the little gap, gulping at the fresh air. Alick lay against her back, his
arm over both her and the child, and they were silent, listening to
Priscilla's singleminded sucking and the intimate rustling and occasional
snapping of the flames. Above them the barn filled with the smoke and
smell of burning hay.

They heard the sound directly over their heads as simply another
voice of destruction; the flames must have broken through the outer
walls, and the building's frame was breaking up. Inside, the hayloft
collapsed, and now the fire was on a level with them, devouring the

floor as it crept toward them in no great rush; it had all the time in the world and reinforcements working in from the outside. The bottom of the door, so close to Jennie's face, shivered under impact after impact. *Let it be quick, let it be quick!* she implored. *God, if you ever do listen, don't let my baby die in agony. Don't let us.*

Alick was gone. "Alick, hold me!" she cried, groping around for him with her free hand, sobbing not much from fear of flames but for loss of him in these last minutes.

In the next instant he was hauling her roughly to her feet, shouting, "Look, Jeannie, *look!*"

The tip end of an ax blade came through the planking at the height of the hasp, was withdrawn, and struck again. They watched with watering eyes, their mouths and the baby's face covered against the smoke, until the final tremendous blow, and the door was torn open with the hasp hanging. They stumbled out into the air and light; behind them the fire went up with a roar. Priscilla, deprived of the breast, began to scream, but the sound of rage, not pain, was as beautiful to Jennie as the sight of the young boy who stood there with a great ax in his hands.

David Evans was skinny and barefoot, wearing ragged shirt and breeches, his hair growing down his neck and long over his ears. His face was wet with sweat, and his mouth was pressed tight like Gwynneth's. His light gray eyes were full of tears. He was shaking.

"Where did Zeb go?" Alick asked him. The boy pointed toward the ell end of the house. "Jeannie, get away from here!" Alick shouted. *"Now."* He ran, and Jennie and the boy followed him. Behind them the smoke poured out in a cloud, and the roar was audible till they were halfway down the path.

Alick was just reaching the bank above the beach, and took a flying leap from the rim and disappeared. David shot off down the field, and Jennie ran as fast as she could. The motion pleased Priscilla, and she stopped crying. At this moment she seemed to weigh no more than a kitten, and Jennie was running as she had in childhood and still sometimes ran in her dreams.

Almost there she saw a mast and furled sail, and then the small wherry anchored a little way off the beach. Now she was at the edge, and stood beside David on the bank and looked down. Zeb was sprawled on his belly; Alick had one knee in his back, the other braced in the pebbles, and he was pounding Zeb's face into the water and gravel.

Suddenly, with a fresh and visible surge of strength, he drove Zeb's head under water and held it there. Zeb's legs thrashed; his hands beat at the shallow water and clawed up fistfuls of gravel. Alick did not speak. Up on the bank Jennie and David watched in their own silence. She knew she was waiting for Zeb's motions to cease as he drowned, and she thought vaguely she should make some conventional gesture of protest; but the smell of Zeb's fire was still in her hair, her clothes, and in the baby's cap and shawl. *We would be dead by now*, she thought. *Turned into charred things.*

All at once Alick sprang up and brushed his hands vigorously together as if to knock off dirt. He looked down at the huge, ungainly shape moving feebly at his feet. "To hell with you," he said. "I'll not soil my hands any more. Let the courts hang you."

Zeb pushed himself up onto his hands and knees, coughing and gagging, and fell flat. Slowly he raised himself again. Vomiting and moaning between spasms, he crawled into the water toward the wherry. He tried to stand upright before he reached it and kept clutching at one thigh as if it pained him. Then he fell again with a splash. He went on his hands and knees all the way to the wherry. By straining his head back, he kept his face just out of the water until he reached the boat and pulled himself up by the gunwale. It took several tries before he could heave himself over the side and fall into the boat and lie there. They could hear his breathing.

Alick picked up his bonnet and brushed it off and put it on.

"And be sure you cock it just so," Jennie said. He looked up at her and grinned.

"So you were watching. Did I not tell you once I would be dealing with Zeb Pulsifer one way or another?" He came up the bank. "Och, he soaked and fouled himself," he said in disgust. "I feel filthy from just laying a hand on him. I will not touch you or the baby till I am scoured clean."

She leaned over and kissed him. "We are alive, Alick."

"Aye, there's that. Thanks to *you*." He put his hand on the boy's shoulder. The light eyes looked solemnly up at him. "Now I must be moving the horse before the fire takes the house."

The barn was engulfed now, and the flames shot high above the house roof; the sound of them reached the shore. Roy was nervously tossing his head. "No wind," Alick said, "and the woods are fairly wet.

It may not spread, but we cannot be trusting in that. Go up to the spruces, Jeannie, and I will meet you there. You, too," he said to David. "There is nothing we can be doing here but ride away from it."

But the boy was staring past him at the house, and involuntarily the adults looked, too. A man appeared on the roof of the ell, carrying a bucket, and another man's head was rising just above the ridgepole.

David ran for the house like an arrow shot from a bow and Alick ran to the frightened horse. When he passed the house, he shouted up to the men on the roof, "I will be there!"

He led the horse down along the edge of the woods and tied him a good distance from the heat and crackle of the fire. Jennie went up the road. No one looked back at the wherry in the cove.

Fifty-Six

JENNIE SAT on a ledge in the field east of the house while Priscilla slept and the barn burned to the ground. The crew on the house roof kept pouring water from the barn well over the shingles. If she'd had a safe place to put Priscilla, she would have happily joined the bucket brigade. She wanted to shout and be strenuous like them; it was as if life had flooded back to her with such force that she ached with it, like a limb that has been numbed and feels the first rush of returning blood.

The strangers had had to make do with two buckets, one leaking, left carelessly (and providentially) by the barn well. Then Alick unlocked the house, and David fetched out more buckets from the pantry. Two fishermen, on their way home upriver, came ashore in the cove and brought two buckets of their own.

When the barn was reduced to smoking embers and a pile of black char shot through with little flares of dying fire, the men came across the field with Alick. David brought a pail of water from the house well, and a dipper, and they all drank deeply.

Until now there'd been no talk among them; everyone had been too busy. Now there were self-introductions and explanations. The fishermen were a father and son named Baxter who lived across the creek on the St. David side. The others hadn't known they were coming to a fire; they were the neighbor Nick Basto, his sons, and his hired man. The boys had been trying for fish off their wharf when they saw Zeb Pulsifer rowing by—there wasn't enough breeze to fill a sail—and they had followed along the shore, out of sight just inside the woods. When they saw him row into the Evans cove, they went back and told their father. The men were busy with a farrowing sow in difficulties, so they hadn't come right along, and Nick had forbidden the boys to go alone for fear of them tangling with Zeb and getting the worst of it; Zeb was known to be too handy with a knife.

When they did come by the woods trail between the two places, they found the barn on fire.

"Great God on high!" said Basto, "I never expected to see anything like that! I'd mistrust Zeb Pulsifer if I saw him setting in church, but I never figgered him for a fire-raiser. I thought he was looking around for anything he could pick up and lug off, and if there warn't anything outside, he'd just as lief break down a door."

"Gave us a turn, too, seeing that rig out by the apple trees," the hired man said. He was gray-haired and thin as a broom handle next to Nick Basto's bulk, and he had run over the roof like a young goat. "Thought somebody was in there. Then we spotted you folk at the shore."

"You ketch him in the act, did you?" Basto asked Alick. "Chase him off?"

"He was catching us in the act," Alick said dryly. "My wife and I were in the barn when he set the hay afire and ran out and locked us in."

"My God!" the older Baxter said. "And the baby, too?" His leathery face looked sick. "We saw him rowing away upstream, making heavy weather of it. I wish we'd have known; we'da given him heavy weather all right."

"David saved us," Jennie said. "He took an ax to the lock."

"That's David for you!" Basto said heartily.

His sons, beefy and high-colored like himself, slapped the boy on the shoulder and ruffled his head, exclaiming, "Good old David!" He grinned and hunched his shoulders under their attentions.

"Where have you been all this time, David?" Basto asked. "We thought you went away with your dad." He shaped and spoke the words with an odd precision, and the boy watched his mouth. It dawned on Jennie that she had not yet heard the boy speak a word. He was a deaf-mute.

While the others watched him with respectful attention, he scraped

a thin layer of moss away from a flat, smooth face of rock. He took a
penknife from his pocket, opened it, and scratched words on the rock,
with the Basto boys watching over his shoulders, and the younger Baxter
craning his neck to see.

"Brush camp!" one of the boys announced. "Old David always has
a brush camp. Good one, too. Ain't that so, Davie? Builds 'em tight,
rain can't get in."

"By the great horn spoon, if this ain't a day!" Nick said. "Zeb Pulsifer
tried to burn three people alive"—he glanced at the baby and visibly
winced—"and David's been here right along, living on rabbits I don't
doubt. He's as smart as an Indian with that bow of his." David's diffident
smile was perilously close to tears. He could not be much more than
twelve, and as far as he knew he had lost his whole family.

Jennie leaned forward and touched his hand. "Do you know about
your mother?" she asked. He nodded reluctantly and looked back at the
shore. She wondered where he had been when the other two were
watching their mother drown herself. "Gwynneth and Geraint are safe,"
she said. "Would you like to go see them?"

This time his nod was emphatic. He watched her mouth as if he
were holding his breath in an anticipation as keen as pain.

"We"—she laid her hand on Alick's sleeve— "we will take you to
them."

Tears spurted into his eyes. He jumped up and ran off across the
field, veered behind the smoking ruins, and up over the rising ground
to the spruce woods.

"He will be back," said Nick Basto. "He's just gone to get his cultch.
It's mighty kind of you folk to take him along. Them young ones was
awful devoted to each other."

"I wonder why he run off from them the way he did," the hired man
said. "I don't figger anyone'll ever know."

The two fishermen left to get home before the tide went out. With
no wind it was a long, hot row even with two pairs of oars. "If we get
there before you do," the father said to Alick, "you want us to set the
constable on Zeb?"

"I am not selfish enough to claim all the pleasure for myself," Alick
said. They laughed and shook hands with him and the Basto crew,
touched their hats to Jennie, and went off down the path. The hired
man and the boys went back to damp down the embers.

"How did it happen you folks were down here this afternoon?" Nick asked. "Why in Tophet would he want to kill you?"

"He has good reason to be not liking me at all," Alick said. "He came upon us this afternoon when we had the General's keys, so he must have believed we had bought it or were about to. He is wanting it for himself."

"*Christ!*" Nick roared, and then slapped his hand across his mouth. "I apologize, ma'am. But Zeb Pulsifer neighbor to me? God forbid!"

"When we were first in the barn, we were hearing some little sounds outside. I think that was when he came up from the shore. He saw the barn open, and heard us talking, and ran away, but not far."

"It had to be the alder swamp below the well," said Jennie. "The birds were carrying on down there, I remember. He went back to the barn while we were in the house. When we were leaving and Alick was about to lock the barn doors, we heard a cat crying in the barn. It was so pathetic, and of course, we couldn't leave her there, so we went in, and he bolted out past us and locked us in." She was proud of being able to tell it so lucidly. "If we had simply driven away instead of being so tenderhearted, I wonder what he would have done."

"Burned the barn down, certainly," Alick said. "He had already started the fire. Then he might have done the same to the house, so we could not be having it. As for *us*," he said ironically, "he would be thinking very hard how else he could be charming us with a new surprise. Instead, the surprise was for him; the lad, David, not with a sling and a stone, but with an ax."

"Ayuh, and he'll be a good witness! He reads and writes like a house afire. Or a barn afire." The spruce wall behind them sent back his shout of laughter. He calmed down, wheezing slightly and wiping his eyes. "Tell me something. *Are* you folks still wanting it after this?"

Jennie looked down into Priscilla's face, waiting for the polite no. There was a long pause. *I don't care*, she thought. *We are alive.*

"I am just thinking," Alick said. "I will have to be building a new barn before we are buying a horse and a cow."

"Amen!" said Basto jubilantly. He shoved a meaty hand at Alick. "Just say the word, Glenroy, and we'll have a barn raising that will shake the rafters of heaven!"

They left David at Rose of Sharon's with his bow, his homemade quiver of arrows slung over his shoulder, and his possessions tied up in an old quilt. He had wanted to bring the big ax, but they convinced him it would be safe in the house for now. "The Lord was watching out for him," Nick Basto said. "Him alone in the woods with that, he could have chopped off his foot out there and died without anybody knowing."

He was safe now; Gwynneth and Geraint knocked him off his feet with their hugs, while Rose of Sharon, her children, and her amiable, slow-witted brother watched with friendly amusement.

"He is a deaf-mute," Jennie said. "There's nothing else wrong in here." She touched her forehead. "He reads and writes. Do you have some paper he can write on tonight? It is important."

"Land of love, I've got some somewhere!" said Rose of Sharon. "Needs feeding up, don't he? Clean enough, though, for living rough all this time. I will say that poor woman did teach her young ones to be clean, even if she was demented."

Alick finally extracted David from the younger two and asked him by way of a slate to write out tonight what he had seen and done this afternoon. "Yes," David wrote in a clear, round hand. "I will come for it tomorrow," Alick said.

When he drove the gig into the stableyard, it felt as if they had left from there on an April afternoon a year ago. Benoni came out and said sociably, "Well, you two made an afternoon of it, didn't you? What's all this about Zeb Pulsifer?"

"Alick will be happy to tell you," Jennie said. She took Priscilla and went through the trees to the cottage. It felt more like home than it ever had, now that home was to be in another place, not back in Northumberland, but down the river. There was much to do first, and she was glad none of it had to be done tonight. She washed and changed Priscilla, and fed her, and carried her up to her cradle. She hung their shawls on the clothesline and tied her bonnet out there by the ribbons. She built the fire. The wash water kept in the big kettle had retained some warmth from the earlier fire, and she filled the pitcher of her toilet set and took it up to her bedroom. She got out clean clothes for Alick and put them on the kitchen table, with a towel. Then she went back upstairs to wash away the afternoon. While she was undressing, she heard him come in and go out again. Priscilla talked to herself in the cradle.

When she was through with washing her body, she turned the remaining water over her hair to rinse away the last wraith of smoke scent, and then walked around the room, naked in the late sunlight, blotting her hair with a towel. She gave herself luxuriously to the small, delicious things of life: the April buds outside the windows, the feel of the sun-warmed floor under her bare soles, and the touch of the air on her unblistered, uncharred skin; Priscilla's drowsy chirpings; Alick's footsteps on the stairs.

He stopped in the doorway at the sight of her. "A *Dia*, Jeannie," he said huskily. "You are so beautiful. It is like the first time. . . . It *is* the first time since we were dying and were brought back to life." He came to her and reverently kissed her breasts, then held her by the shoulders and kissed her mouth. "This is for the first time, too, my Jeannie," he whispered.

There were two familiar signals from downstairs: the knock of a stick against the front door and one authoritative bass bark.

"The General and his aide-de-camp," said Jeannie.

"So he has heard, and now we talk. Will you come down?"

"Yes, but not like this." He laughed and drew her to him, and they kissed again, and then he ran down the stairs.

Epilogue

THE ACCOUNT OF David Evans:

I saw my Da go. It was before daylight. I ran after the wagon for a long time, but he would not stop for me. I was so tired I fell down before he got to the bridge. I slept in the woods, and then I went home. Nobody saw me, but I saw them taking my mother out of the water, and then they took her away, and my brother and sister. I got the food from the house and my bow and arrows and went to my brush camp. I have gone in the house a few times. Once when it was cold, I had a fire. Then they fixed the windows, so I could not.

I saw everybody who came to our house. Today I saw the people ride in with the horse the man tied under an apple tree. The people are named Glenroy. I saw the big man, too. He was outside the barn when they were in it, and then he ran away. He hid by the well, and then he went into the woods and came back to the barn that way. I saw him, but he didn't see me. He was in it when the people named Glenroy went in it again. He ran out and locked the door. I did not know about the fire then, but it was wrong to lock them in there. I went to my brush camp to get my ax to break off the lock. When I came back, he knew I was there. He tried to take my ax away and I hit him in the leg but not hard enough. I reckon it hurt him some because he could not run very fast and Mr. Glenroy could catch him, so I did good after all.

"And so you did, David, so you did," Jennie said. They were reading it in bed the next night.

"The Bible is telling of an angel who stood outside Eden with a flaming sword," said Alick. "We are knowing of an angel who cleaved a path through the flames with an ax." He blew out the candle and took her in his arms.

"Alick, what made you decide to buy the property?" she asked.

"When we came out alive, and after I was half killing a man, and all the time we were soaking down the roof, I was knowing we had been given a world, or the stuff to make one for all of us: you, me, Priscilla, and the others to come. I have not the second sight, but I am telling you I saw it all, and in that place."

He gave her a little squeeze. "What are you thinking? Are you happy?"

"My thoughts are too deep for mere words," she said, "and happiness is like the froth on the waves, and the sun glancing off them. But yes, my darling, I am happy."

"What are you thinking now?" he asked again.

"About all the others to come," she murmured. "For the first time I am seeing us as ancestors."

"But for tonight," he said, "we will be lovers, just."

Catalog *

If you are interested in a list of fine Paperback
books, covering a wide range of subjects
and interests, send your name and address,
requesting your free catalog, to:

McGraw-Hill Paperbacks
1221 Avenue of Americas
New York, N.Y. 10020